POKÉMON™

ADVENTURES

GOLD & SILVER

Pokémon ADVENTURES
Volume 10
Perfect Square Edition

Story by HIDENORI KUSAKA
Art by SATOSHI YAMAMOTO

© 2010 The Pokémon Company International.
© 1995-2010 Nintendo/Creatures Inc./GAME FREAK inc.
TM, ®, and character names are trademarks of Nintendo.
POCKET MONSTERS SPECIAL Vol. 10
by Hidenori KUSAKA, Satoshi YAMAMOTO
© 1997 Hidenori KUSAKA, Satoshi YAMAMOTO
All rights reserved.
Original Japanese edition published by SHOGAKUKAN.
English translation rights in the United States of America, Canada, the United Kingdom,
Ireland, Australia, New Zealand and India arranged with SHOGAKUKAN.

English Adaptation/Gerard Jones
Translation/Kaori Inoue
Touch-up & Lettering/Annaliese Christman
Design/Sam Elzway
Editor/Annette Roman

Printed in the U.S.A.

Published by VIZ Media, LLC
P.O. Box 77010
San Francisco, CA 94107

10 9
First printing, December 2010
Ninth printing, June 2017

www.perfectsquare.com   www.viz.com

Pokémon™ Adventures

Gold & Silver

10
Volume Ten

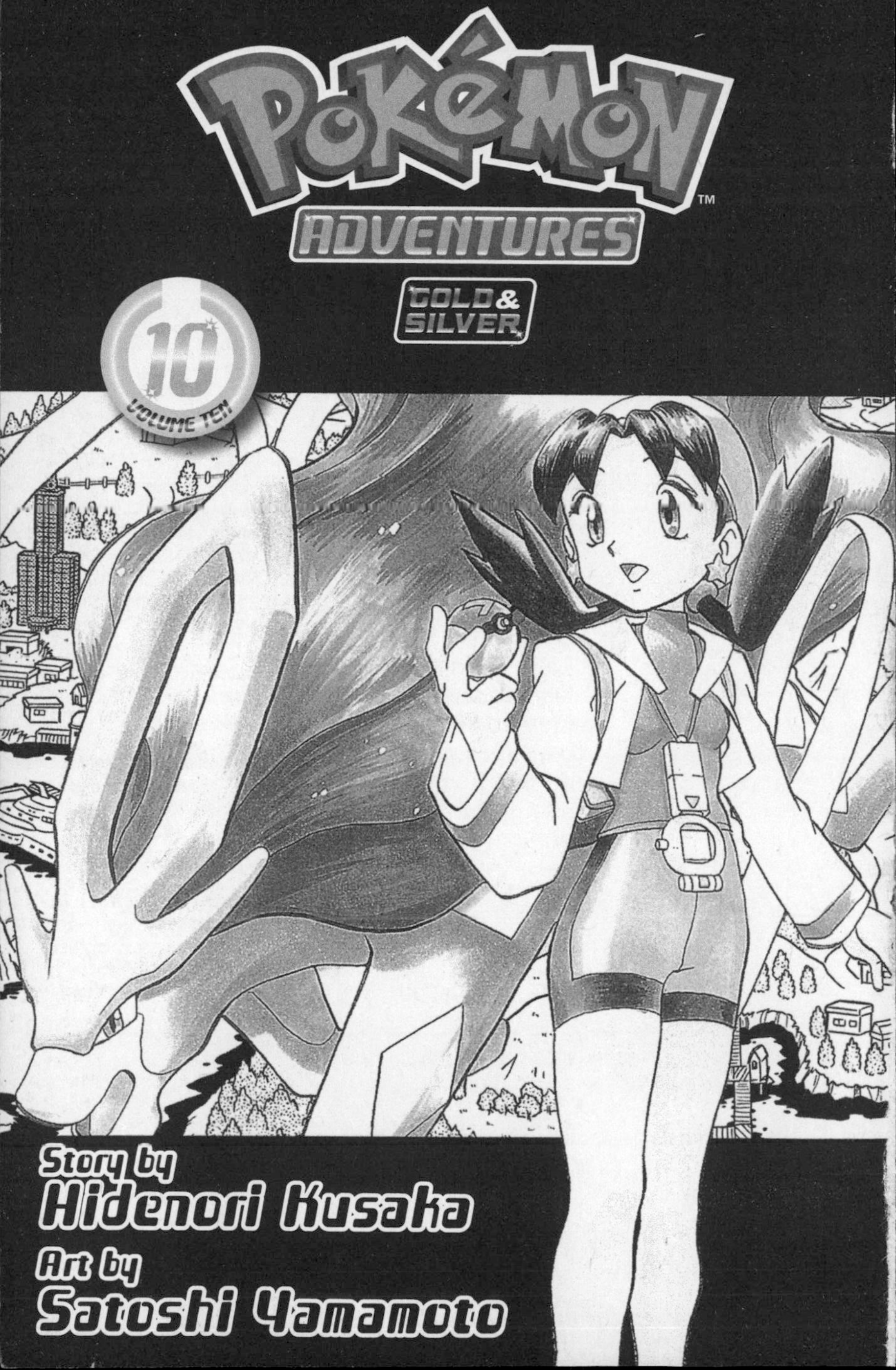

Story by
Hidenori Kusaka
Art by
Satoshi Yamamoto

POKÉMO

CHARACTERS

THUS FAR…

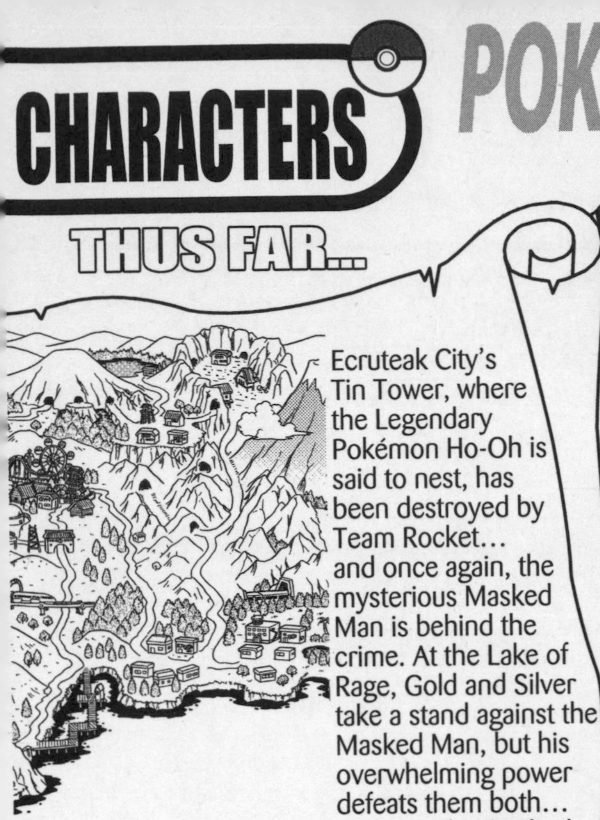

Ecruteak City's Tin Tower, where the Legendary Pokémon Ho-Oh is said to nest, has been destroyed by Team Rocket… and once again, the mysterious Masked Man is behind the crime. At the Lake of Rage, Gold and Silver take a stand against the Masked Man, but his overwhelming power defeats them both… and now they've both gone missing!

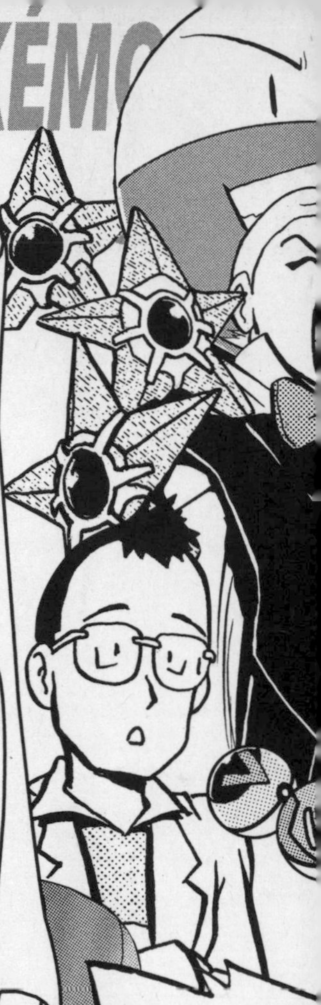

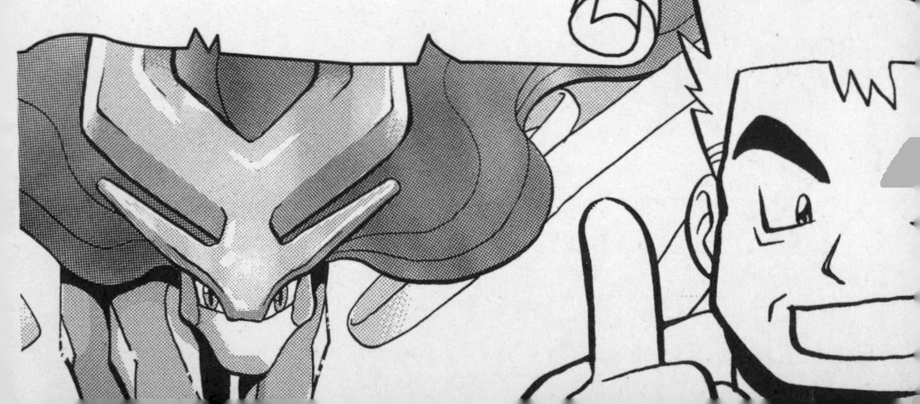

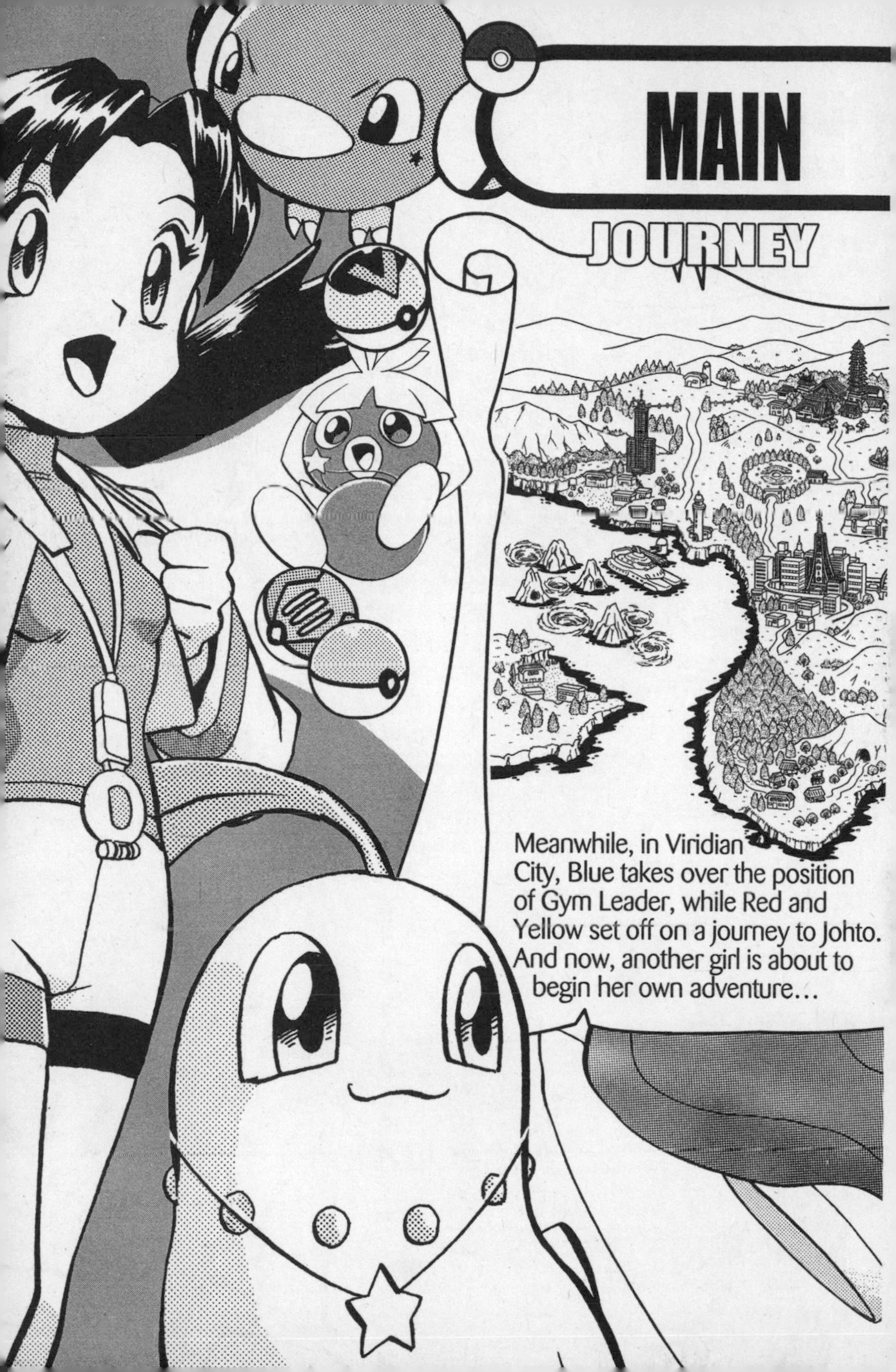
MAIN
JOURNEY
Meanwhile, in Viridian City, Blue takes over the position of Gym Leader, while Red and Yellow set off on a journey to Johto. And now, another girl is about to begin her own adventure...

CONTENTS

CRYSTAL

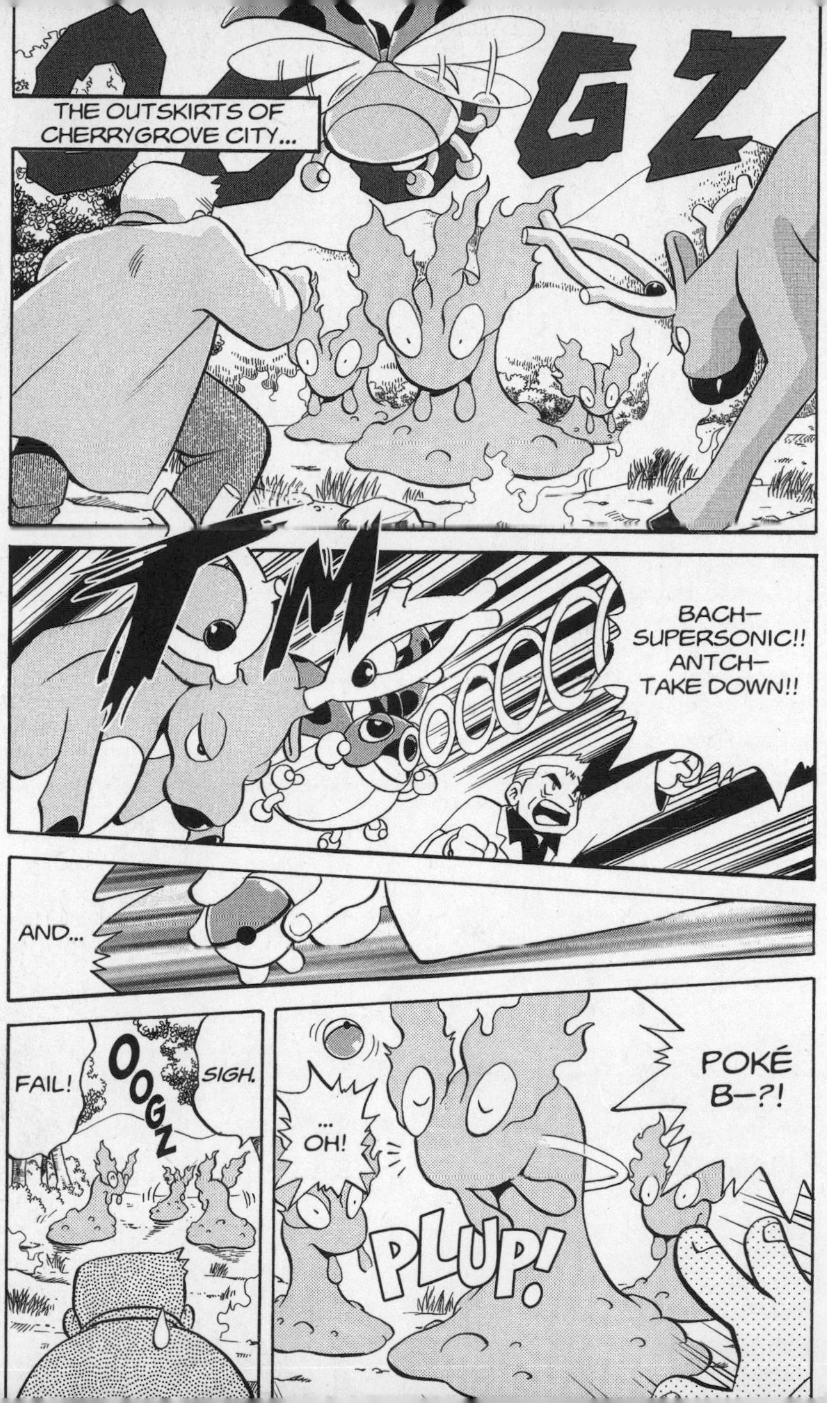

OOGZ
THE OUTSKIRTS OF CHERRYGROVE CITY...
BACH— SUPERSONIC!! ANTCH— TAKE DOWN!!
AND...
POKÉ B—?!
...OH!
PLUP!
SIGH.
OOGZ
FAIL!

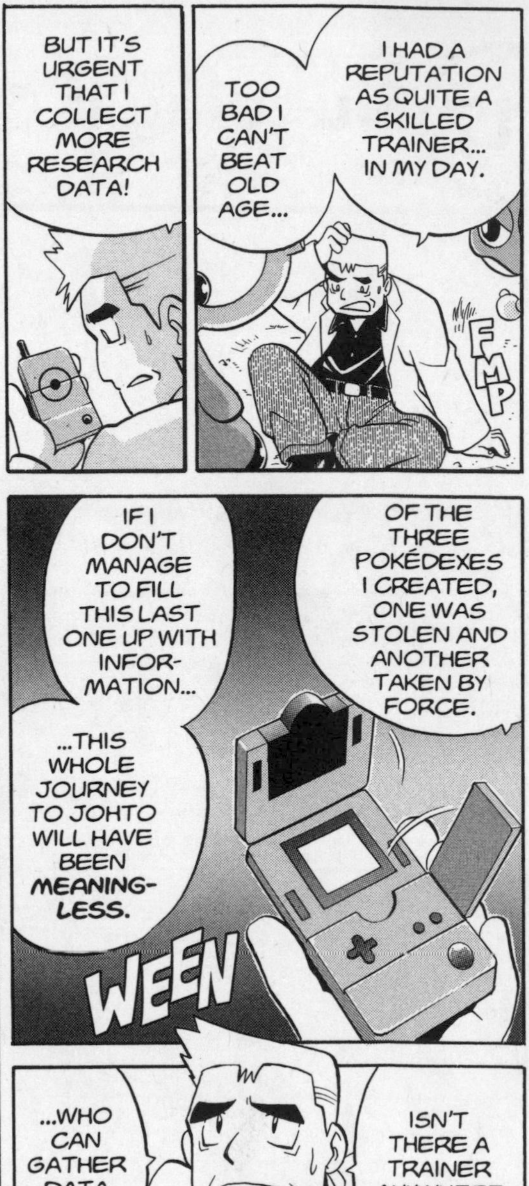
I HAD A REPUTATION AS QUITE A SKILLED TRAINER... IN MY DAY.
TOO BAD I CAN'T BEAT OLD AGE...
FMP
BUT IT'S URGENT THAT I COLLECT MORE RESEARCH DATA!
OF THE THREE POKÉDEXES I CREATED, ONE WAS STOLEN AND ANOTHER TAKEN BY FORCE.
IF I DON'T MANAGE TO FILL THIS LAST ONE UP WITH INFOR-MATION...
...THIS WHOLE JOURNEY TO JOHTO WILL HAVE BEEN **MEANING-LESS.**
WEEN
ISN'T THERE A TRAINER ANYWHERE ...
...WHO CAN GATHER DATA FOR ME?
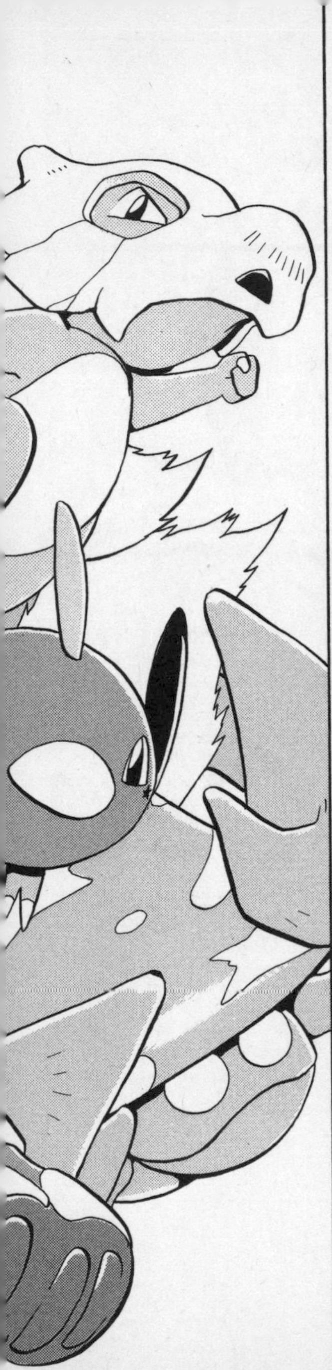

117 Slugging It Out with Slugma

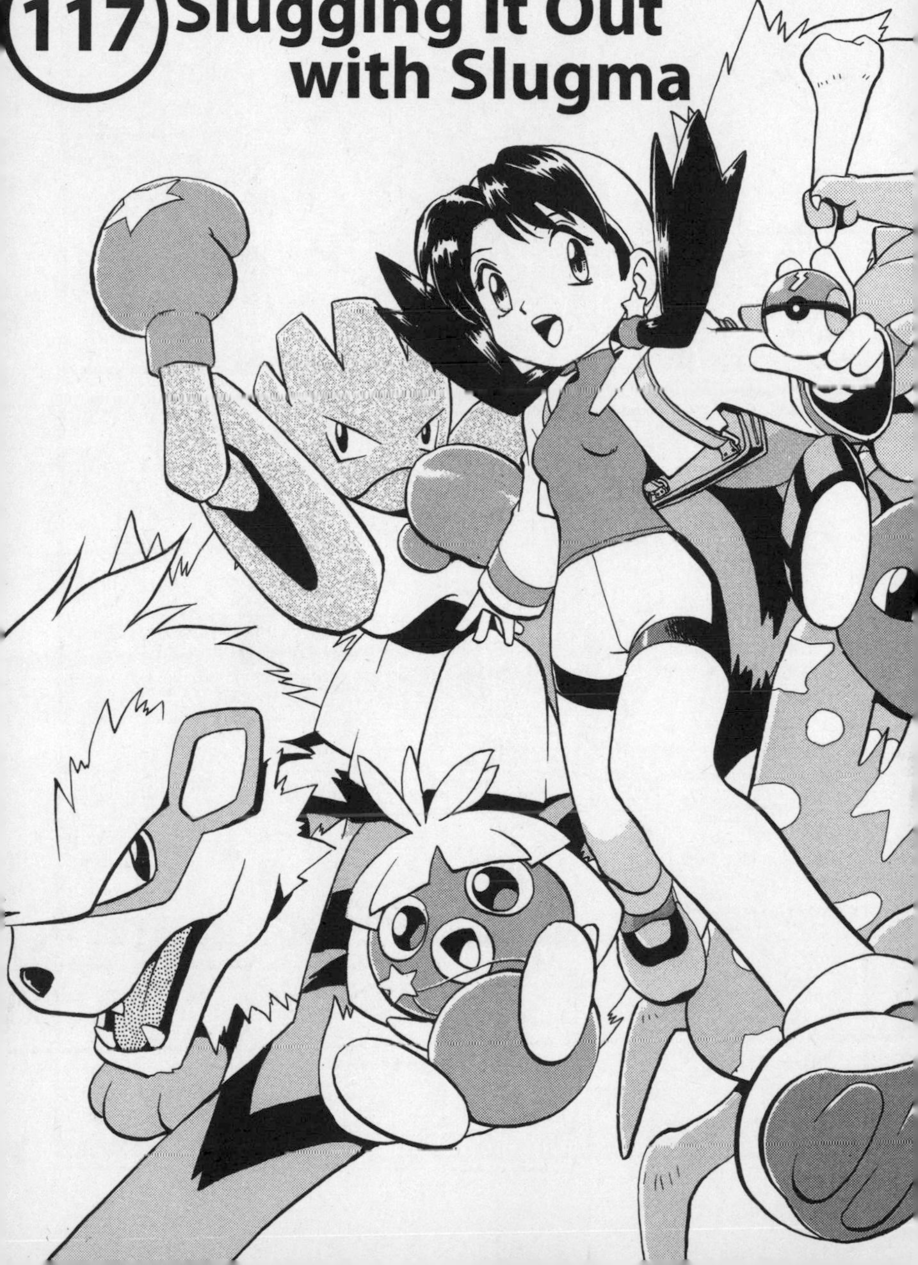

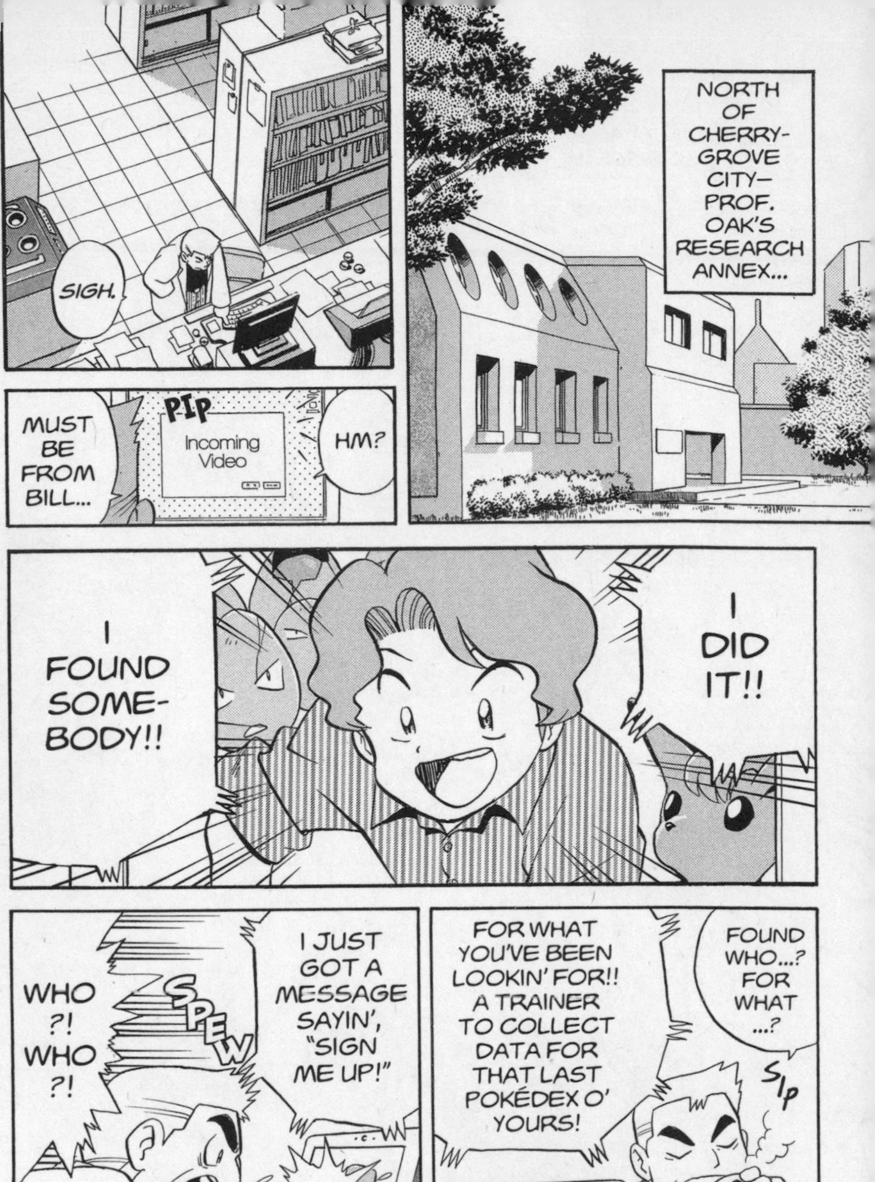

NORTH OF CHERRY-GROVE CITY—PROF. OAK'S RESEARCH ANNEX...
SIGH.
PIP
HM?
Incoming Video
MUST BE FROM BILL...
I DID IT!!
I FOUND SOME-BODY!!
FOUND WHO...? FOR WHAT ...?
SLP
FOR WHAT YOU'VE BEEN LOOKIN' FOR!! A TRAINER TO COLLECT DATA FOR THAT LAST POKÉDEX O' YOURS!
I JUST GOT A MESSAGE SAYIN', "SIGN ME UP!"
SPEW
WHO ?! WHO ?!
AGH!

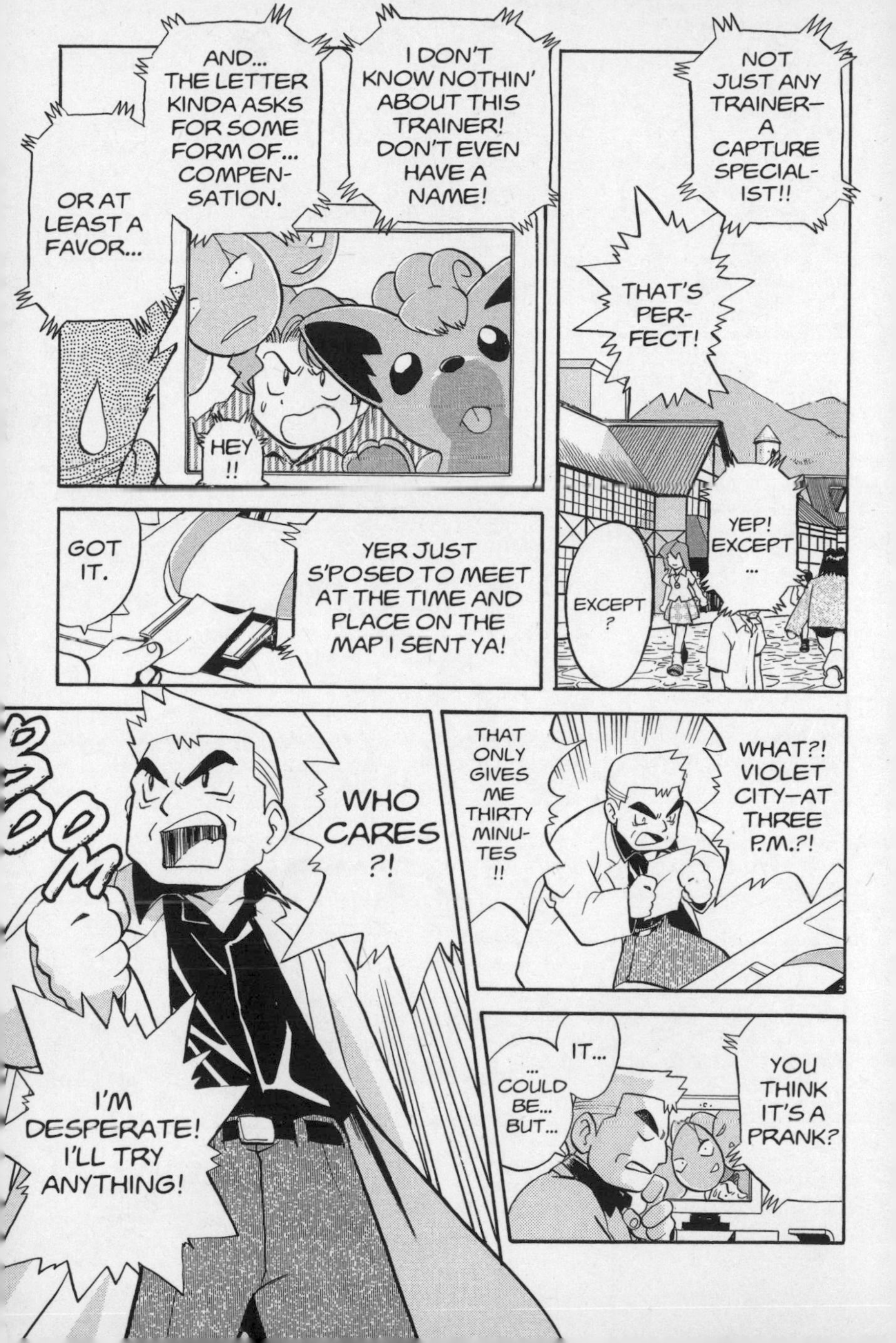
NOT JUST ANY TRAINER—A CAPTURE SPECIAL-IST!!
THAT'S PER-FECT!
YEP! EXCEPT ...
EXCEPT ?
I DON'T KNOW NOTHIN' ABOUT THIS TRAINER! DON'T EVEN HAVE A NAME!
AND... THE LETTER KINDA ASKS FOR SOME FORM OF... COMPEN-SATION.
OR AT LEAST A FAVOR...
HEY !!
YER JUST S'POSED TO MEET AT THE TIME AND PLACE ON THE MAP I SENT YA!
GOT IT.
WHAT?! VIOLET CITY—AT THREE P.M.?!
THAT ONLY GIVES ME THIRTY MINU-TES !!
YOU THINK IT'S A PRANK?
IT...
... COULD BE... BUT...
BOOM
WHO CARES ?!
I'M DESPERATE! I'LL TRY ANYTHING!

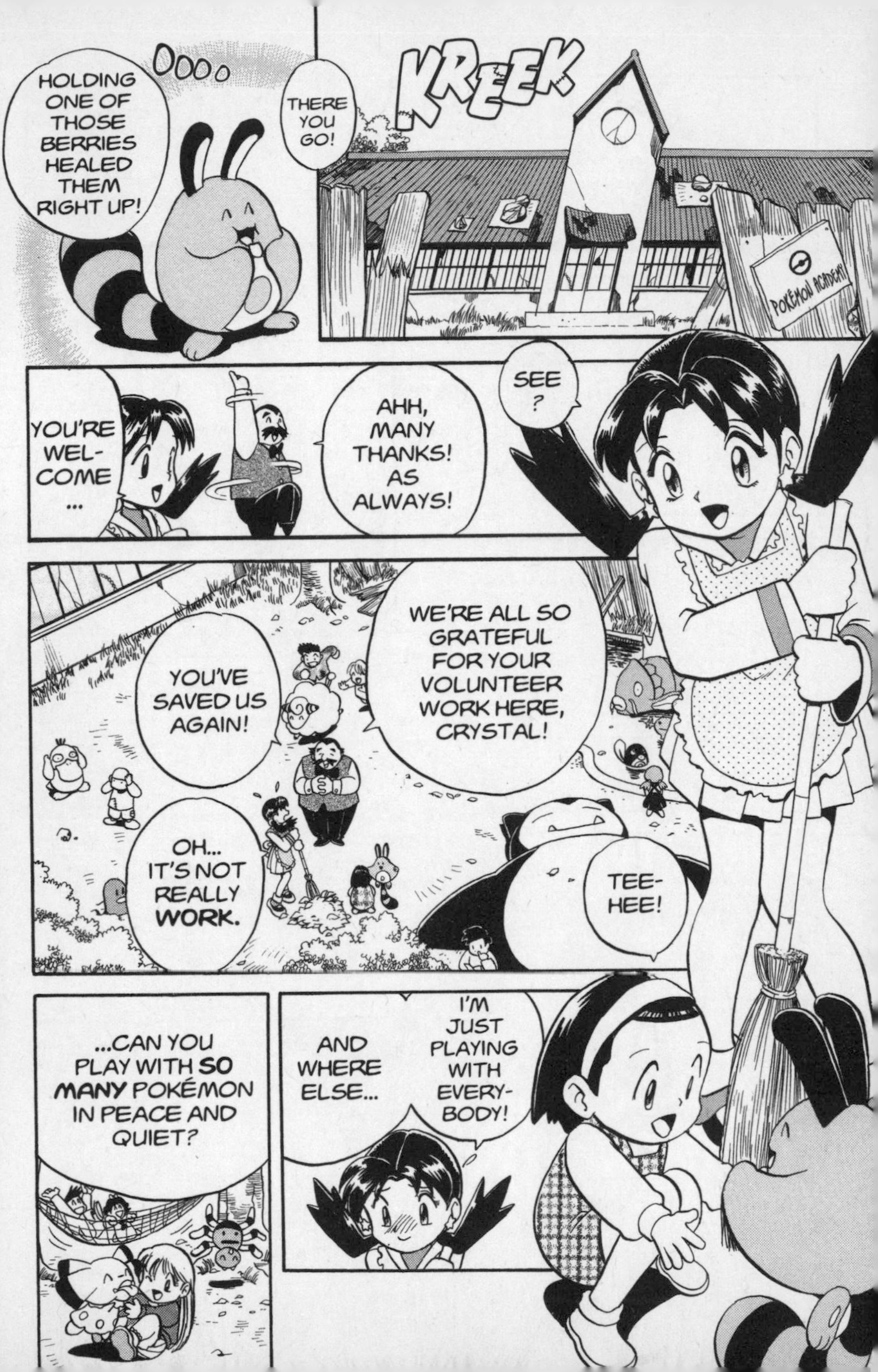
KREEK
THERE YOU GO!
POKÉMON ACADEMY
OOOO
HOLDING ONE OF THOSE BERRIES HEALED THEM RIGHT UP!
SEE?
AHH, MANY THANKS! AS ALWAYS!
YOU'RE WEL- COME ...
WE'RE ALL SO GRATEFUL FOR YOUR VOLUNTEER WORK HERE, CRYSTAL!
YOU'VE SAVED US AGAIN!
OH... IT'S NOT REALLY **WORK.**
TEE- HEE!
I'M JUST PLAYING WITH EVERY- BODY!
AND WHERE ELSE...
...CAN YOU PLAY WITH **SO MANY** POKÉMON IN PEACE AND QUIET?

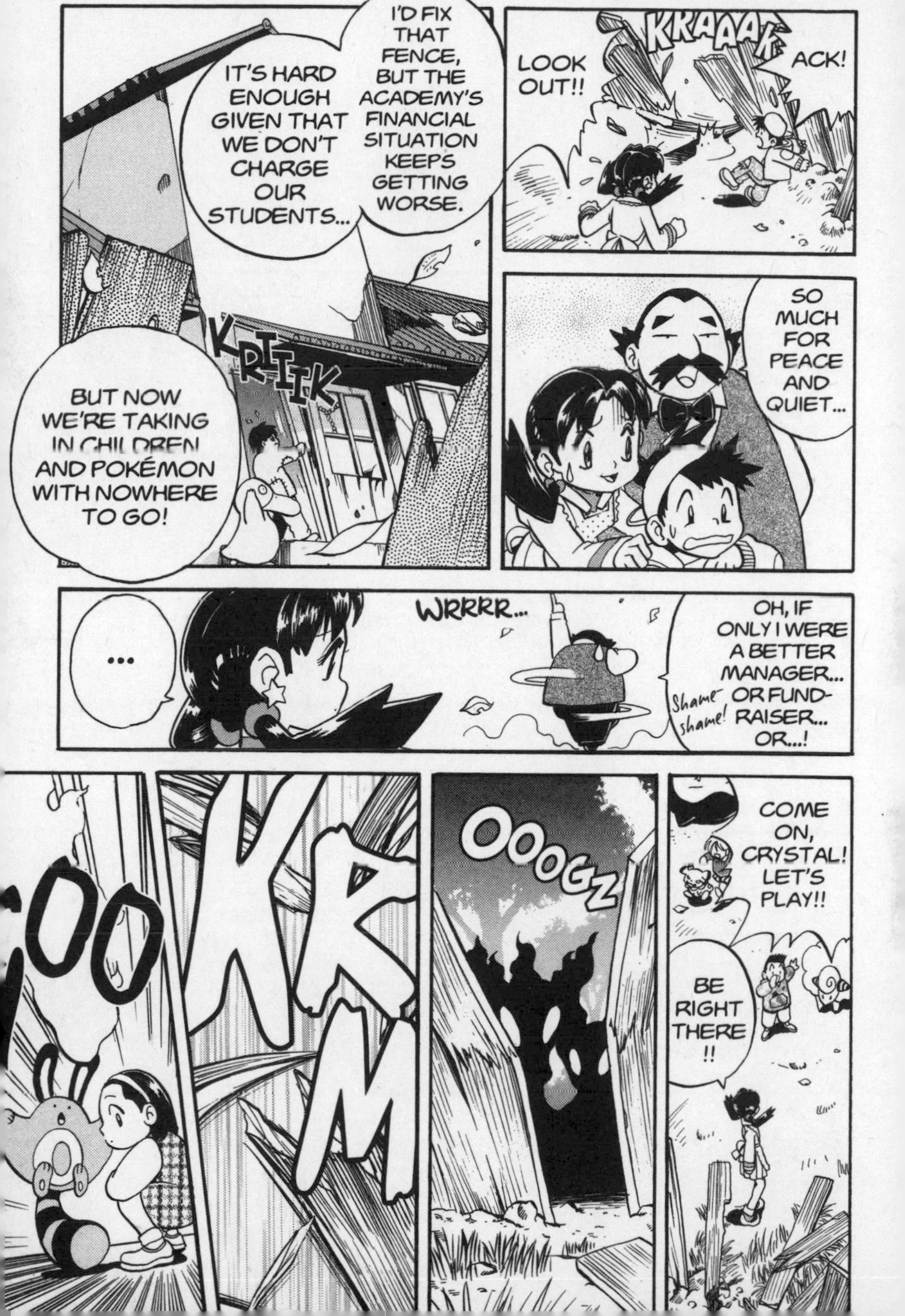
KRAAAK
ACK!
LOOK OUT!!
SO MUCH FOR PEACE AND QUIET...
I'D FIX THAT FENCE, BUT THE ACADEMY'S FINANCIAL SITUATION KEEPS GETTING WORSE.
IT'S HARD ENOUGH GIVEN THAT WE DON'T CHARGE OUR STUDENTS...
KRTIIK
BUT NOW WE'RE TAKING IN CHILDREN AND POKÉMON WITH NOWHERE TO GO!
OH, IF ONLY I WERE A BETTER MANAGER... OR FUND-RAISER... OR...!
Shame shame!
WRRRR...
...
COME ON, CRYSTAL! LET'S PLAY!!
BE RIGHT THERE!!
OOOGZ
KRM
COO

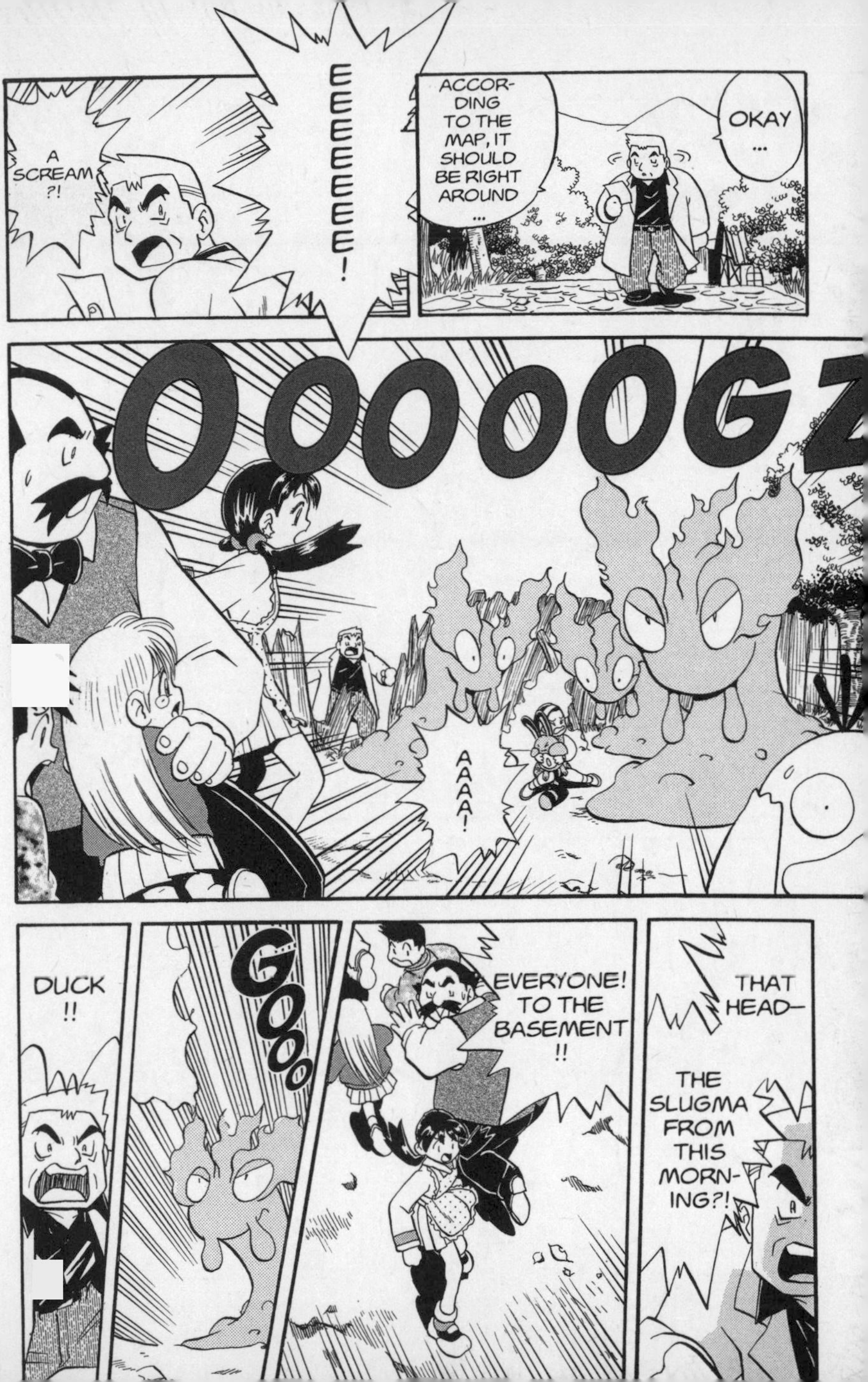
OKAY ...
ACCORDING TO THE MAP, IT SHOULD BE RIGHT AROUND ...
EEEEEEEEE!
A SCREAM ?!
OOOOOGZ
AAAA!
THAT HEAD—
THE SLUGMA FROM THIS MORNING?!
EVERYONE! TO THE BASEMENT !!
GOOO
DUCK !!

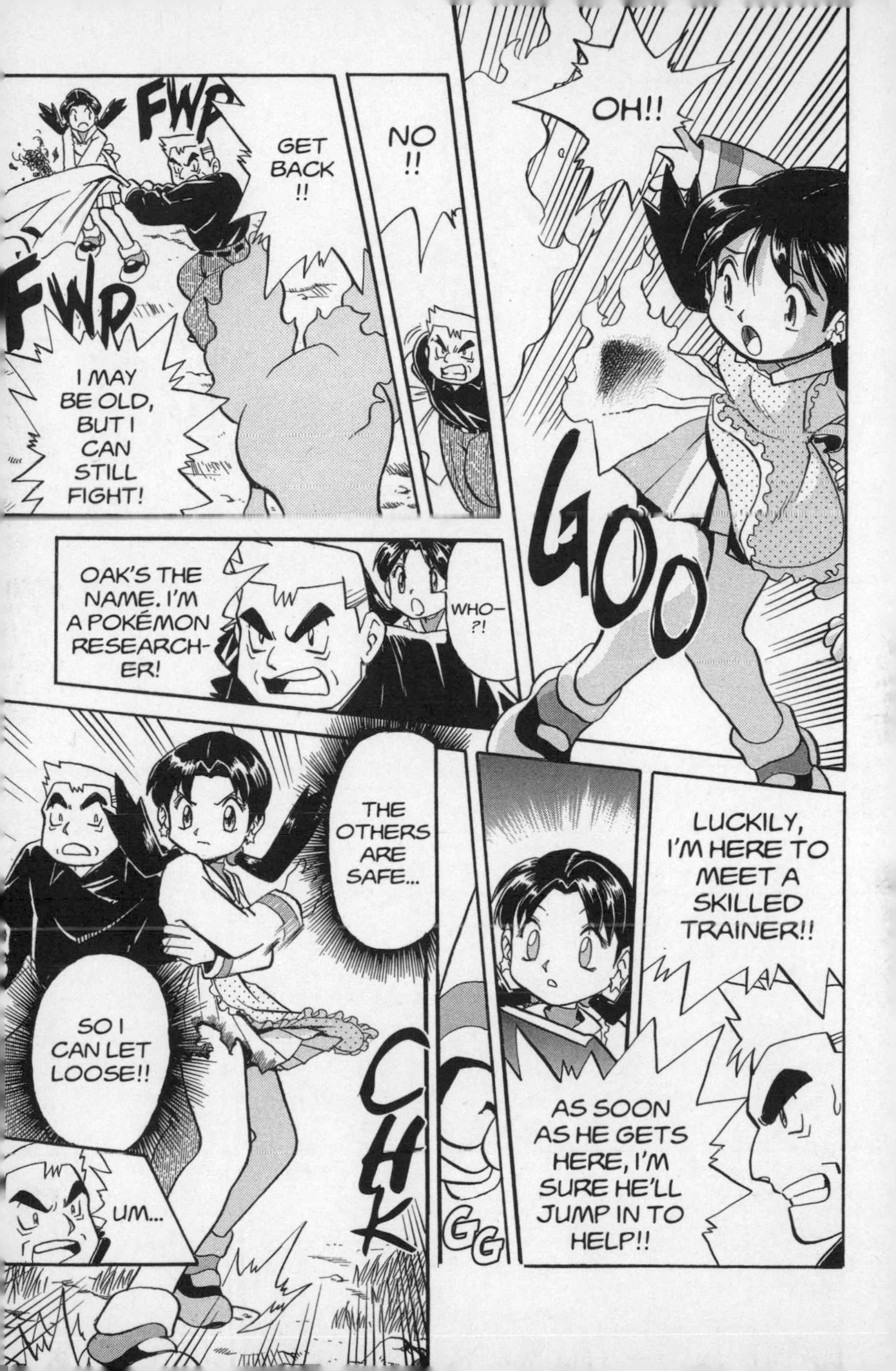
OH!!
GOO
NO !!
GET BACK !!
FWP
FWP
I MAY BE OLD, BUT I CAN STILL FIGHT!
WHO-?!
OAK'S THE NAME. I'M A POKÉMON RESEARCHER!
LUCKILY, I'M HERE TO MEET A SKILLED TRAINER!!
AS SOON AS HE GETS HERE, I'M SURE HE'LL JUMP IN TO HELP!!
GG
THE OTHERS ARE SAFE...
CHK
SO I CAN LET LOOSE!!
UM...

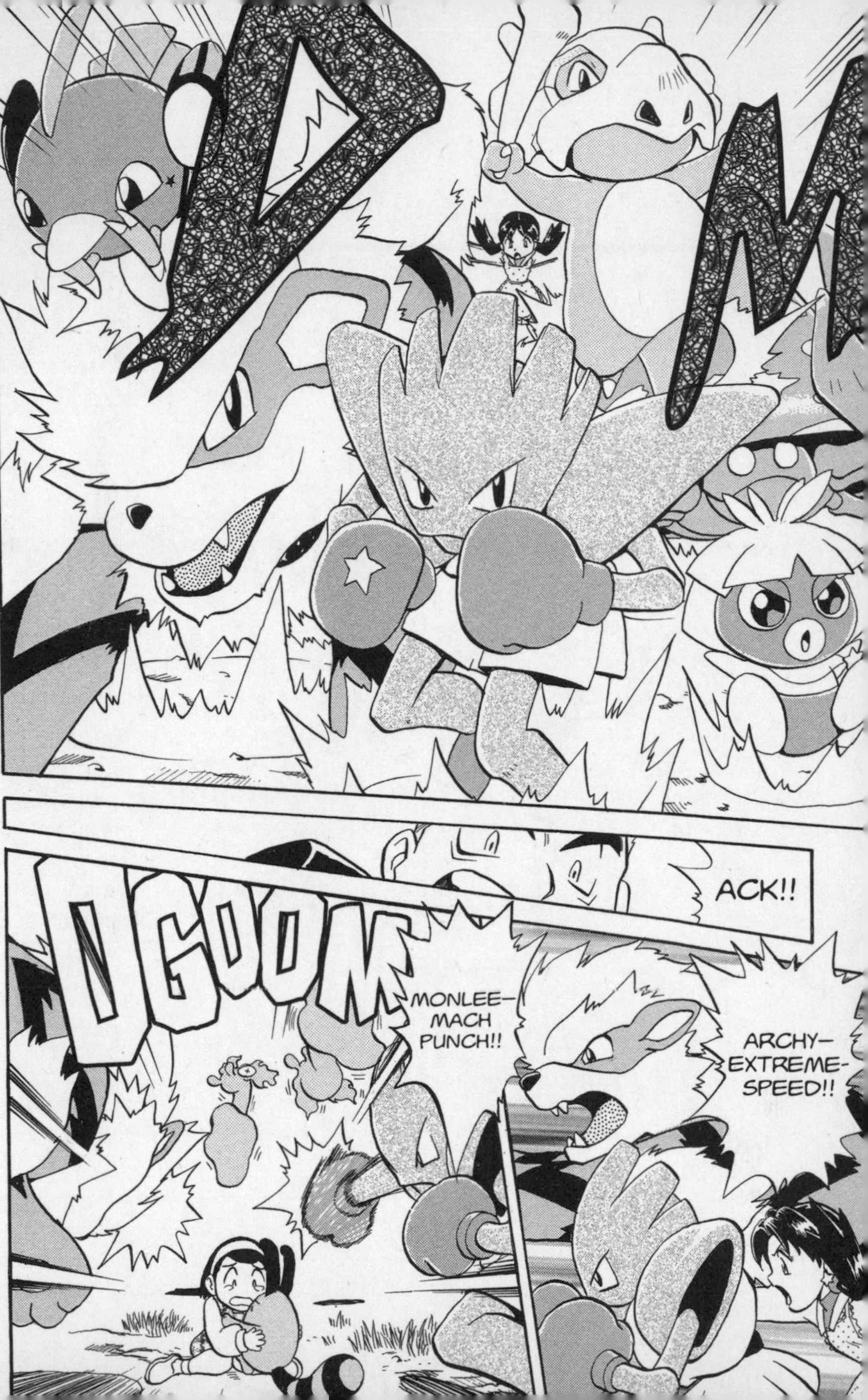
ACK!!
ARCHY—EXTREME-SPEED!!
MONLEE—MACH PUNCH!!
DGOOM

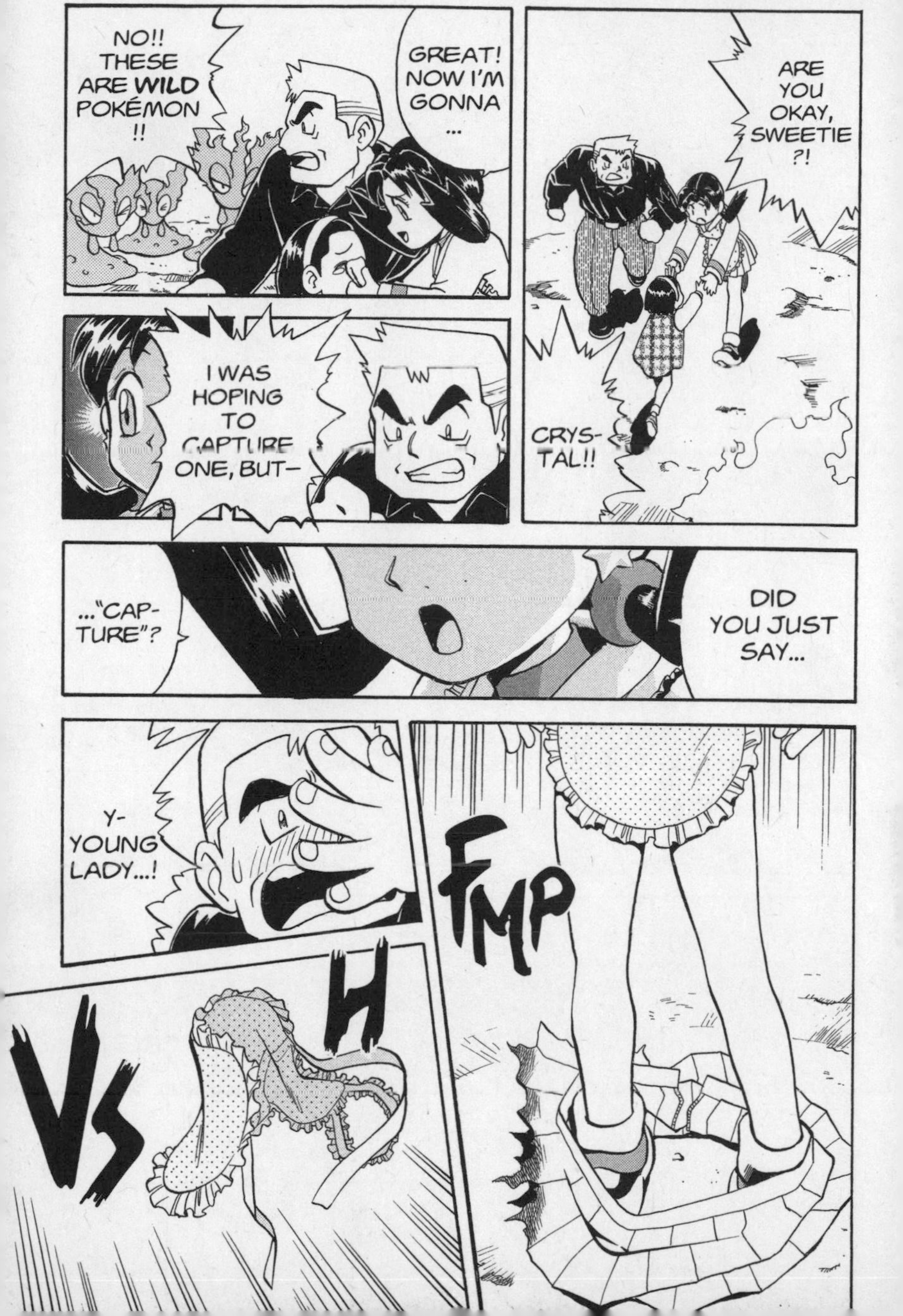
ARE YOU OKAY, SWEETIE?!
CRYS-TAL!!
GREAT! NOW I'M GONNA ...
NO!! THESE ARE **WILD** POKÉMON !!
I WAS HOPING TO CAPTURE ONE, BUT–
DID YOU JUST SAY...
..."CAP-TURE"?
FMP
Y-YOUNG LADY...!
VS
H

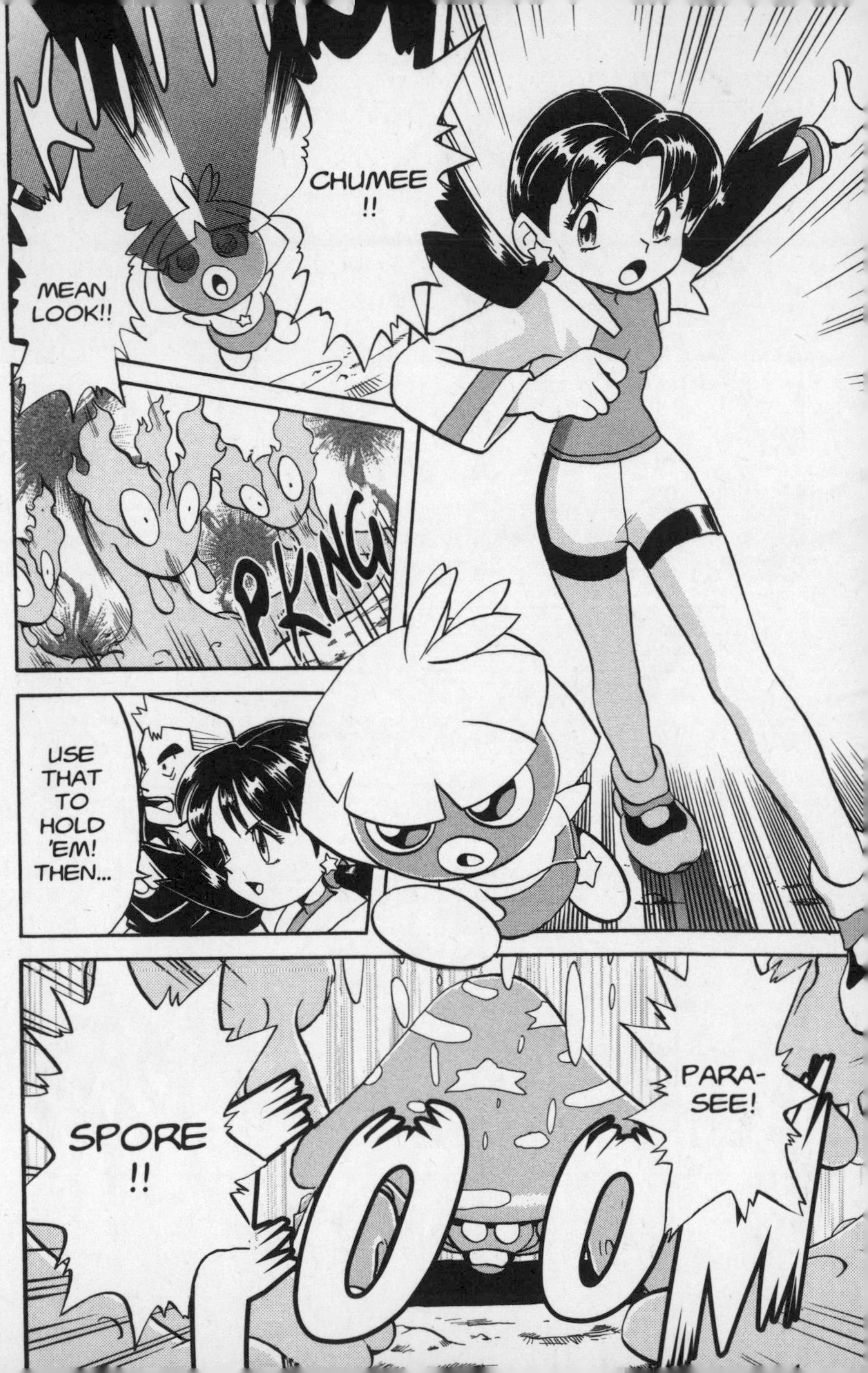
CHUMEE !!
MEAN LOOK!!
P-KING
USE THAT TO HOLD 'EM! THEN...
PARA-SEE!
SPORE !!

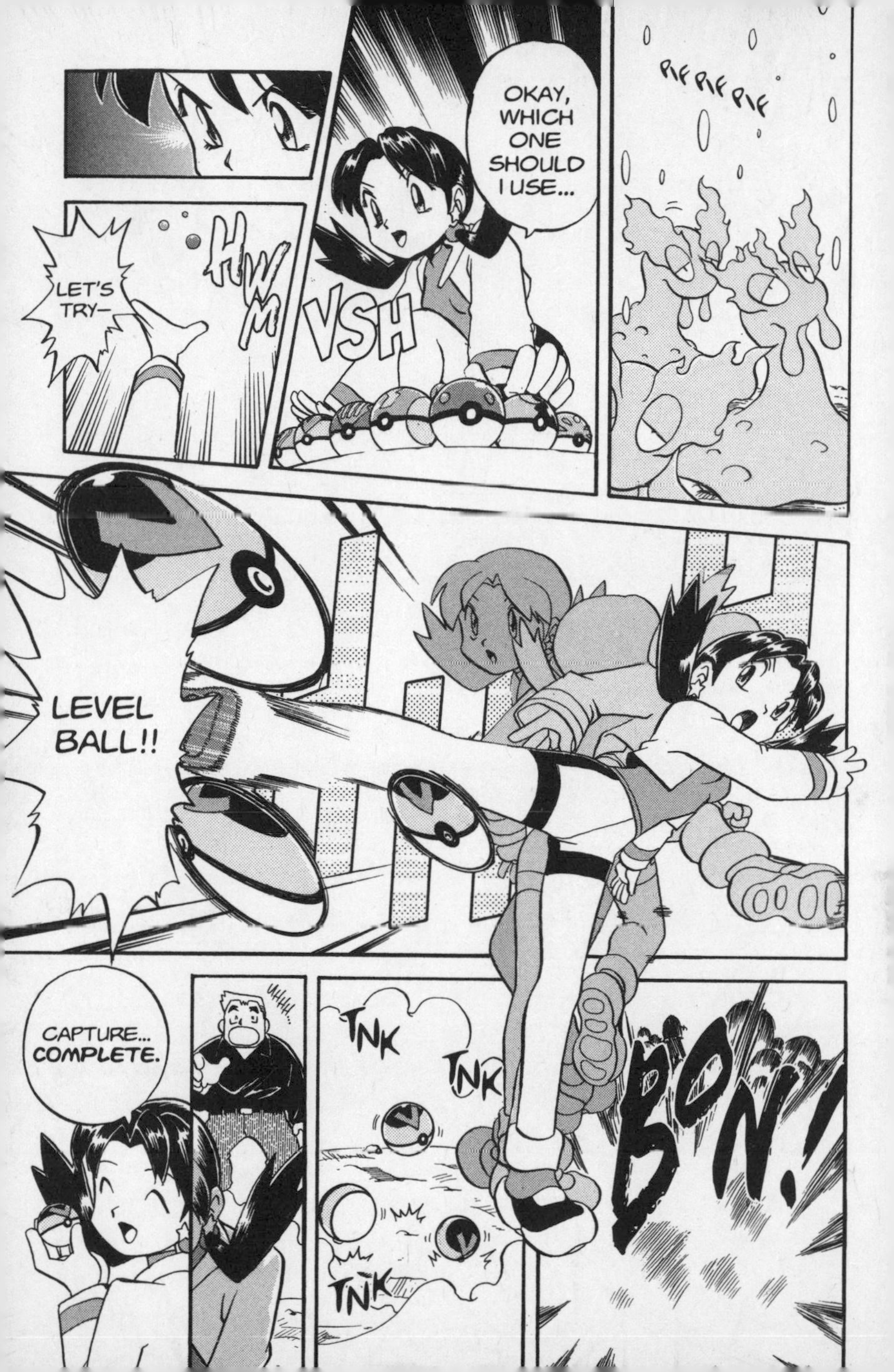
PIF PIF PIF
OKAY, WHICH ONE SHOULD I USE...
VSH
HWM
LET'S TRY—
LEVEL BALL!!
BON!!
TNK
TNK
TNK
CAPTURE... COMPLETE.

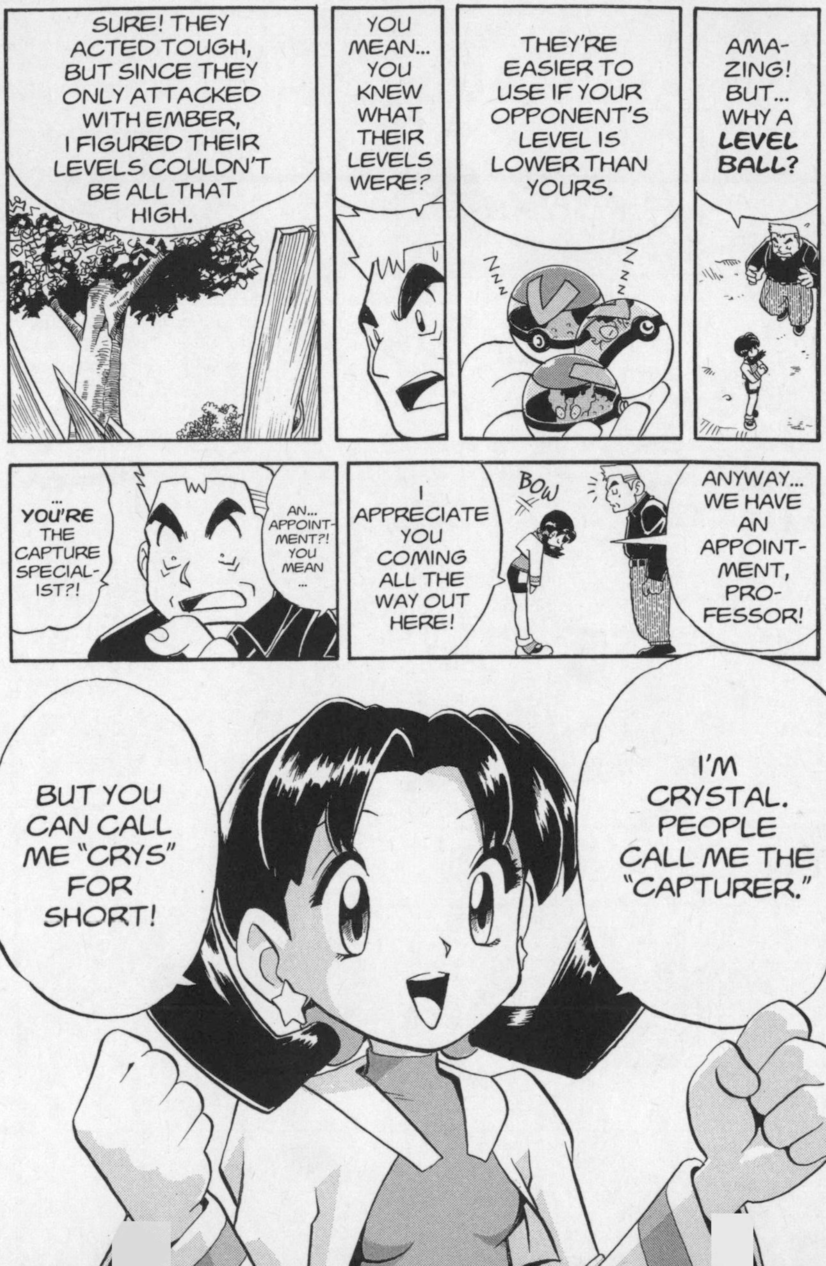
AMAZING! BUT... WHY A **LEVEL BALL?**
THEY'RE EASIER TO USE IF YOUR OPPONENT'S LEVEL IS LOWER THAN YOURS.
YOU MEAN... YOU KNEW WHAT THEIR LEVELS WERE?
SURE! THEY ACTED TOUGH, BUT SINCE THEY ONLY ATTACKED WITH EMBER, I FIGURED THEIR LEVELS COULDN'T BE ALL THAT HIGH.
ANYWAY... WE HAVE AN APPOINTMENT, PROFESSOR!
BOW
I APPRECIATE YOU COMING ALL THE WAY OUT HERE!
AN... APPOINTMENT?! YOU MEAN ...
... **YOU'RE** THE CAPTURE SPECIALIST?!
I'M CRYSTAL. PEOPLE CALL ME THE "CAPTURER."
BUT YOU CAN CALL ME "CRYS" FOR SHORT!

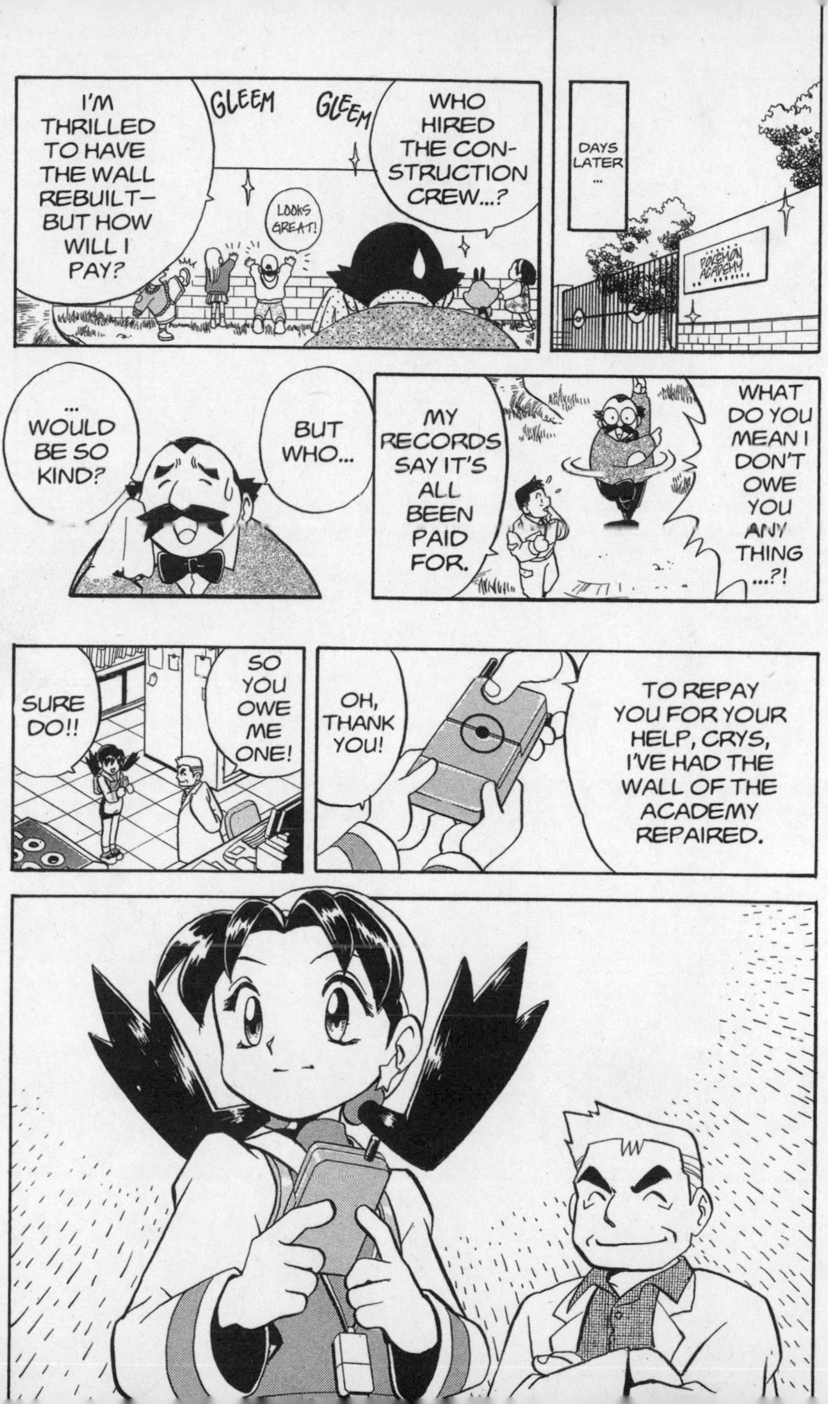
DAYS LATER ...
POKéMON ACADEMY
WHO HIRED THE CON-STRUCTION CREW...?
GLEEM
GLEEM
LOOKS GREAT!
I'M THRILLED TO HAVE THE WALL REBUILT—BUT HOW WILL I PAY?
WHAT DO YOU MEAN I DON'T OWE YOU ANY THING ...?!
MY RECORDS SAY IT'S ALL BEEN PAID FOR.
BUT WHO...
... WOULD BE SO KIND?
TO REPAY YOU FOR YOUR HELP, CRYS, I'VE HAD THE WALL OF THE ACADEMY REPAIRED.
OH, THANK YOU!
SO YOU OWE ME ONE!
SURE DO!!

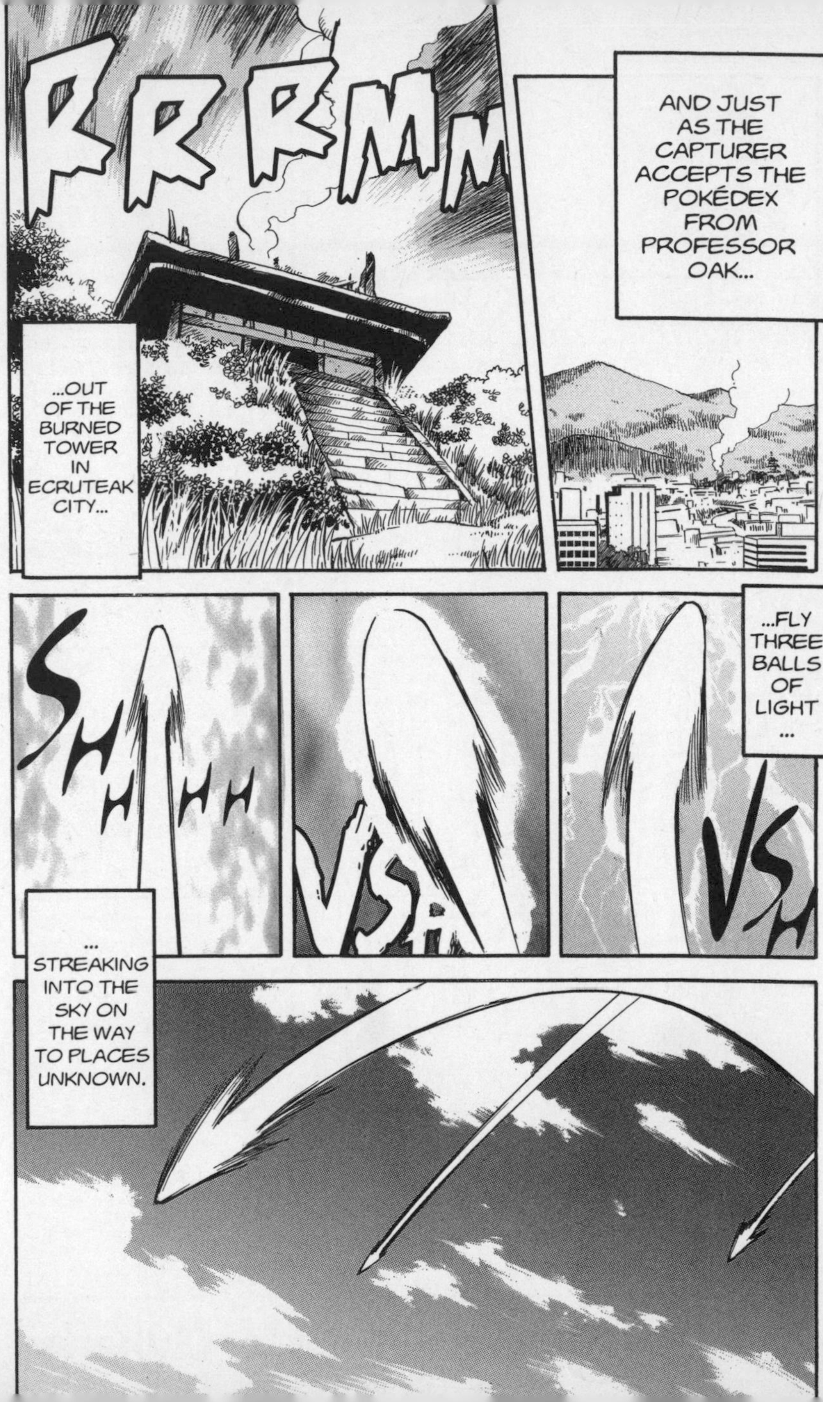
AND JUST AS THE CAPTURER ACCEPTS THE POKÉDEX FROM PROFESSOR OAK...
RRRMM
...OUT OF THE BURNED TOWER IN ECRUTEAK CITY...
...FLY THREE BALLS OF LIGHT ...
VSH
SHHHH
... STREAKING INTO THE SKY ON THE WAY TO PLACES UNKNOWN.

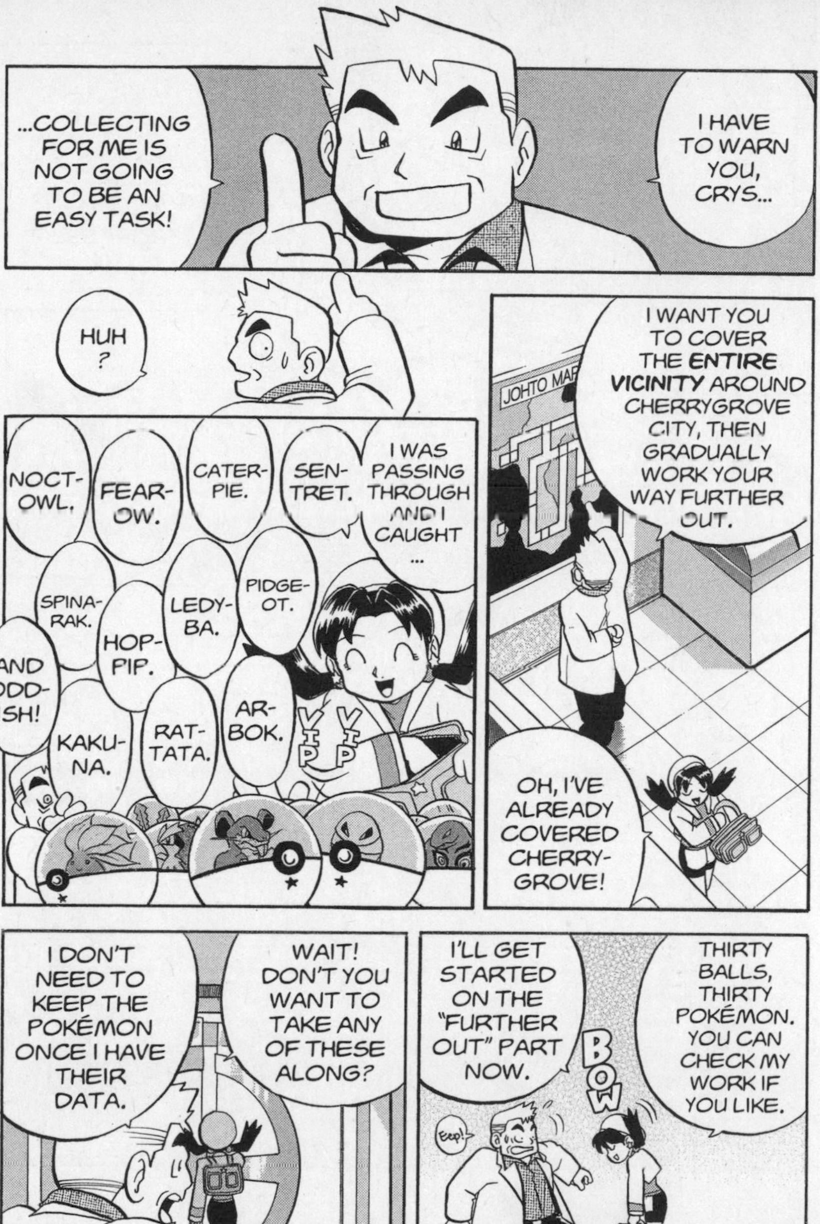
I HAVE TO WARN YOU, CRYS...
...COLLECTING FOR ME IS NOT GOING TO BE AN EASY TASK!
I WANT YOU TO COVER THE **ENTIRE VICINITY** AROUND CHERRYGROVE CITY, THEN GRADUALLY WORK YOUR WAY FURTHER OUT.
OH, I'VE ALREADY COVERED CHERRY-GROVE!
HUH?
I WAS PASSING THROUGH AND I CAUGHT...
SEN-TRET.
CATER-PIE.
FEAR-OW.
NOCT-OWL.
PIDGE-OT.
LEDY-BA.
HOP-PIP.
SPINA-RAK.
AR-BOK.
RAT-TATA.
KAKU-NA.
AND ODD-ISH!
VIP
VIP
THIRTY BALLS, THIRTY POKÉMON. YOU CAN CHECK MY WORK IF YOU LIKE.
I'LL GET STARTED ON THE "FURTHER OUT" PART NOW.
BOW
Eep!
WAIT! DON'T YOU WANT TO TAKE ANY OF THESE ALONG?
I DON'T NEED TO KEEP THE POKÉMON ONCE I HAVE THEIR DATA.

118 Three Cheers for Chikorita

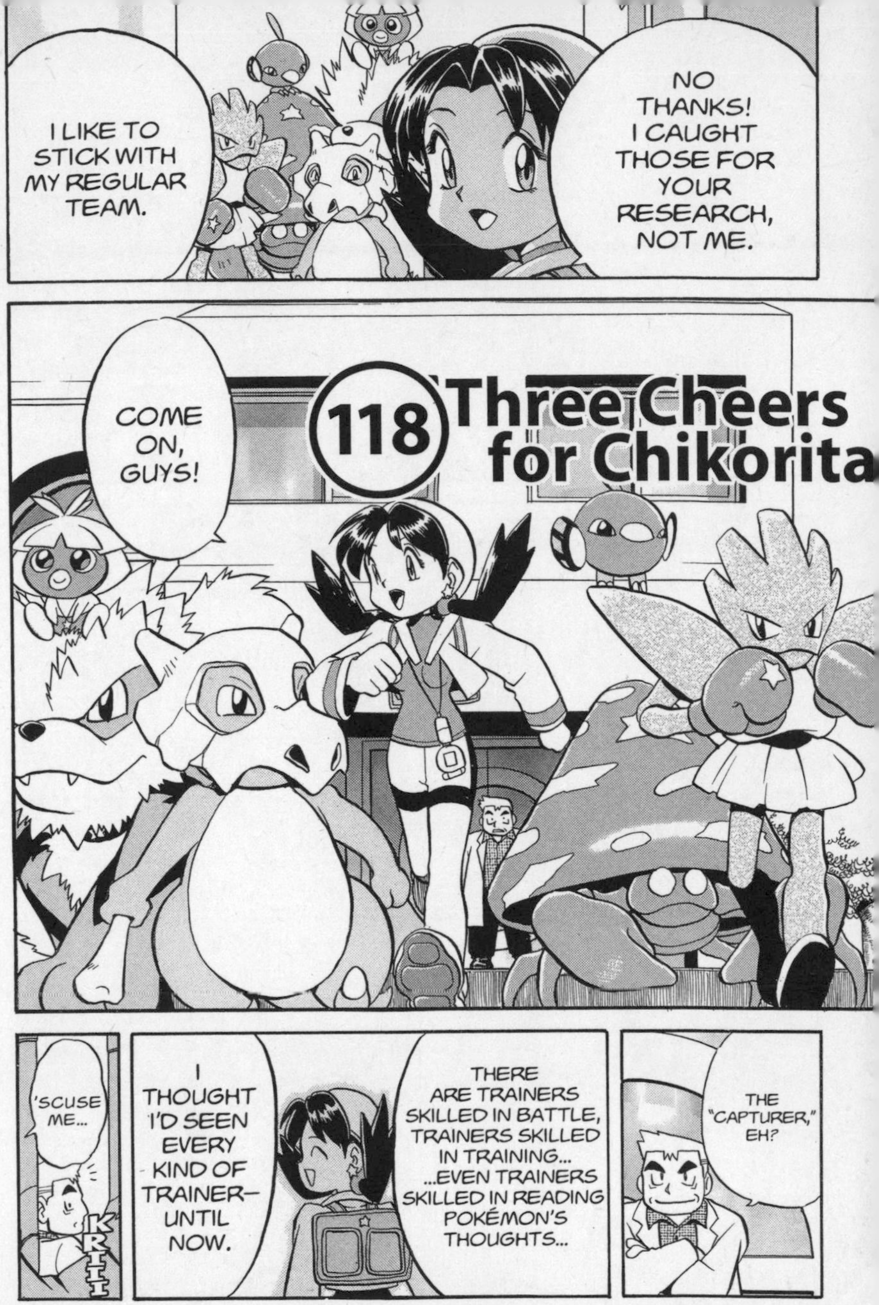
NO THANKS! I CAUGHT THOSE FOR YOUR RESEARCH, NOT ME.
I LIKE TO STICK WITH MY REGULAR TEAM.
118 Three Cheers for Chikorita
COME ON, GUYS!
THE "CAPTURER," EH?
THERE ARE TRAINERS SKILLED IN BATTLE, TRAINERS SKILLED IN TRAINING... ...EVEN TRAINERS SKILLED IN READING POKÉMON'S THOUGHTS...
I THOUGHT I'D SEEN EVERY KIND OF TRAINER—UNTIL NOW.
'SCUSE ME...
KRIII

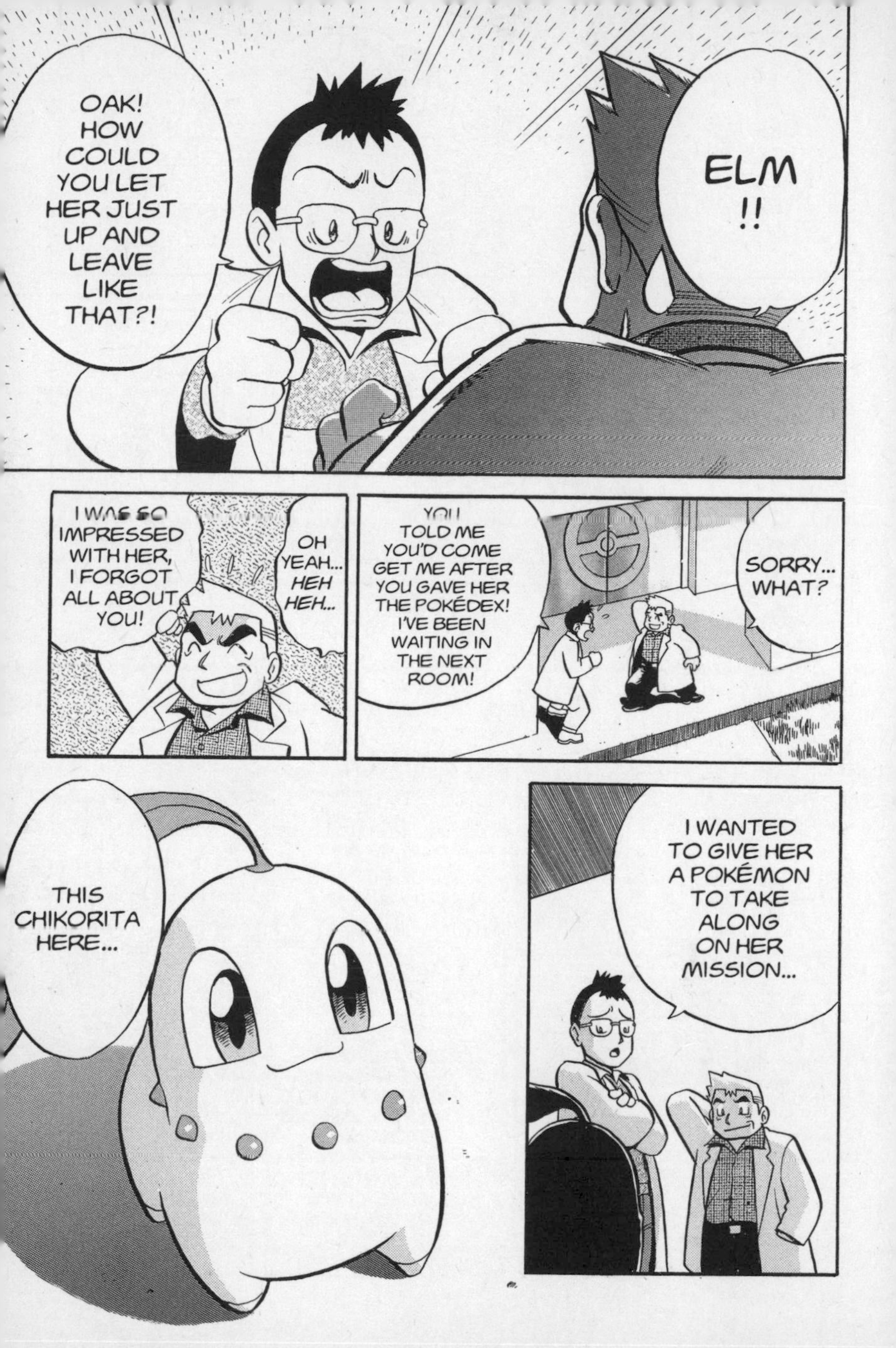
ELM!!
OAK! HOW COULD YOU LET HER JUST UP AND LEAVE LIKE THAT?!
SORRY... WHAT?
YOU TOLD ME YOU'D COME GET ME AFTER YOU GAVE HER THE POKÉDEX! I'VE BEEN WAITING IN THE NEXT ROOM!
OH YEAH... HEH HEH...
I WAS SO IMPRESSED WITH HER, I FORGOT ALL ABOUT YOU!
I WANTED TO GIVE HER A POKÉMON TO TAKE ALONG ON HER MISSION...
THIS CHIKORITA HERE...

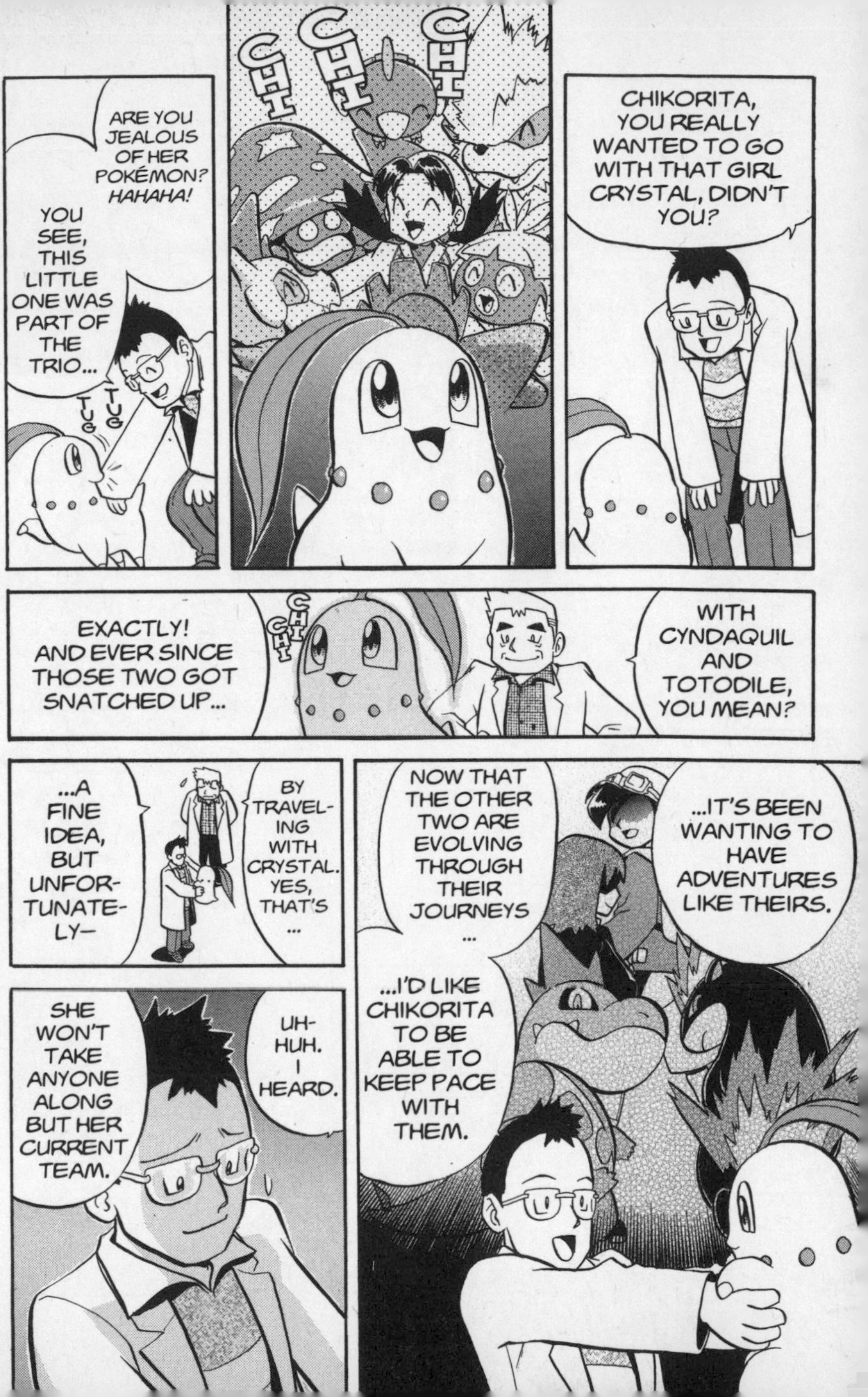
CHIKORITA, YOU REALLY WANTED TO GO WITH THAT GIRL CRYSTAL, DIDN'T YOU?
CHI CHI CHI
ARE YOU JEALOUS OF HER POKÉMON? *HAHAHA!*
YOU SEE, THIS LITTLE ONE WAS PART OF THE TRIO...
TUG TUG
WITH CYNDAQUIL AND TOTODILE, YOU MEAN?
CHI CHI
EXACTLY! AND EVER SINCE THOSE TWO GOT SNATCHED UP...
...IT'S BEEN WANTING TO HAVE ADVENTURES LIKE THEIRS.
NOW THAT THE OTHER TWO ARE EVOLVING THROUGH THEIR JOURNEYS...
...I'D LIKE CHIKORITA TO BE ABLE TO KEEP PACE WITH THEM.
BY TRAVEL-ING WITH CRYSTAL. YES, THAT'S...
...A FINE IDEA, BUT UNFOR-TUNATE-LY—
UH-HUH. I HEARD.
SHE WON'T TAKE ANYONE ALONG BUT HER CURRENT TEAM.

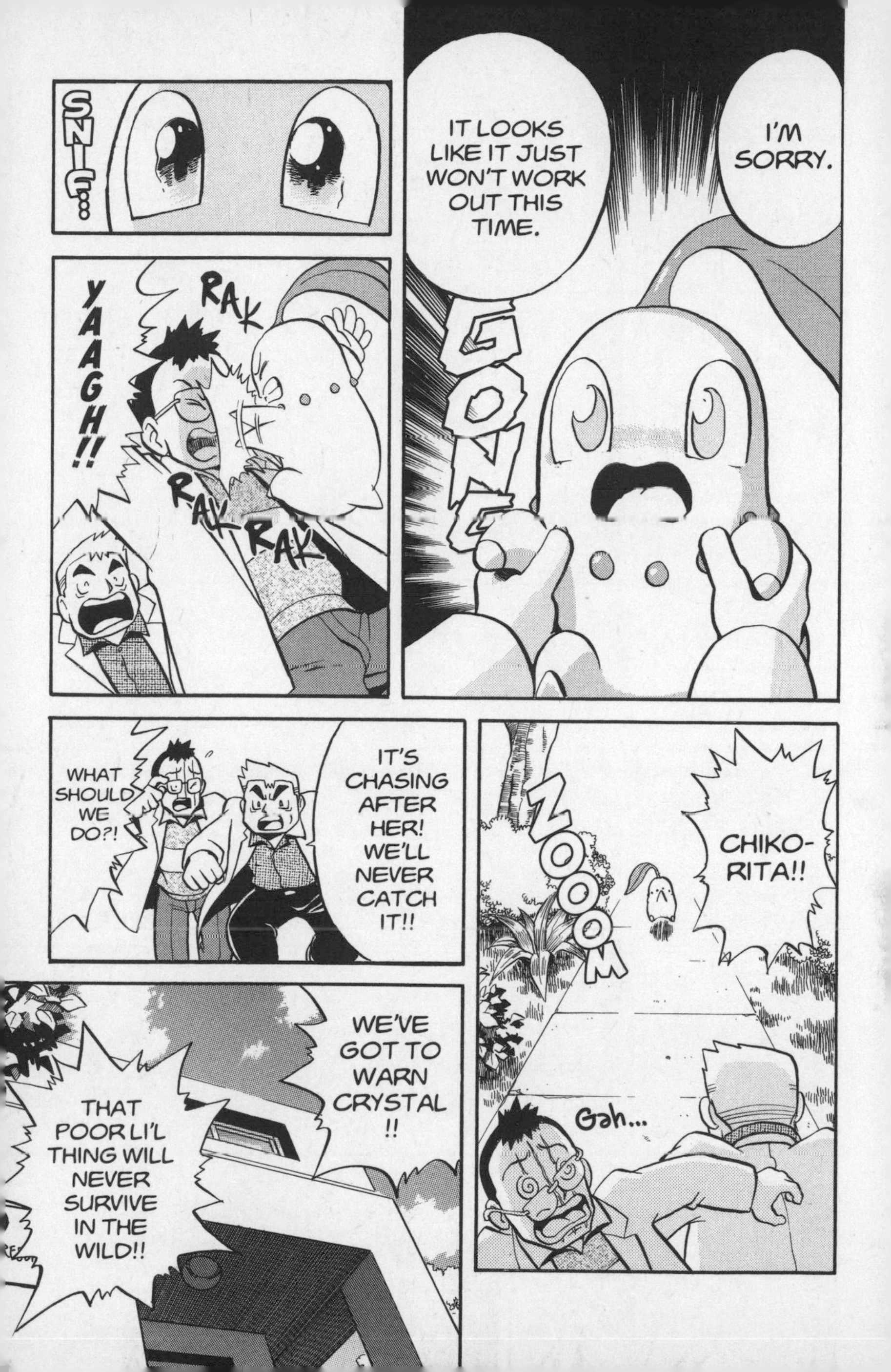
I'M SORRY.
IT LOOKS LIKE IT JUST WON'T WORK OUT THIS TIME.
GONG
SNIF...
YAAAGH!!
RAK
RAK
RAK
CHIKO-RITA!!
ZOOOOM
Gah...
IT'S CHASING AFTER HER! WE'LL NEVER CATCH IT!!
WHAT SHOULD WE DO?!
WE'VE GOT TO WARN CRYSTAL!!
THAT POOR LI'L THING WILL NEVER SURVIVE IN THE WILD!!

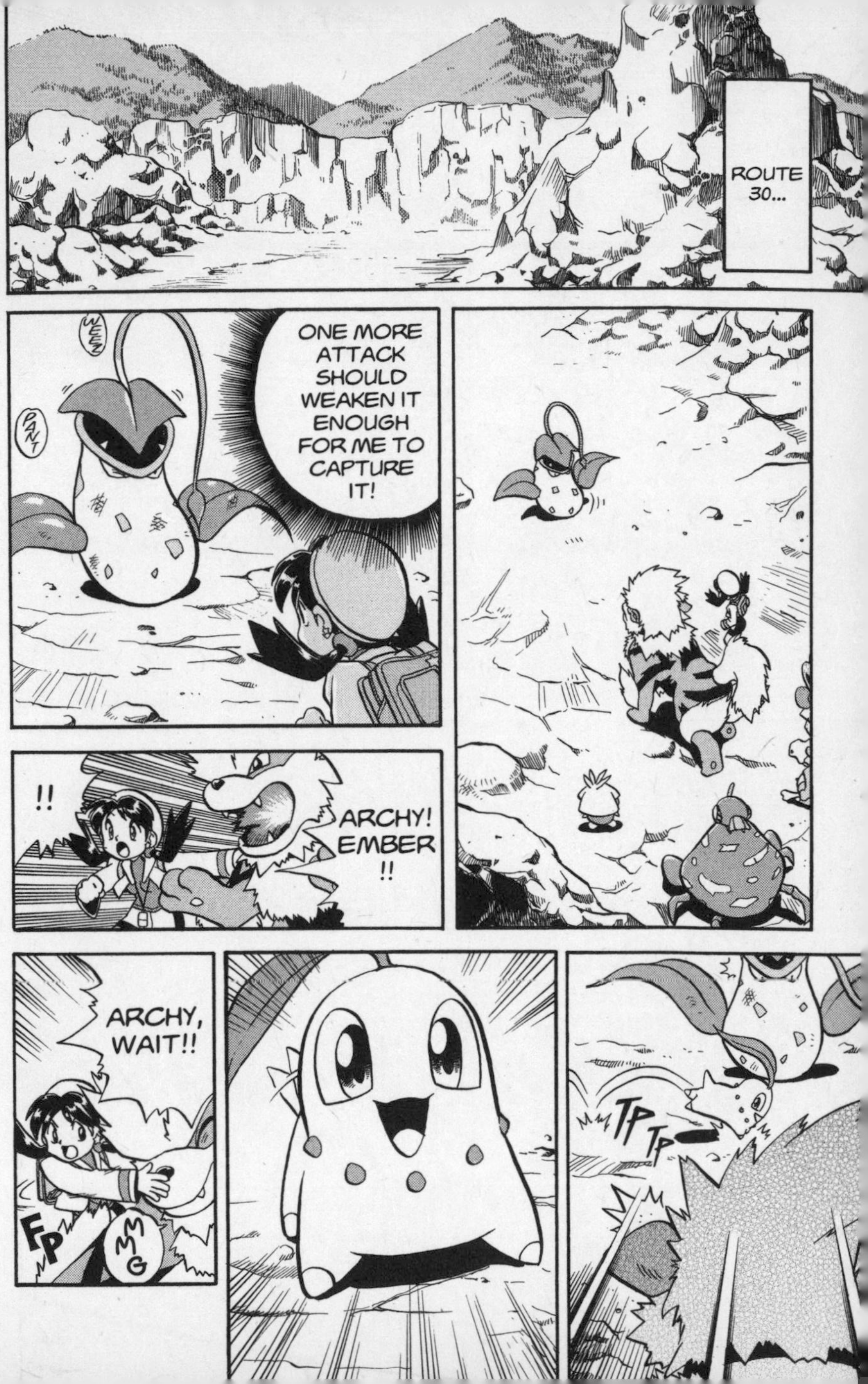
ROUTE 30...
ONE MORE ATTACK SHOULD WEAKEN IT ENOUGH FOR ME TO CAPTURE IT!
WEEZ
PANT
ARCHY! EMBER!!
!!
TP TP
ARCHY, WAIT!!
FP
MMMG

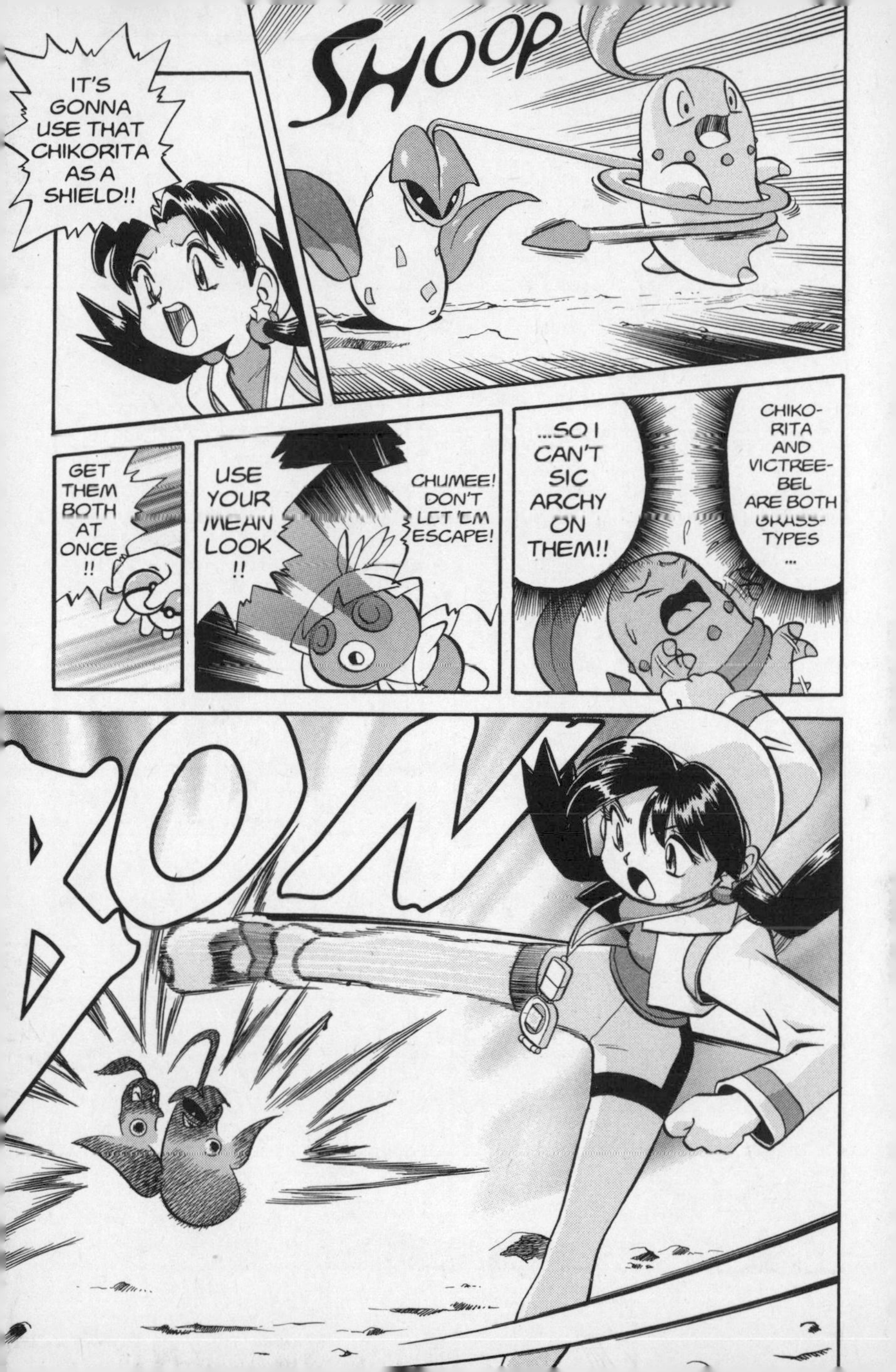
SHOOP
IT'S GONNA USE THAT CHIKORITA AS A SHIELD!!
CHIKO-RITA AND VICTREE-BEL ARE BOTH GRASS-TYPES ...
...SO I CAN'T SIC ARCHY ON THEM!!
CHUMEE! DON'T LET 'EM ESCAPE!
USE YOUR MEAN LOOK!!
GET THEM BOTH AT ONCE!!

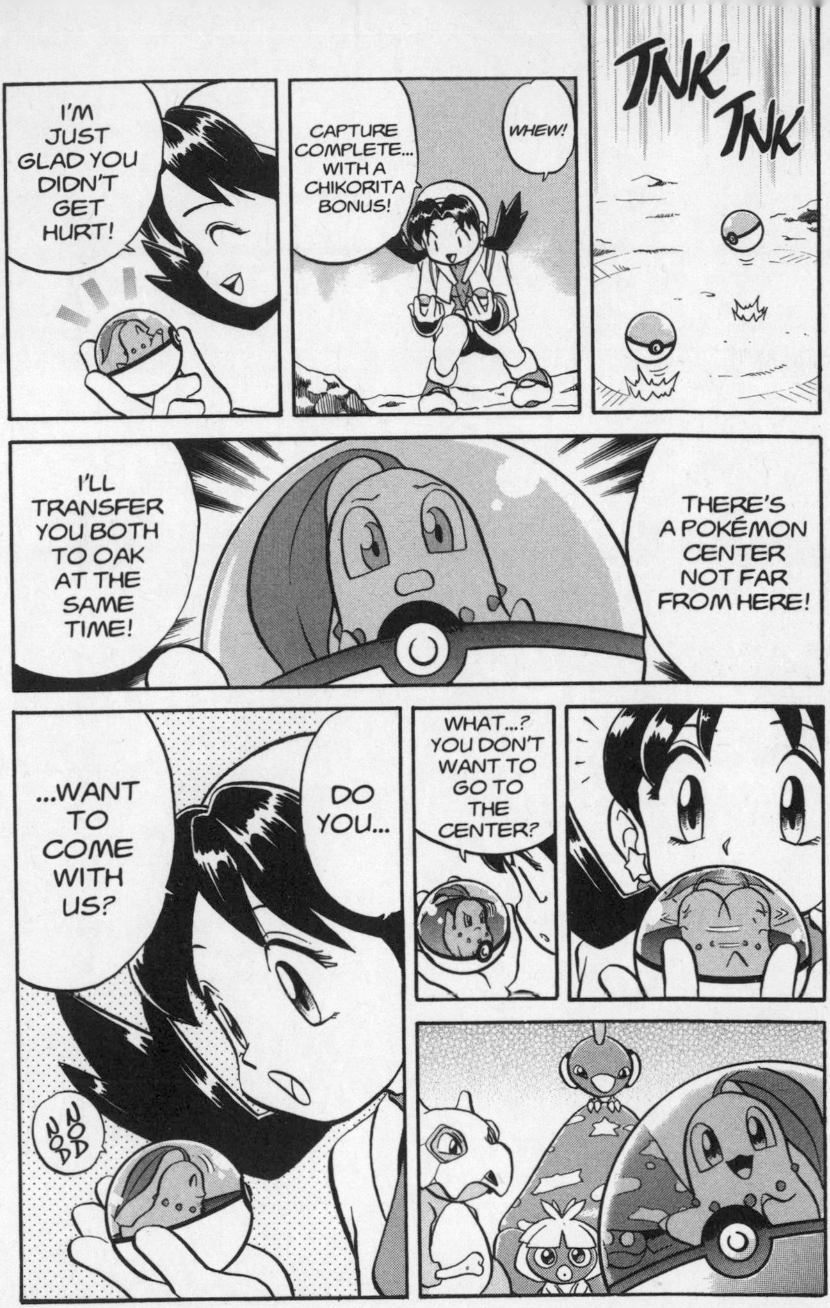
TNK TNK
WHEW!
CAPTURE COMPLETE... WITH A CHIKORITA BONUS!
I'M JUST GLAD YOU DIDN'T GET HURT!
THERE'S A POKÉMON CENTER NOT FAR FROM HERE!
I'LL TRANSFER YOU BOTH TO OAK AT THE SAME TIME!
WHAT...? YOU DON'T WANT TO GO TO THE CENTER?
DO YOU...
...WANT TO COME WITH US?
NOD NOD

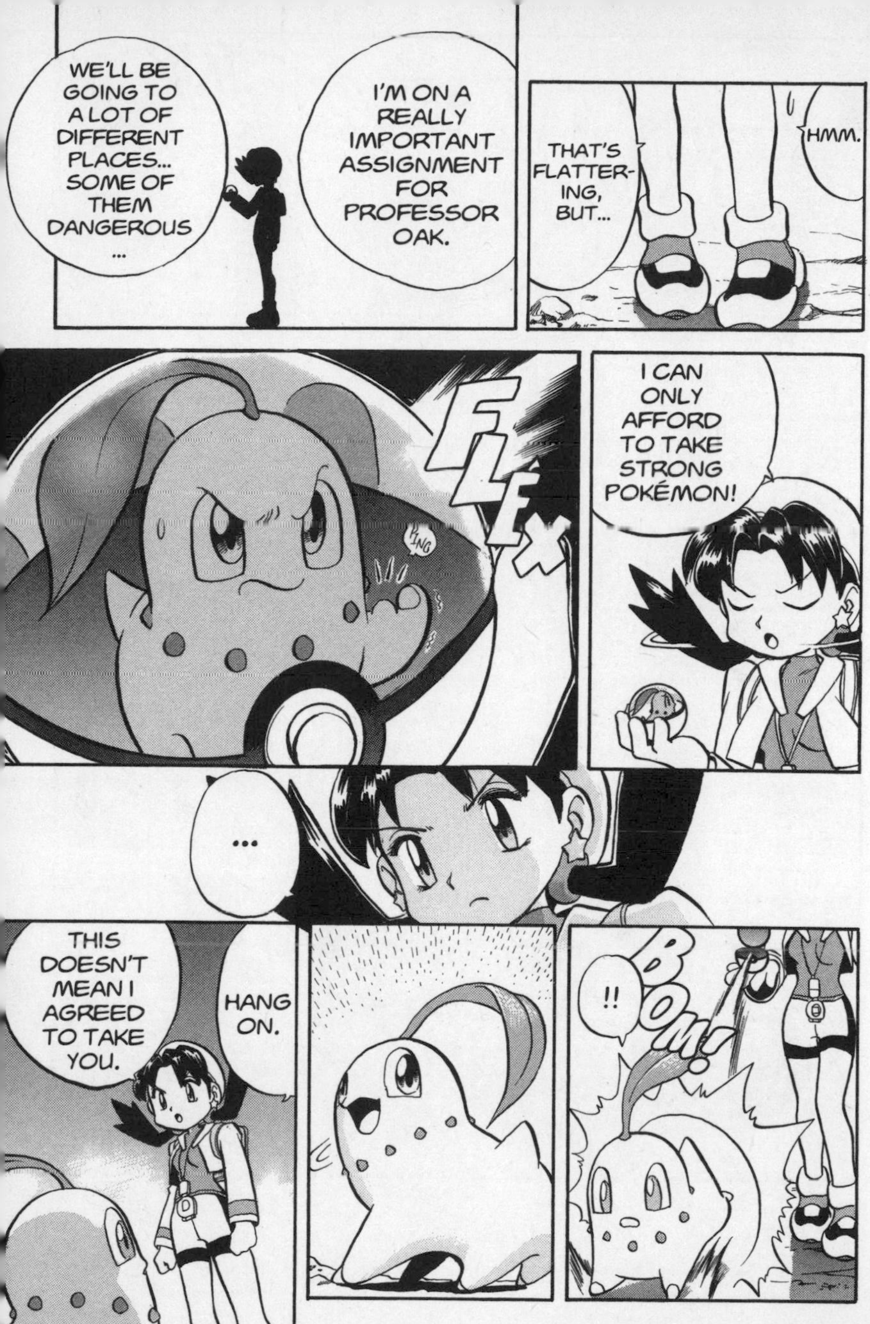
HMM.
THAT'S FLATTER-ING, BUT...
I'M ON A REALLY IMPORTANT ASSIGNMENT FOR PROFESSOR OAK.
WE'LL BE GOING TO A LOT OF DIFFERENT PLACES... SOME OF THEM DANGEROUS ...
I CAN ONLY AFFORD TO TAKE STRONG POKÉMON!
FLEX
...
BOOM!
!!
HANG ON.
THIS DOESN'T MEAN I AGREED TO TAKE YOU.

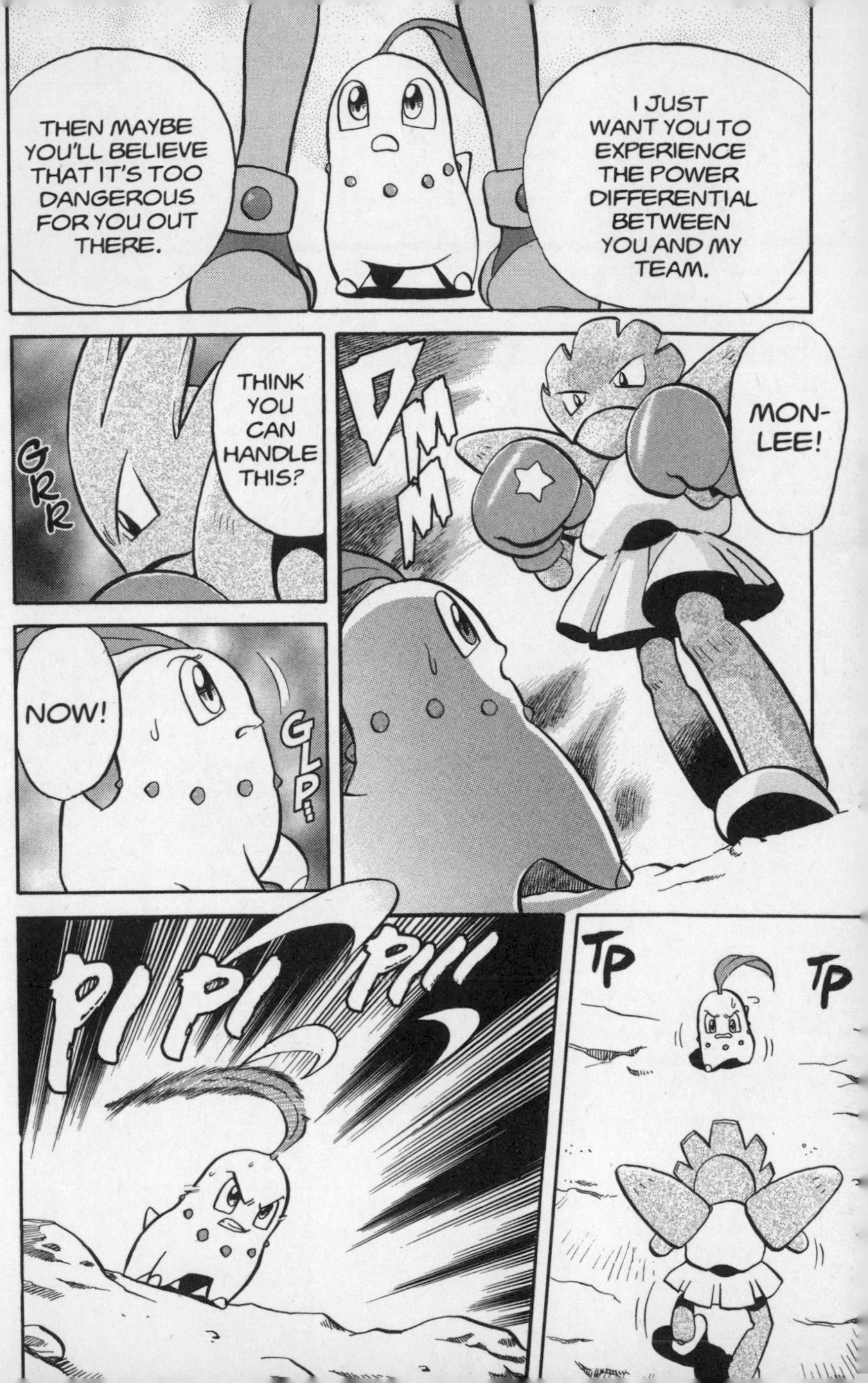
I JUST WANT YOU TO EXPERIENCE THE POWER DIFFERENTIAL BETWEEN YOU AND MY TEAM.
THEN MAYBE YOU'LL BELIEVE THAT IT'S TOO DANGEROUS FOR YOU OUT THERE.
MON-LEE!
DMMM
THINK YOU CAN HANDLE THIS?
GRR
NOW!
GLP!
TP
TP
PI PI PII

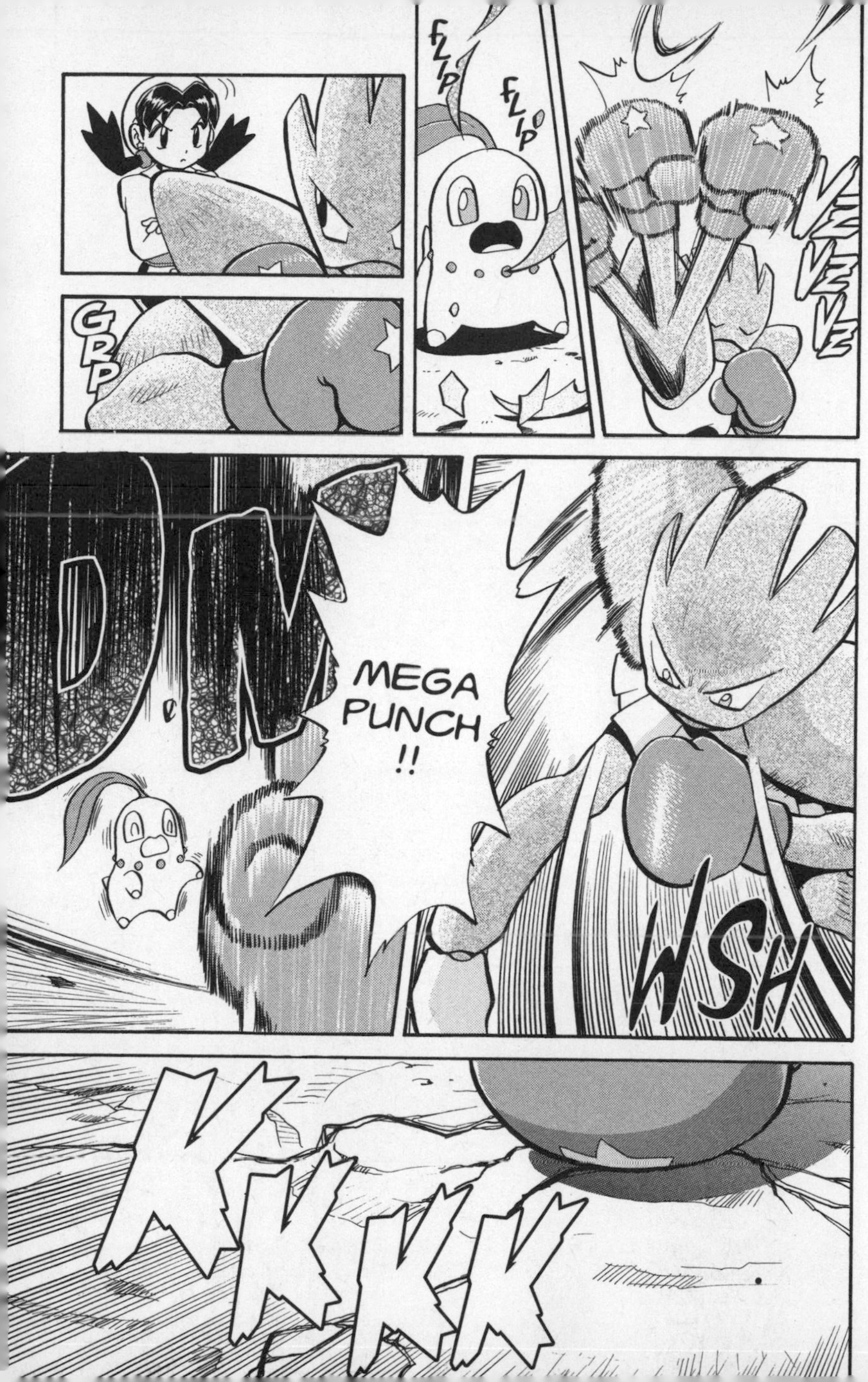

VE VE VE
FLIP
FLIP
GRP
MEGA PUNCH !!
DM
WSH
KKKK

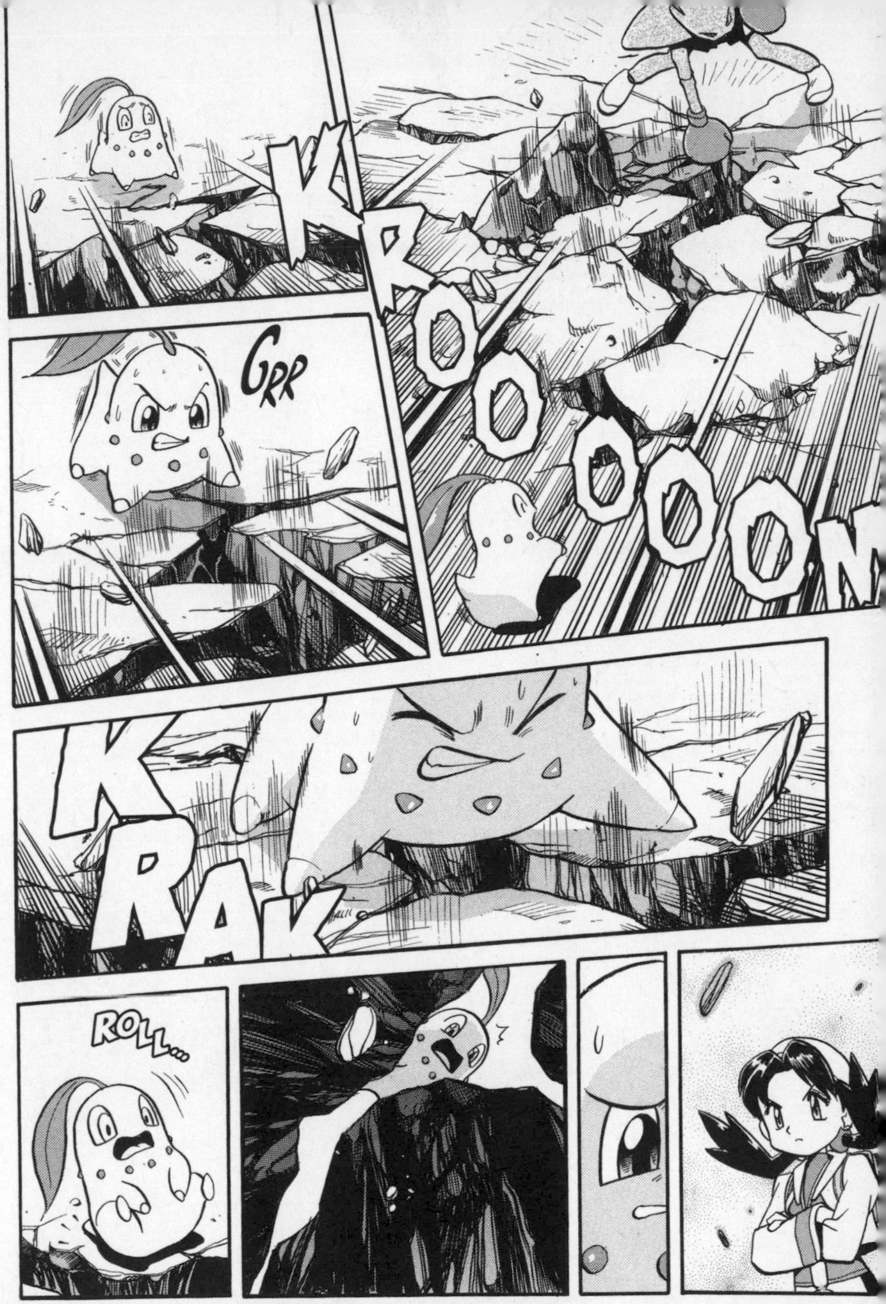
KROOOOOM
GRR
KRAK
ROLL...

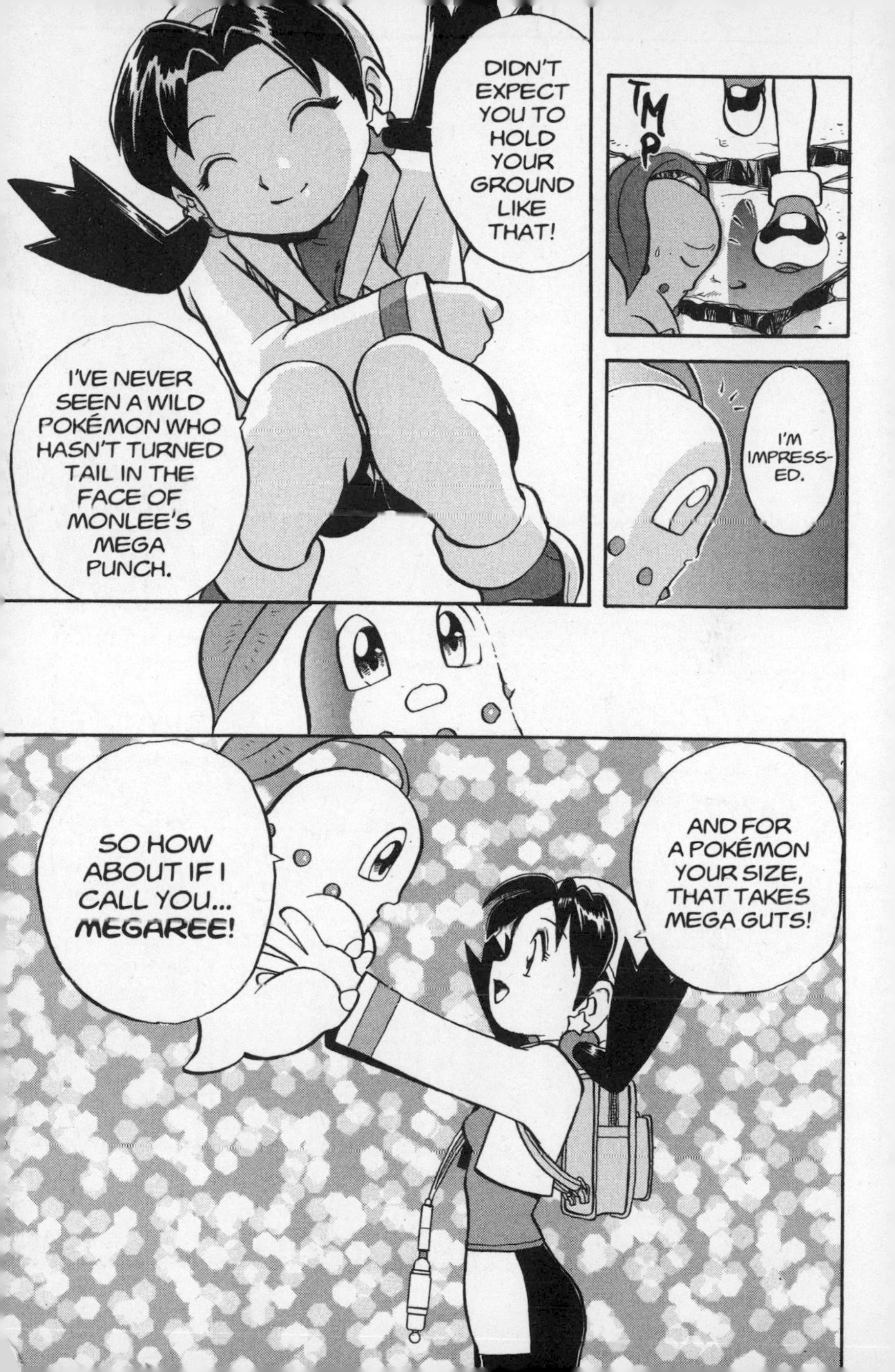
TMP
I'M IMPRESS-ED.
DIDN'T EXPECT YOU TO HOLD YOUR GROUND LIKE THAT!
I'VE NEVER SEEN A WILD POKÉMON WHO HASN'T TURNED TAIL IN THE FACE OF MONLEE'S MEGA PUNCH.
AND FOR A POKÉMON YOUR SIZE, THAT TAKES MEGA GUTS!
SO HOW ABOUT IF I CALL YOU... MEGAREE!

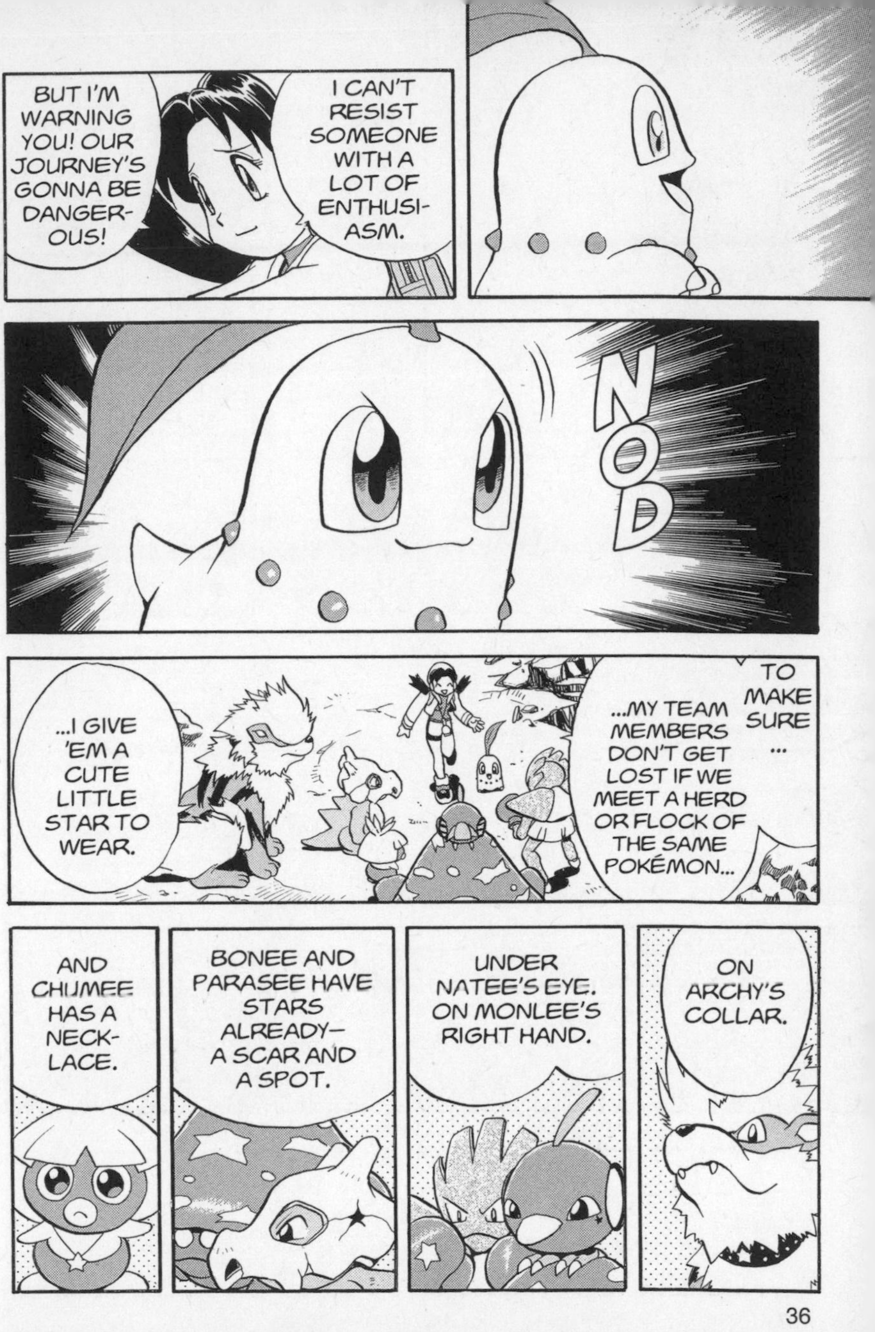

I CAN'T RESIST SOMEONE WITH A LOT OF ENTHUSI-ASM.
BUT I'M WARNING YOU! OUR JOURNEY'S GONNA BE DANGER-OUS!
NOD
TO MAKE SURE ...
...MY TEAM MEMBERS DON'T GET LOST IF WE MEET A HERD OR FLOCK OF THE SAME POKÉMON...
...I GIVE 'EM A CUTE LITTLE STAR TO WEAR.
ON ARCHY'S COLLAR.
UNDER NATEE'S EYE. ON MONLEE'S RIGHT HAND.
BONEE AND PARASEE HAVE STARS ALREADY— A SCAR AND A SPOT.
AND CHUMEE HAS A NECK-LACE.

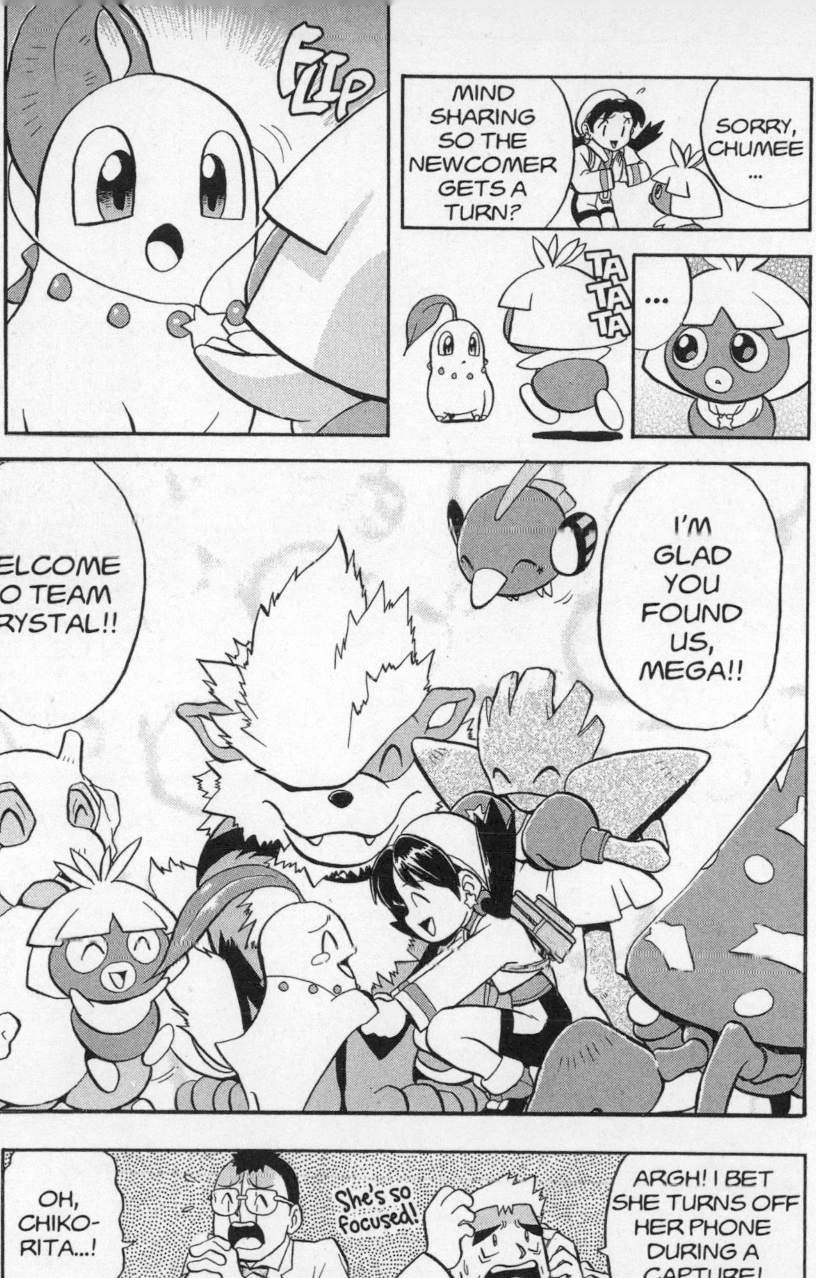
SORRY, CHUMEE ...
MIND SHARING SO THE NEWCOMER GETS A TURN?
...
TA TA TA
FLIP
I'M GLAD YOU FOUND US, MEGA!!
WELCOME TO TEAM CRYSTAL!!
ARGH! I BET SHE TURNS OFF HER PHONE DURING A CAPTURE!
She's so focused!
OH, CHIKO-RITA...!

(119) A Flaaffy Kerfuffle

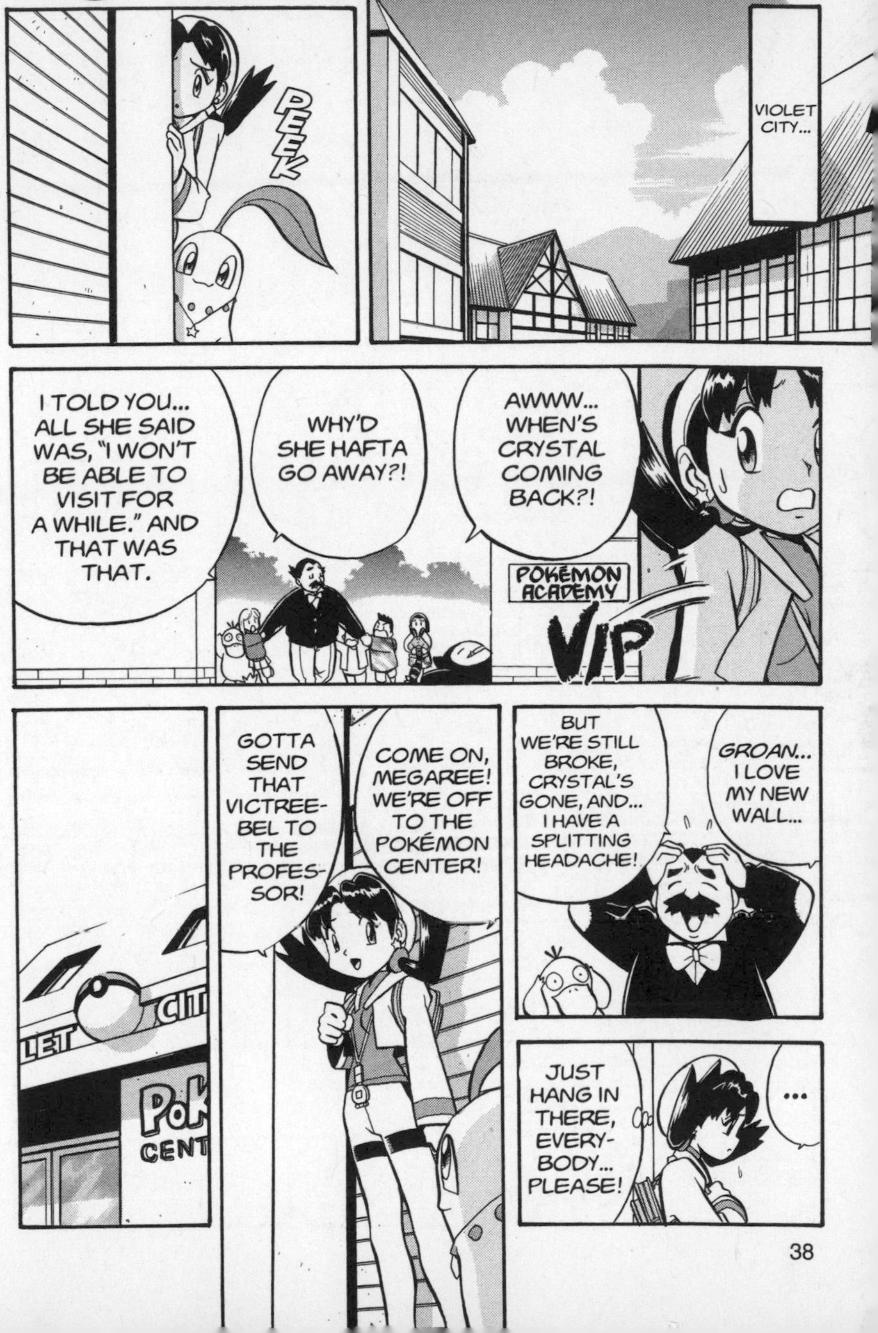
VIOLET CITY...
PEEK
POKÉMON ACADEMY
VIP
AWWW... WHEN'S CRYSTAL COMING BACK?!
WHY'D SHE HAFTA GO AWAY?!
I TOLD YOU... ALL SHE SAID WAS, "I WON'T BE ABLE TO VISIT FOR A WHILE." AND THAT WAS THAT.
GROAN... I LOVE MY NEW WALL...
BUT WE'RE STILL BROKE, CRYSTAL'S GONE, AND... I HAVE A SPLITTING HEADACHE!
...
JUST HANG IN THERE, EVERY-BODY... PLEASE!
COME ON, MEGAREE! WE'RE OFF TO THE POKÉMON CENTER!
GOTTA SEND THAT VICTREE-BEL TO THE PROFES-SOR!
LET
CIT
PoK
CENT

119 A Flaaffy Kerfuffle

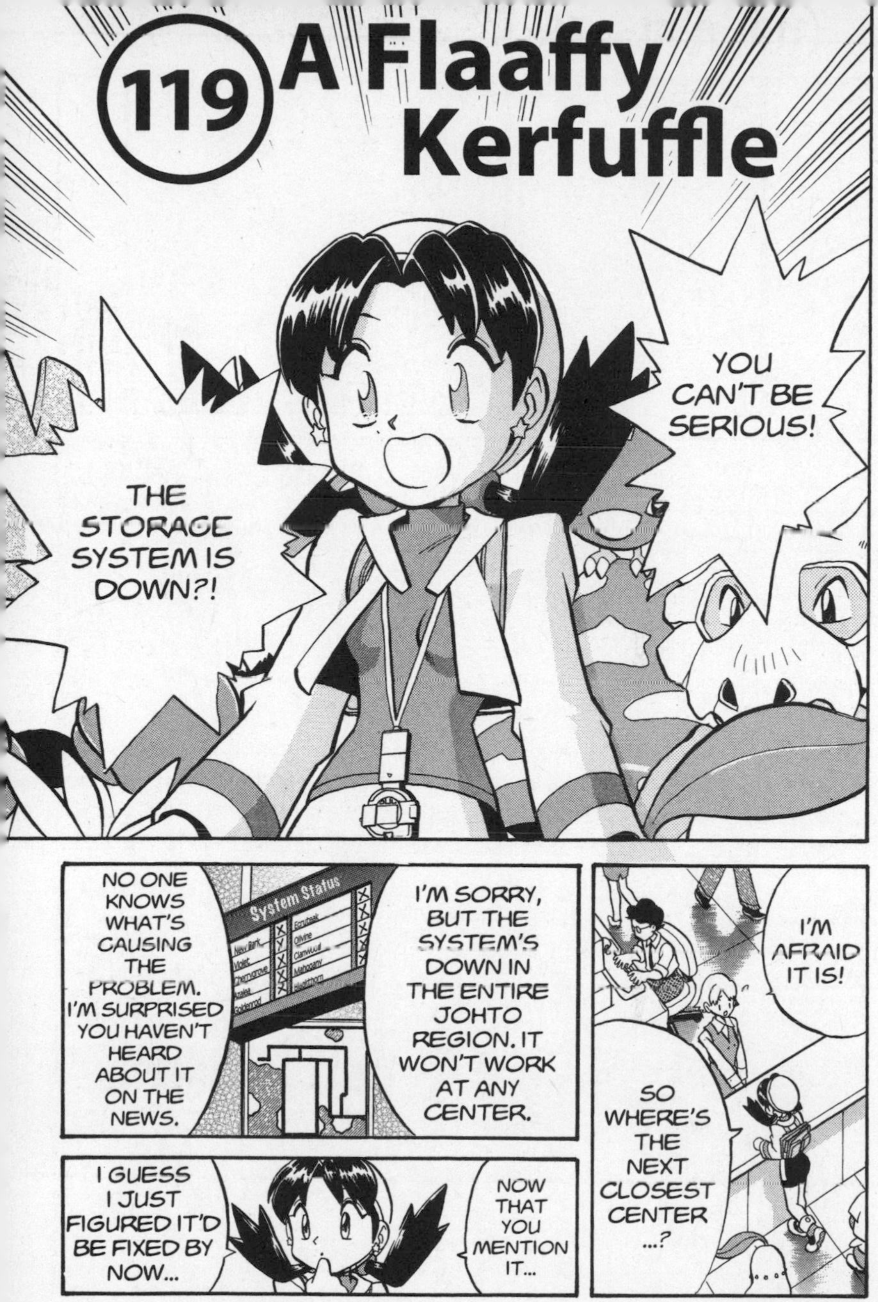

YOU CAN'T BE SERIOUS!
THE STORAGE SYSTEM IS DOWN?!
I'M AFRAID IT IS!
SO WHERE'S THE NEXT CLOSEST CENTER ...?
I'M SORRY, BUT THE SYSTEM'S DOWN IN THE ENTIRE JOHTO REGION. IT WON'T WORK AT ANY CENTER.
System Status
NO ONE KNOWS WHAT'S CAUSING THE PROBLEM. I'M SURPRISED YOU HAVEN'T HEARD ABOUT IT ON THE NEWS.
NOW THAT YOU MENTION IT...
I GUESS I JUST FIGURED IT'D BE FIXED BY NOW...

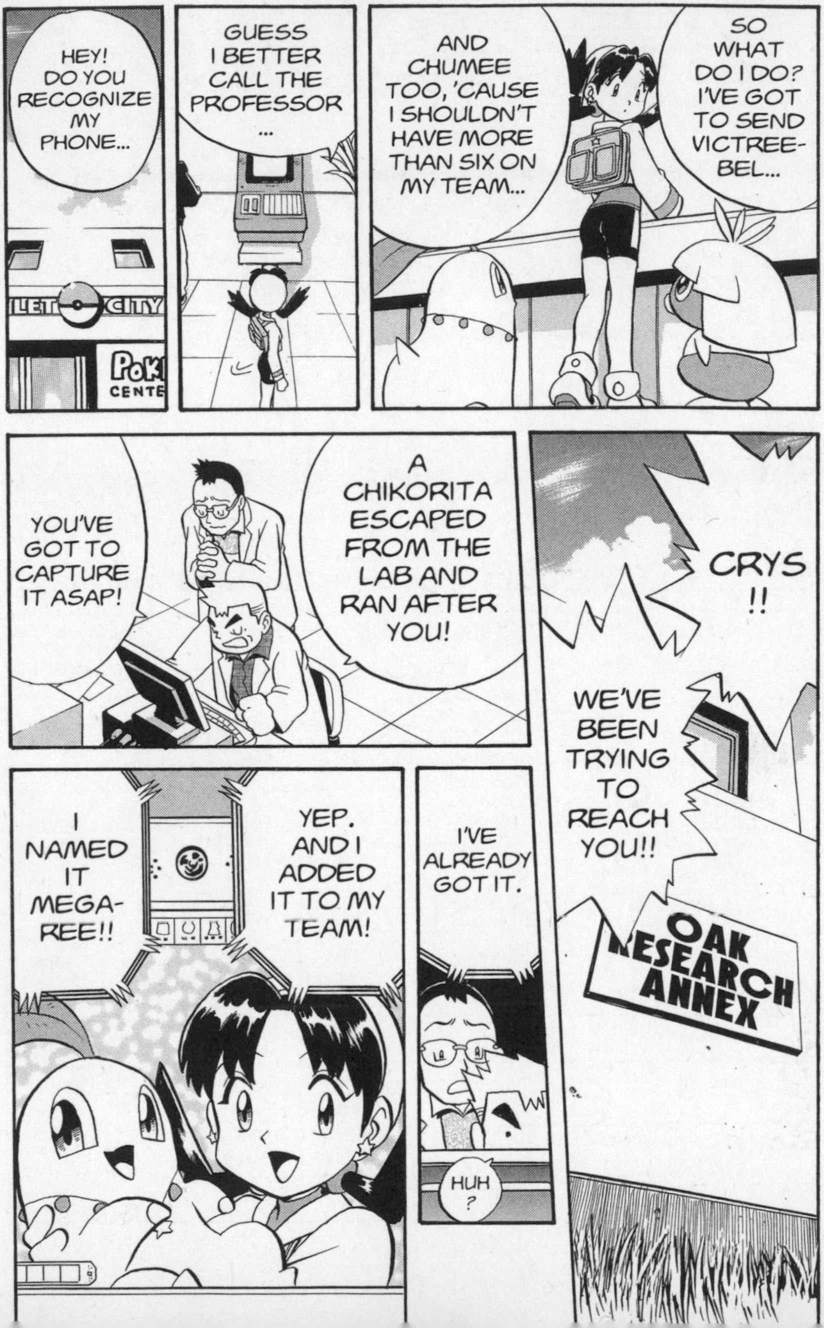
SO WHAT DO I DO? I'VE GOT TO SEND VICTREE-BEL...
AND CHUMEE TOO, 'CAUSE I SHOULDN'T HAVE MORE THAN SIX ON MY TEAM...
GUESS I BETTER CALL THE PROFESSOR ...
HEY! DO YOU RECOGNIZE MY PHONE...
LET CITY
POKé CENTE
CRYS !!
WE'VE BEEN TRYING TO REACH YOU!!
OAK RESEARCH ANNEX
A CHIKORITA ESCAPED FROM THE LAB AND RAN AFTER YOU!
YOU'VE GOT TO CAPTURE IT ASAP!
I'VE ALREADY GOT IT.
HUH ?
YEP. AND I ADDED IT TO MY TEAM!
I NAMED IT MEGA-REE!!

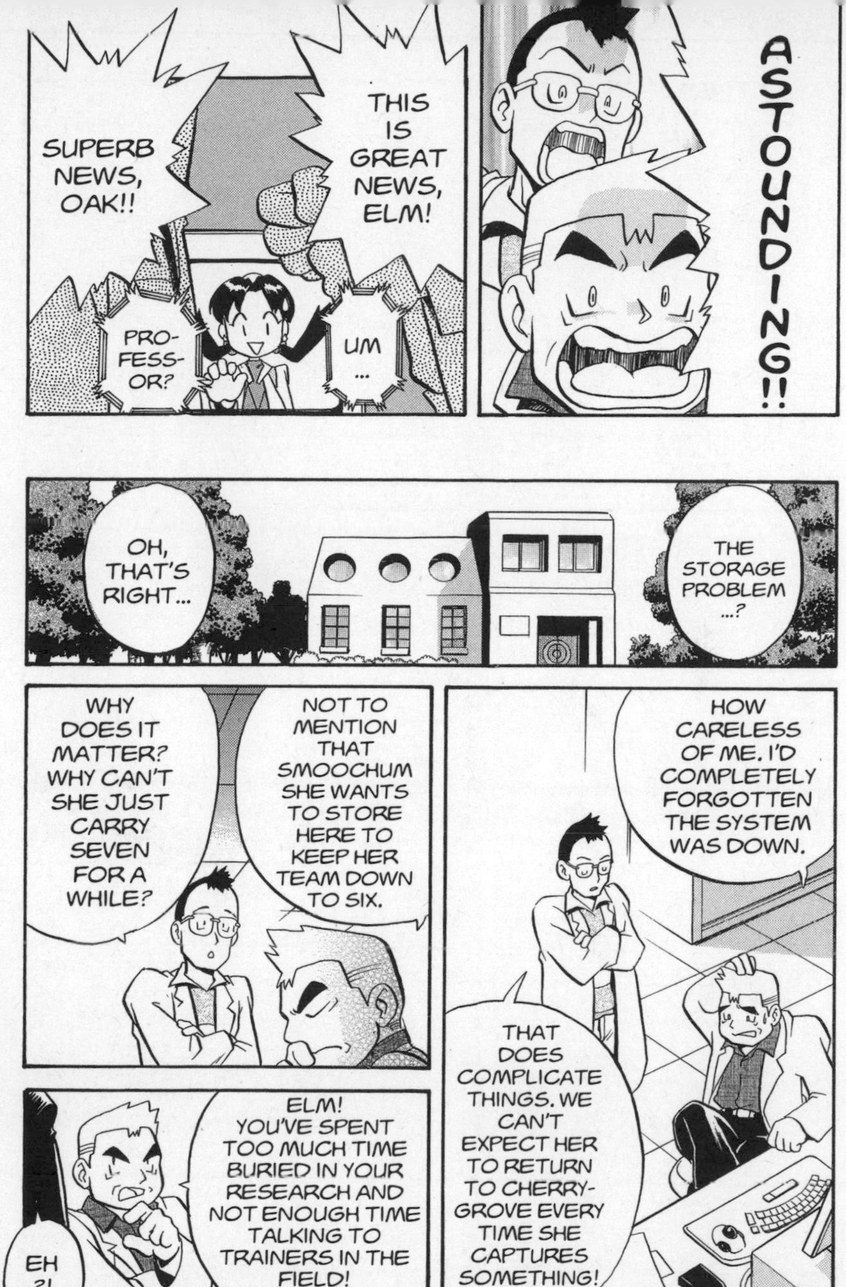
ASTOUNDING!!
THIS IS GREAT NEWS, ELM!
SUPERB NEWS, OAK!!
UM ...
PRO-FESS-OR?
THE STORAGE PROBLEM ...?
OH, THAT'S RIGHT...
HOW CARELESS OF ME. I'D COMPLETELY FORGOTTEN THE SYSTEM WAS DOWN.
THAT DOES COMPLICATE THINGS. WE CAN'T EXPECT HER TO RETURN TO CHERRY-GROVE EVERY TIME SHE CAPTURES SOMETHING!
NOT TO MENTION THAT SMOOCHUM SHE WANTS TO STORE HERE TO KEEP HER TEAM DOWN TO SIX.
WHY DOES IT MATTER? WHY CAN'T SHE JUST CARRY SEVEN FOR A WHILE?
ELM! YOU'VE SPENT TOO MUCH TIME BURIED IN YOUR RESEARCH AND NOT ENOUGH TIME TALKING TO TRAINERS IN THE FIELD!
EH ?!

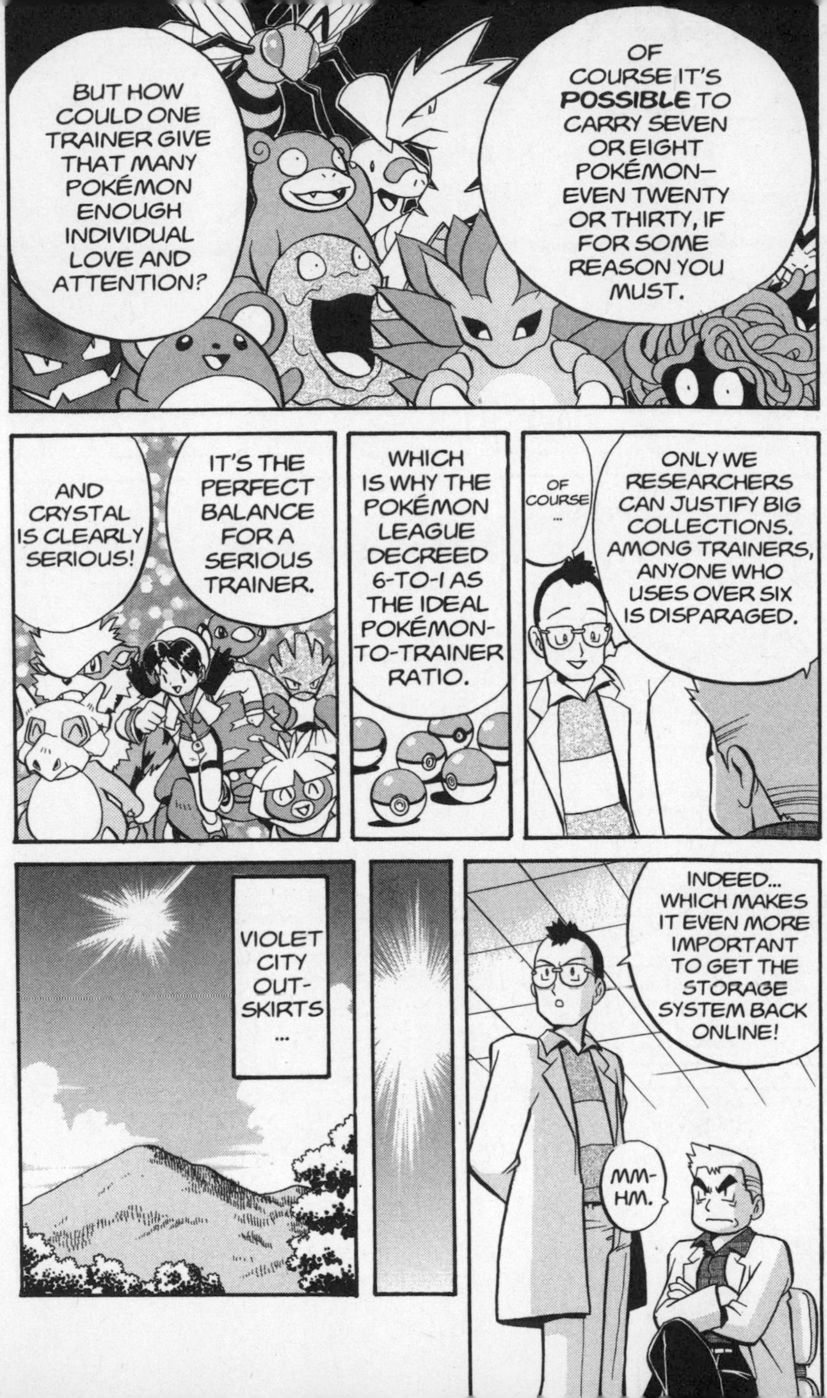
OF COURSE IT'S **POSSIBLE** TO CARRY SEVEN OR EIGHT POKÉMON—EVEN TWENTY OR THIRTY, IF FOR SOME REASON YOU MUST.
BUT HOW COULD ONE TRAINER GIVE THAT MANY POKÉMON ENOUGH INDIVIDUAL LOVE AND ATTENTION?
ONLY WE RESEARCHERS CAN JUSTIFY BIG COLLECTIONS. AMONG TRAINERS, ANYONE WHO USES OVER SIX IS DISPARAGED.
OF COURSE...
WHICH IS WHY THE POKÉMON LEAGUE DECREED 6-TO-1 AS THE IDEAL POKÉMON-TO-TRAINER RATIO.
IT'S THE PERFECT BALANCE FOR A SERIOUS TRAINER.
AND CRYSTAL IS CLEARLY SERIOUS!
INDEED... WHICH MAKES IT EVEN MORE IMPORTANT TO GET THE STORAGE SYSTEM BACK ONLINE!
MM-HM.
VIOLET CITY OUT-SKIRTS ...

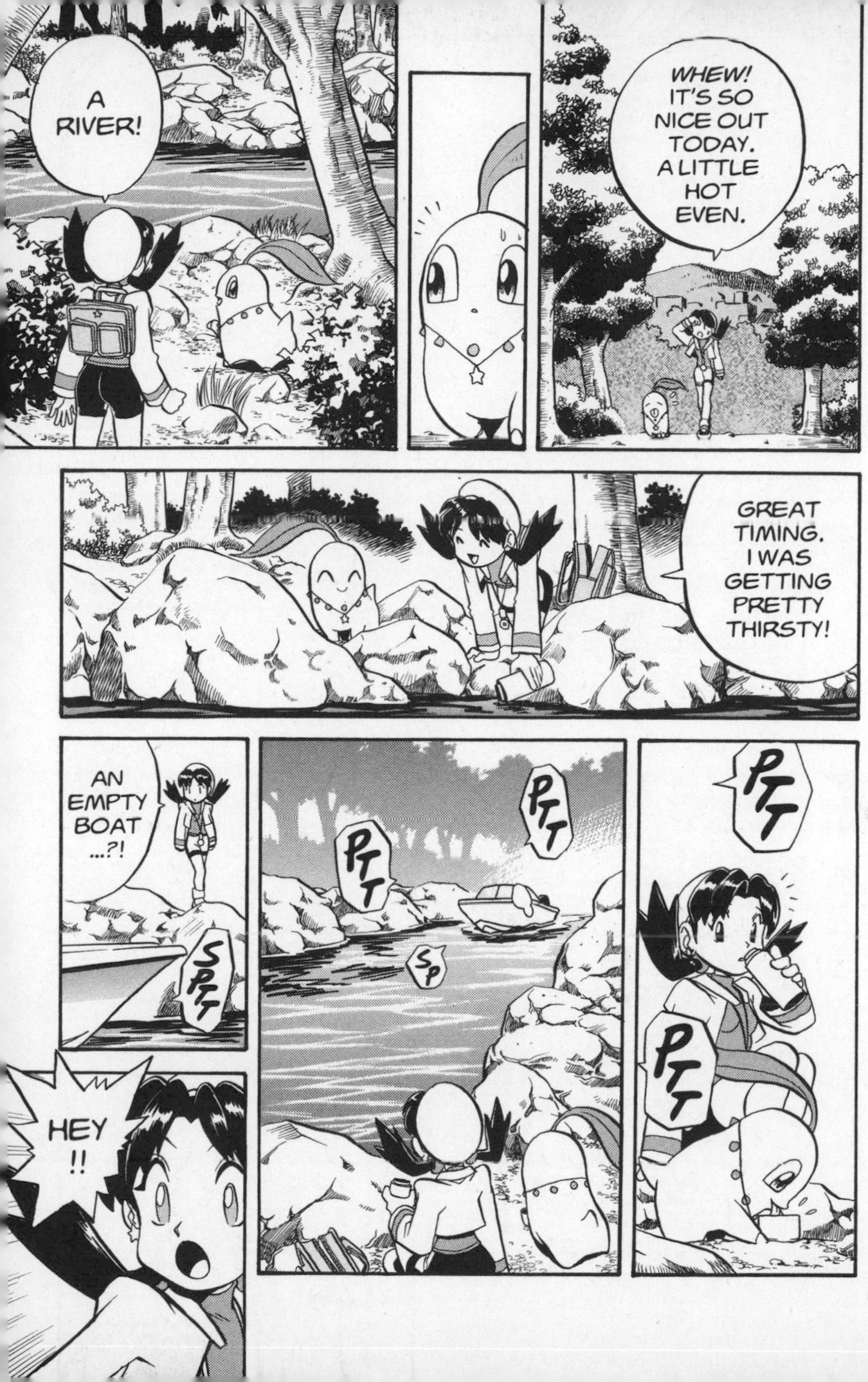
WHEW! IT'S SO NICE OUT TODAY. A LITTLE HOT EVEN.
A RIVER!
GREAT TIMING. I WAS GETTING PRETTY THIRSTY!
PTT
PTT
PTT
PTT
SP
AN EMPTY BOAT ...?!
SPTT
HEY !!

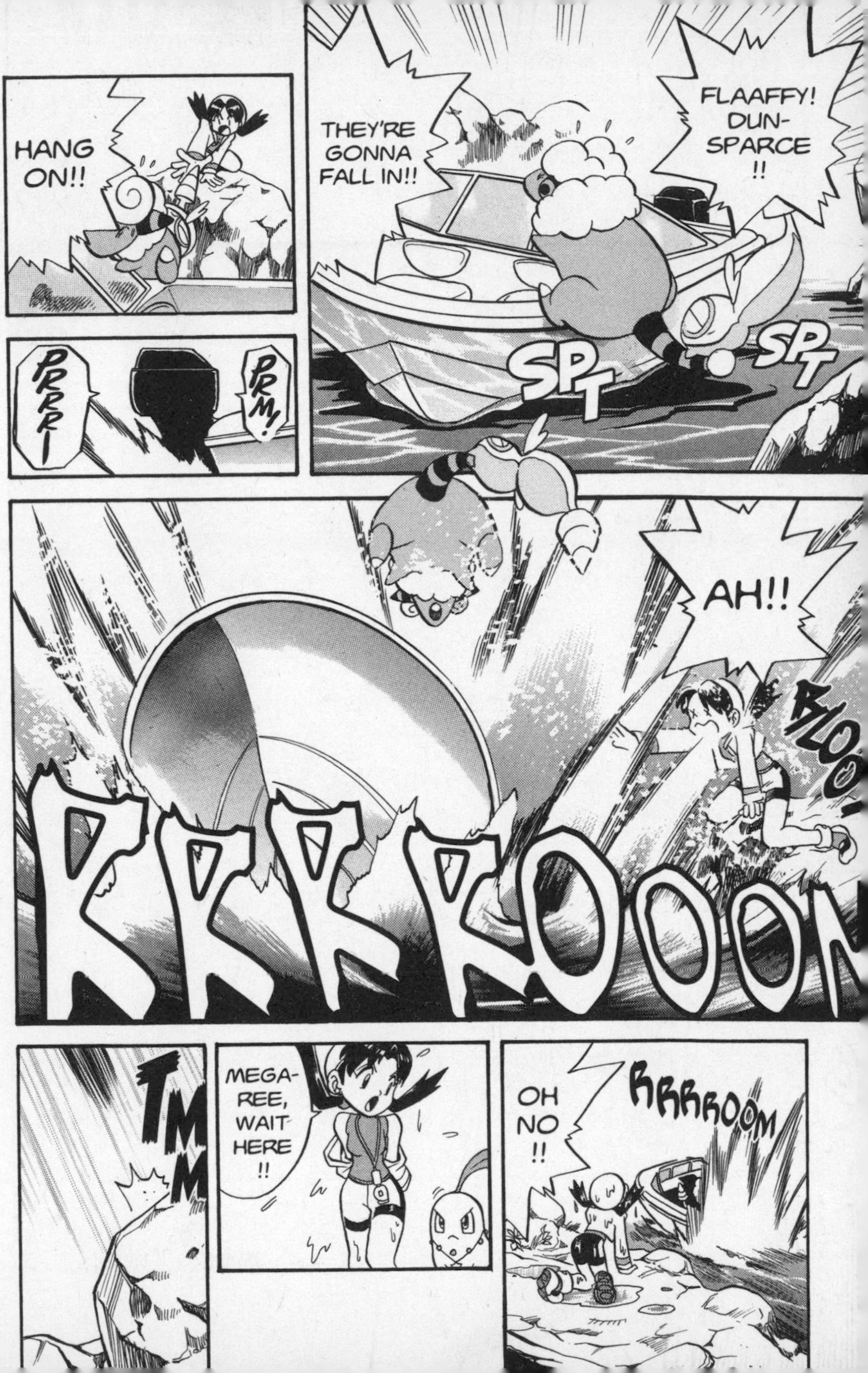
FLAAFFY! DUN-SPARCE !!
THEY'RE GONNA FALL IN!!
SPT
SPT
HANG ON!!
PRM!
PRRRI
AH!!
BLOO
KRRROOO
RRRROOM
OH NO !!
MEGA-REE, WAIT HERE !!
TMM

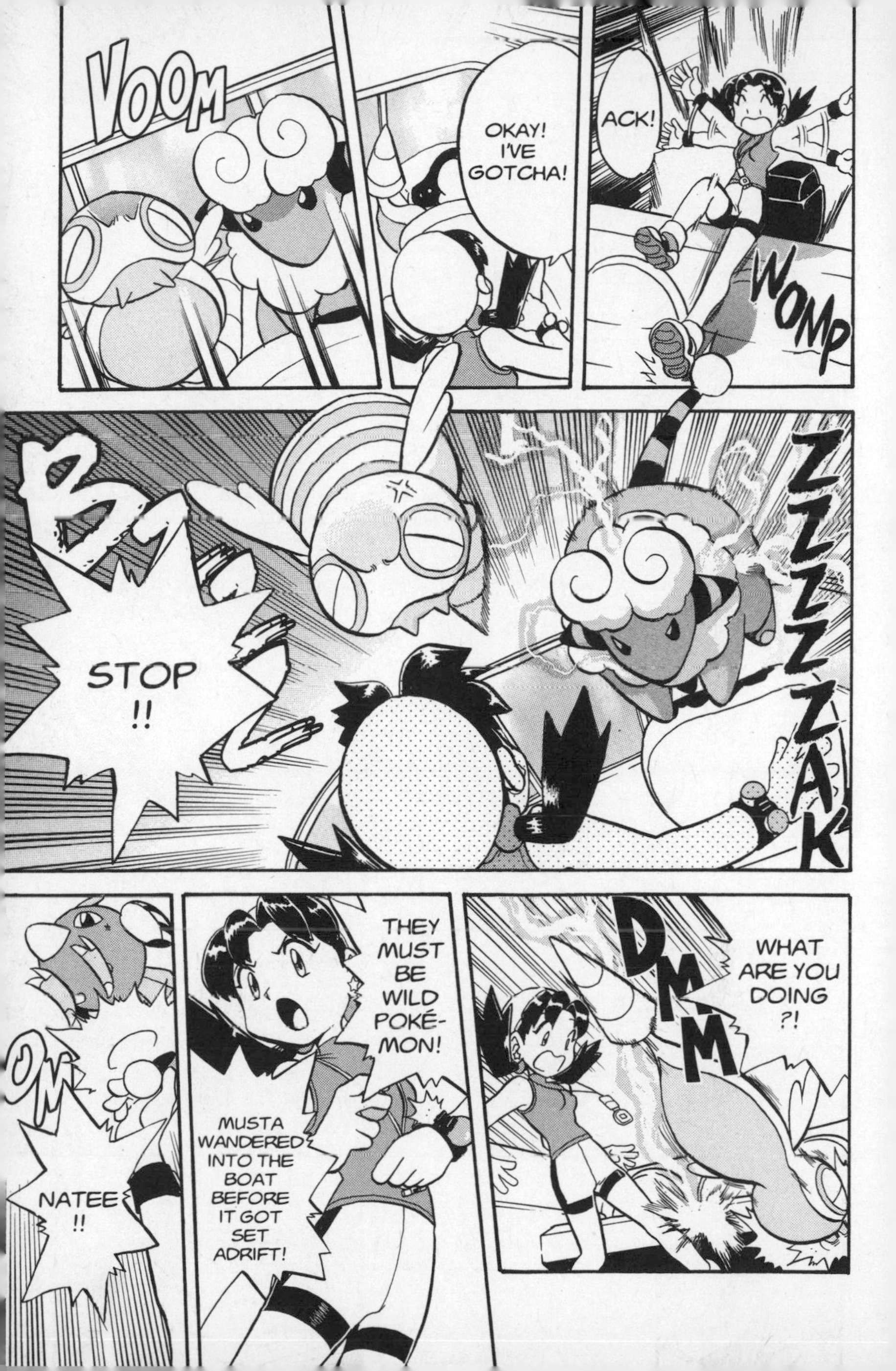

ACK!
WOMP
OKAY! I'VE GOTCHA!
VOOM
ZZZZZAK
STOP !!
DMMM
WHAT ARE YOU DOING ?!
THEY MUST BE WILD POKÉ-MON!
MUSTA WANDERED INTO THE BOAT BEFORE IT GOT SET ADRIFT!
NATEE !!

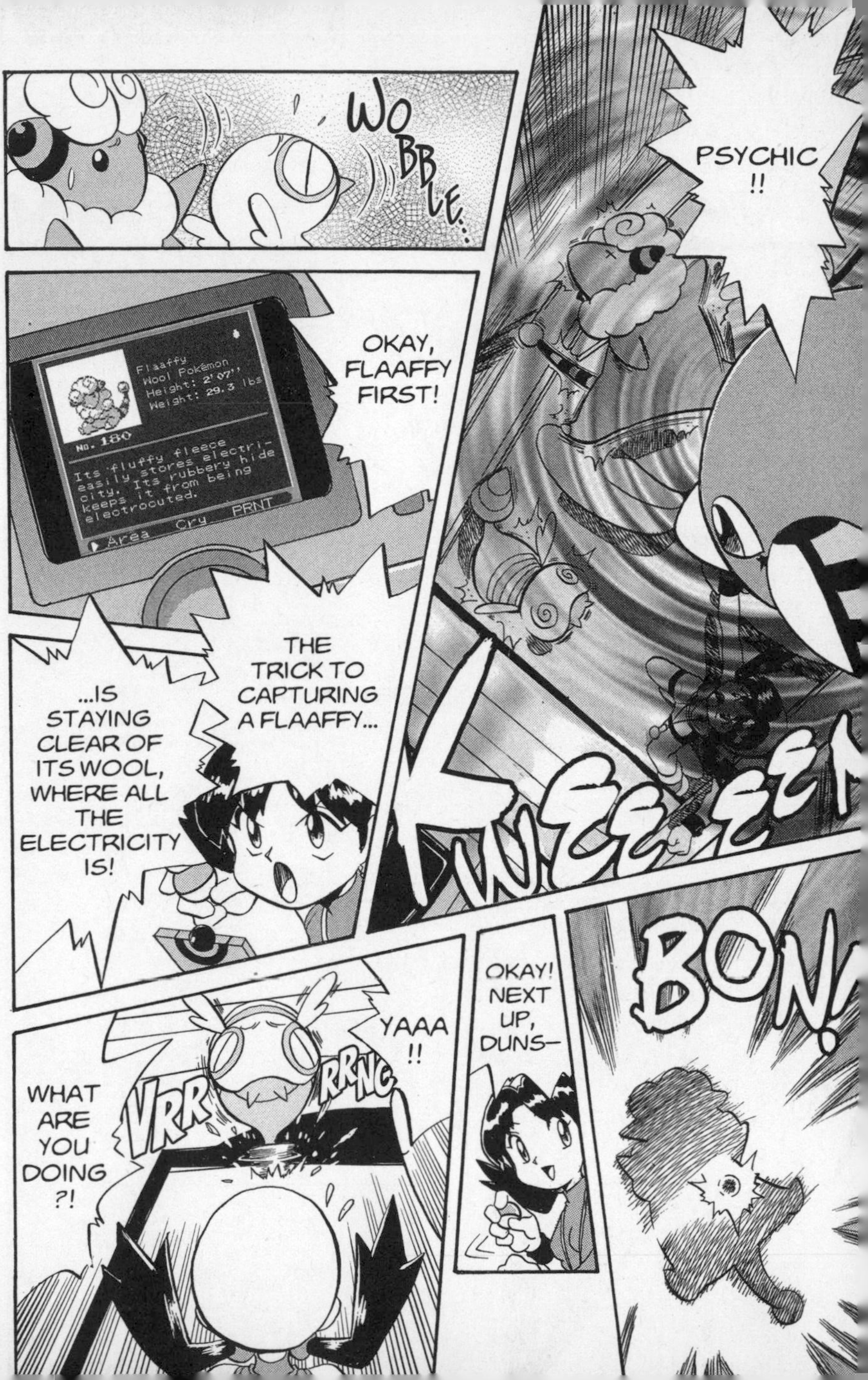
PSYCHIC !!
WEEEEEN
WOBBLE...
Flaaffy
Wool Pokémon
Height: 2'07''
Weight: 29.3 lbs
No. 180
Its fluffy fleece easily stores electricity. Its rubbery hide keeps it from being electrocuted.
Area Cry PRNT
OKAY, FLAAFFY FIRST!
THE TRICK TO CAPTURING A FLAAFFY...
...IS STAYING CLEAR OF ITS WOOL, WHERE ALL THE ELECTRICITY IS!
BON!
OKAY! NEXT UP, DUNS—
YAAA !!
VRR
RRRNG
WHAT ARE YOU DOING ?!

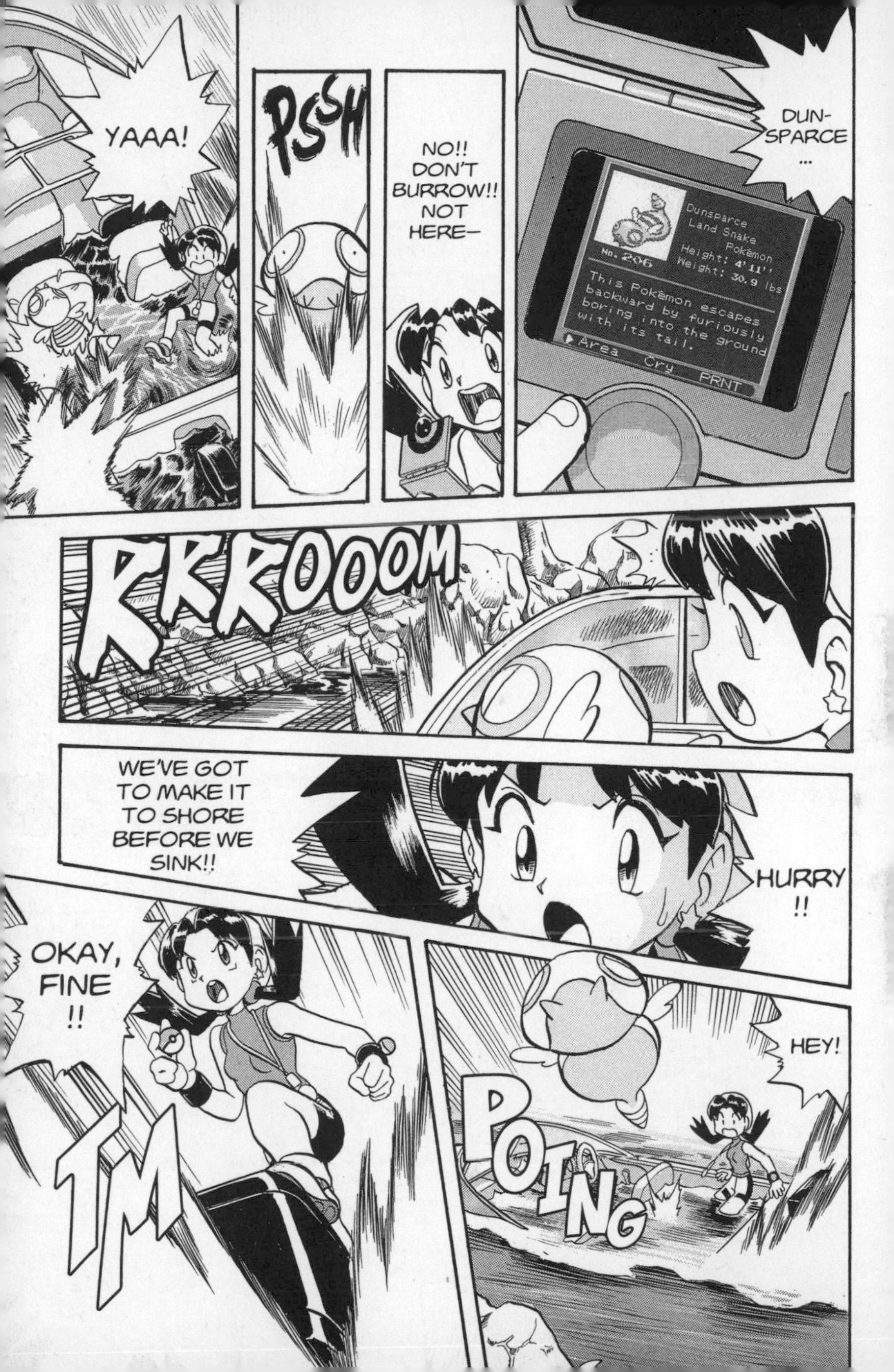
DUN-SPARCE ...
Dunsparce
Land Snake Pokémon
No. 206
Height: 4'11''
Weight: 30.9 lbs
This Pokémon escapes backward by furiously boring into the ground with its tail.
Area Cry PRNT
NO!! DON'T BURROW!! NOT HERE—
PSSH
YAAA!
RRROOOM
WE'VE GOT TO MAKE IT TO SHORE BEFORE WE SINK!!
HURRY!!
HEY!
POING
OKAY, FINE!!
TM

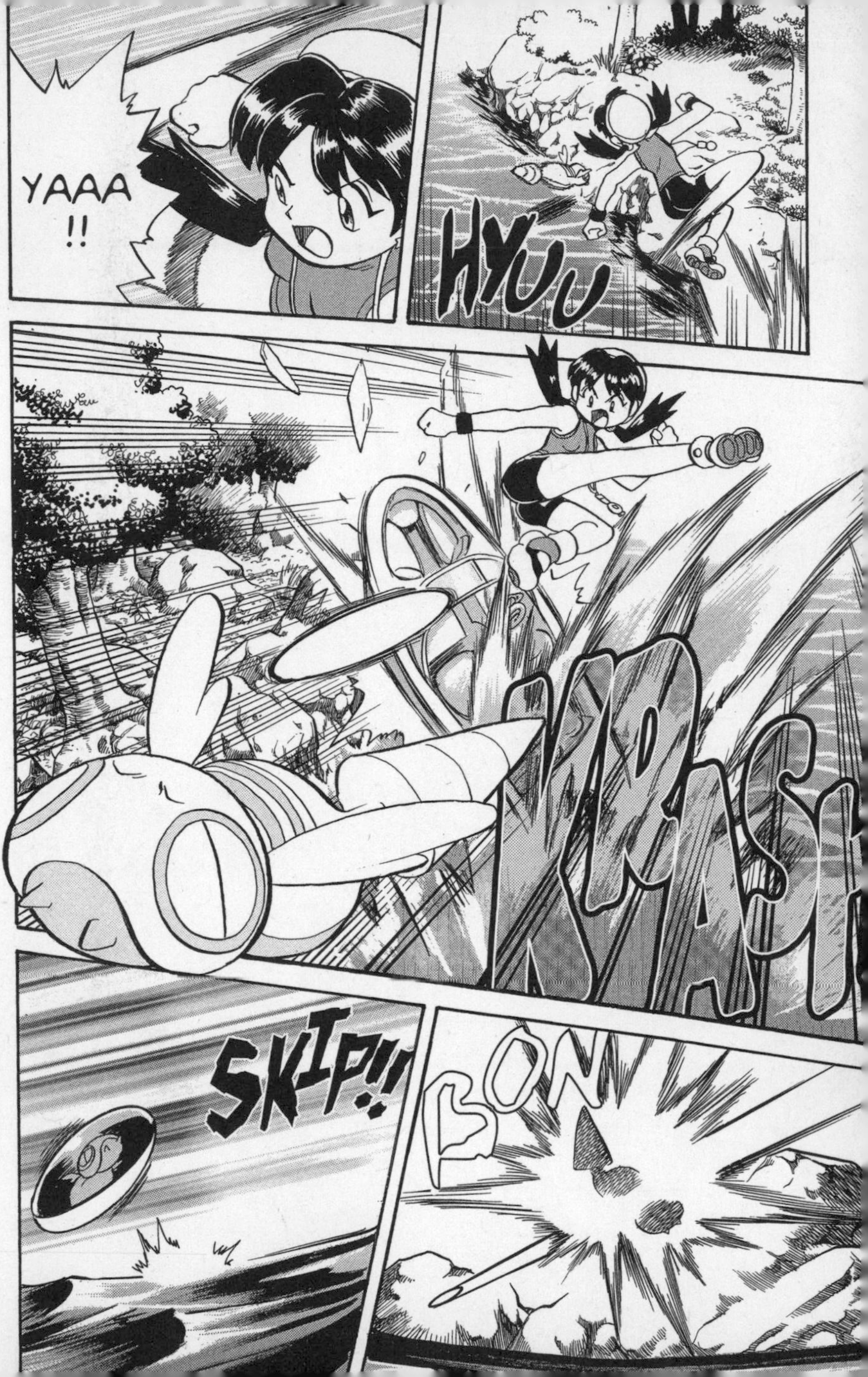
HYUU
YAAA !!
KRASH
BON
SKIP!!

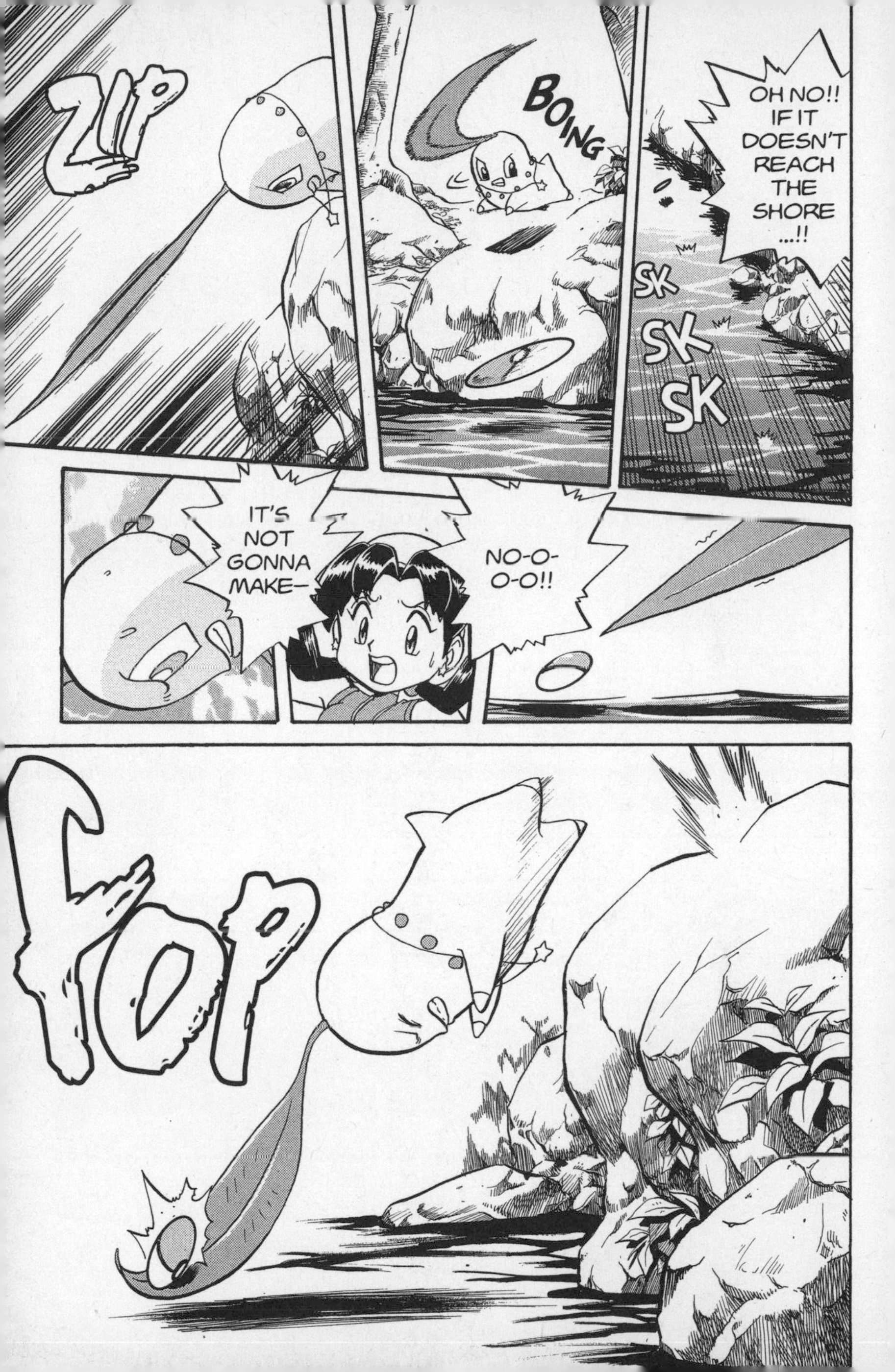

OH NO!! IF IT DOESN'T REACH THE SHORE ...!!
SK
SK
SK
BOING
ZIP
IT'S NOT GONNA MAKE—
NO-O-O-O!!
FOP

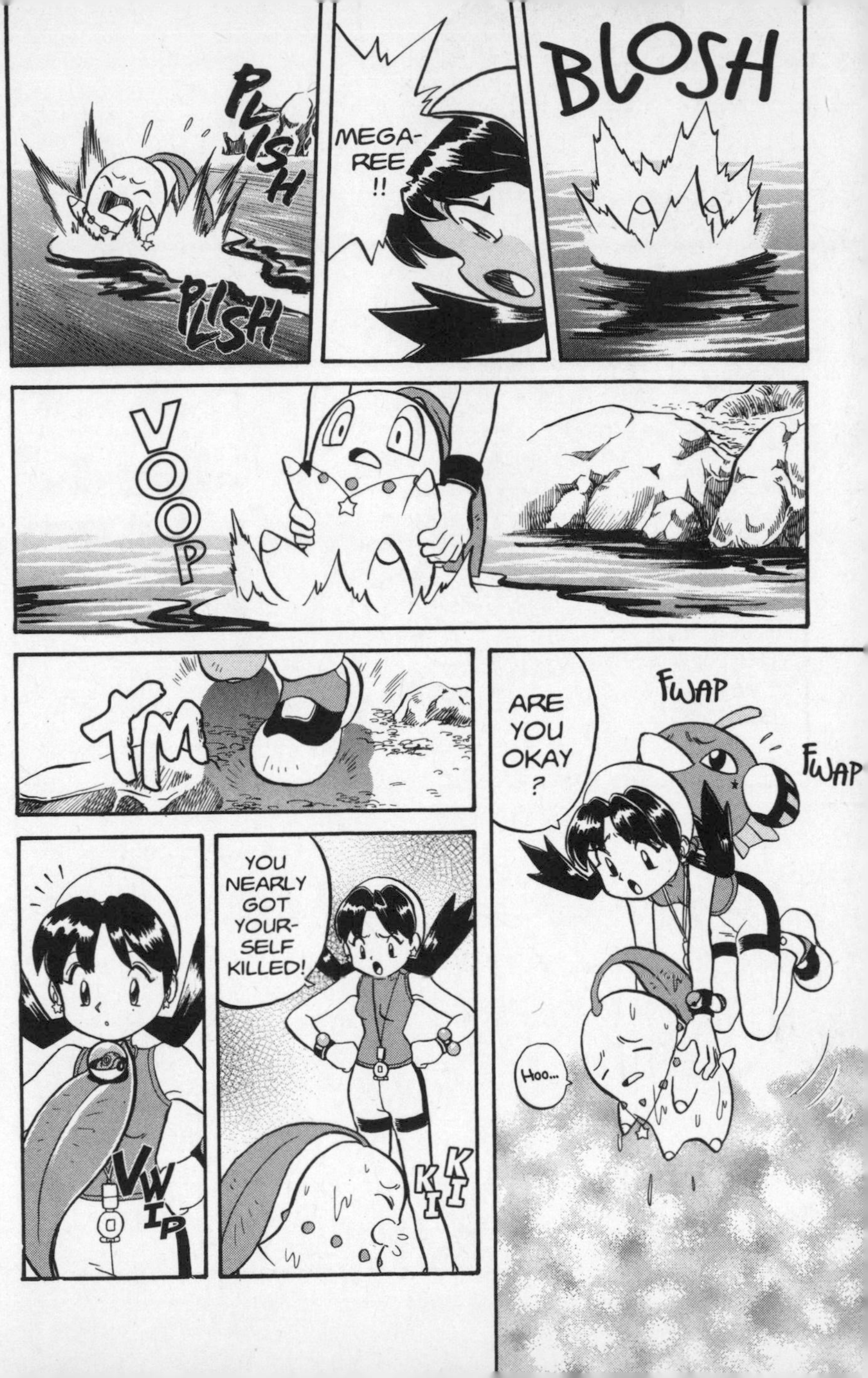
BLOSH
MEGA-REE !!
PLISH
PLISH
VOOP
ARE YOU OKAY ?
FWAP
FWAP
Hoo...
TM
YOU NEARLY GOT YOURSELF KILLED!
KI KI
VWIP

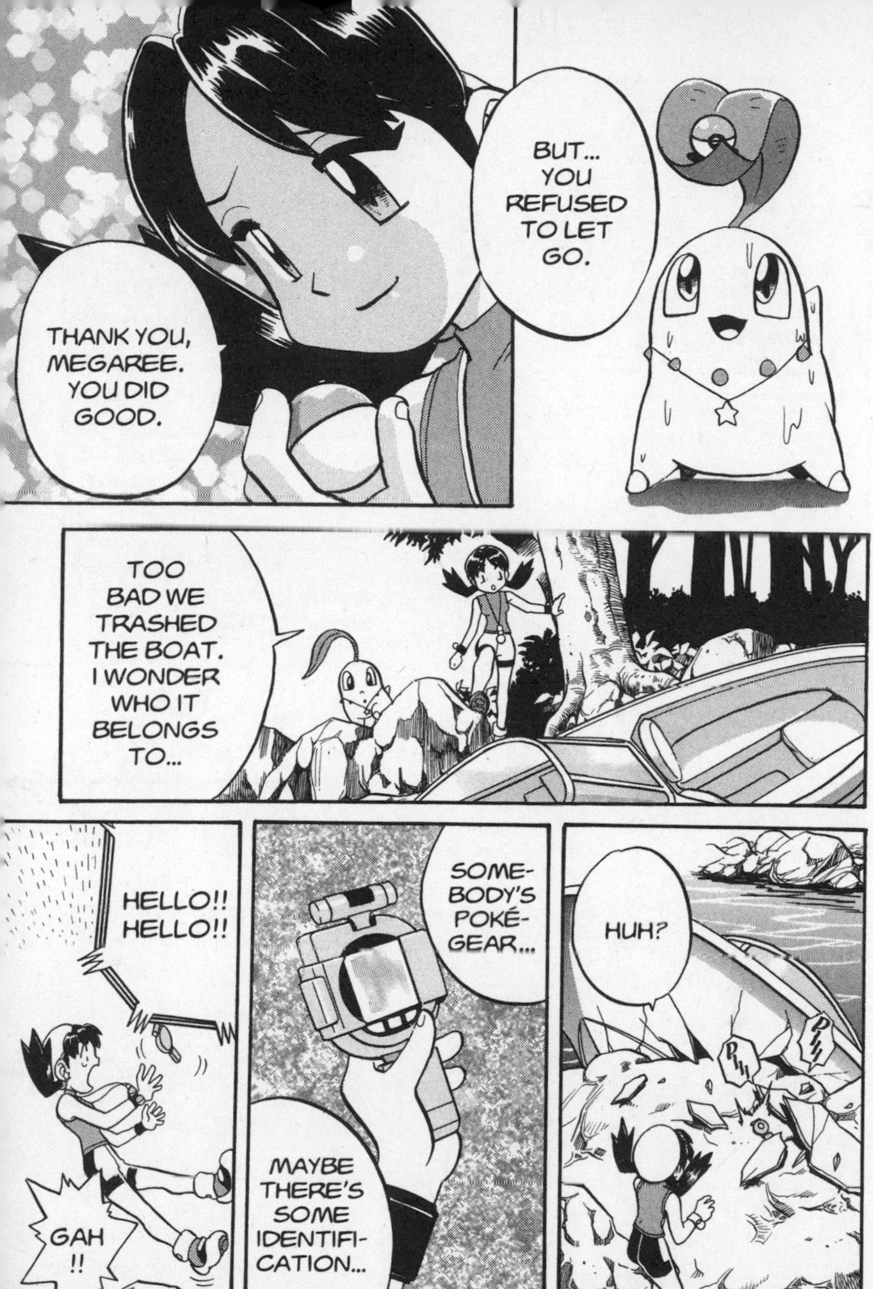
BUT... YOU REFUSED TO LET GO.
THANK YOU, MEGAREE. YOU DID GOOD.
TOO BAD WE TRASHED THE BOAT. I WONDER WHO IT BELONGS TO...
HUH?
SOME-BODY'S POKÉ-GEAR...
MAYBE THERE'S SOME IDENTIFI-CATION...
HELLO!! HELLO!!
GAH !!

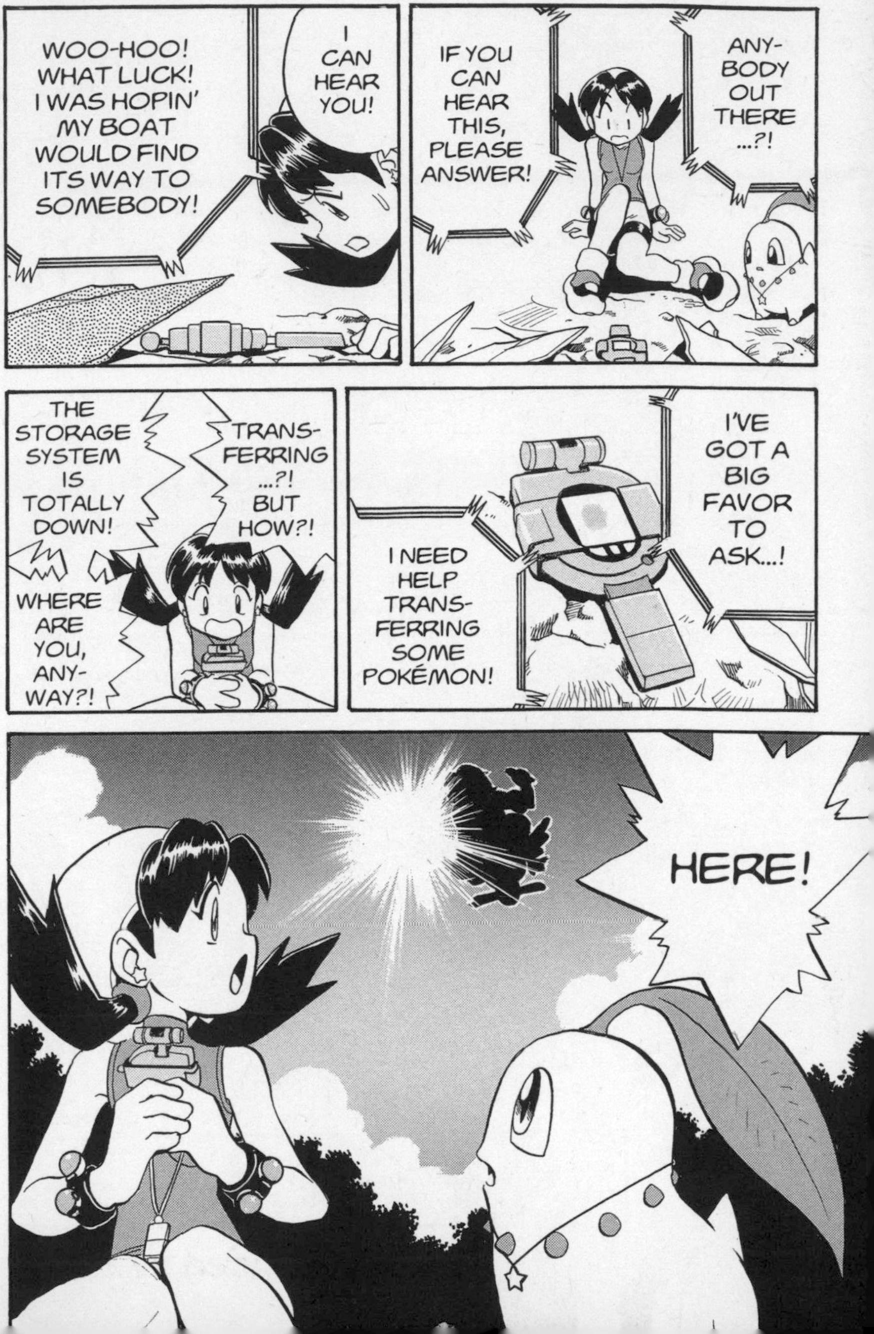
ANY-BODY OUT THERE ...?!
IF YOU CAN HEAR THIS, PLEASE ANSWER!
I CAN HEAR YOU!
WOO-HOO! WHAT LUCK! I WAS HOPIN' MY BOAT WOULD FIND ITS WAY TO SOMEBODY!
I'VE GOT A BIG FAVOR TO ASK...!
I NEED HELP TRANS-FERRING SOME POKÉMON!
TRANS-FERRING ...?! BUT HOW?!
THE STORAGE SYSTEM IS TOTALLY DOWN!
WHERE ARE YOU, ANY-WAY?!
HERE!

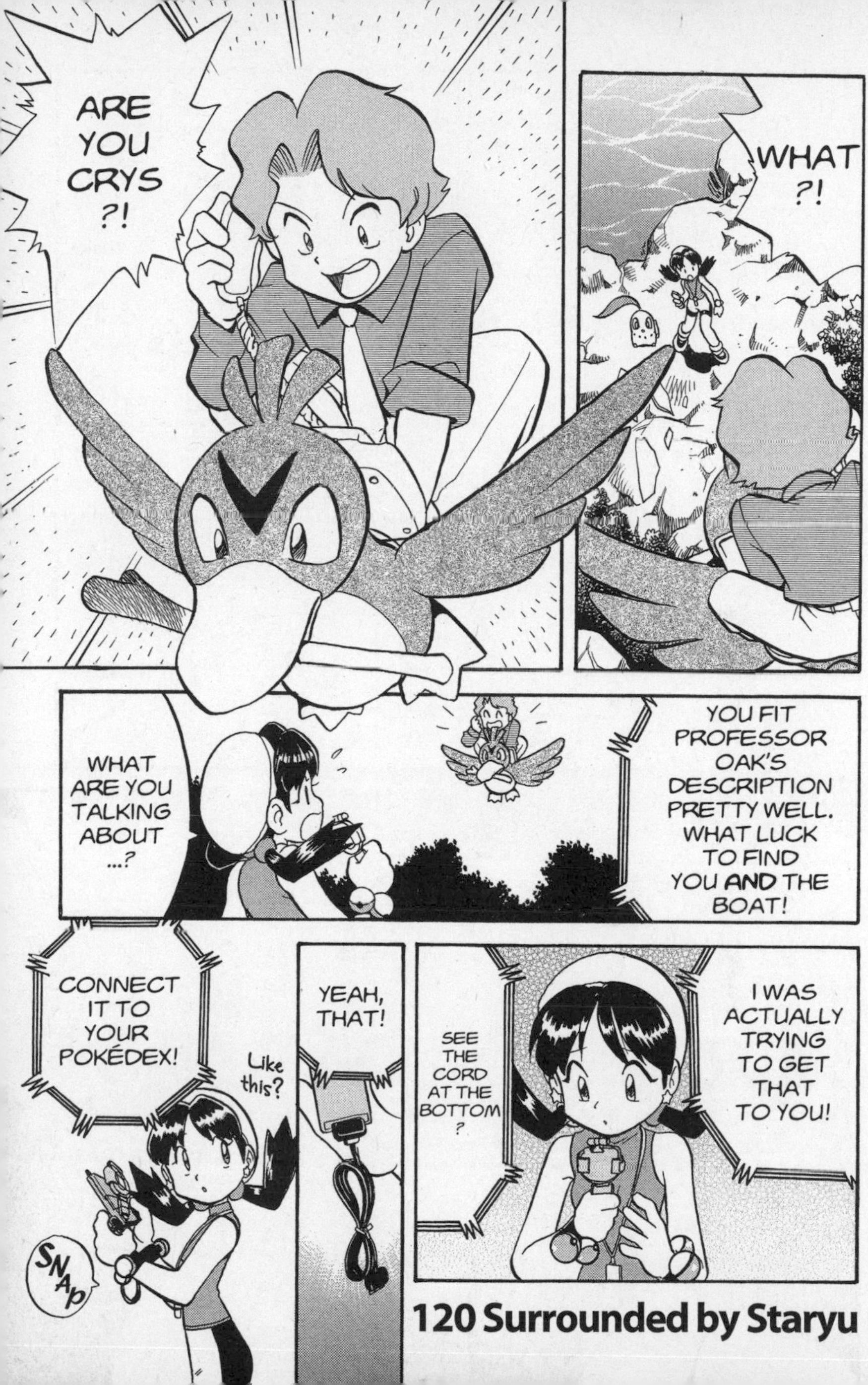
WHAT ?!
ARE YOU CRYS ?!
YOU FIT PROFESSOR OAK'S DESCRIPTION PRETTY WELL. WHAT LUCK TO FIND YOU **AND** THE BOAT!
WHAT ARE YOU TALKING ABOUT ...?
I WAS ACTUALLY TRYING TO GET THAT TO YOU!
SEE THE CORD AT THE BOTTOM ?
YEAH, THAT!
CONNECT IT TO YOUR POKÉDEX!
Like this?
SNAP

120 Surrounded by Staryu

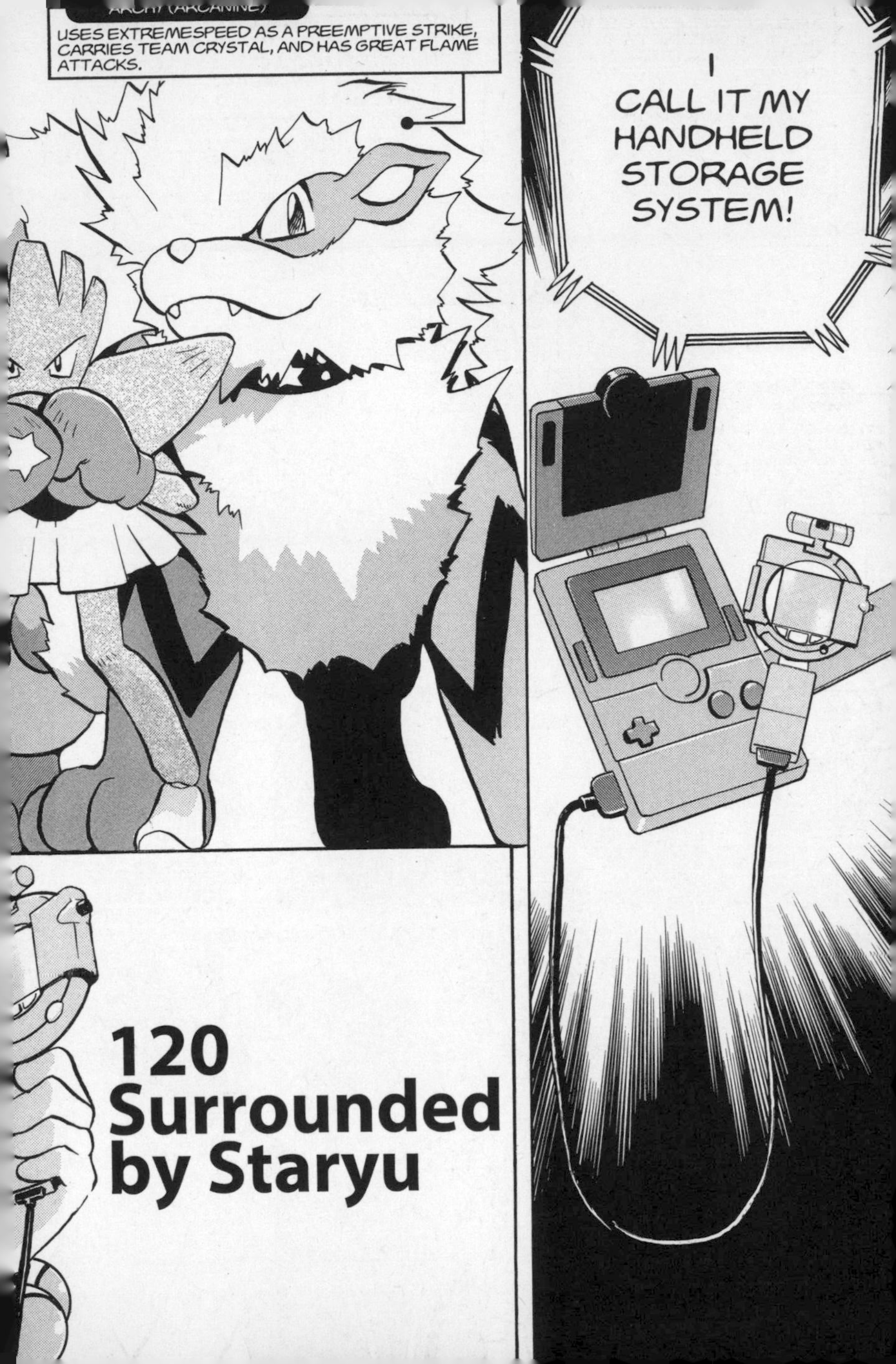
I CALL IT MY HANDHELD STORAGE SYSTEM!
USES EXTREMESPEED AS A PREEMPTIVE STRIKE, CARRIES TEAM CRYSTAL, AND HAS GREAT FLAME ATTACKS.
120 Surrounded by Staryu

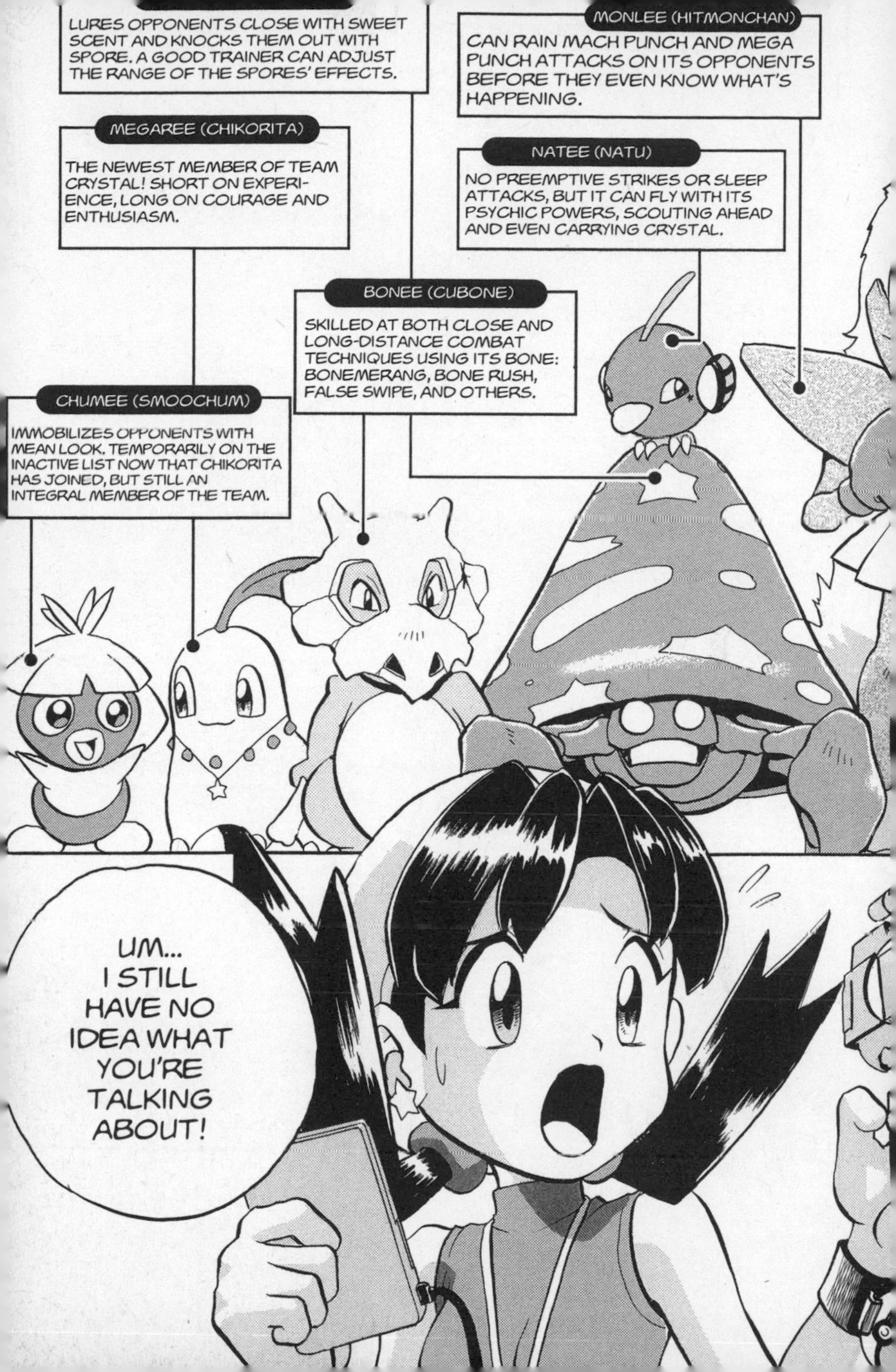
MONLEE (HITMONCHAN)
CAN RAIN MACH PUNCH AND MEGA PUNCH ATTACKS ON ITS OPPONENTS BEFORE THEY EVEN KNOW WHAT'S HAPPENING.
LURES OPPONENTS CLOSE WITH SWEET SCENT AND KNOCKS THEM OUT WITH SPORE. A GOOD TRAINER CAN ADJUST THE RANGE OF THE SPORES' EFFECTS.
NATEE (NATU)
NO PREEMPTIVE STRIKES OR SLEEP ATTACKS, BUT IT CAN FLY WITH ITS PSYCHIC POWERS, SCOUTING AHEAD AND EVEN CARRYING CRYSTAL.
MEGAREE (CHIKORITA)
THE NEWEST MEMBER OF TEAM CRYSTAL! SHORT ON EXPERI-ENCE, LONG ON COURAGE AND ENTHUSIASM.
BONEE (CUBONE)
SKILLED AT BOTH CLOSE AND LONG-DISTANCE COMBAT TECHNIQUES USING ITS BONE: BONEMERANG, BONE RUSH, FALSE SWIPE, AND OTHERS.
CHUMEE (SMOOCHUM)
IMMOBILIZES OPPONENTS WITH MEAN LOOK. TEMPORARILY ON THE INACTIVE LIST NOW THAT CHIKORITA HAS JOINED, BUT STILL AN INTEGRAL MEMBER OF THE TEAM.
UM... I STILL HAVE NO IDEA WHAT YOU'RE TALKING ABOUT!

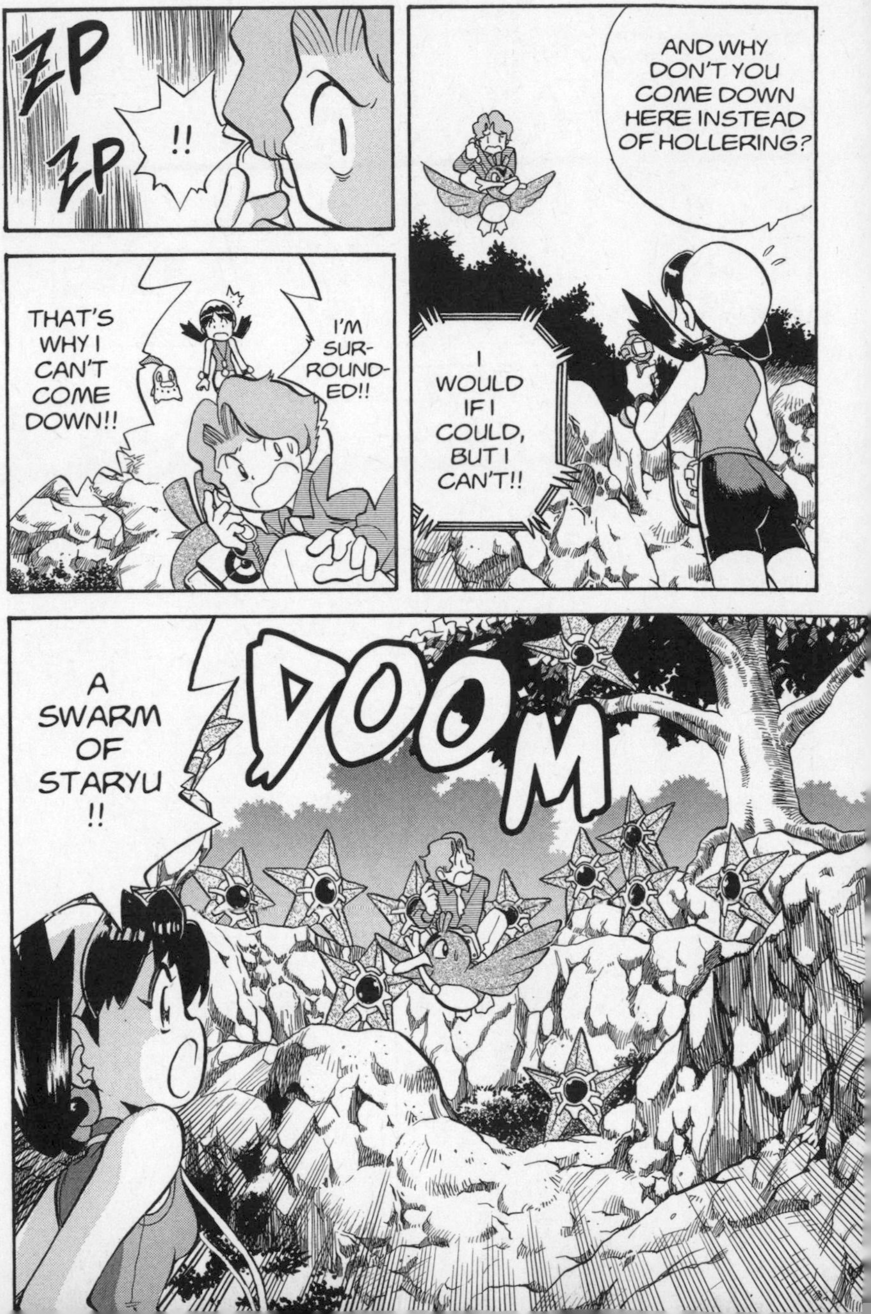
AND WHY DON'T YOU COME DOWN HERE INSTEAD OF HOLLERING?
I WOULD IF I COULD, BUT I CAN'T!!
ZP ZP
!!
I'M SUR-ROUND-ED!!
THAT'S WHY I CAN'T COME DOWN!!
DOOM
A SWARM OF STARYU !!

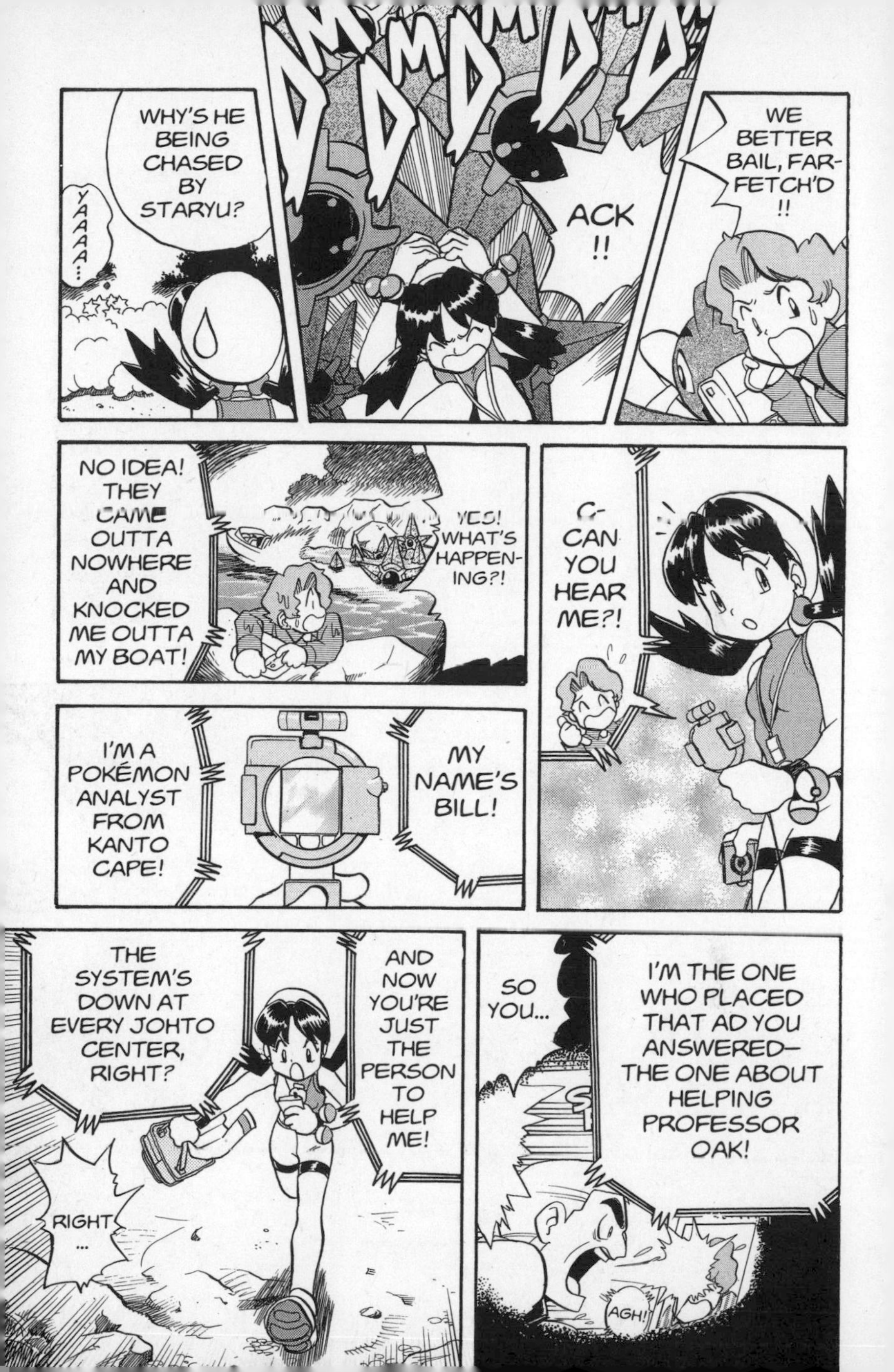
WE BETTER BAIL, FAR-FETCH'D !!
ACK !!
WHY'S HE BEING CHASED BY STARYU?
YAAAA...
C-CAN YOU HEAR ME?!
YES! WHAT'S HAPPENING?!
NO IDEA! THEY CAME OUTTA NOWHERE AND KNOCKED ME OUTTA MY BOAT!
MY NAME'S BILL!
I'M A POKÉMON ANALYST FROM KANTO CAPE!
I'M THE ONE WHO PLACED THAT AD YOU ANSWERED— THE ONE ABOUT HELPING PROFESSOR OAK!
SO YOU...
AGH!
AND NOW YOU'RE JUST THE PERSON TO HELP ME!
THE SYSTEM'S DOWN AT EVERY JOHTO CENTER, RIGHT?
RIGHT...

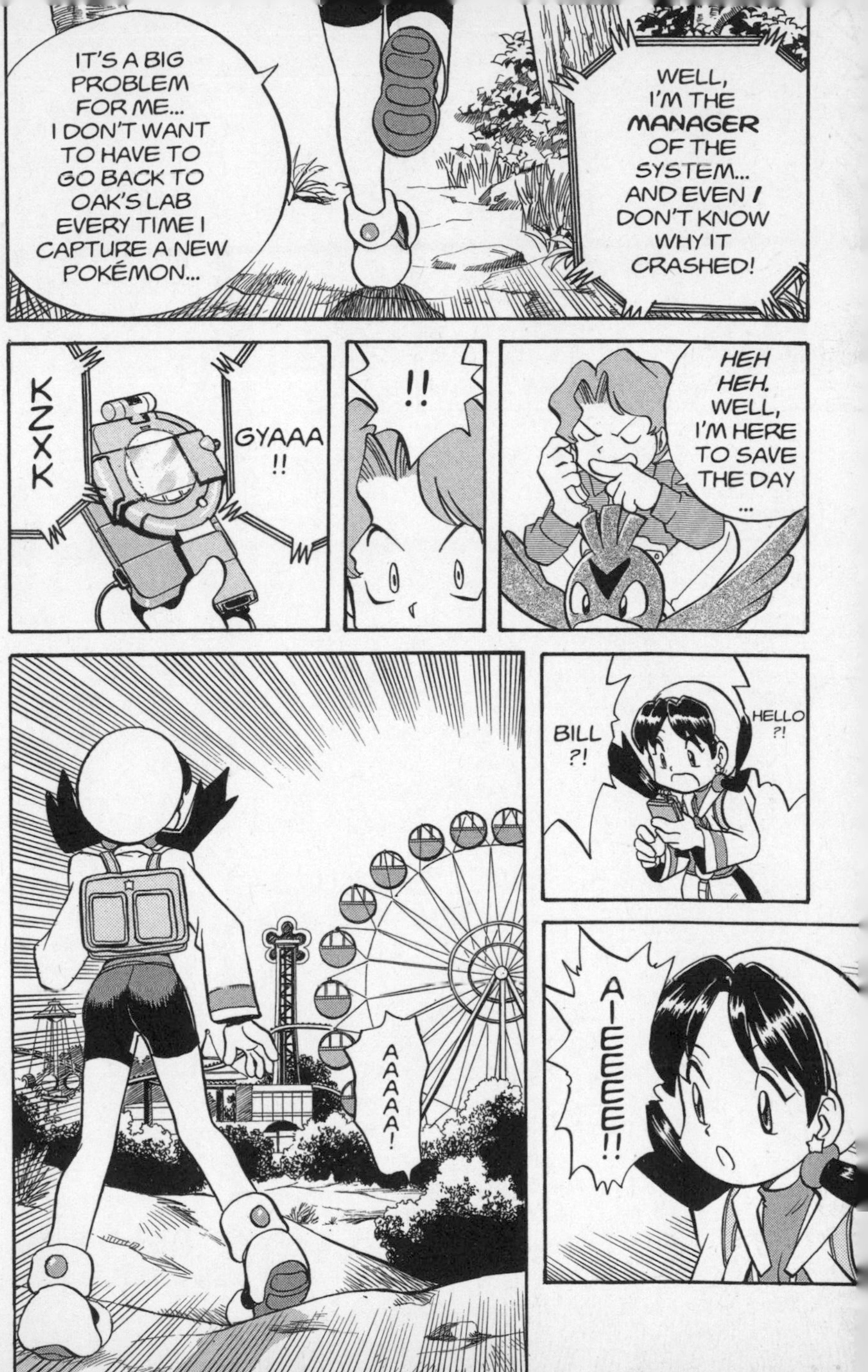
WELL, I'M THE **MANAGER** OF THE SYSTEM... AND EVEN ***I*** DON'T KNOW WHY IT CRASHED!
IT'S A BIG PROBLEM FOR ME... I DON'T WANT TO HAVE TO GO BACK TO OAK'S LAB EVERY TIME I CAPTURE A NEW POKÉMON...
HEH HEH. WELL, I'M HERE TO SAVE THE DAY...
!!
GYAAA !!
KZXK
HELLO ?!
BILL ?!
AIEEEE!!
AAAAA!

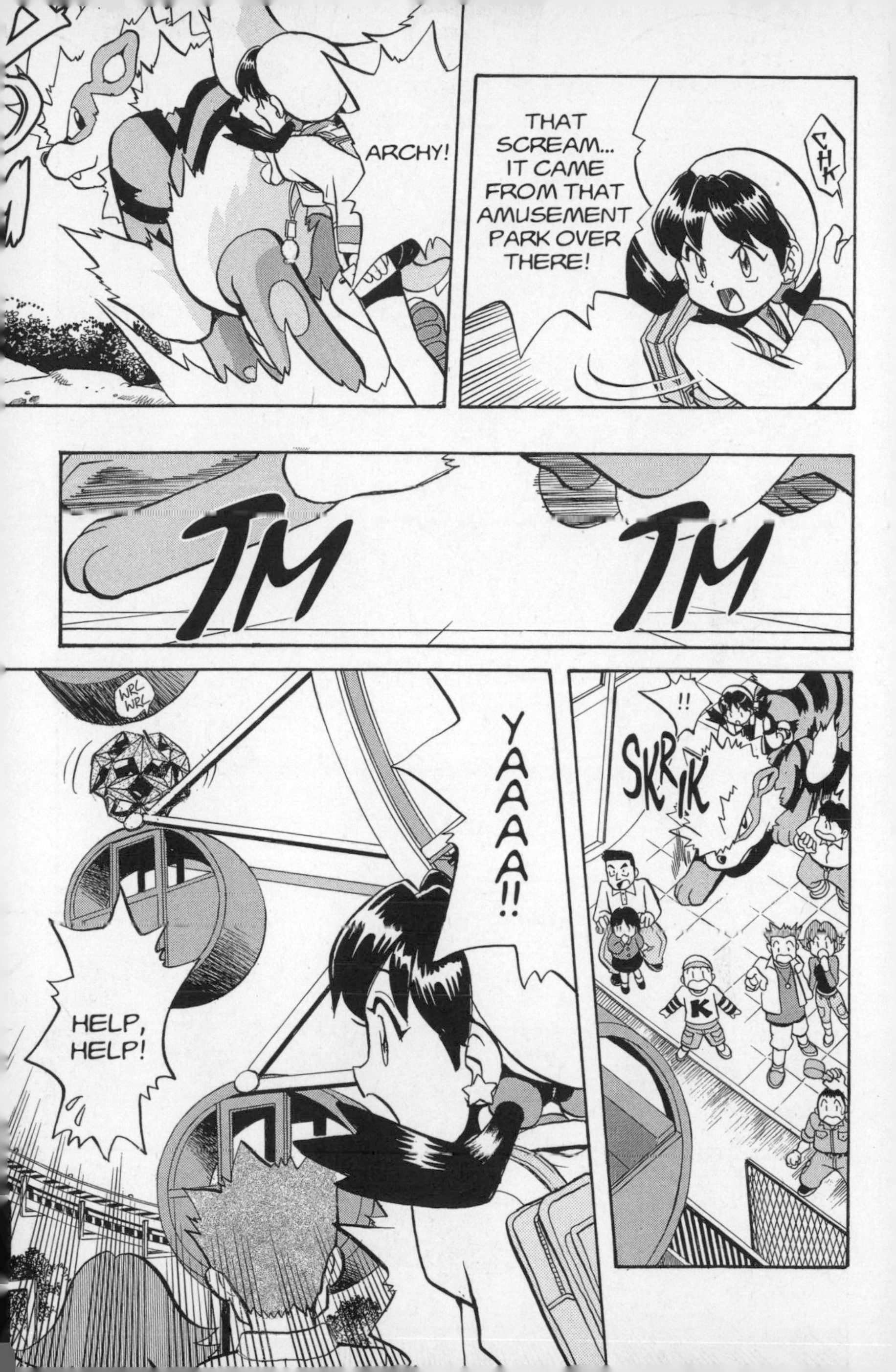
CHK
THAT SCREAM... IT CAME FROM THAT AMUSEMENT PARK OVER THERE!
ARCHY!
TM TM
!!
SKRIK!
WRL WRL
YAAAAA!!
HELP, HELP!

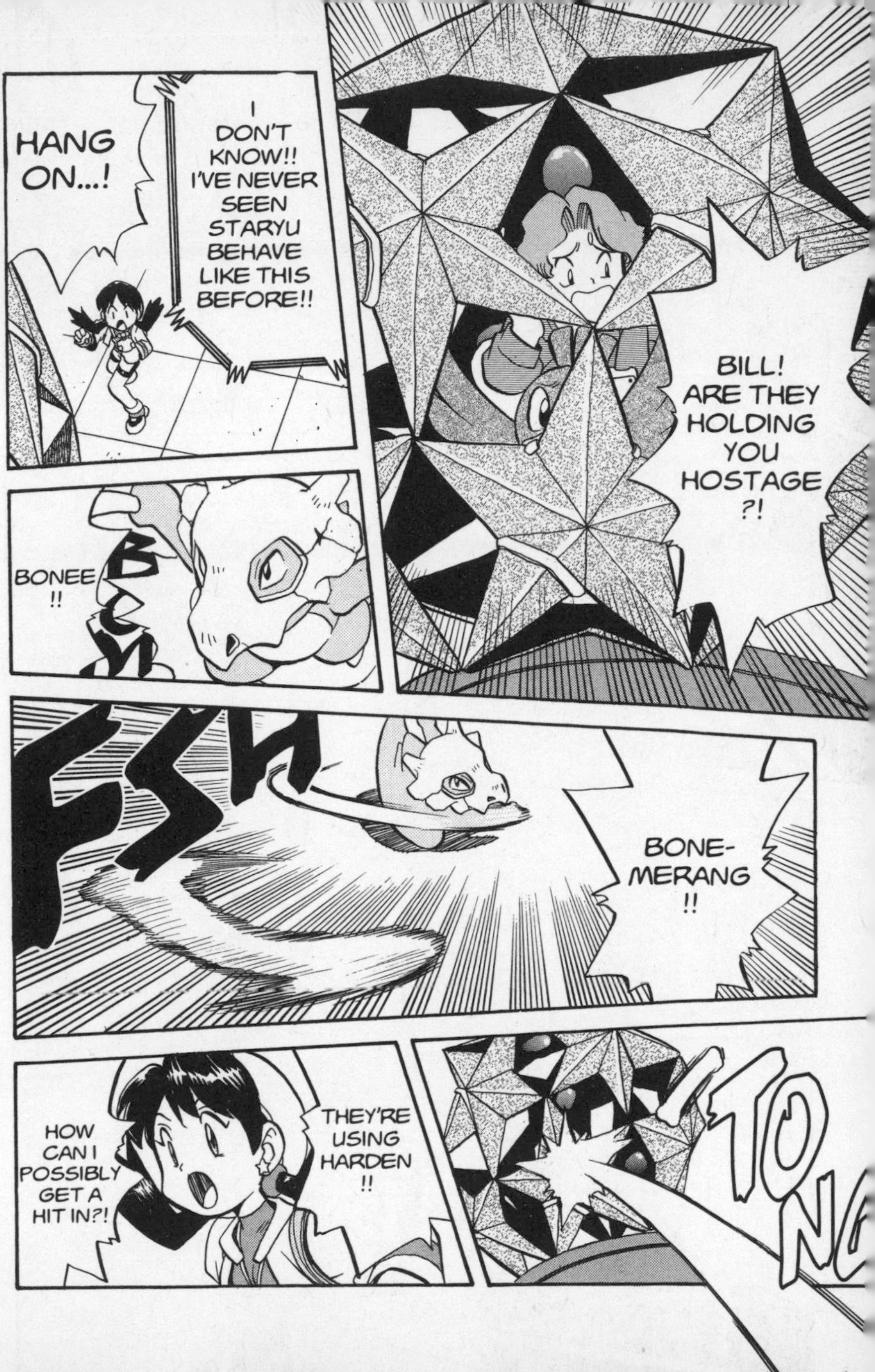
BILL! ARE THEY HOLDING YOU HOSTAGE ?!
I DON'T KNOW!! I'VE NEVER SEEN STARYU BEHAVE LIKE THIS BEFORE!!
HANG ON...!
BONEE !!
FSH
BONE-MERANG !!
THEY'RE USING HARDEN !!
HOW CAN I POSSIBLY GET A HIT IN?!

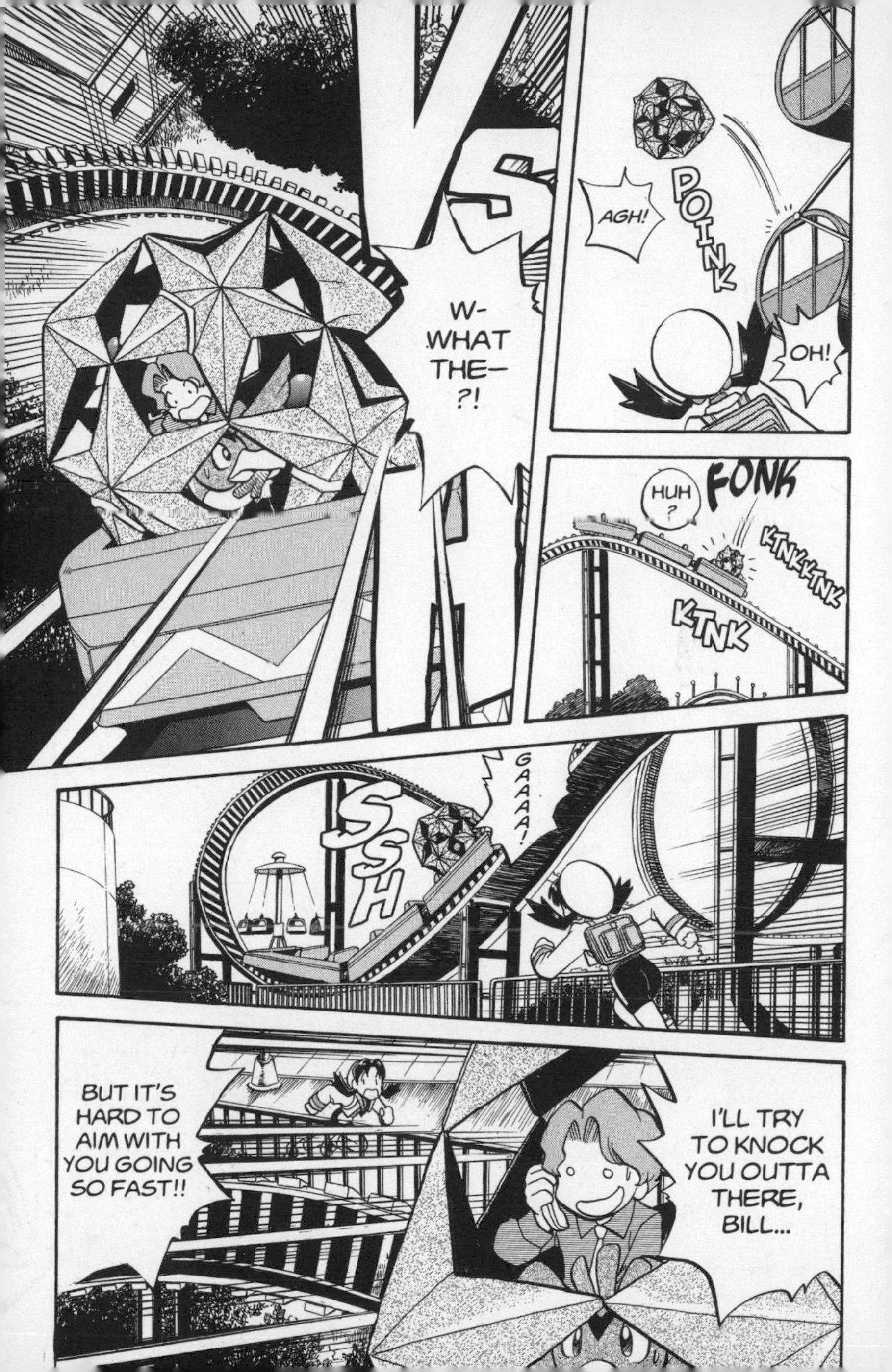
POINK
AGH!
OH!
FONK
HUH?
KTNK KTNK
KTNK
W-WHAT THE—?!
GAAAA!
SSH
I'LL TRY TO KNOCK YOU OUTTA THERE, BILL...
BUT IT'S HARD TO AIM WITH YOU GOING SO FAST!!

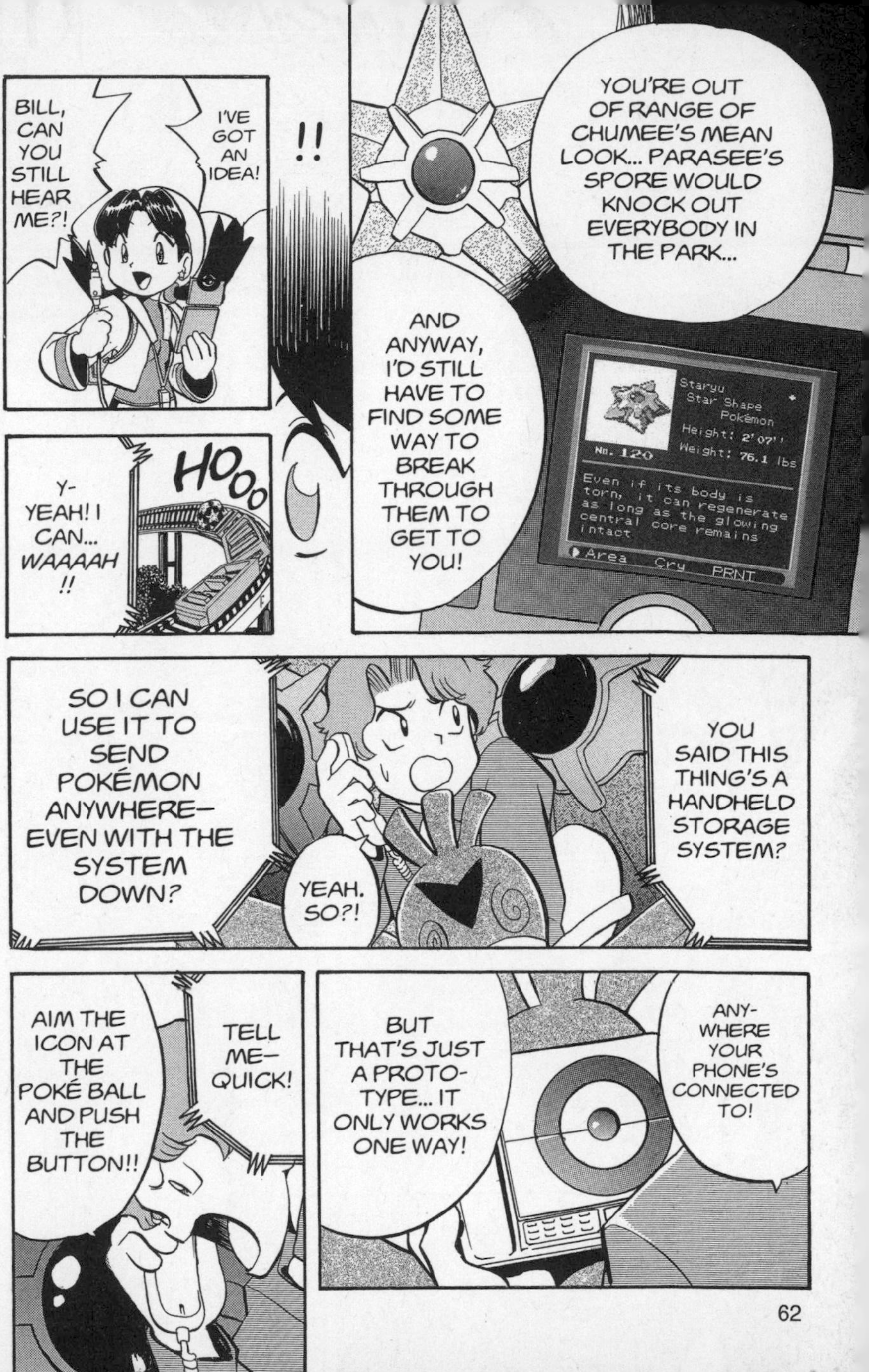
YOU'RE OUT OF RANGE OF CHUMEE'S MEAN LOOK... PARASEE'S SPORE WOULD KNOCK OUT EVERYBODY IN THE PARK...
AND ANYWAY, I'D STILL HAVE TO FIND SOME WAY TO BREAK THROUGH THEM TO GET TO YOU!
Staryu
Star Shape Pokémon
Height: 2'07''
Weight: 76.1 lbs
No. 120
Even if its body is torn, it can regenerate as long as the glowing central core remains intact
Area Cry PRNT
!!
BILL, CAN YOU STILL HEAR ME?!
I'VE GOT AN IDEA!
HOOOO
Y-YEAH! I CAN... WAAAAH!!
YOU SAID THIS THING'S A HANDHELD STORAGE SYSTEM?
YEAH. SO?!
SO I CAN USE IT TO SEND POKÉMON ANYWHERE—EVEN WITH THE SYSTEM DOWN?
ANY-WHERE YOUR PHONE'S CONNECTED TO!
BUT THAT'S JUST A PROTO-TYPE... IT ONLY WORKS ONE WAY!
TELL ME—QUICK!
AIM THE ICON AT THE POKÉ BALL AND PUSH THE BUTTON!!

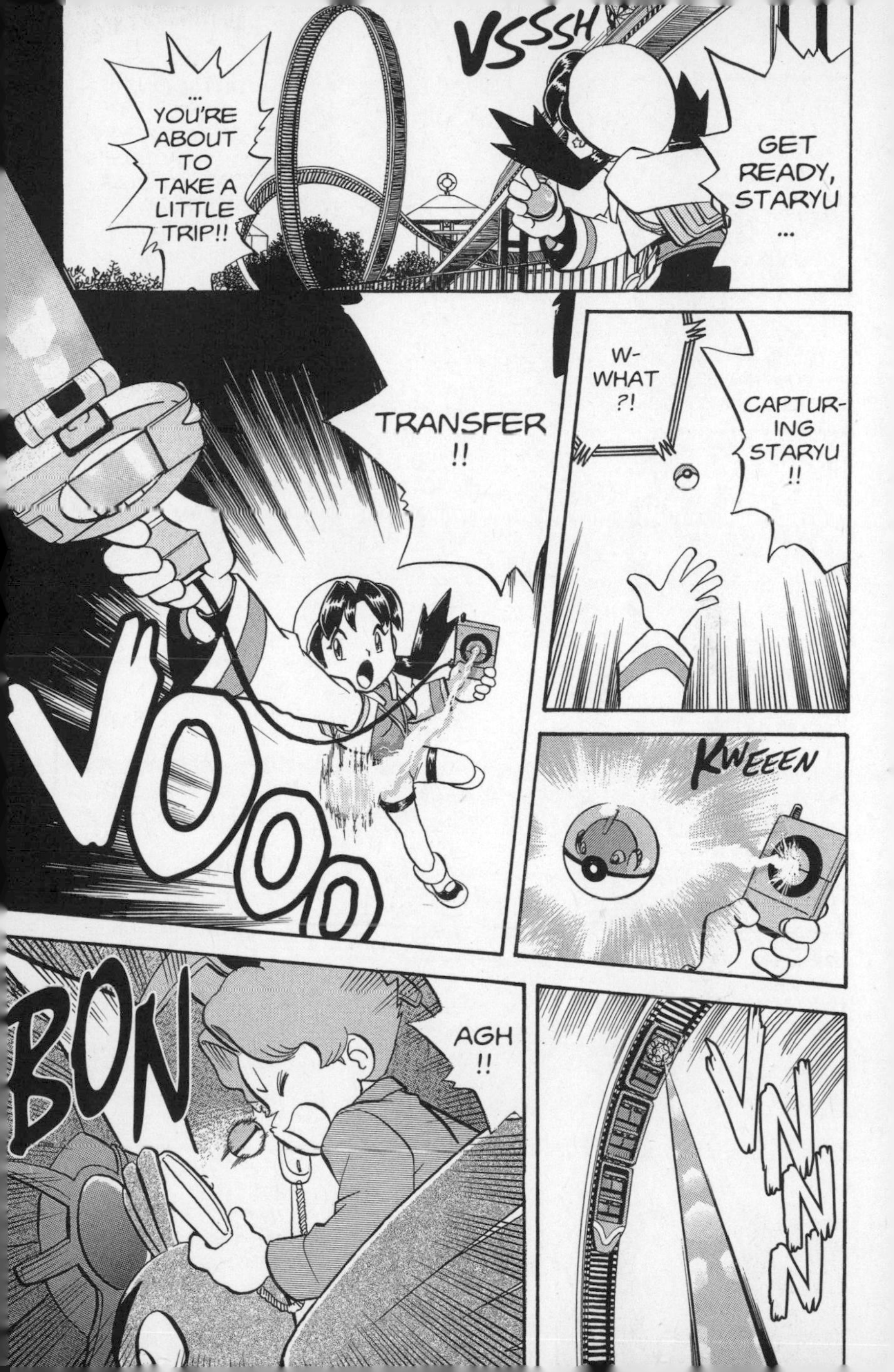
VSSSH
GET READY, STARYU ...
... YOU'RE ABOUT TO TAKE A LITTLE TRIP!!
CAPTURING STARYU!!
W-WHAT?!
KWEEEN
TRANSFER!!
VOOOO
VNNN
AGH!!
BON

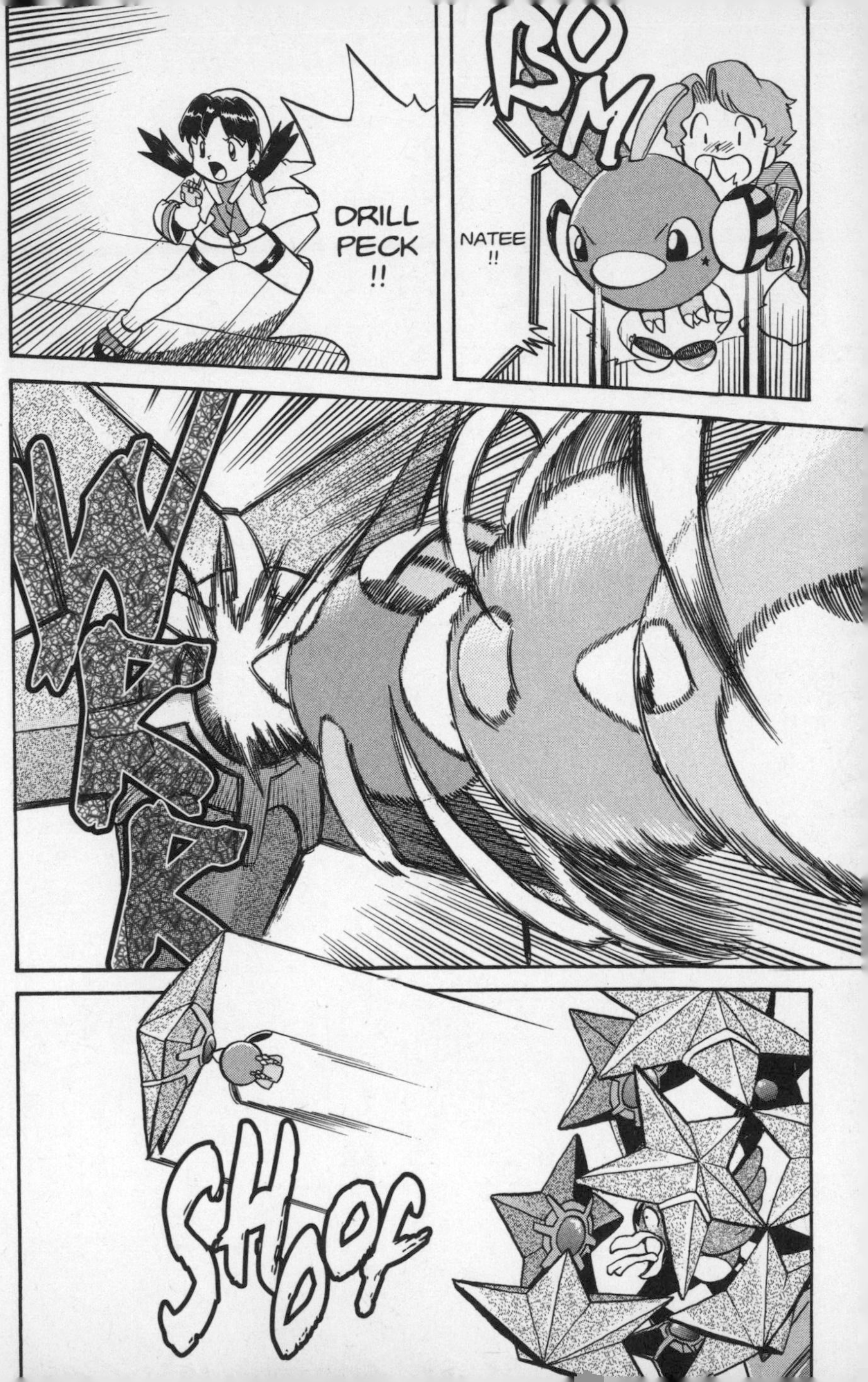
NATEE !!
DRILL PECK !!

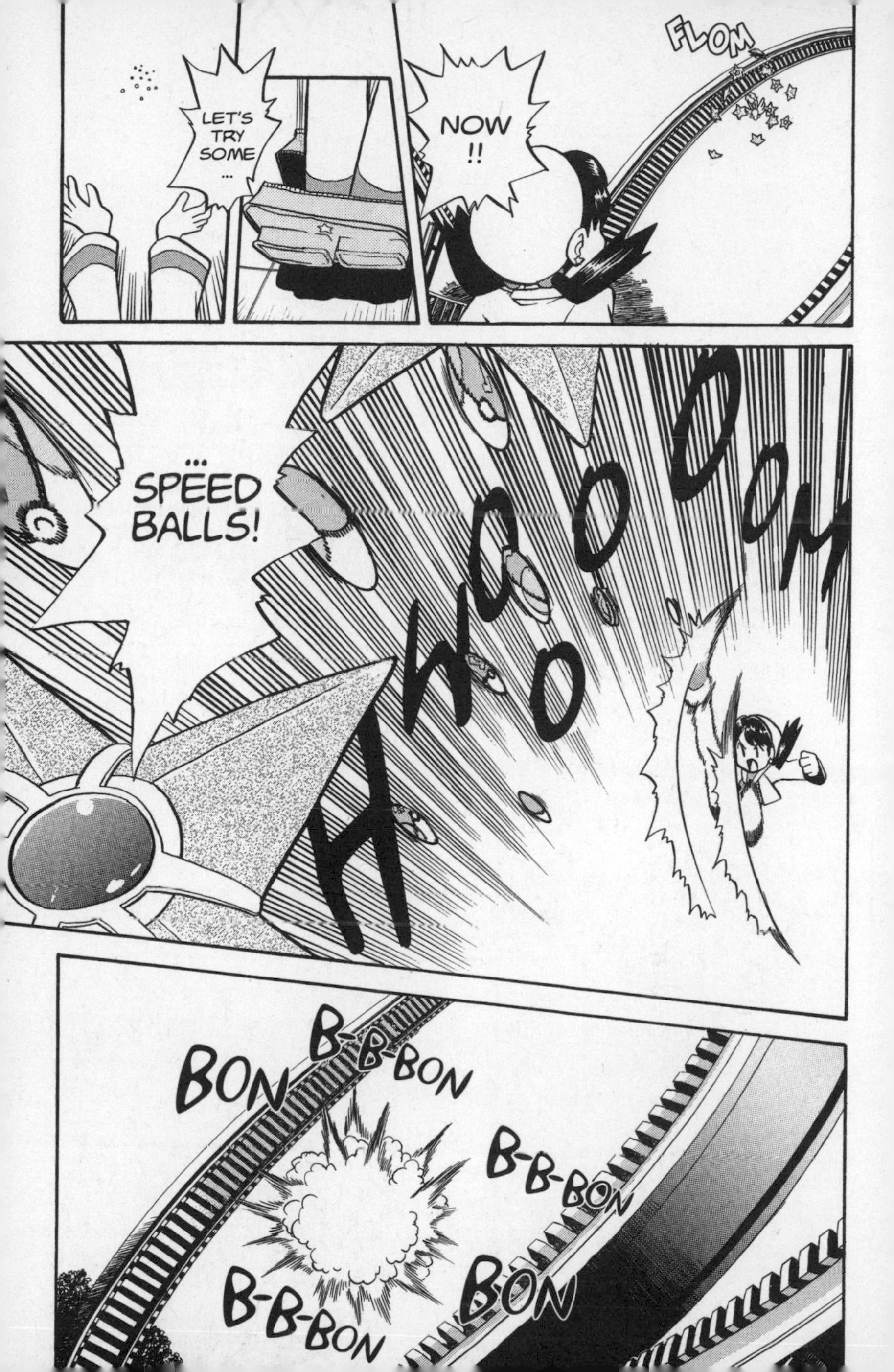
FLOM
NOW !!
LET'S TRY SOME ...
... SPEED BALLS!
HWOOOOOM
B-B-BON
BON
B-B-BON
BON
B-B-BON

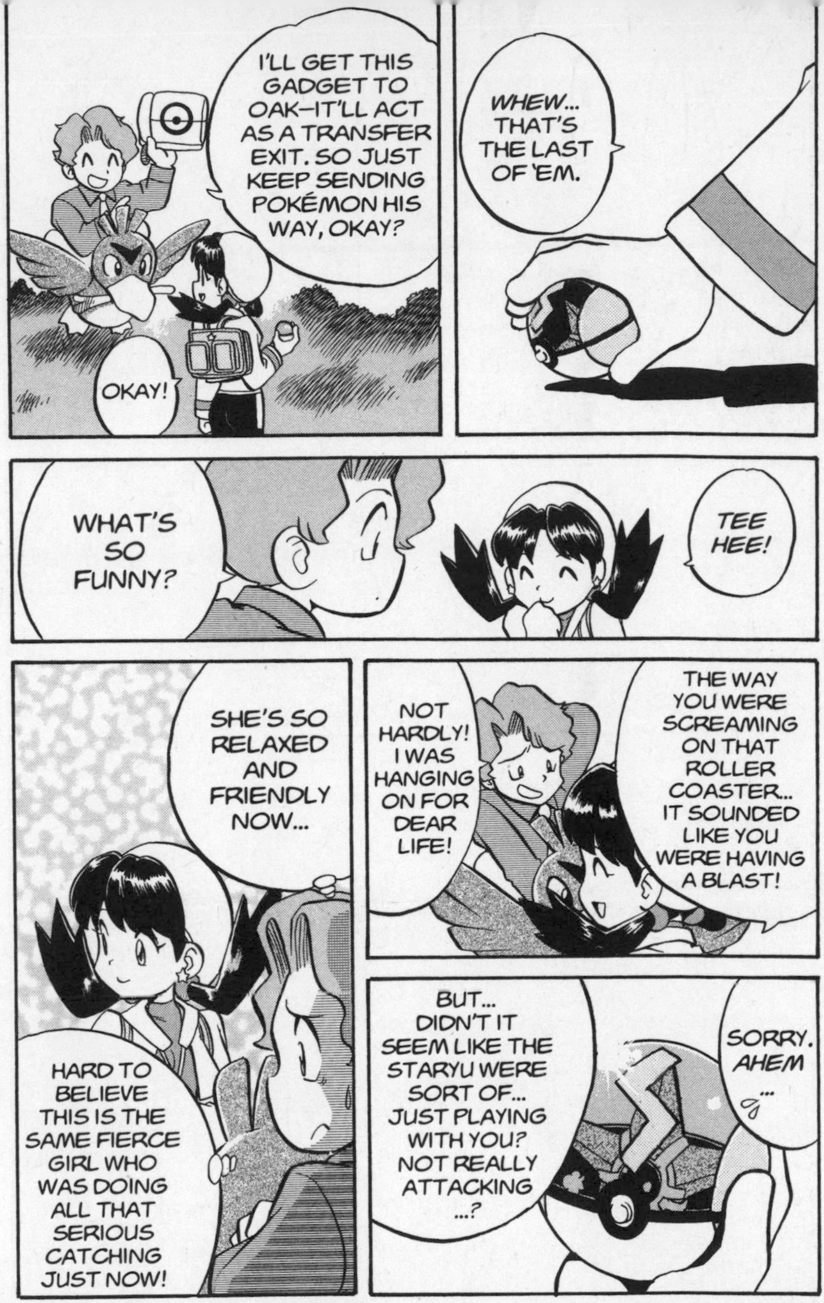
WHEW... THAT'S THE LAST OF 'EM.
I'LL GET THIS GADGET TO OAK—IT'LL ACT AS A TRANSFER EXIT. SO JUST KEEP SENDING POKÉMON HIS WAY, OKAY?
OKAY!
TEE HEE!
WHAT'S SO FUNNY?
THE WAY YOU WERE SCREAMING ON THAT ROLLER COASTER... IT SOUNDED LIKE YOU WERE HAVING A BLAST!
NOT HARDLY! I WAS HANGING ON FOR DEAR LIFE!
SORRY. AHEM...
BUT... DIDN'T IT SEEM LIKE THE STARYU WERE SORT OF... JUST PLAYING WITH YOU? NOT REALLY ATTACKING ...?
SHE'S SO RELAXED AND FRIENDLY NOW...
HARD TO BELIEVE THIS IS THE SAME FIERCE GIRL WHO WAS DOING ALL THAT SERIOUS CATCHING JUST NOW!

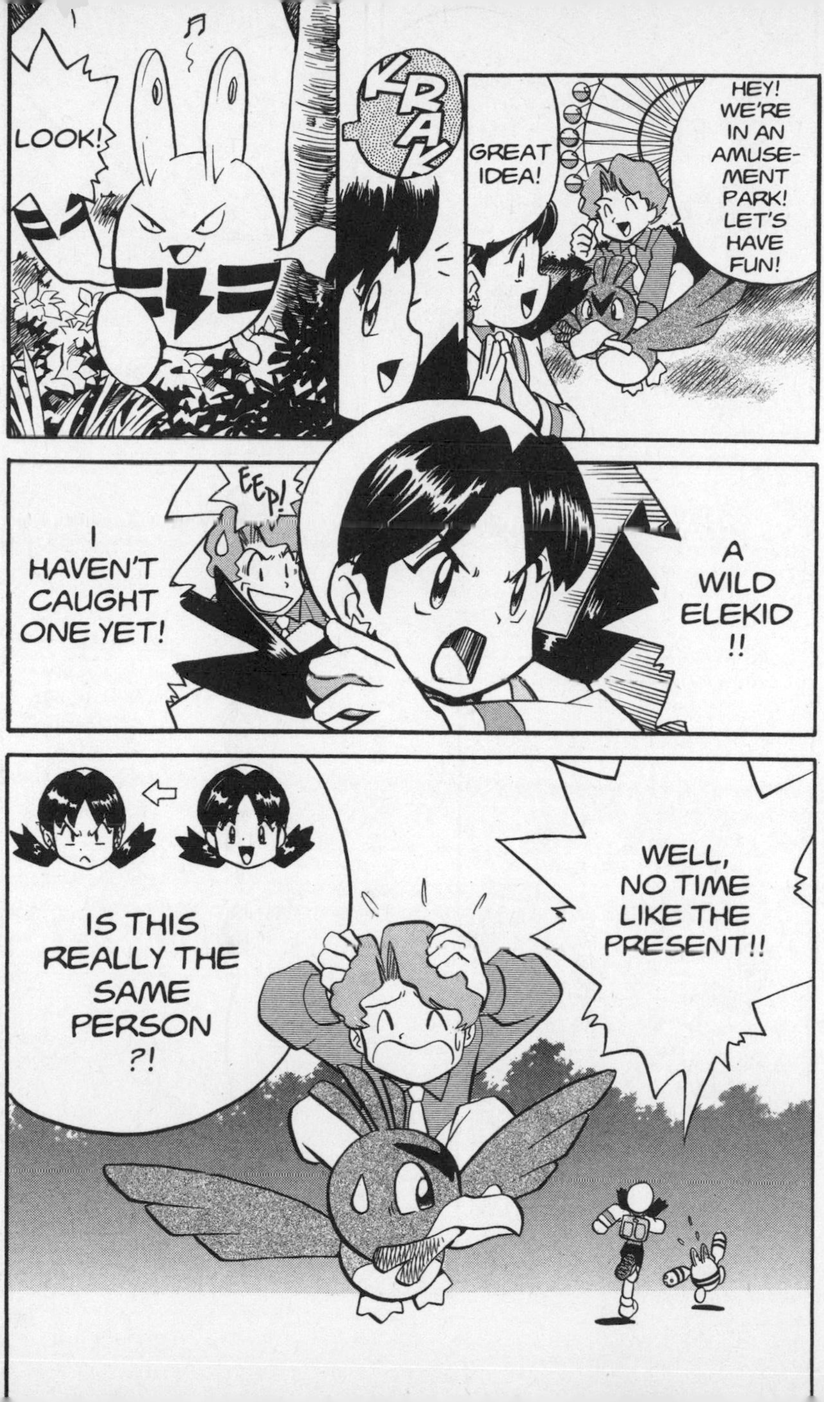
HEY! WE'RE IN AN AMUSEMENT PARK! LET'S HAVE FUN!
GREAT IDEA!
KRAK
LOOK!
A WILD ELEKID!!
EEP!
I HAVEN'T CAUGHT ONE YET!
WELL, NO TIME LIKE THE PRESENT!!
IS THIS REALLY THE SAME PERSON ?!

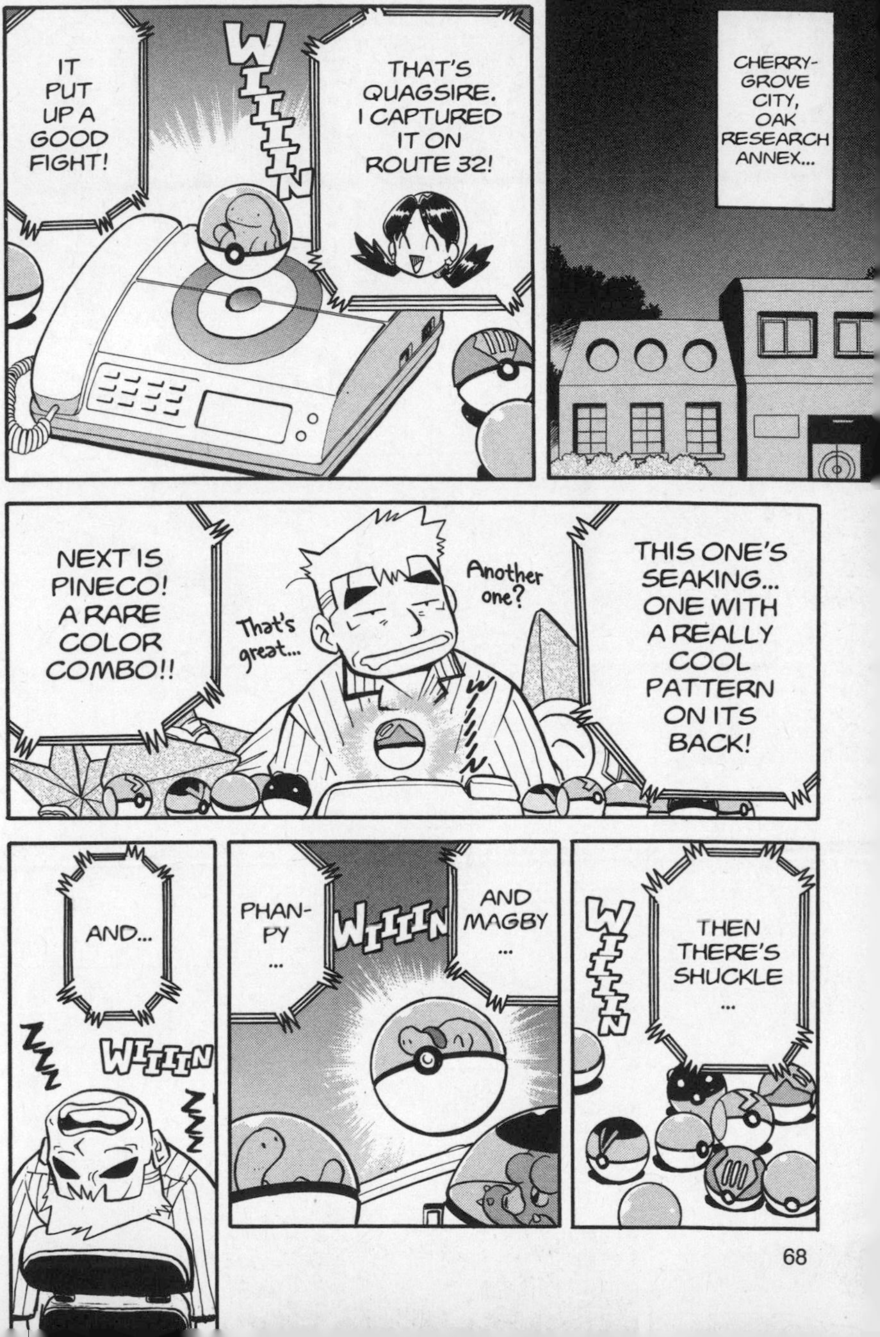
CHERRY-GROVE CITY, OAK RESEARCH ANNEX...
THAT'S QUAGSIRE. I CAPTURED IT ON ROUTE 32!
WIIIIN
IT PUT UP A GOOD FIGHT!
THIS ONE'S SEAKING... ONE WITH A REALLY COOL PATTERN ON ITS BACK!
Another one?
That's great...
NEXT IS PINECO! A RARE COLOR COMBO!!
WIIIIN
THEN THERE'S SHUCKLE ...
AND MAGBY ...
WIIIIN
PHAN-PY ...
AND...
WIIIIN

121 Off Course with Corsola

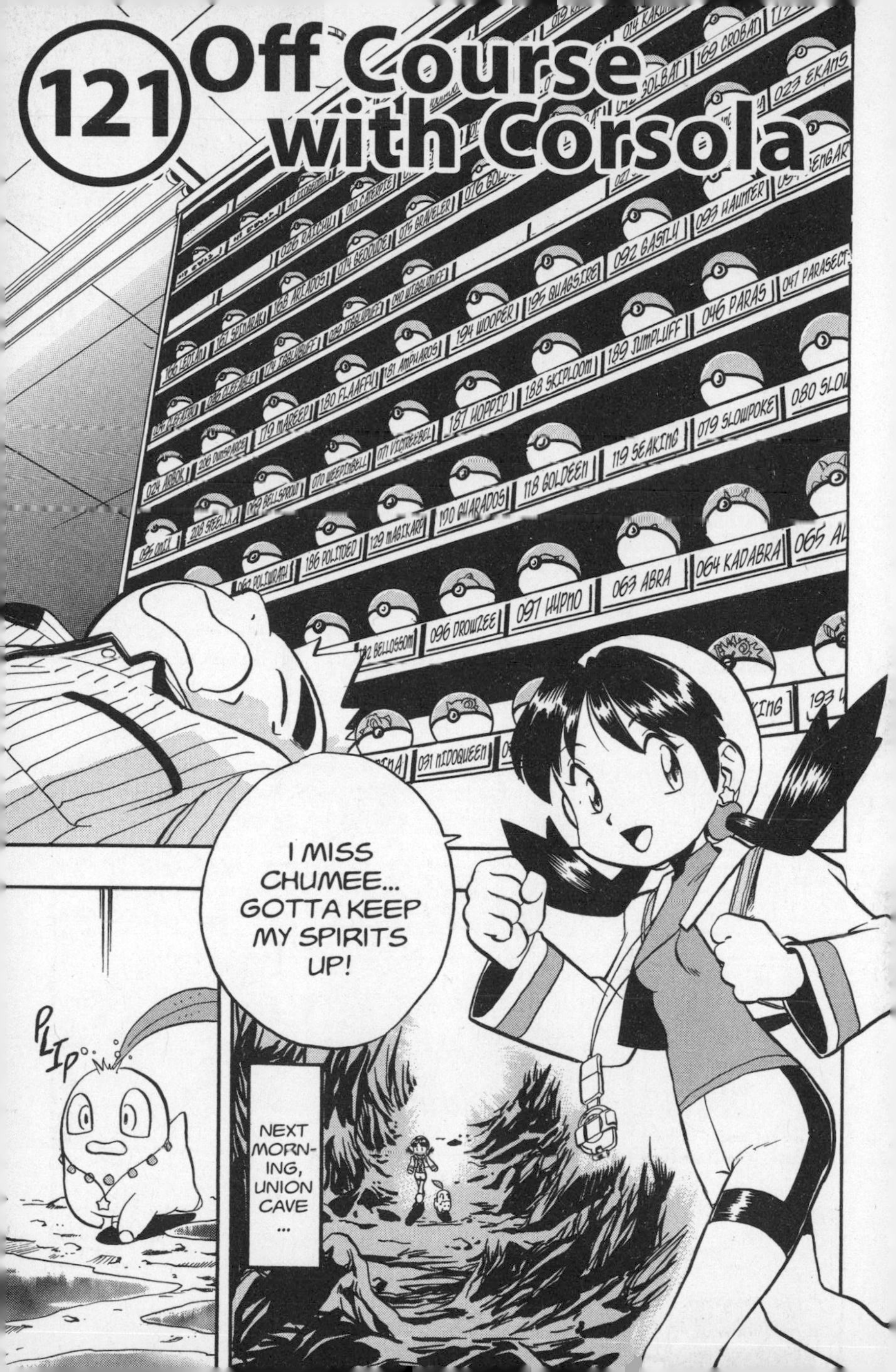
I MISS CHUMEE... GOTTA KEEP MY SPIRITS UP!
NEXT MORNING, UNION CAVE...
PLIP

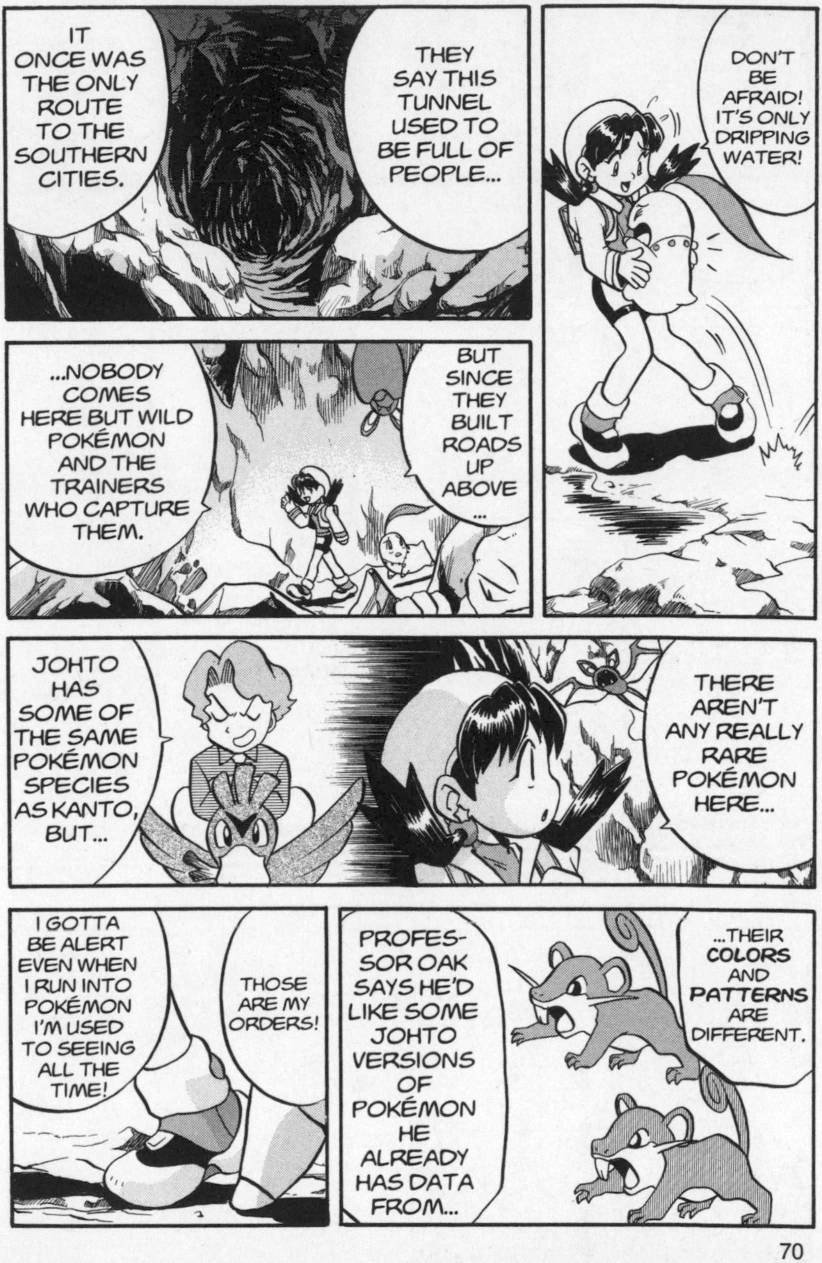
DON'T BE AFRAID! IT'S ONLY DRIPPING WATER!
THEY SAY THIS TUNNEL USED TO BE FULL OF PEOPLE...
IT ONCE WAS THE ONLY ROUTE TO THE SOUTHERN CITIES.
BUT SINCE THEY BUILT ROADS UP ABOVE ...
...NOBODY COMES HERE BUT WILD POKÉMON AND THE TRAINERS WHO CAPTURE THEM.
THERE AREN'T ANY REALLY RARE POKÉMON HERE...
JOHTO HAS SOME OF THE SAME POKÉMON SPECIES AS KANTO, BUT...
...THEIR **COLORS** AND **PATTERNS** ARE DIFFERENT.
PROFES-SOR OAK SAYS HE'D LIKE SOME JOHTO VERSIONS OF POKÉMON HE ALREADY HAS DATA FROM...
THOSE ARE MY ORDERS!
I GOTTA BE ALERT EVEN WHEN I RUN INTO POKÉMON I'M USED TO SEEING ALL THE TIME!

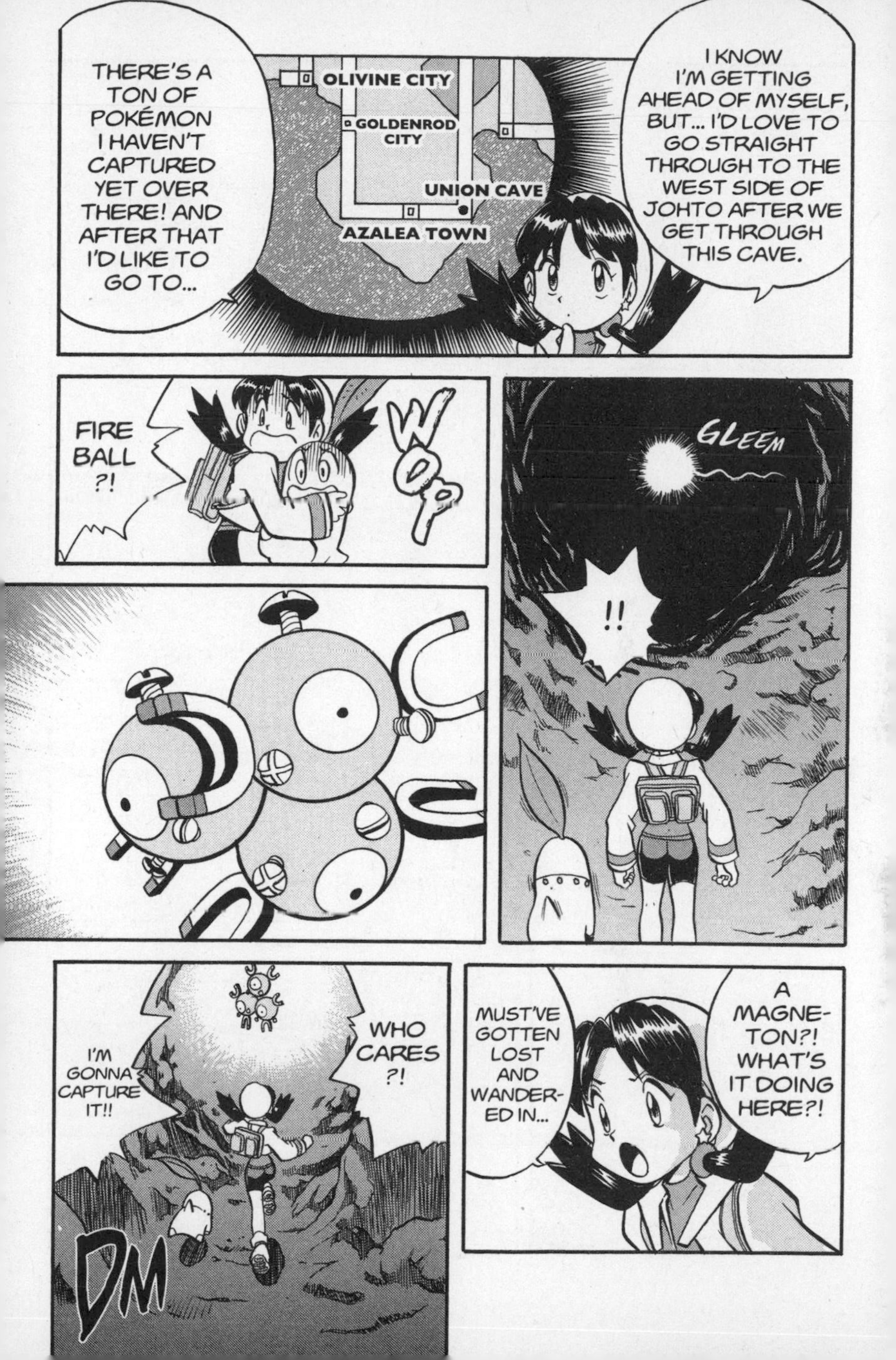
I KNOW I'M GETTING AHEAD OF MYSELF, BUT... I'D LOVE TO GO STRAIGHT THROUGH TO THE WEST SIDE OF JOHTO AFTER WE GET THROUGH THIS CAVE.
OLIVINE CITY
GOLDENROD CITY
UNION CAVE
AZALEA TOWN
THERE'S A TON OF POKÉMON I HAVEN'T CAPTURED YET OVER THERE! AND AFTER THAT I'D LIKE TO GO TO...
GLEEM
!!
FIRE BALL ?!
WOP
A MAGNETON?! WHAT'S IT DOING HERE?!
MUST'VE GOTTEN LOST AND WANDERED IN...
WHO CARES ?!
I'M GONNA CAPTURE IT!!
DM

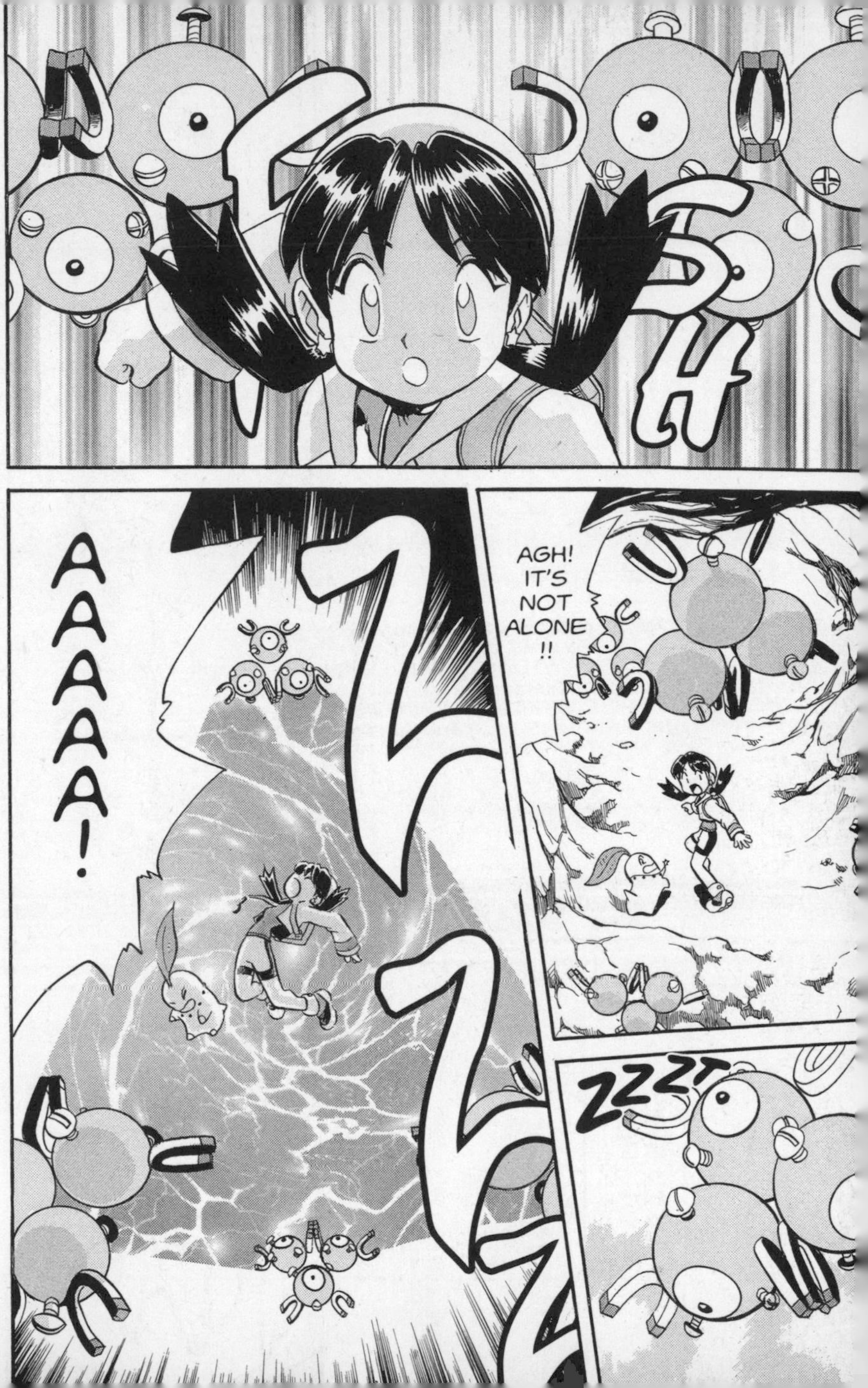
SH
AGH! IT'S NOT ALONE !!
ZZZT
AAAAA!

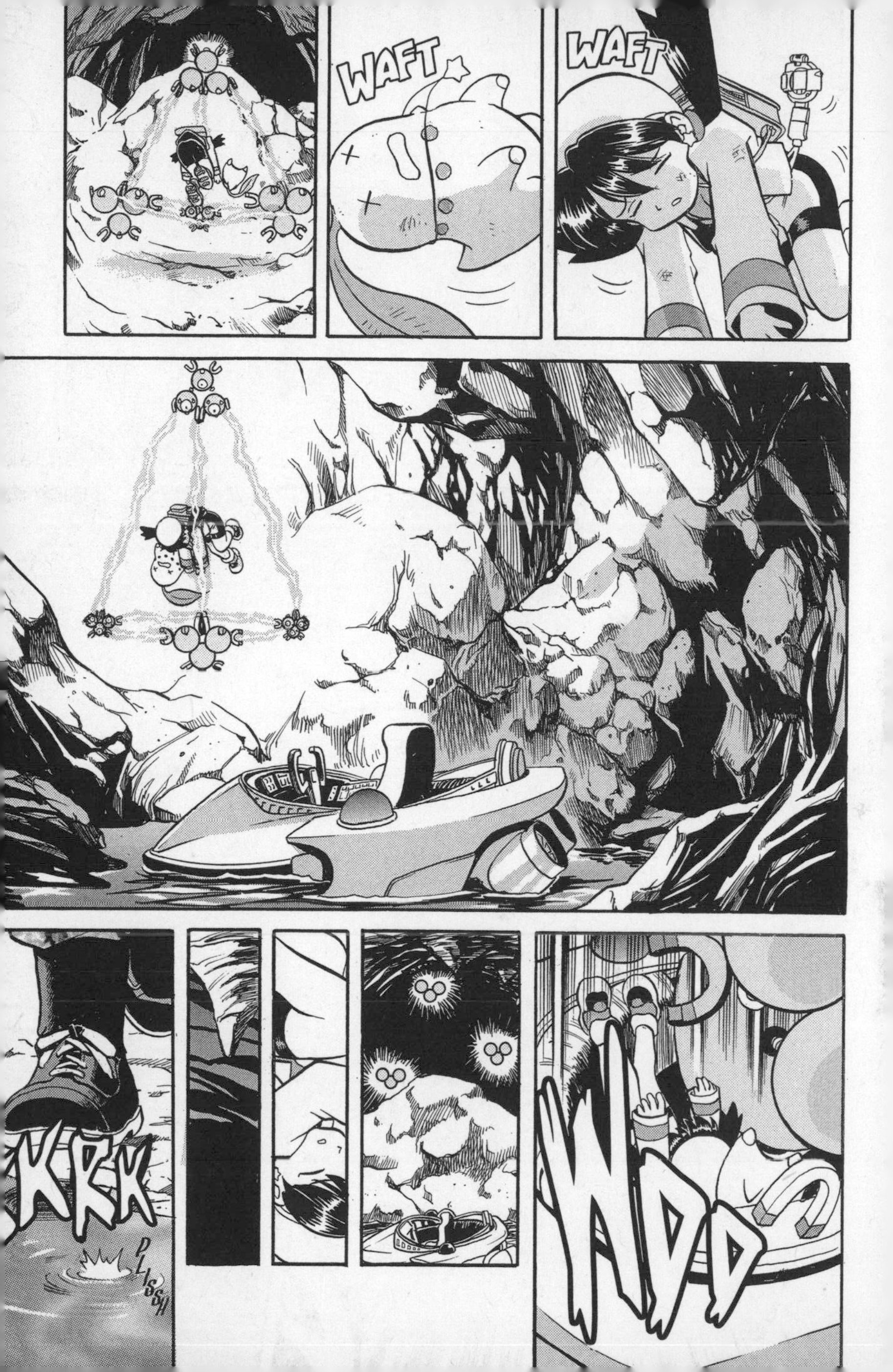

WAFT
WAFT
WOO
KRK
PLISSH

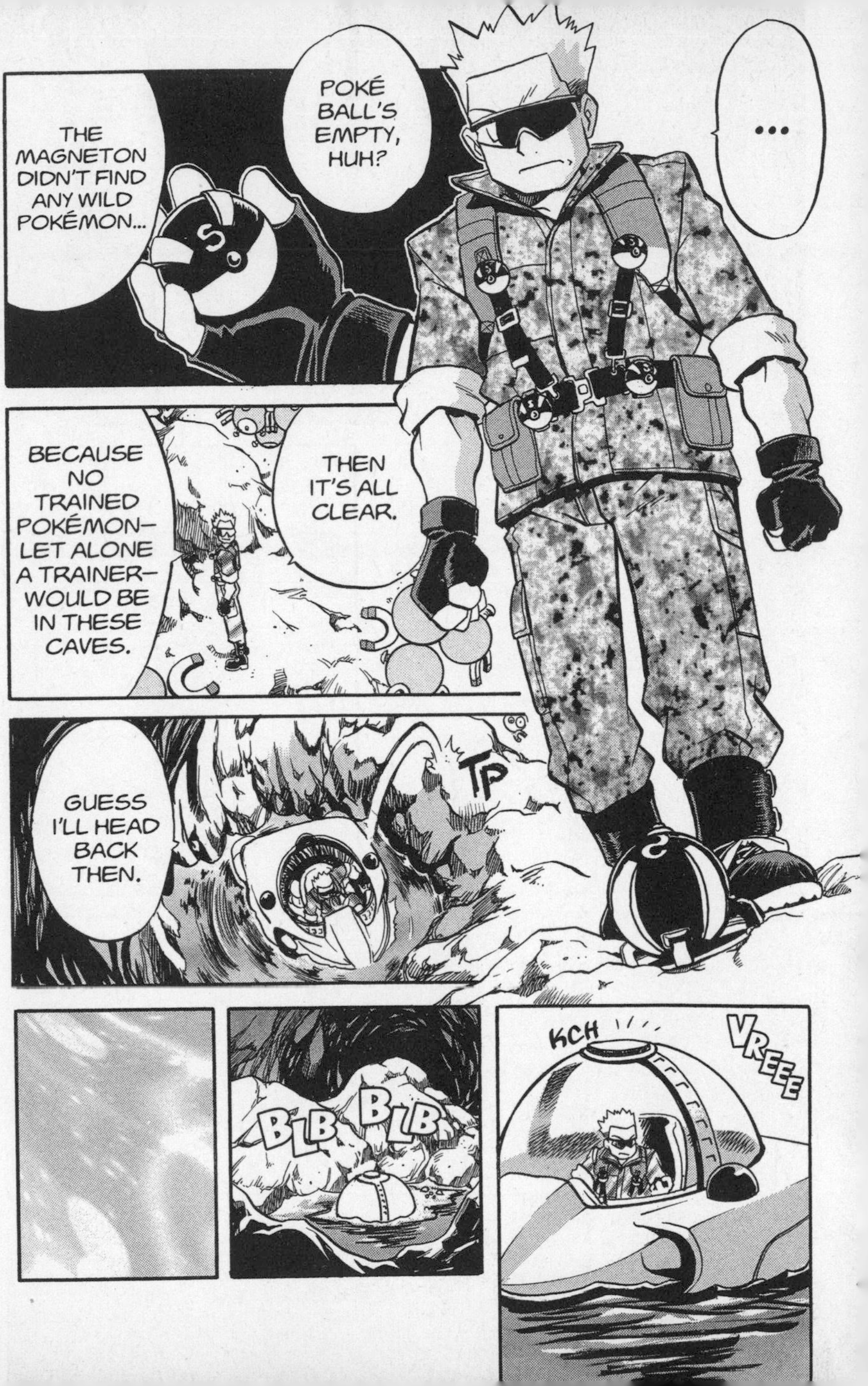
...
POKÉ BALL'S EMPTY, HUH?
THE MAGNETON DIDN'T FIND ANY WILD POKÉMON...
THEN IT'S ALL CLEAR.
BECAUSE NO TRAINED POKÉMON—LET ALONE A TRAINER—WOULD BE IN THESE CAVES.
TP
GUESS I'LL HEAD BACK THEN.
VREEE
KCH
BLB BLB

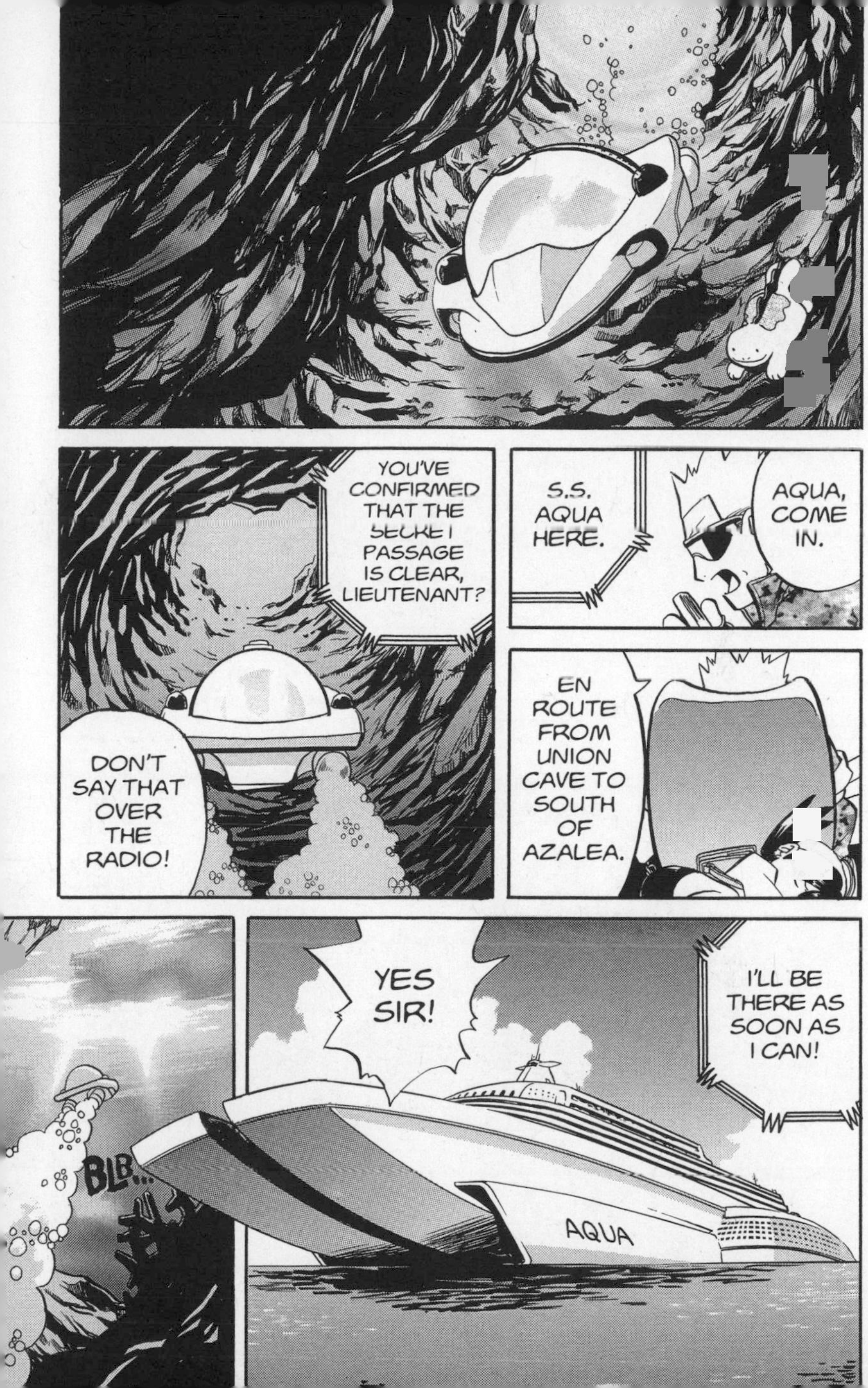
AQUA, COME IN.
S.S. AQUA HERE.
EN ROUTE FROM UNION CAVE TO SOUTH OF AZALEA.
YOU'VE CONFIRMED THAT THE SECRET PASSAGE IS CLEAR, LIEUTENANT?
DON'T SAY THAT OVER THE RADIO!
I'LL BE THERE AS SOON AS I CAN!
YES SIR!
AQUA
BLB...

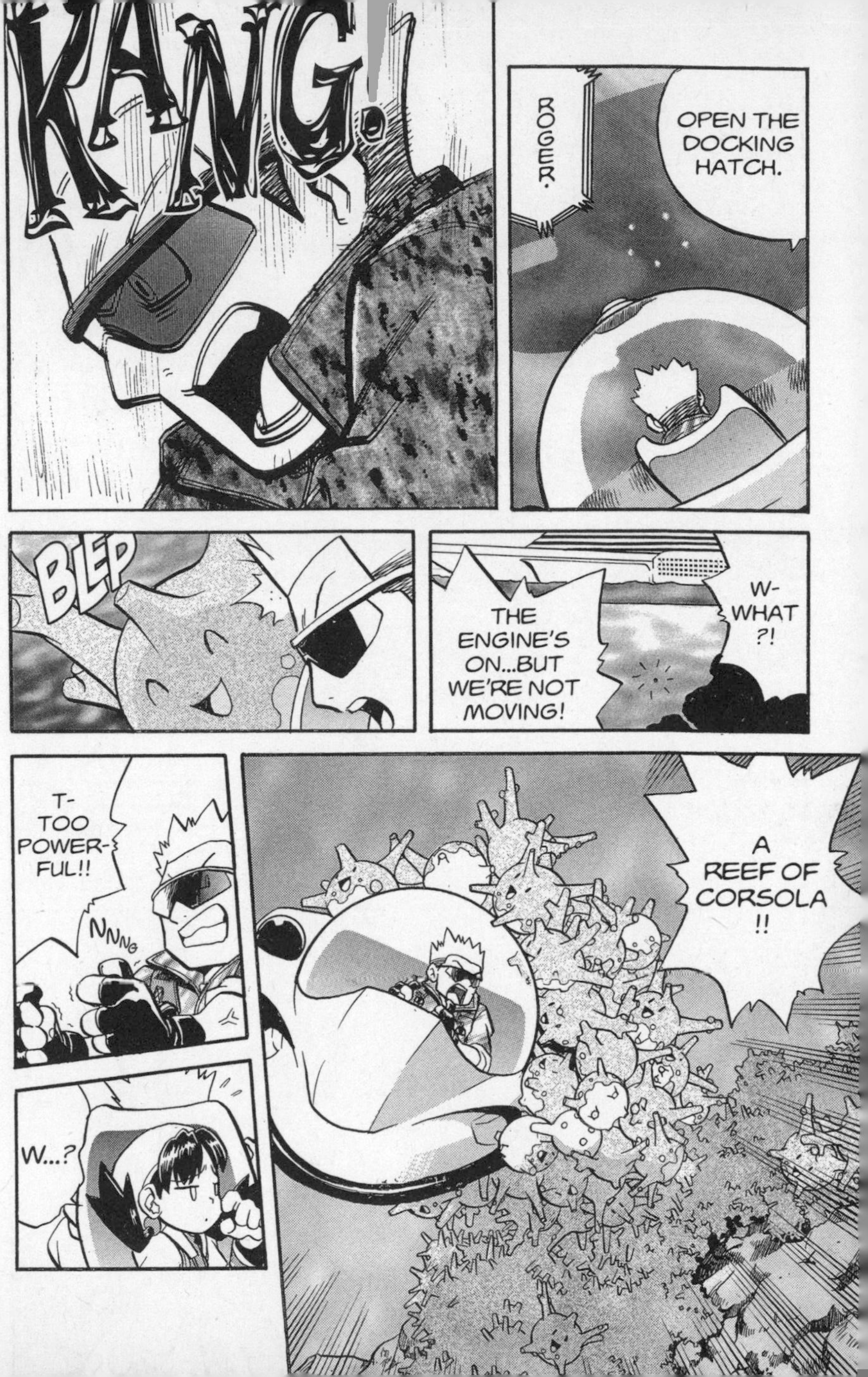
OPEN THE DOCKING HATCH.
ROGER.
KANG!
W-WHAT?!
THE ENGINE'S ON...BUT WE'RE NOT MOVING!
BLEP
A REEF OF CORSOLA!!
T-TOO POWER-FUL!!
NNNG
W...?

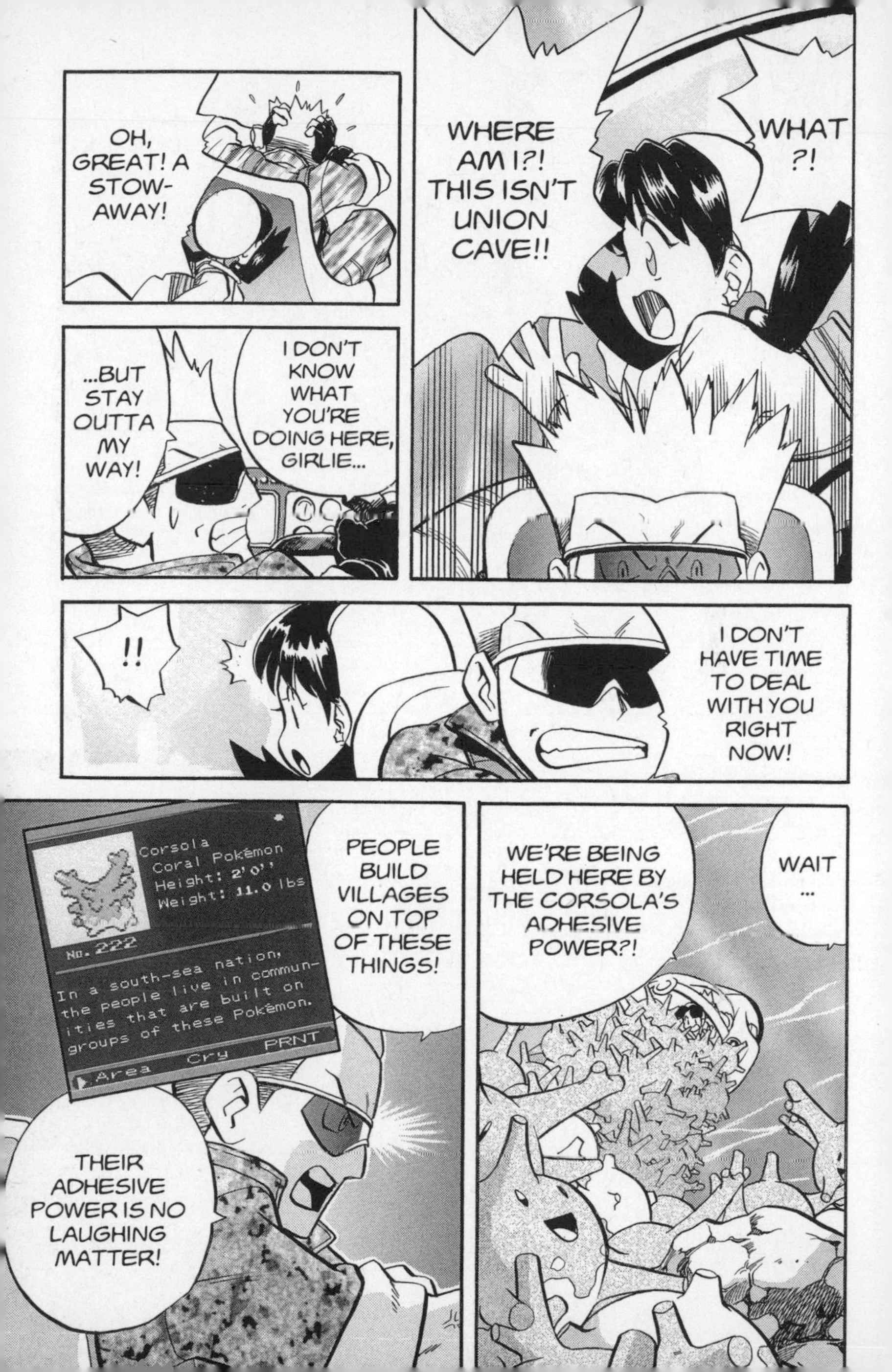
WHAT?!
WHERE AM I?! THIS ISN'T UNION CAVE!!
OH, GREAT! A STOW-AWAY!
I DON'T KNOW WHAT YOU'RE DOING HERE, GIRLIE...
...BUT STAY OUTTA MY WAY!
I DON'T HAVE TIME TO DEAL WITH YOU RIGHT NOW!
!!
WAIT ...
WE'RE BEING HELD HERE BY THE CORSOLA'S ADHESIVE POWER?!
PEOPLE BUILD VILLAGES ON TOP OF THESE THINGS!
Corsola
Coral Pokémon
Height: 2'0''
Weight: 11.0 lbs
No. 222
In a south-sea nation, the people live in communities that are built on groups of these Pokémon.
Area Cry PRNT
THEIR ADHESIVE POWER IS NO LAUGHING MATTER!

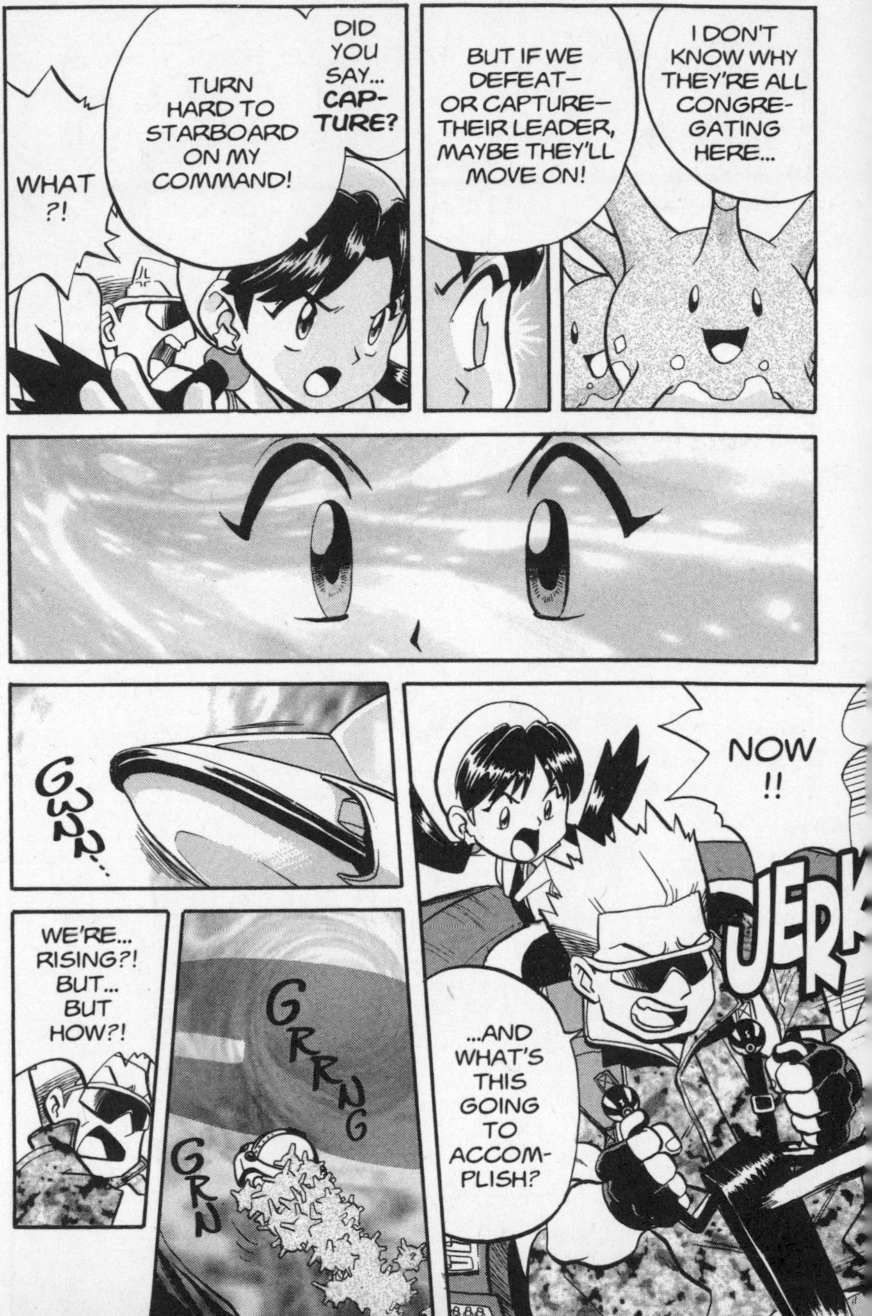
I DON'T KNOW WHY THEY'RE ALL CONGREGATING HERE...
BUT IF WE DEFEAT—OR CAPTURE—THEIR LEADER, MAYBE THEY'LL MOVE ON!
DID YOU SAY... **CAPTURE?**
TURN HARD TO STARBOARD ON MY COMMAND!
WHAT?!
NOW!!
JERK
...AND WHAT'S THIS GOING TO ACCOMPLISH?
GWNN...
GRRNG
GRN
WE'RE... RISING?! BUT... BUT HOW?!

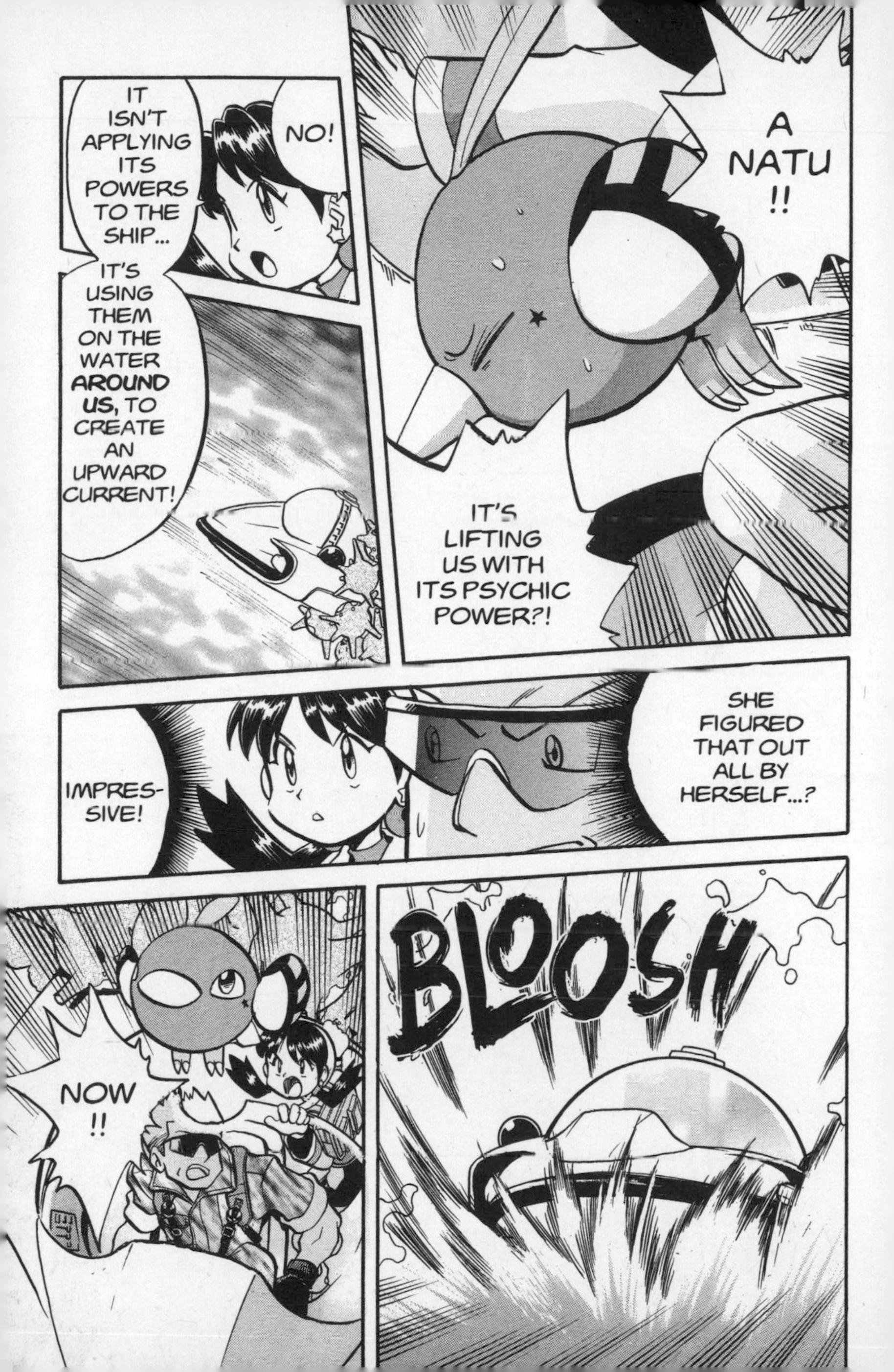
A NATU !!
IT'S LIFTING US WITH ITS PSYCHIC POWER?!
NO!
IT ISN'T APPLYING ITS POWERS TO THE SHIP...
IT'S USING THEM ON THE WATER **AROUND US,** TO CREATE AN UPWARD CURRENT!
SHE FIGURED THAT OUT ALL BY HERSELF...?
IMPRES-SIVE!
BLOOSH
NOW !!

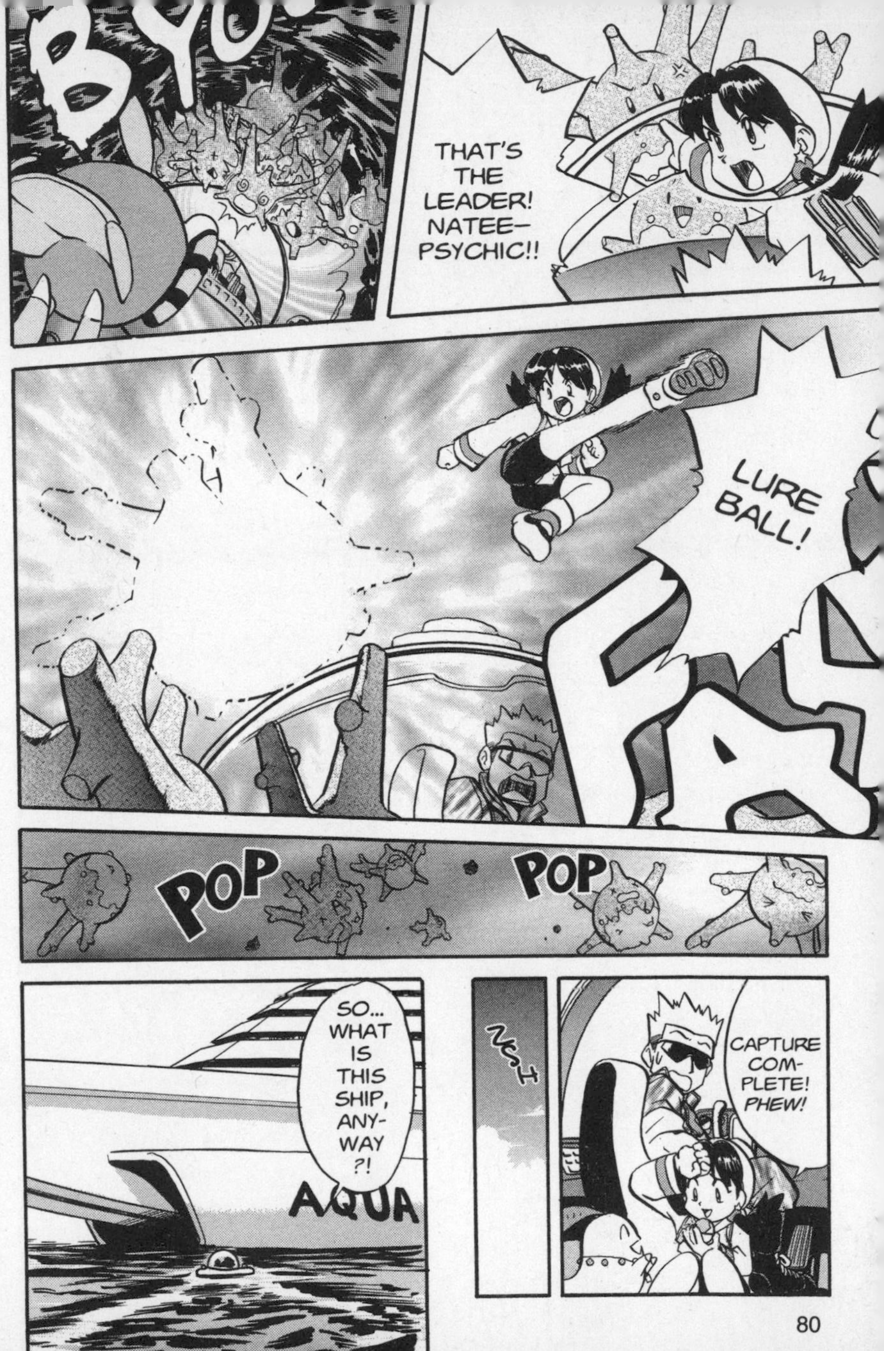
THAT'S THE LEADER! NATEE—PSYCHIC!!
BYO
LURE BALL!
POP
POP
CAPTURE COM-PLETE! PHEW!
SO... WHAT IS THIS SHIP, ANYWAY?!
AQUA

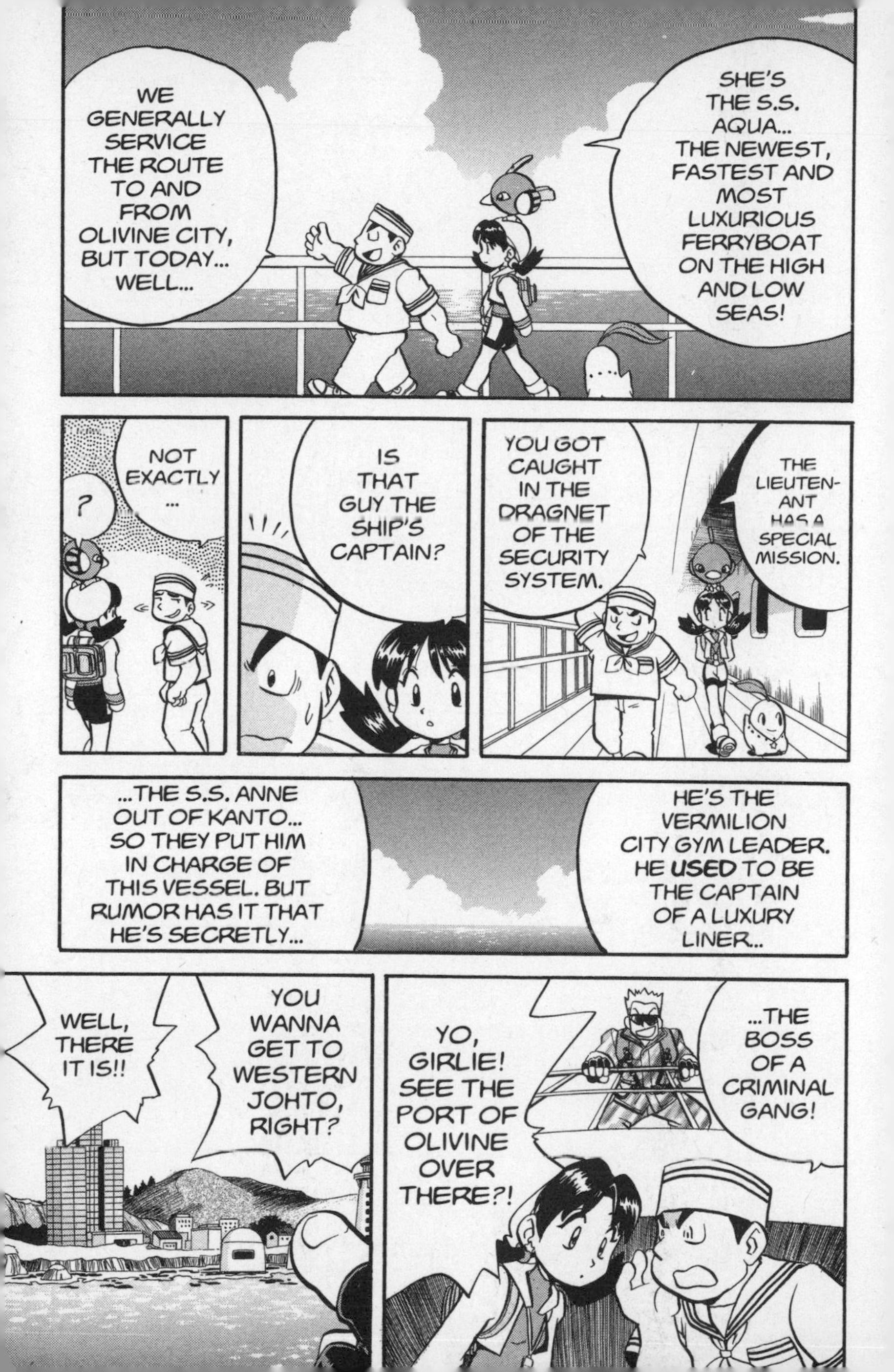
SHE'S THE S.S. AQUA... THE NEWEST, FASTEST AND MOST LUXURIOUS FERRYBOAT ON THE HIGH AND LOW SEAS!
WE GENERALLY SERVICE THE ROUTE TO AND FROM OLIVINE CITY, BUT TODAY... WELL...
THE LIEUTENANT HAS A SPECIAL MISSION.
YOU GOT CAUGHT IN THE DRAGNET OF THE SECURITY SYSTEM.
IS THAT GUY THE SHIP'S CAPTAIN?
NOT EXACTLY ...
?
HE'S THE VERMILION CITY GYM LEADER. HE **USED** TO BE THE CAPTAIN OF A LUXURY LINER...
...THE S.S. ANNE OUT OF KANTO... SO THEY PUT HIM IN CHARGE OF THIS VESSEL. BUT RUMOR HAS IT THAT HE'S SECRETLY...
...THE BOSS OF A CRIMINAL GANG!
YO, GIRLIE! SEE THE PORT OF OLIVINE OVER THERE?!
YOU WANNA GET TO WESTERN JOHTO, RIGHT?
WELL, THERE IT IS!!

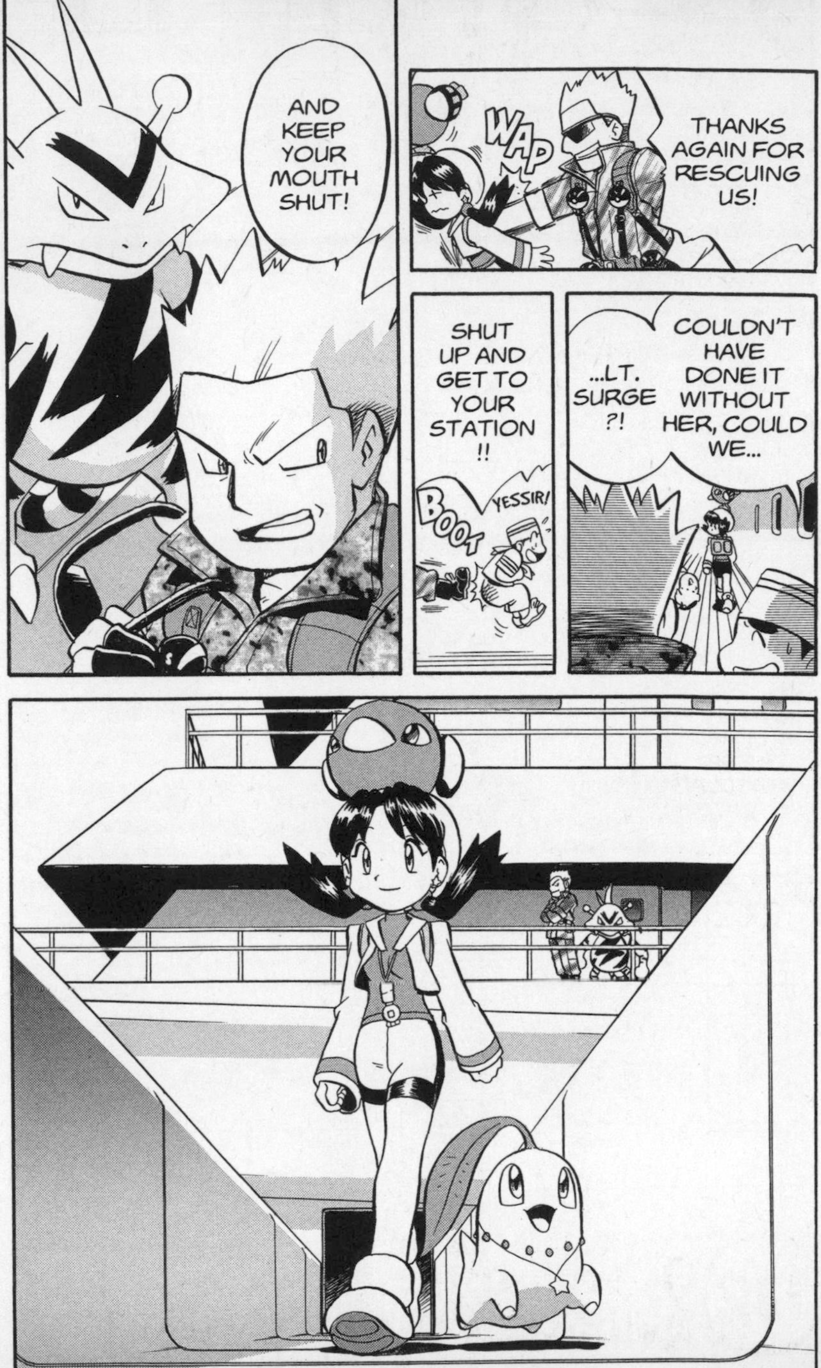
THANKS AGAIN FOR RESCUING US!
WAP
COULDN'T HAVE DONE IT WITHOUT HER, COULD WE...
...LT. SURGE ?!
SHUT UP AND GET TO YOUR STATION !!
YESSIR!
BOOOT
AND KEEP YOUR MOUTH SHUT!

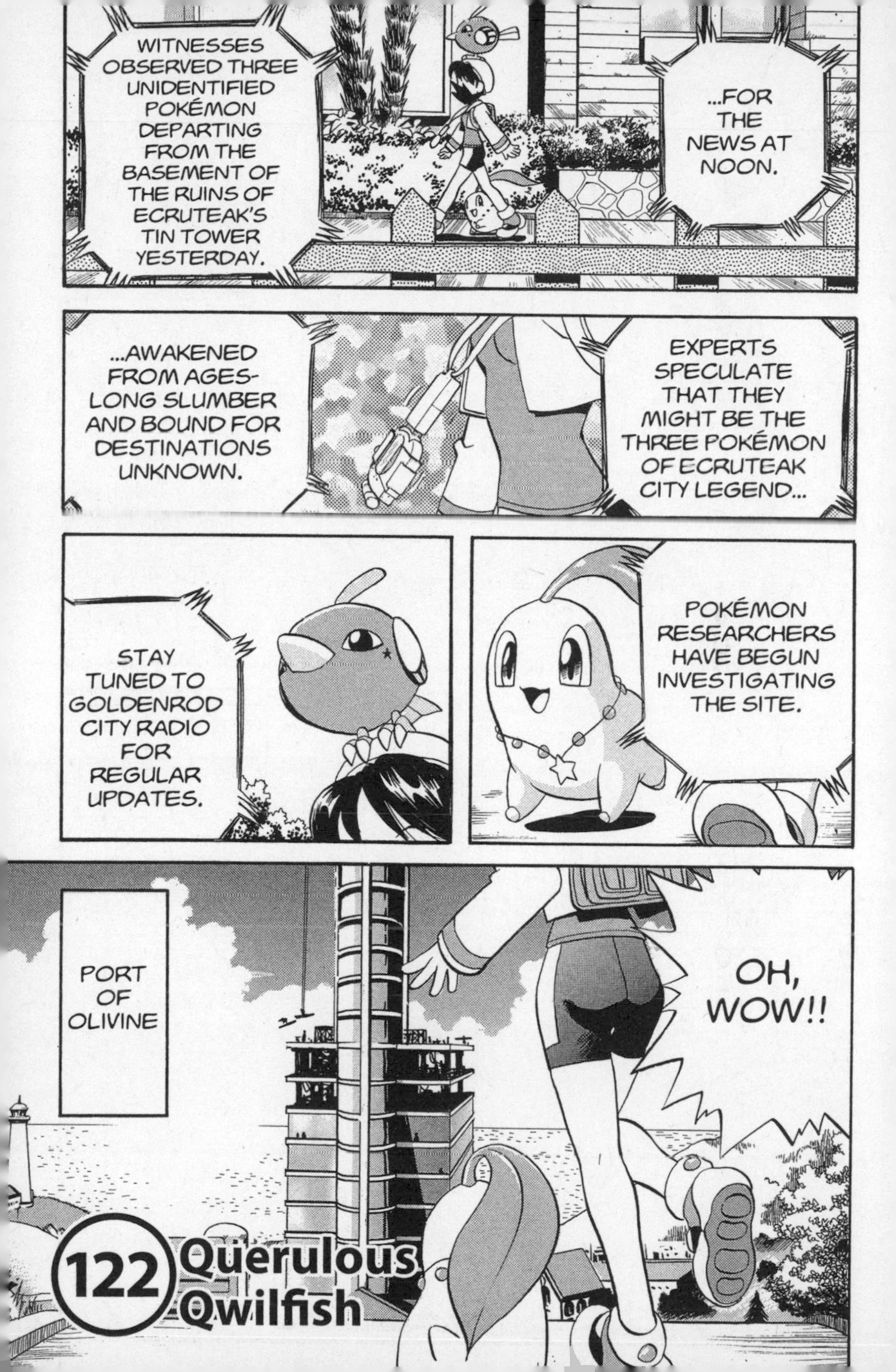
...FOR THE NEWS AT NOON.
WITNESSES OBSERVED THREE UNIDENTIFIED POKÉMON DEPARTING FROM THE BASEMENT OF THE RUINS OF ECRUTEAK'S TIN TOWER YESTERDAY.
EXPERTS SPECULATE THAT THEY MIGHT BE THE THREE POKÉMON OF ECRUTEAK CITY LEGEND...
...AWAKENED FROM AGES-LONG SLUMBER AND BOUND FOR DESTINATIONS UNKNOWN.
POKÉMON RESEARCHERS HAVE BEGUN INVESTIGATING THE SITE.
STAY TUNED TO GOLDENROD CITY RADIO FOR REGULAR UPDATES.
OH, WOW!!
PORT OF OLIVINE
122 Querulous Qwilfish

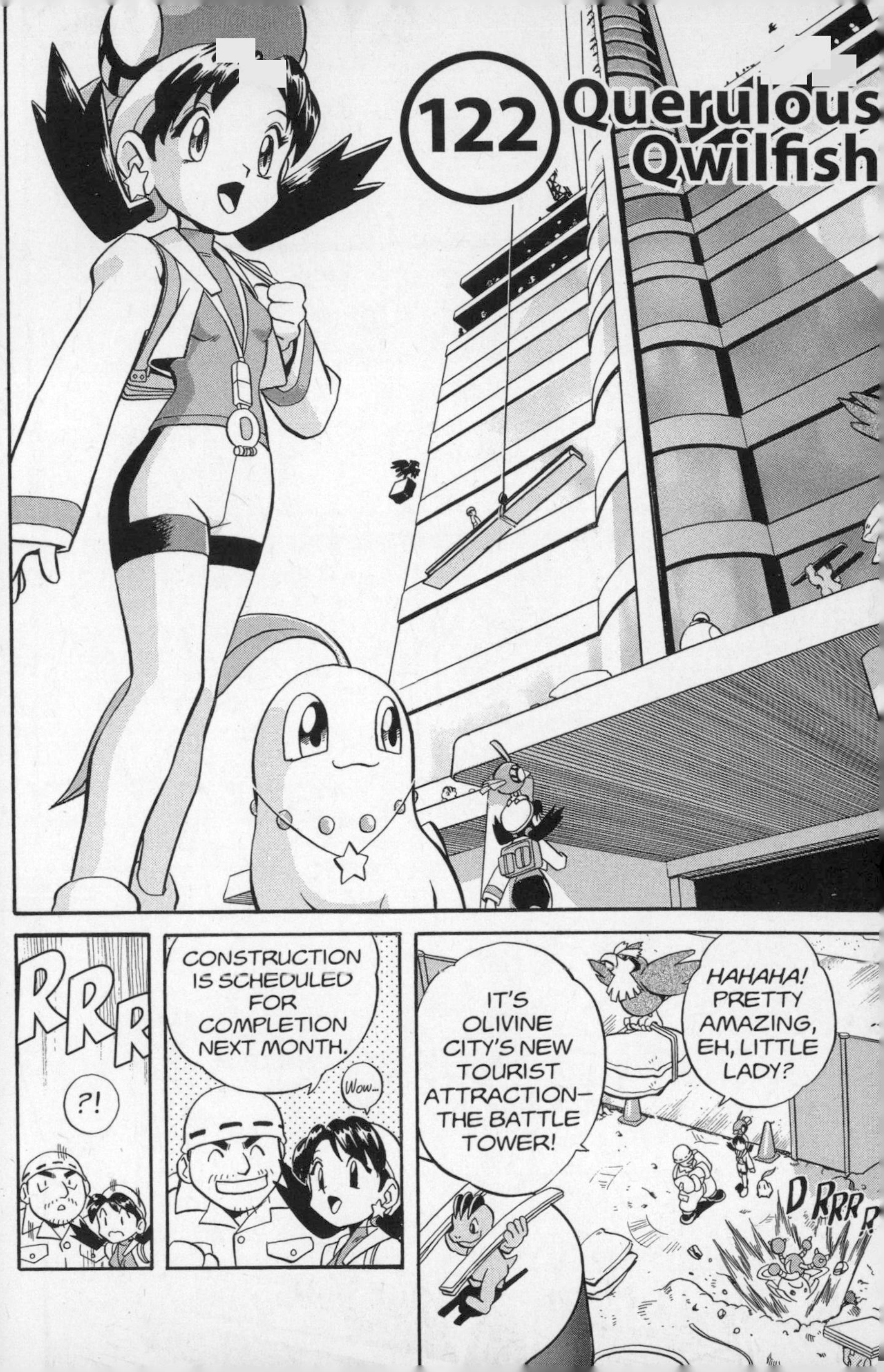
122 Querulous Qwilfish
HAHAHA! PRETTY AMAZING, EH, LITTLE LADY?
IT'S OLIVINE CITY'S NEW TOURIST ATTRACTION— THE BATTLE TOWER!
DRRRR
CONSTRUCTION IS SCHEDULED FOR COMPLETION NEXT MONTH.
Wow...
RRRR
?!

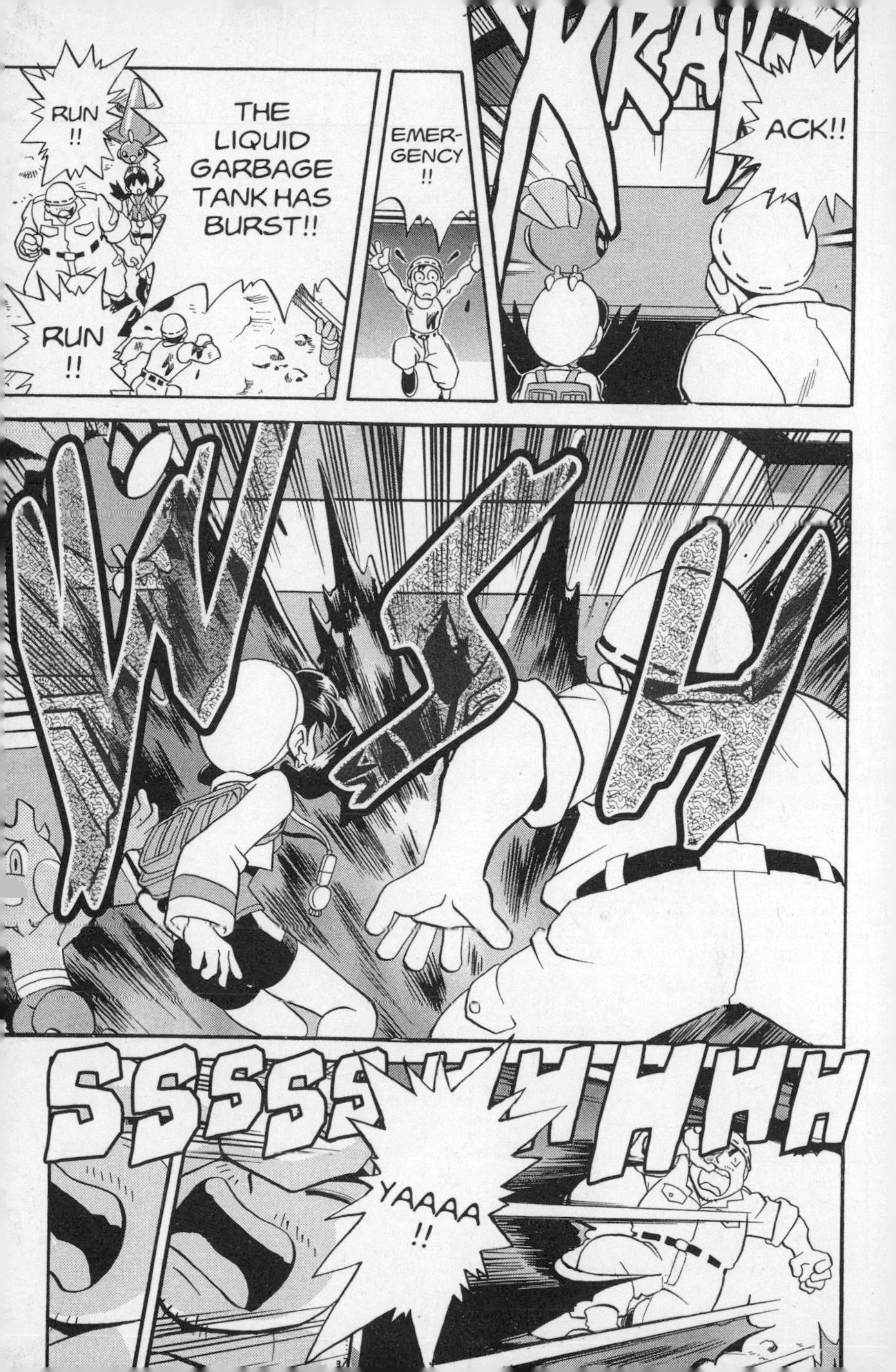
ACK!!
EMER-
GENCY
!!
THE LIQUID GARBAGE TANK HAS BURST!!
RUN
!!
RUN
!!
YAAAA
!!

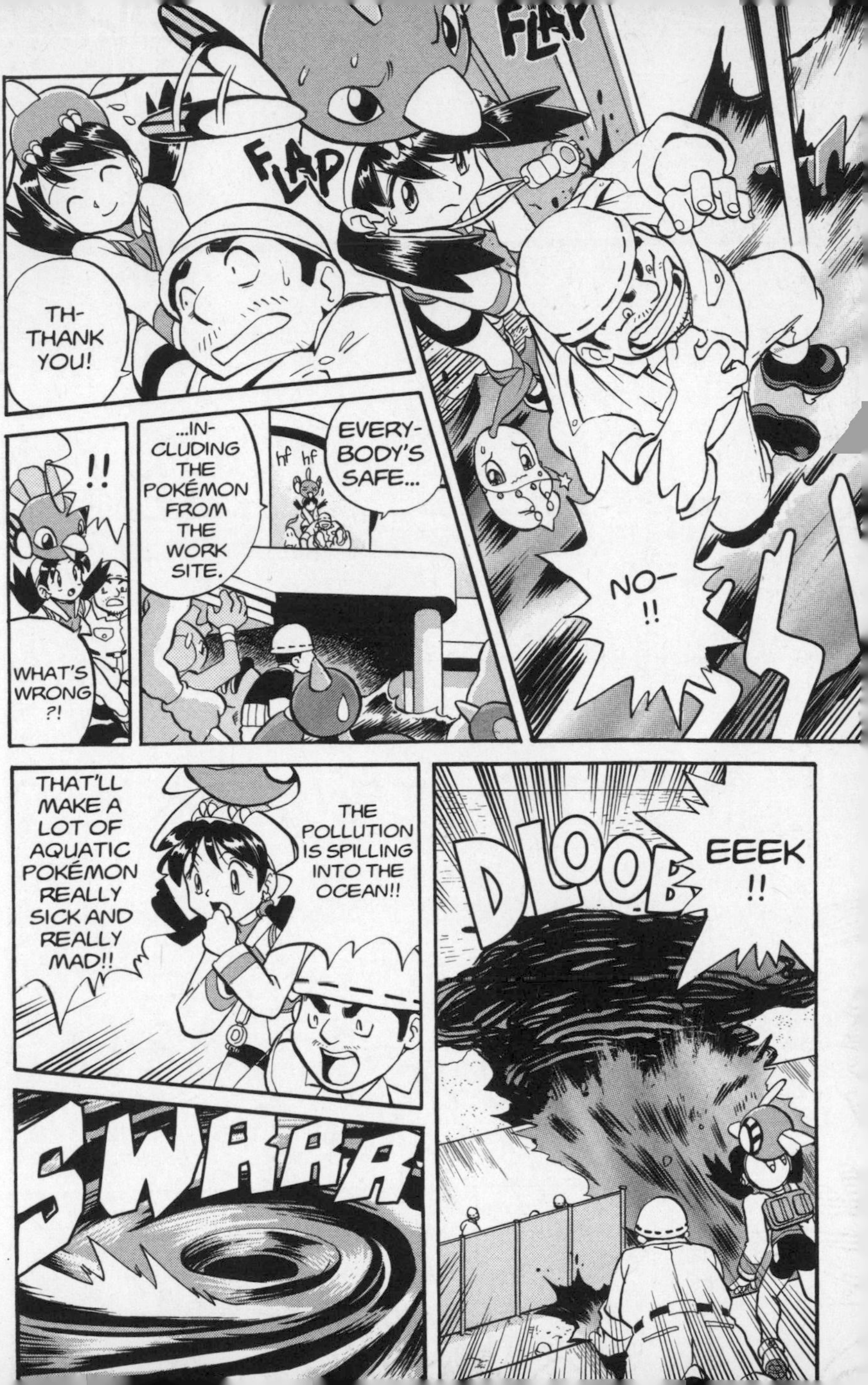
FLAP
NO— !!
FLAP
TH-THANK YOU!
EVERYBODY'S SAFE...
hf hf
...INCLUDING THE POKÉMON FROM THE WORK SITE.
!!
WHAT'S WRONG ?!
DLOOB
EEEK !!
THE POLLUTION IS SPILLING INTO THE OCEAN!!
THAT'LL MAKE A LOT OF AQUATIC POKÉMON REALLY SICK AND REALLY MAD!!
SWRRR

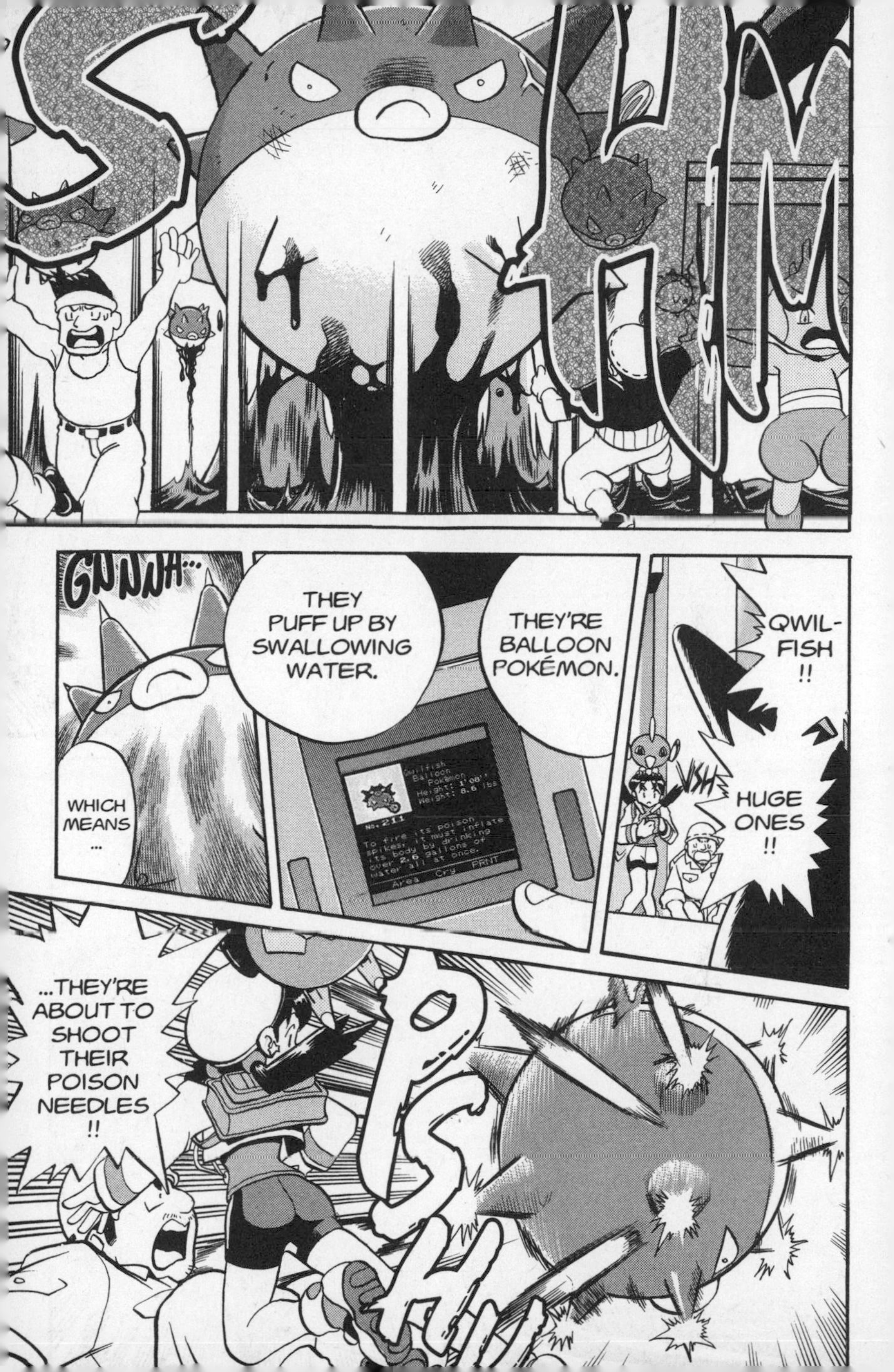
QWIL-FISH !!
VSH
HUGE ONES !!
THEY'RE BALLOON POKÉMON.
THEY PUFF UP BY SWALLOWING WATER.
Qwilfish Balloon Pokémon Height: 1'08" Weight: 8.6 lbs
No.211
To fire its poison spikes, it must inflate its body by drinking over 2.6 gallons of water all at once.
Area Cry PRNT
GNNNH...
WHICH MEANS ...
...THEY'RE ABOUT TO SHOOT THEIR POISON NEEDLES !!

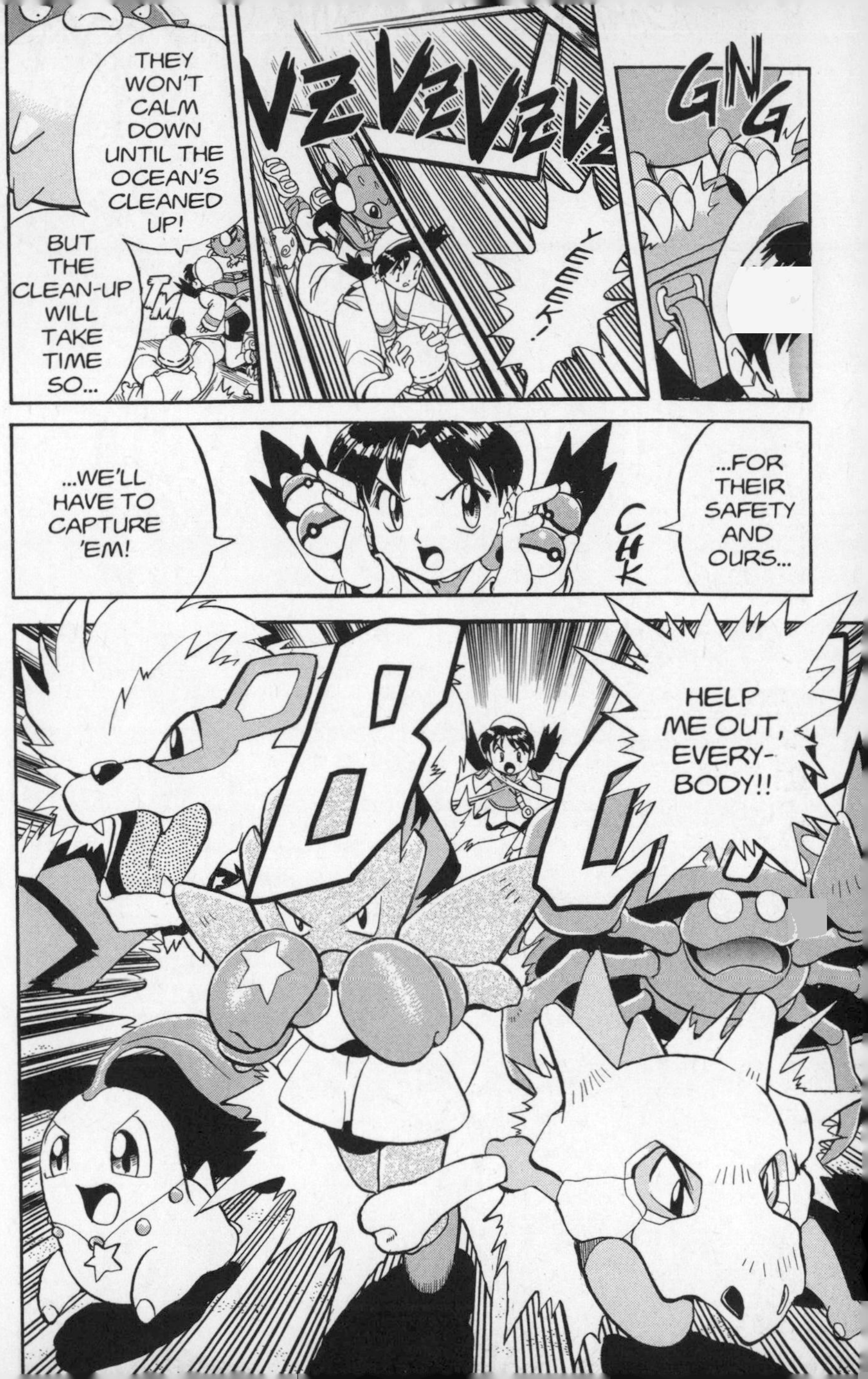
GNG
VZVZVZVZ
YEEEEK!
THEY WON'T CALM DOWN UNTIL THE OCEAN'S CLEANED UP!
BUT THE CLEAN-UP WILL TAKE TIME SO...
...FOR THEIR SAFETY AND OURS...
CHK
...WE'LL HAVE TO CAPTURE 'EM!
HELP ME OUT, EVERY-BODY!!

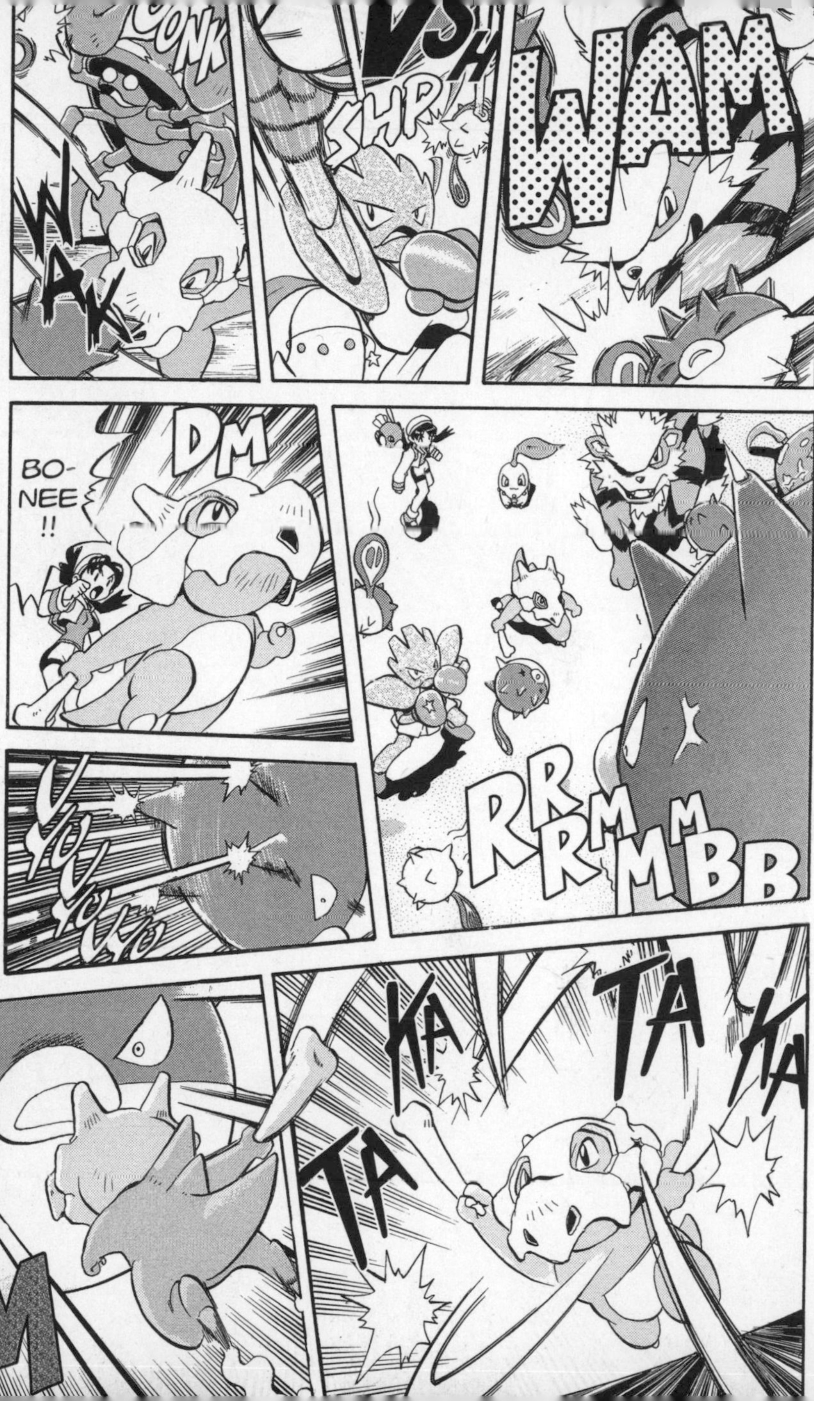
WAM
VSH
SHP
CONK
WAK
RRRMMMMBB
DM
BO-
NEE
!!
KA
TA
KA
TA
TM

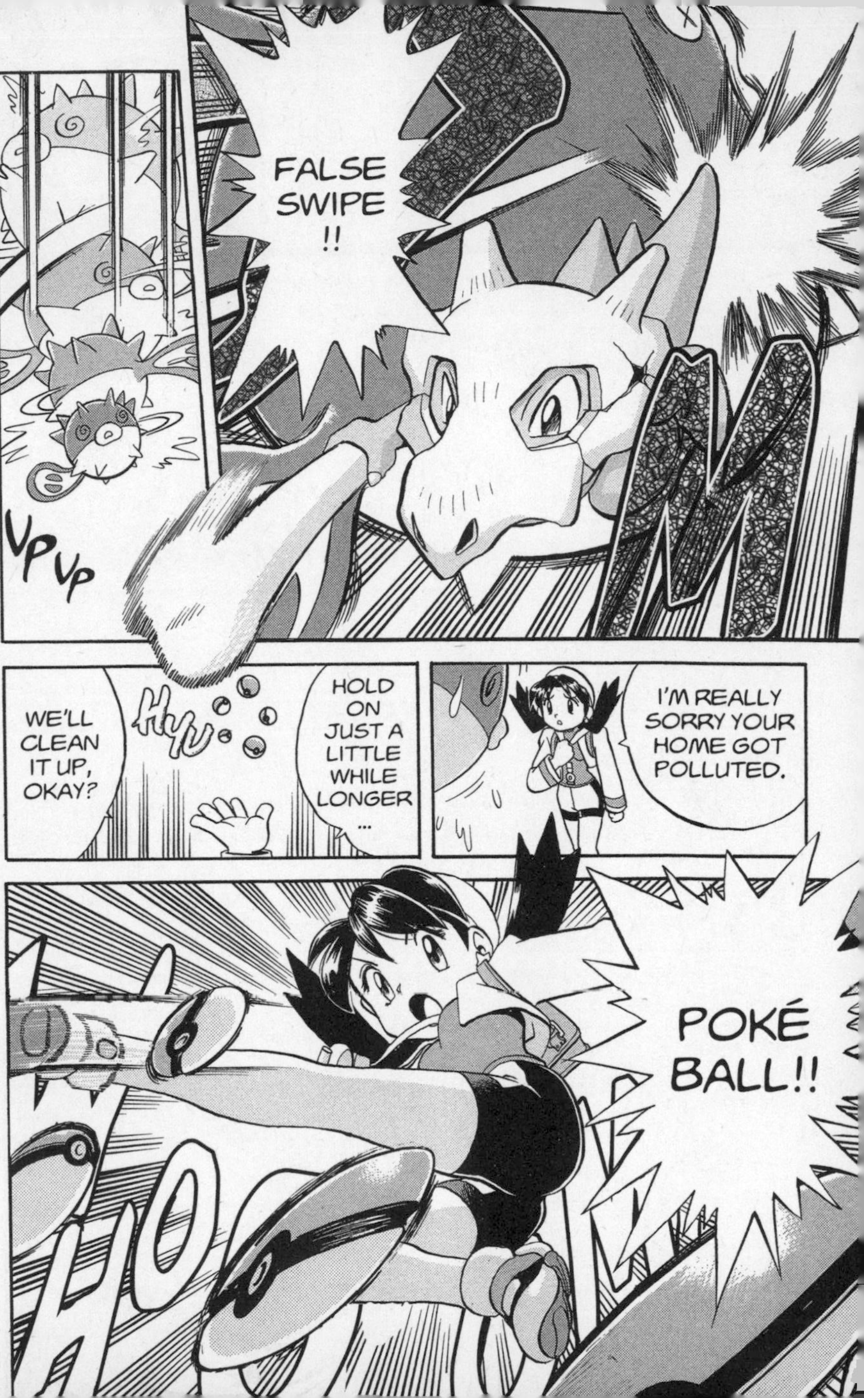
FALSE SWIPE !!
VP VP
I'M REALLY SORRY YOUR HOME GOT POLLUTED.
HOLD ON JUST A LITTLE WHILE LONGER ...
HYU
WE'LL CLEAN IT UP, OKAY?
POKÉ BALL!!

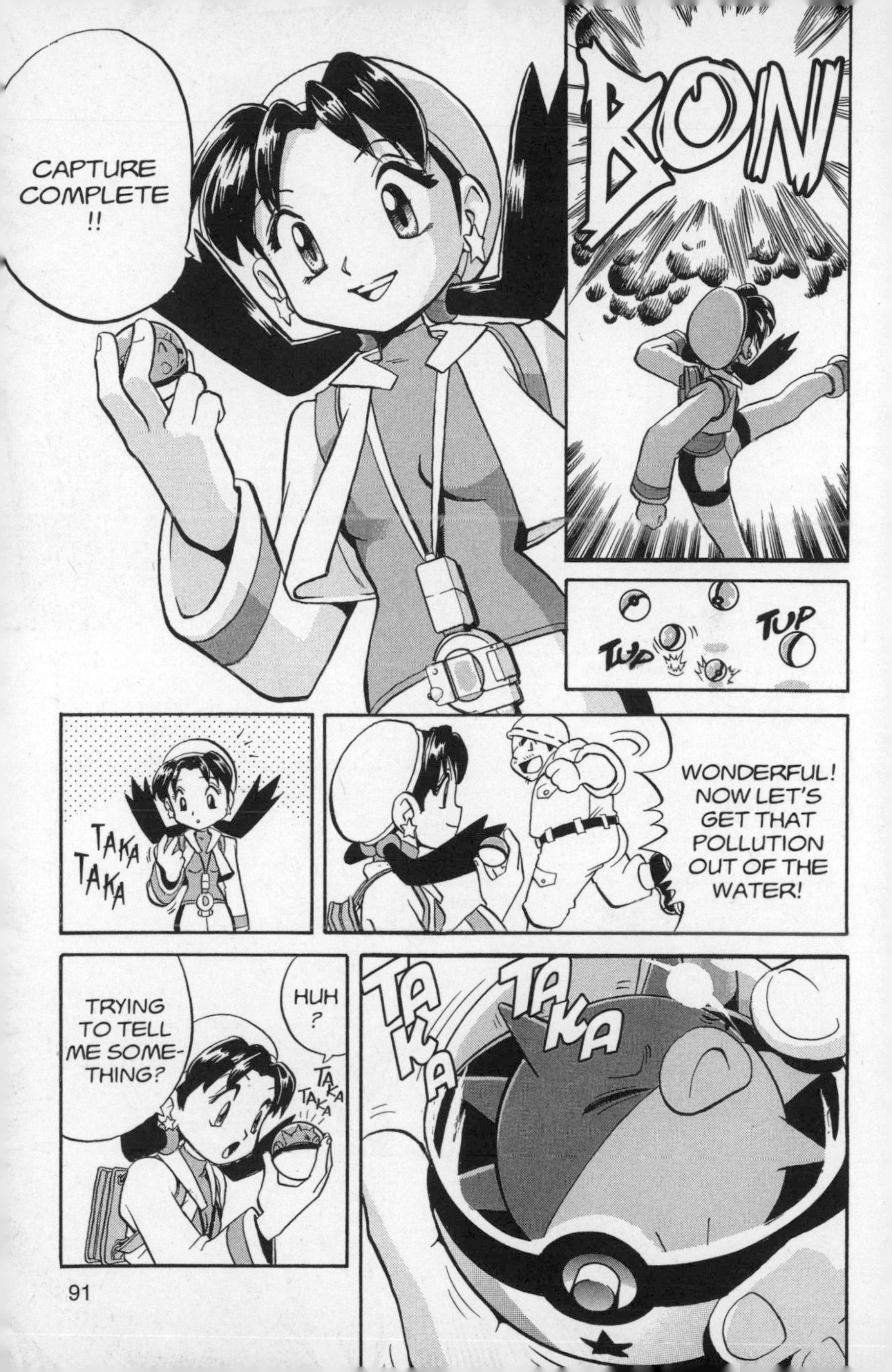
BON
TUP
TUP
CAPTURE COMPLETE !!
WONDERFUL! NOW LET'S GET THAT POLLUTION OUT OF THE WATER!
TAKA TAKA
TAKA TAKA TAKA
HUH?
TRYING TO TELL ME SOME-THING?
TAKA TAKA

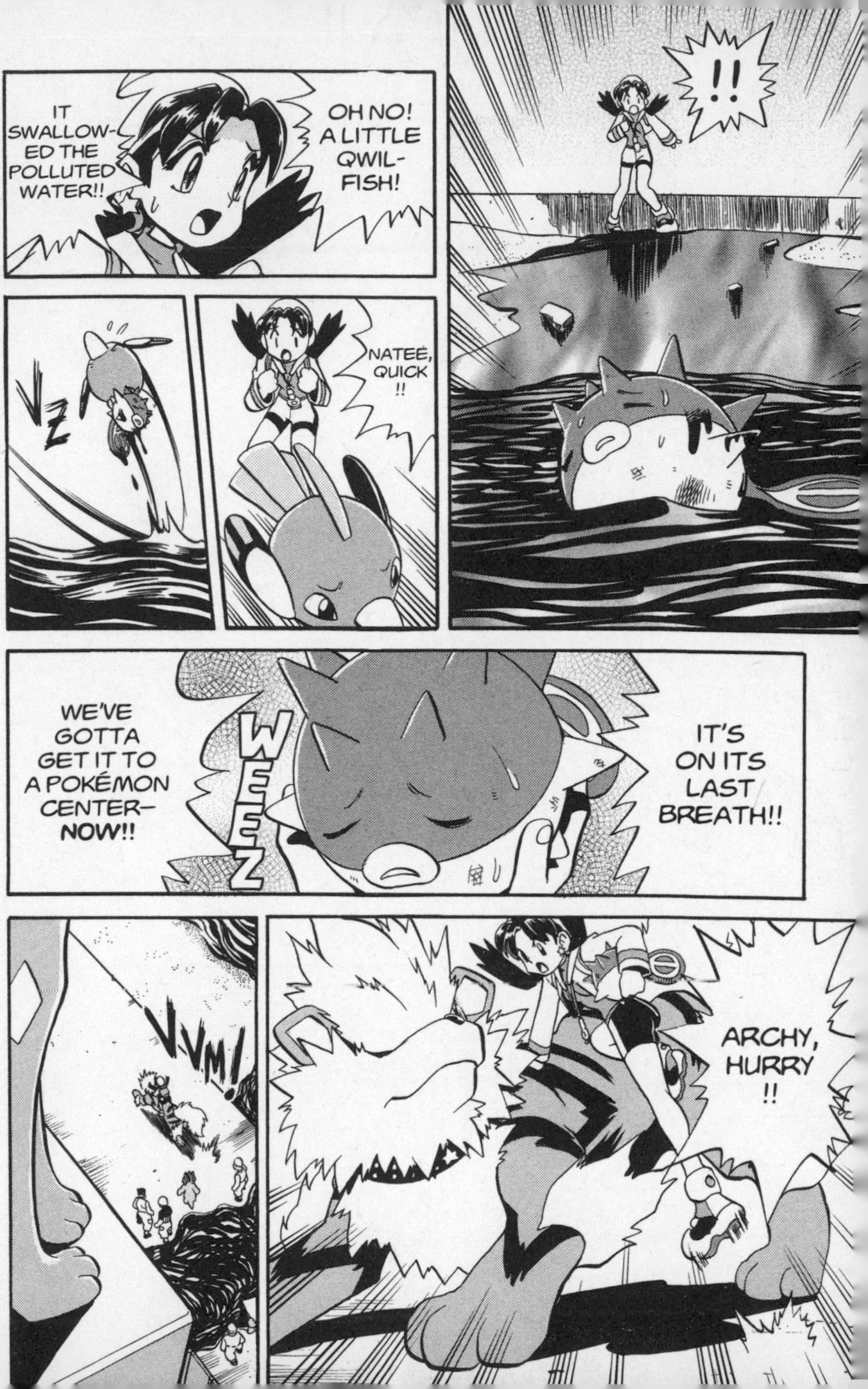
!!
OH NO! A LITTLE QWIL-FISH!
IT SWALLOW-ED THE POLLUTED WATER!!
NATEE, QUICK!!
VZ
IT'S ON ITS LAST BREATH!!
WEEZ
WE'VE GOTTA GET IT TO A POKÉMON CENTER—NOW!!
ARCHY, HURRY!!
VVM!

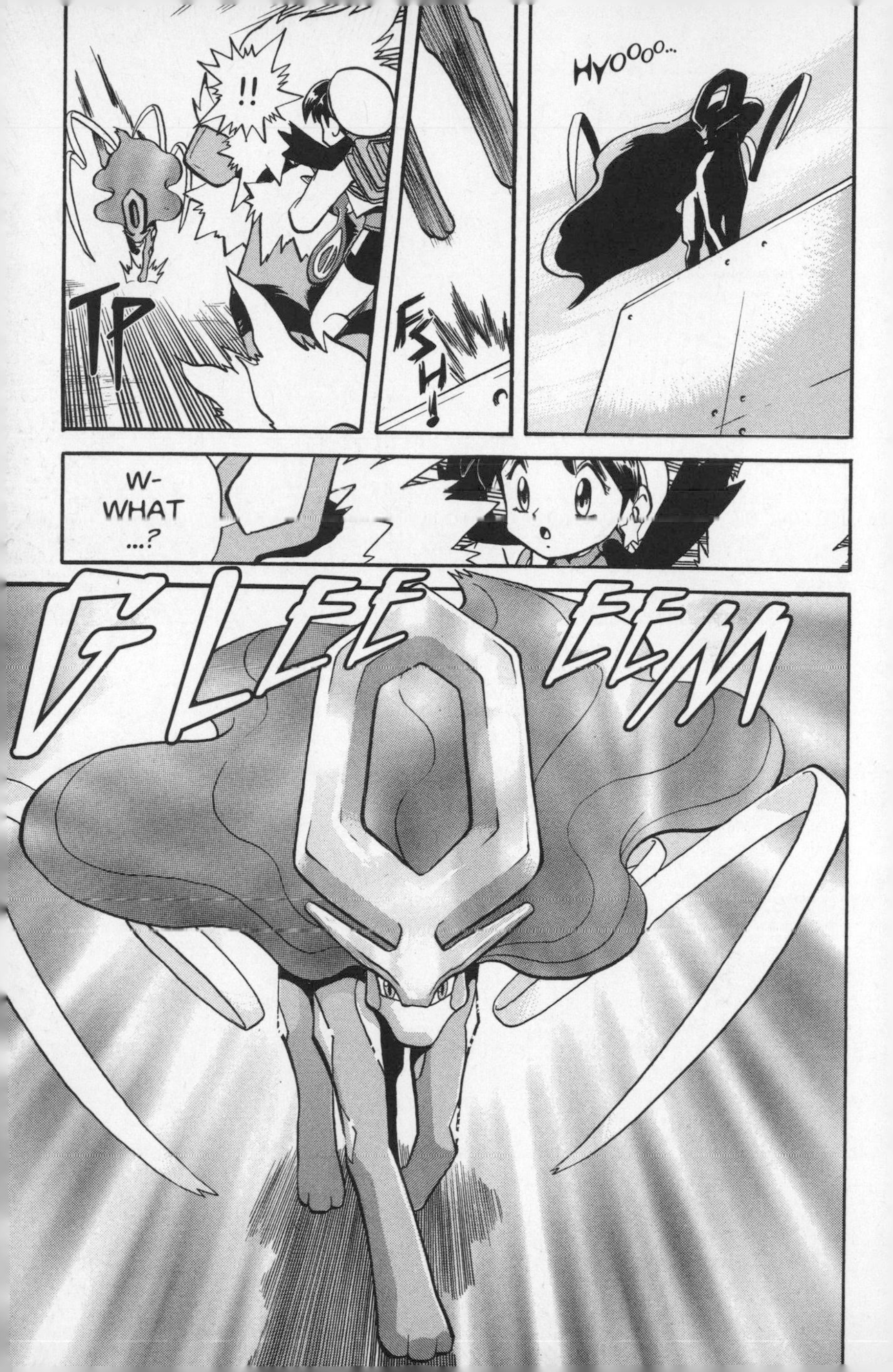
HYOOOO...
FSH!
!!
TP
W-WHAT ...?
G'LEE EEM

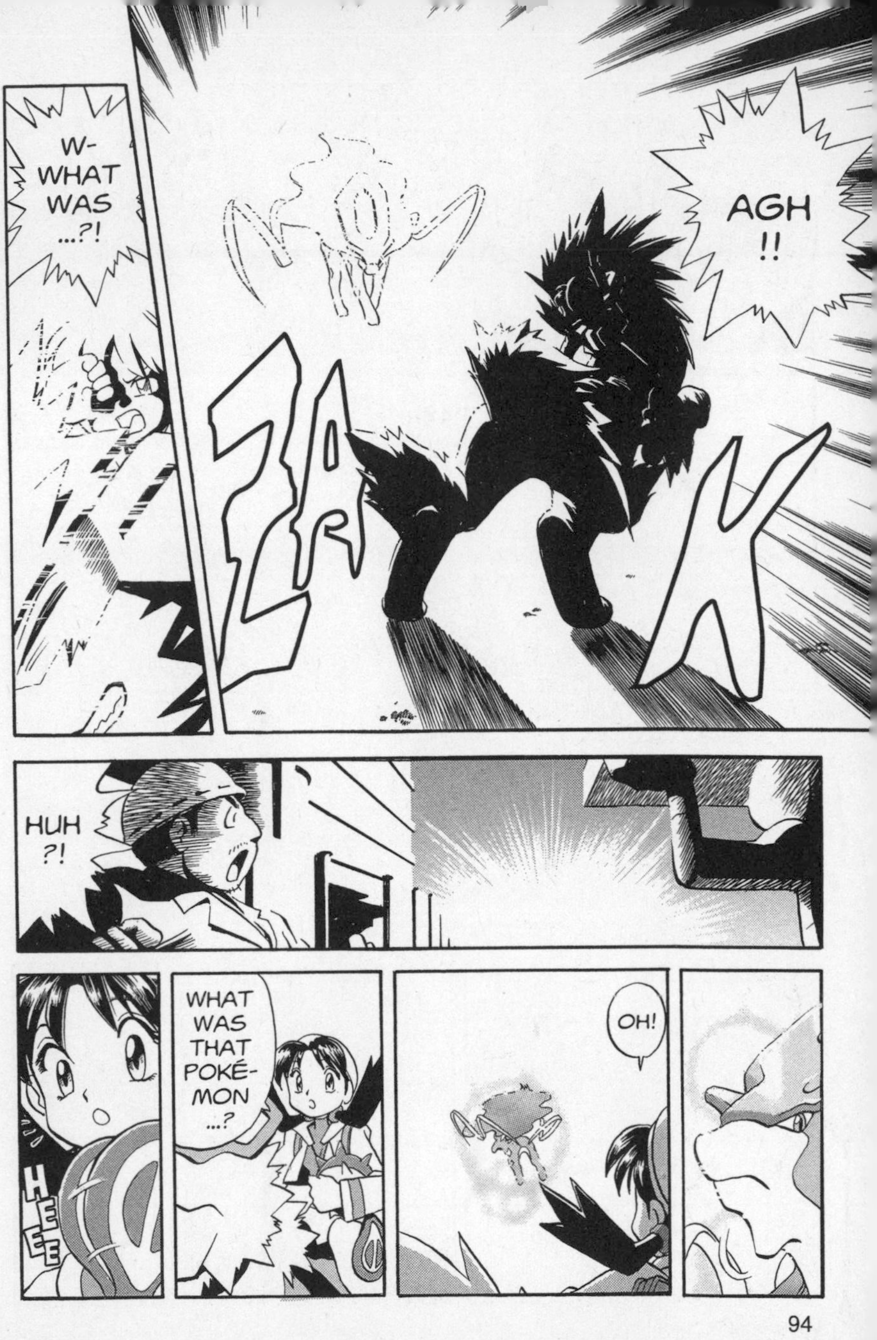
AGH!!
ZAK
W-WHAT WAS ...?!
HUH?!
OH!
WHAT WAS THAT POKÉMON ...?
HEEE

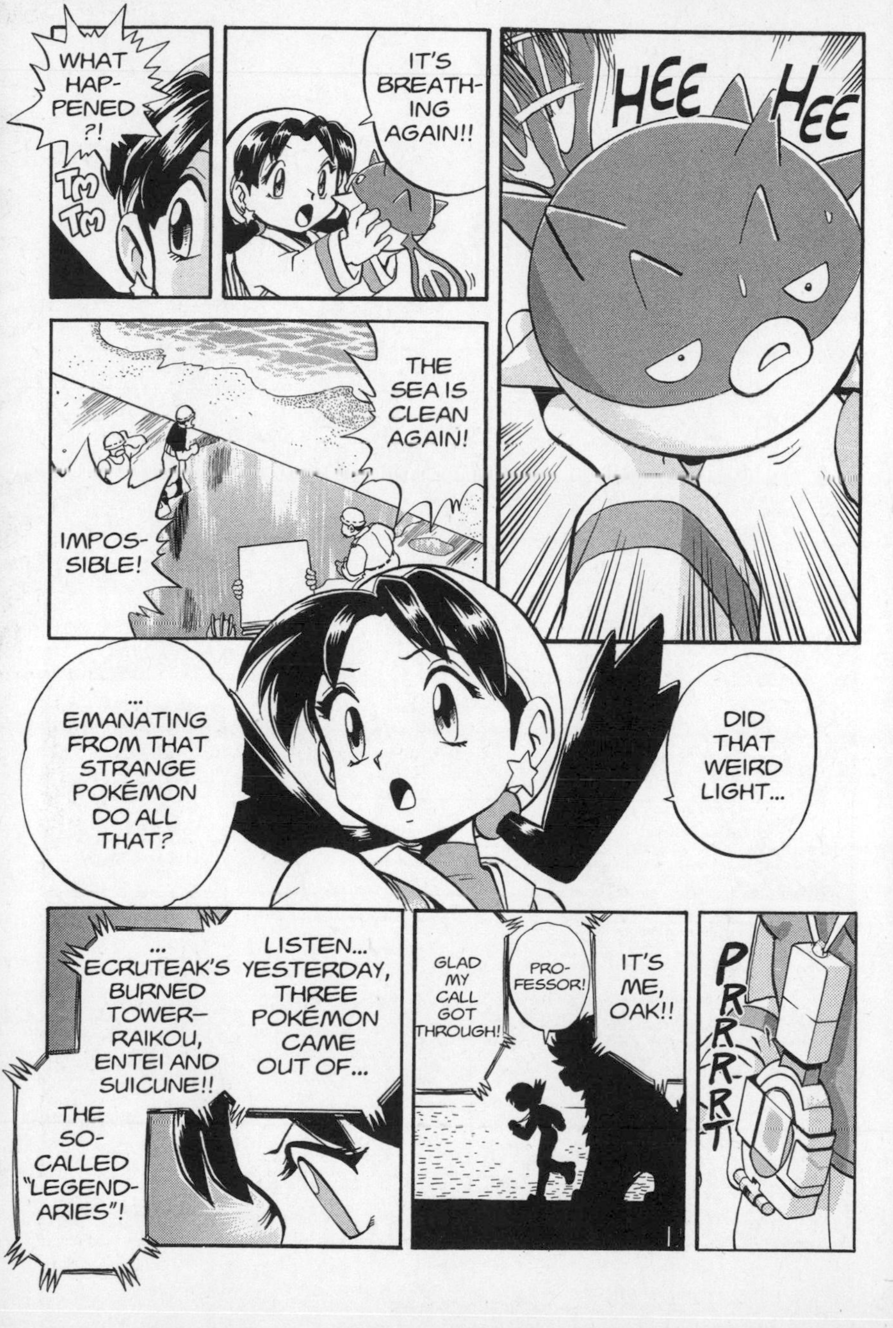
HEE HEE
IT'S BREATHING AGAIN!!
WHAT HAPPENED?!
TM TM
THE SEA IS CLEAN AGAIN!
IMPOSSIBLE!
DID THAT WEIRD LIGHT...
...EMANATING FROM THAT STRANGE POKÉMON DO ALL THAT?
PRRRRT
IT'S ME, OAK!!
PROFESSOR!
GLAD MY CALL GOT THROUGH!
LISTEN... YESTERDAY, THREE POKÉMON CAME OUT OF...
...ECRUTEAK'S BURNED TOWER—RAIKOU, ENTEI AND SUICUNE!!
THE SO-CALLED "LEGENDARIES"!

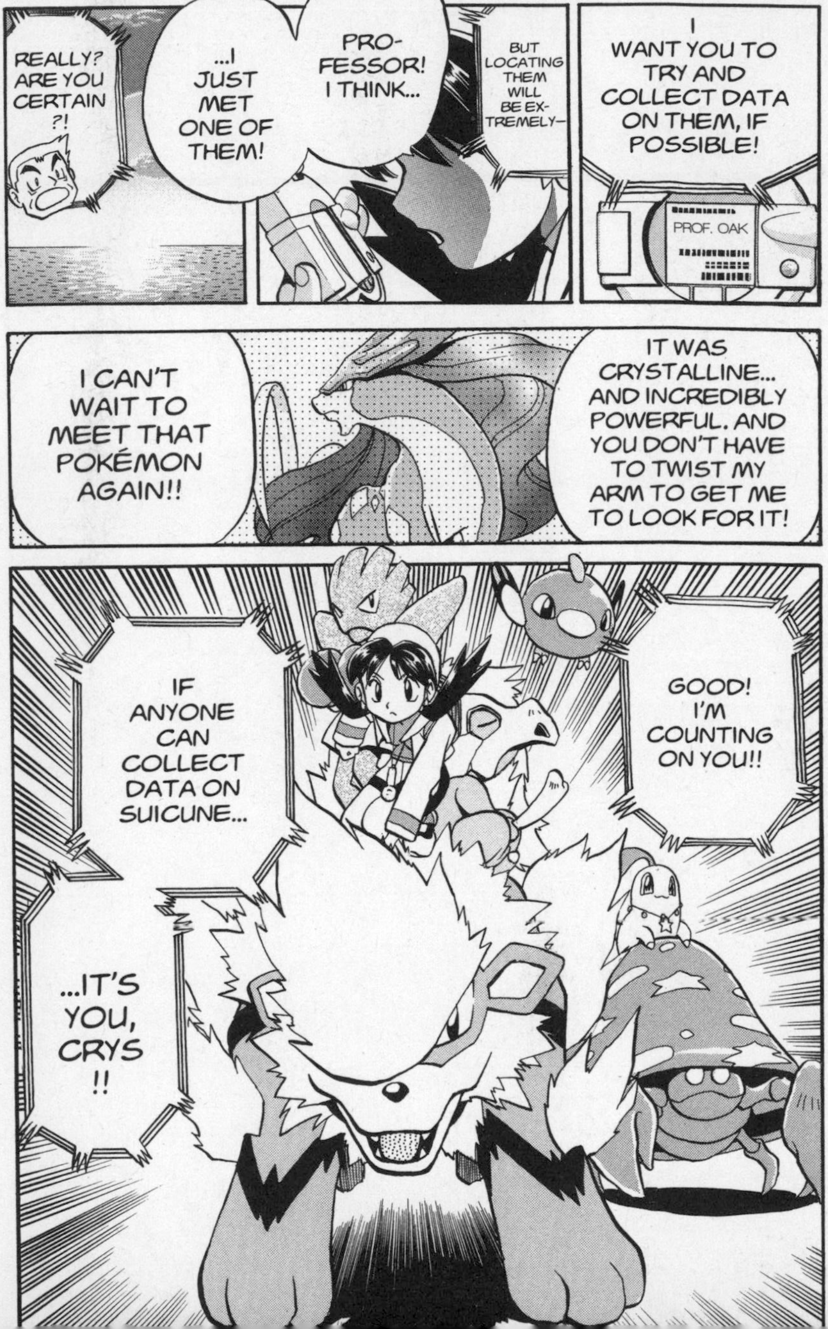
I WANT YOU TO TRY AND COLLECT DATA ON THEM, IF POSSIBLE!
PROF. OAK
BUT LOCATING THEM WILL BE EX-TREMELY—
PRO-FESSOR! I THINK...
...I JUST MET ONE OF THEM!
REALLY? ARE YOU CERTAIN ?!
IT WAS CRYSTALLINE... AND INCREDIBLY POWERFUL. AND YOU DON'T HAVE TO TWIST MY ARM TO GET ME TO LOOK FOR IT!
I CAN'T WAIT TO MEET THAT POKÉMON AGAIN!!
GOOD! I'M COUNTING ON YOU!!
IF ANYONE CAN COLLECT DATA ON SUICUNE...
...IT'S YOU, CRYS !!

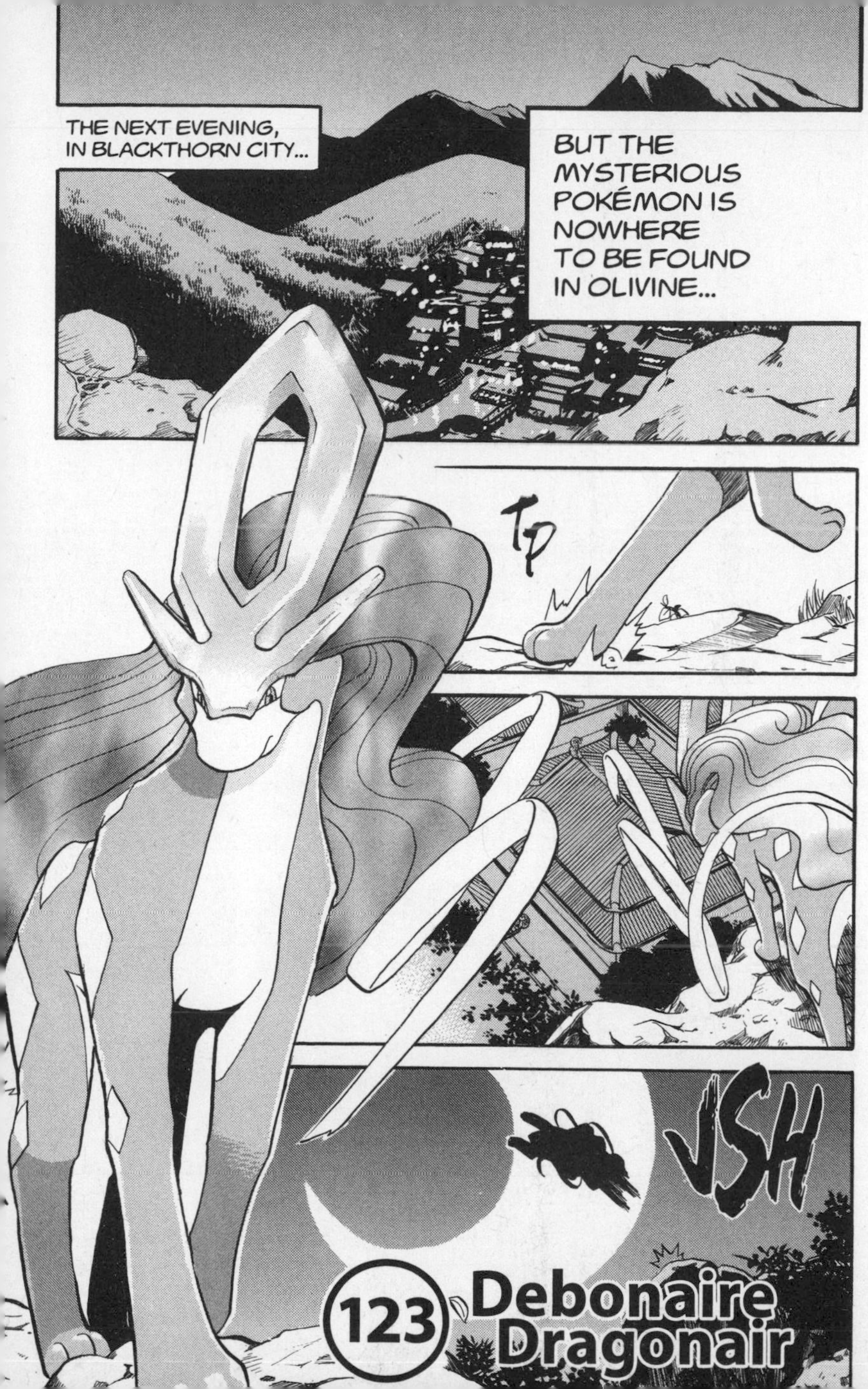
BUT THE MYSTERIOUS POKÉMON IS NOWHERE TO BE FOUND IN OLIVINE...
THE NEXT EVENING, IN BLACKTHORN CITY...
TP
VSH
123
Debonaire Dragonair

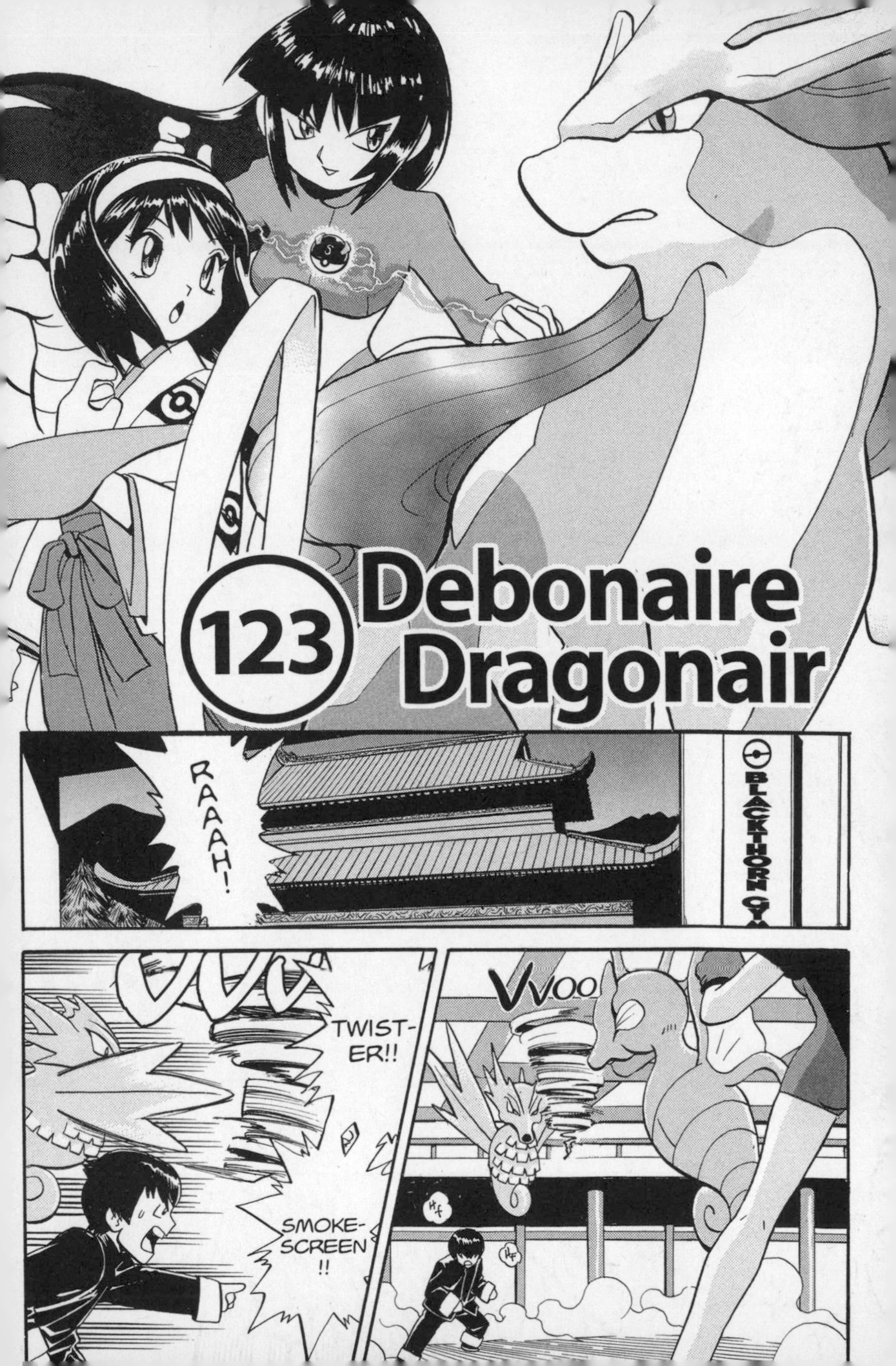
123
Debonaire Dragonair
RAAAH!
BLACKTHORN GYM
VVOO
TWIST-ER!!
SMOKE-SCREEN!!

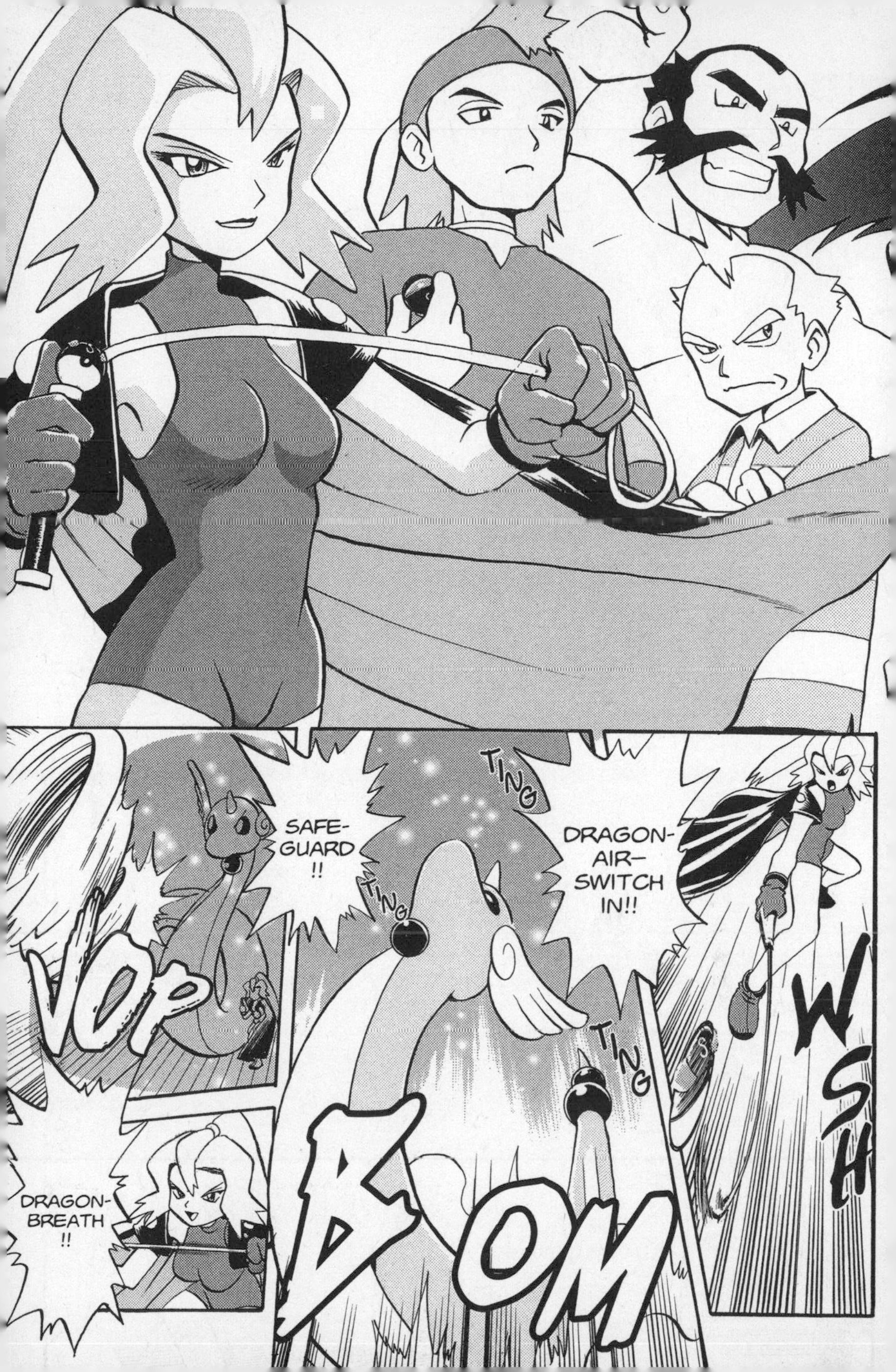
DRAGON-AIR-SWITCH IN!!
WSH
TING
SAFE-GUARD !!
TING
TING
BOOM
VOP
DRAGON-BREATH !!

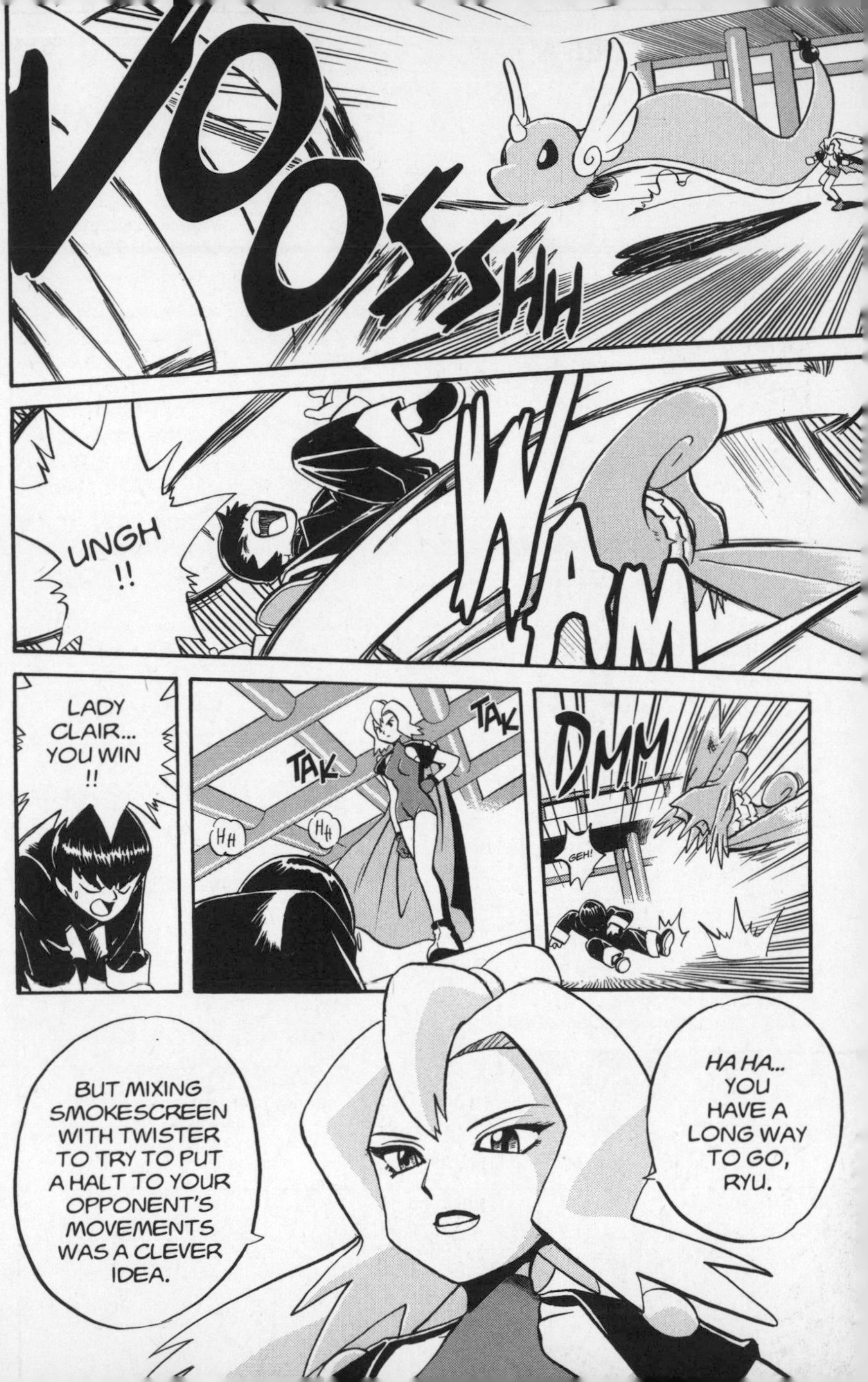
VOOSSHH
WAM
UNGH !!
DMM
GEH!
TAK
TAK
HH
HH
LADY CLAIR... YOU WIN !!
HA HA... YOU HAVE A LONG WAY TO GO, RYU.
BUT MIXING SMOKESCREEN WITH TWISTER TO TRY TO PUT A HALT TO YOUR OPPONENT'S MOVEMENTS WAS A CLEVER IDEA.

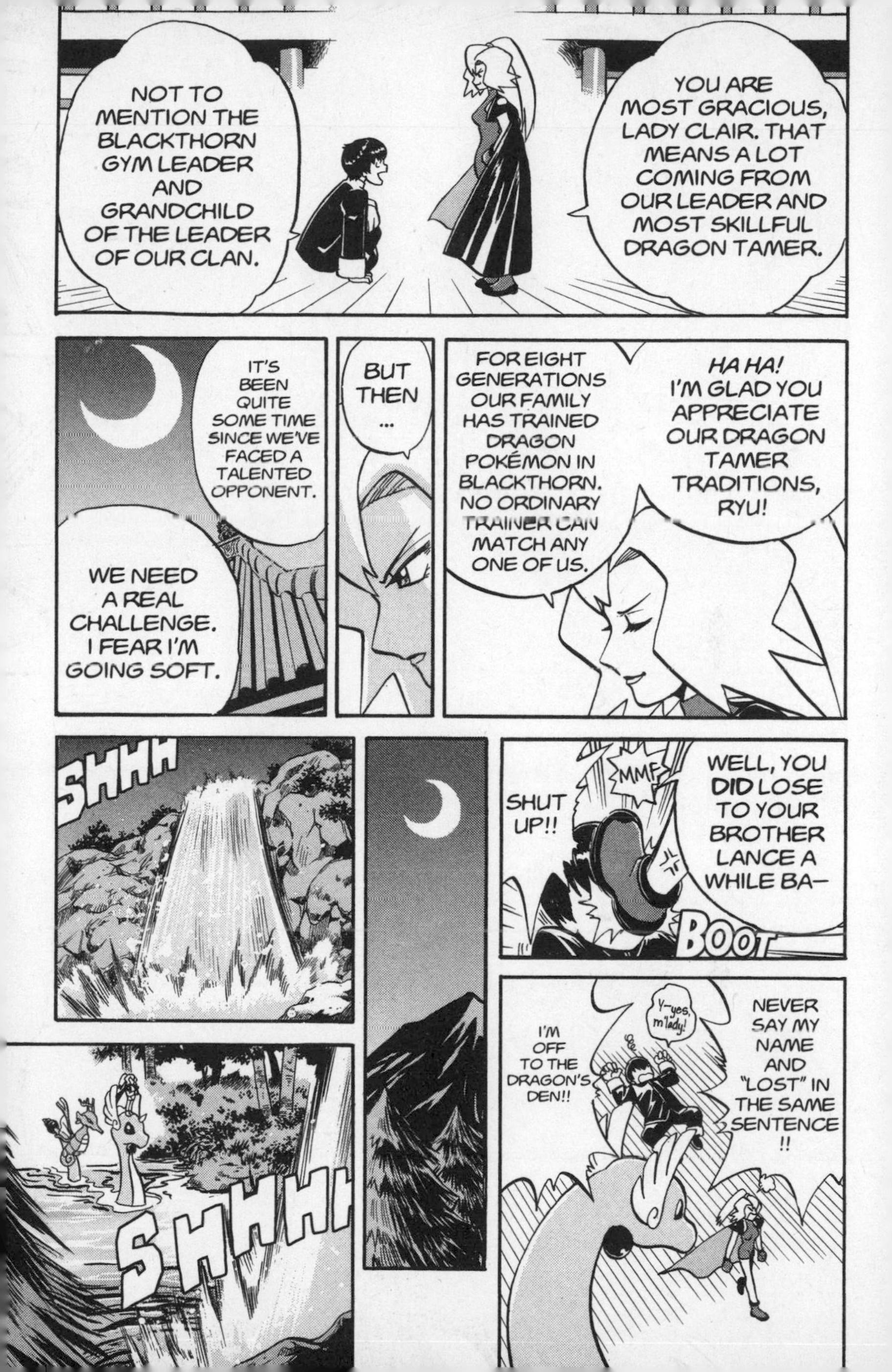
YOU ARE MOST GRACIOUS, LADY CLAIR. THAT MEANS A LOT COMING FROM OUR LEADER AND MOST SKILLFUL DRAGON TAMER.
NOT TO MENTION THE BLACKTHORN GYM LEADER AND GRANDCHILD OF THE LEADER OF OUR CLAN.
HA HA! I'M GLAD YOU APPRECIATE OUR DRAGON TAMER TRADITIONS, RYU!
FOR EIGHT GENERATIONS OUR FAMILY HAS TRAINED DRAGON POKÉMON IN BLACKTHORN. NO ORDINARY TRAINER CAN MATCH ANY ONE OF US.
BUT THEN ...
IT'S BEEN QUITE SOME TIME SINCE WE'VE FACED A TALENTED OPPONENT.
WE NEED A REAL CHALLENGE. I FEAR I'M GOING SOFT.
WELL, YOU DID LOSE TO YOUR BROTHER LANCE A WHILE BA—
MMF
BOOT
SHUT UP!!
NEVER SAY MY NAME AND "LOST" IN THE SAME SENTENCE !!
Y—yes, m'lady!
I'M OFF TO THE DRAGON'S DEN!!
SHHH
SHHHH

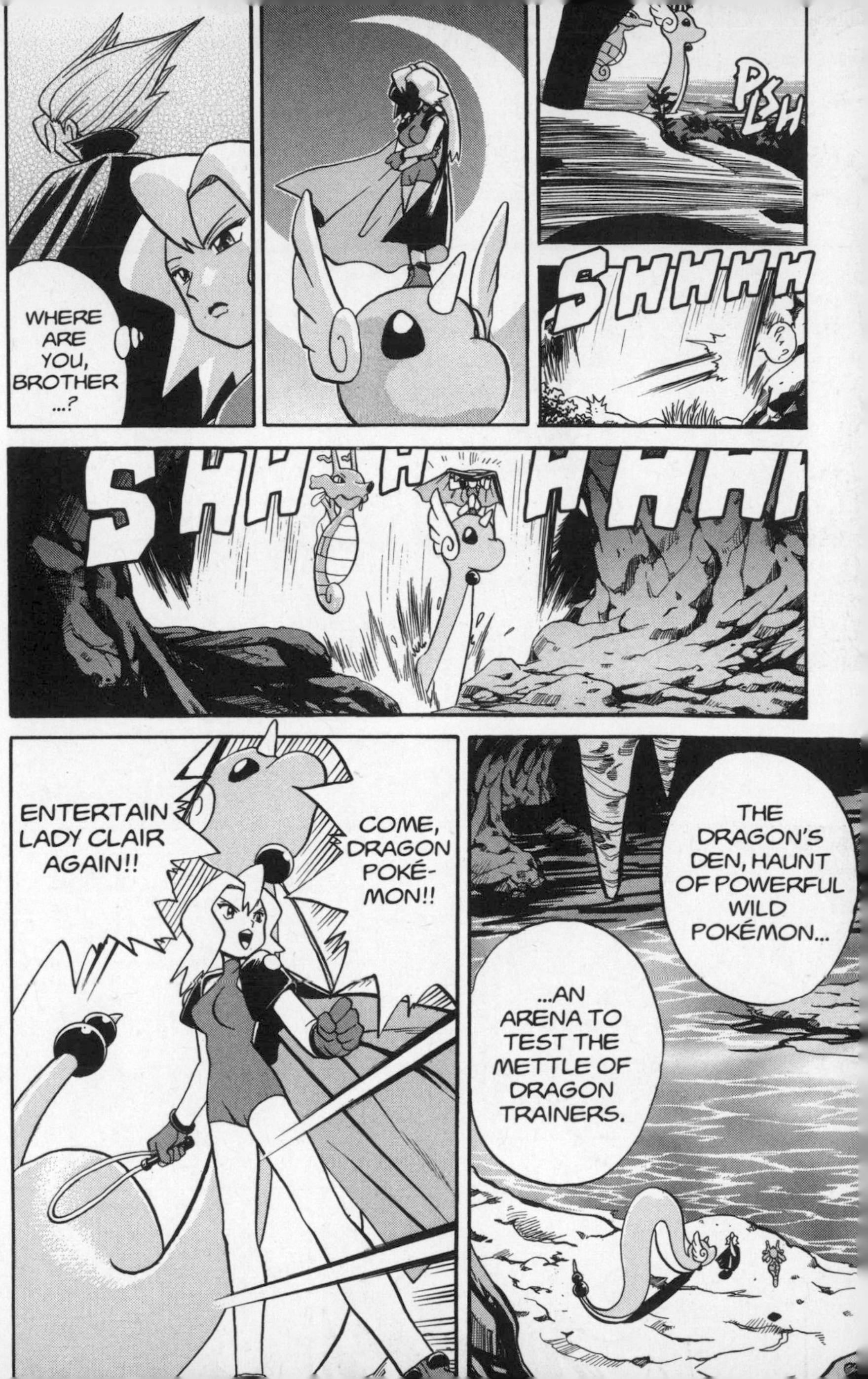
PLSH
SHHHHH
WHERE ARE YOU, BROTHER ...?
SHHHHHHHHHH
THE DRAGON'S DEN, HAUNT OF POWERFUL WILD POKÉMON...
...AN ARENA TO TEST THE METTLE OF DRAGON TRAINERS.
COME, DRAGON POKÉ-MON!!
ENTERTAIN LADY CLAIR AGAIN!!

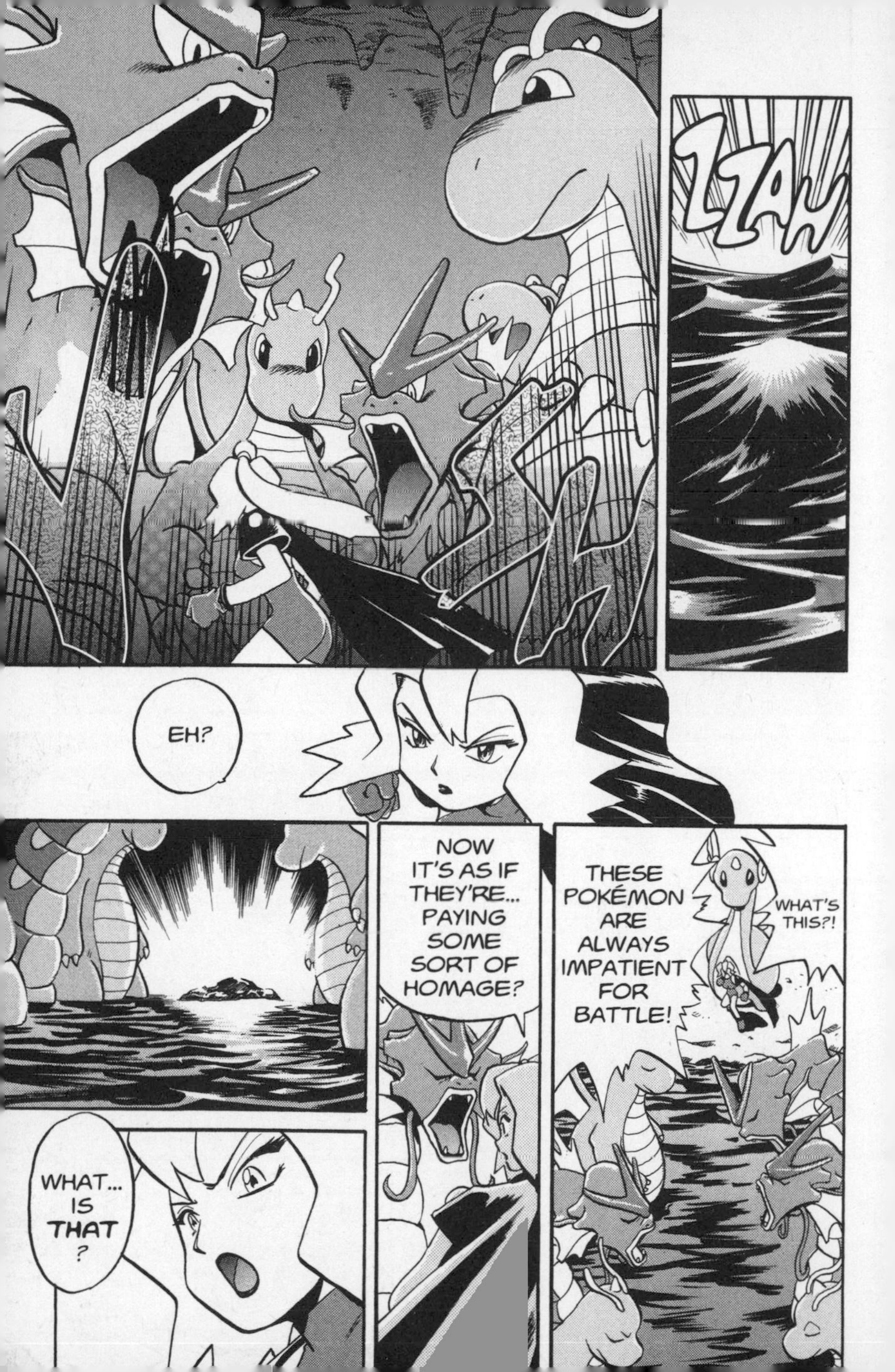
ZZAH
EH?
WHAT'S THIS?!
THESE POKÉMON ARE ALWAYS IMPATIENT FOR BATTLE!
NOW IT'S AS IF THEY'RE... PAYING SOME SORT OF HOMAGE?
WHAT... IS THAT?

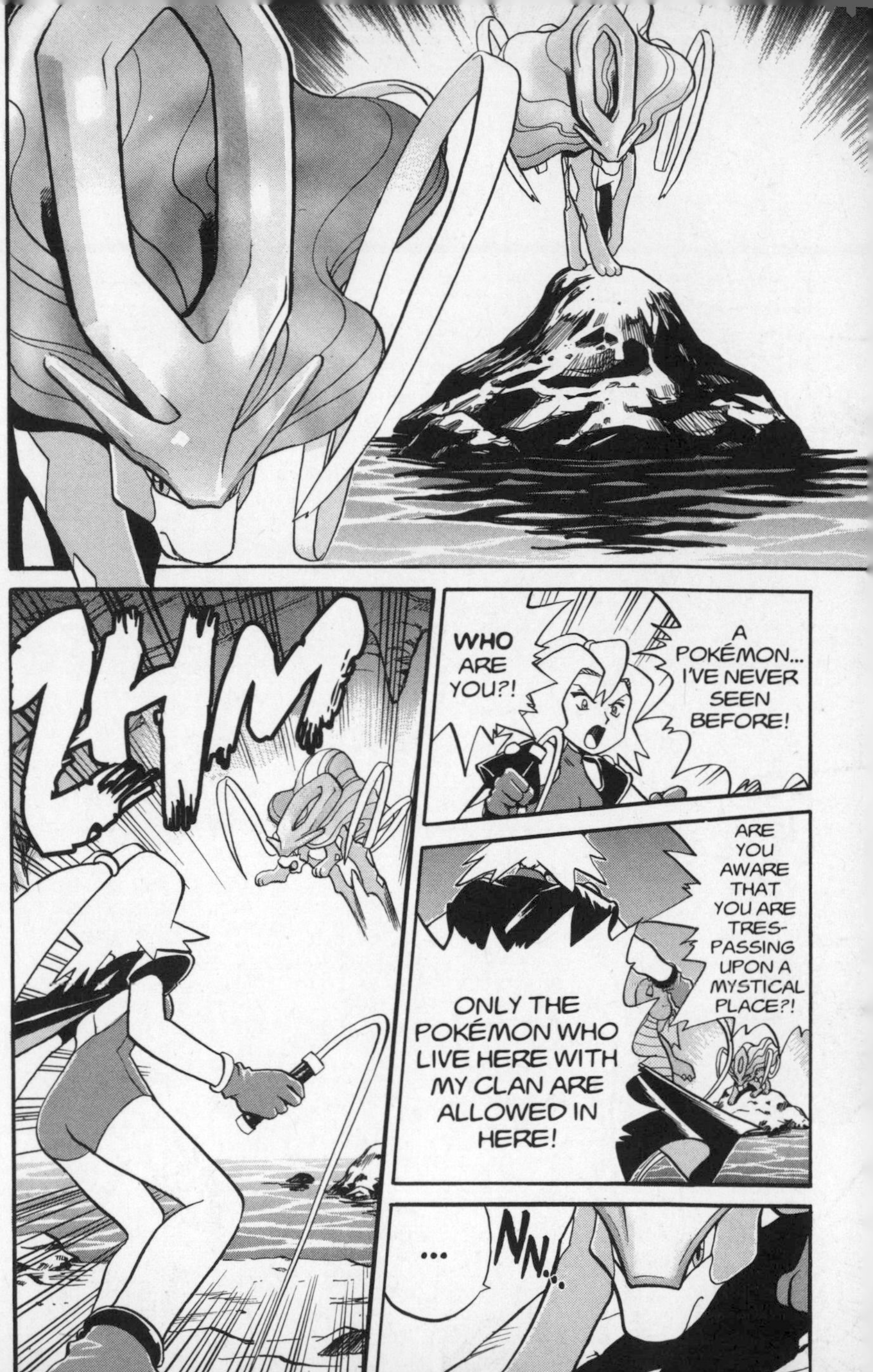
A POKÉMON... I'VE NEVER SEEN BEFORE!
WHO ARE YOU?!
ARE YOU AWARE THAT YOU ARE TRES-PASSING UPON A MYSTICAL PLACE?!
ONLY THE POKÉMON WHO LIVE HERE WITH MY CLAN ARE ALLOWED IN HERE!
NN..!
...
ZHM

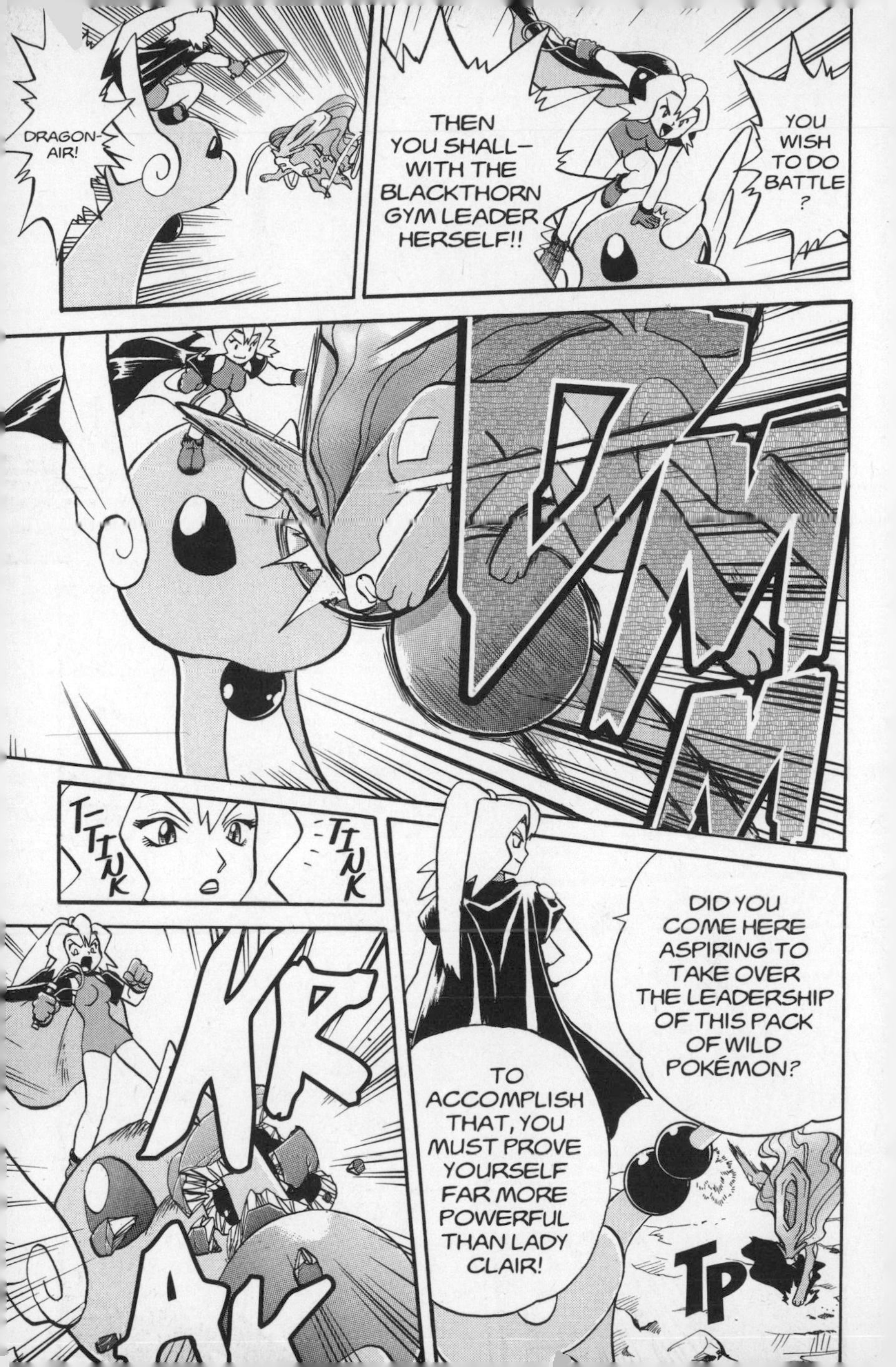
YOU WISH TO DO BATTLE?
THEN YOU SHALL—WITH THE BLACKTHORN GYM LEADER HERSELF!!
DRAGON-AIR!
DID YOU COME HERE ASPIRING TO TAKE OVER THE LEADERSHIP OF THIS PACK OF WILD POKÉMON?
TO ACCOMPLISH THAT, YOU MUST PROVE YOURSELF FAR MORE POWERFUL THAN LADY CLAIR!
TP
TINK
T-TINK

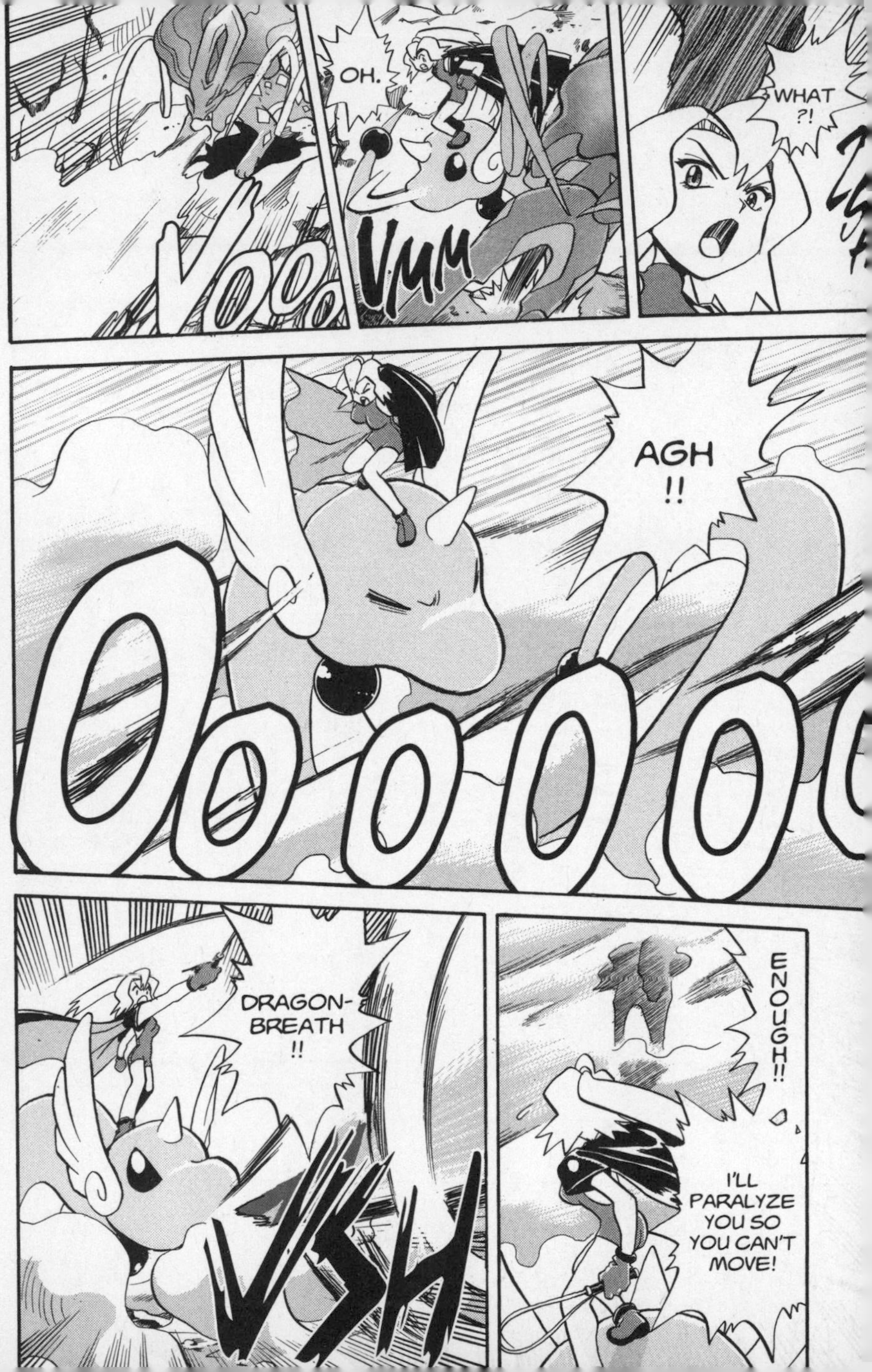
WHAT ?!
OH.
VUM
VOOO
AGH !!
OOOOOO
ENOUGH!!
I'LL PARALYZE YOU SO YOU CAN'T MOVE!
DRAGON-BREATH !!
VSSH

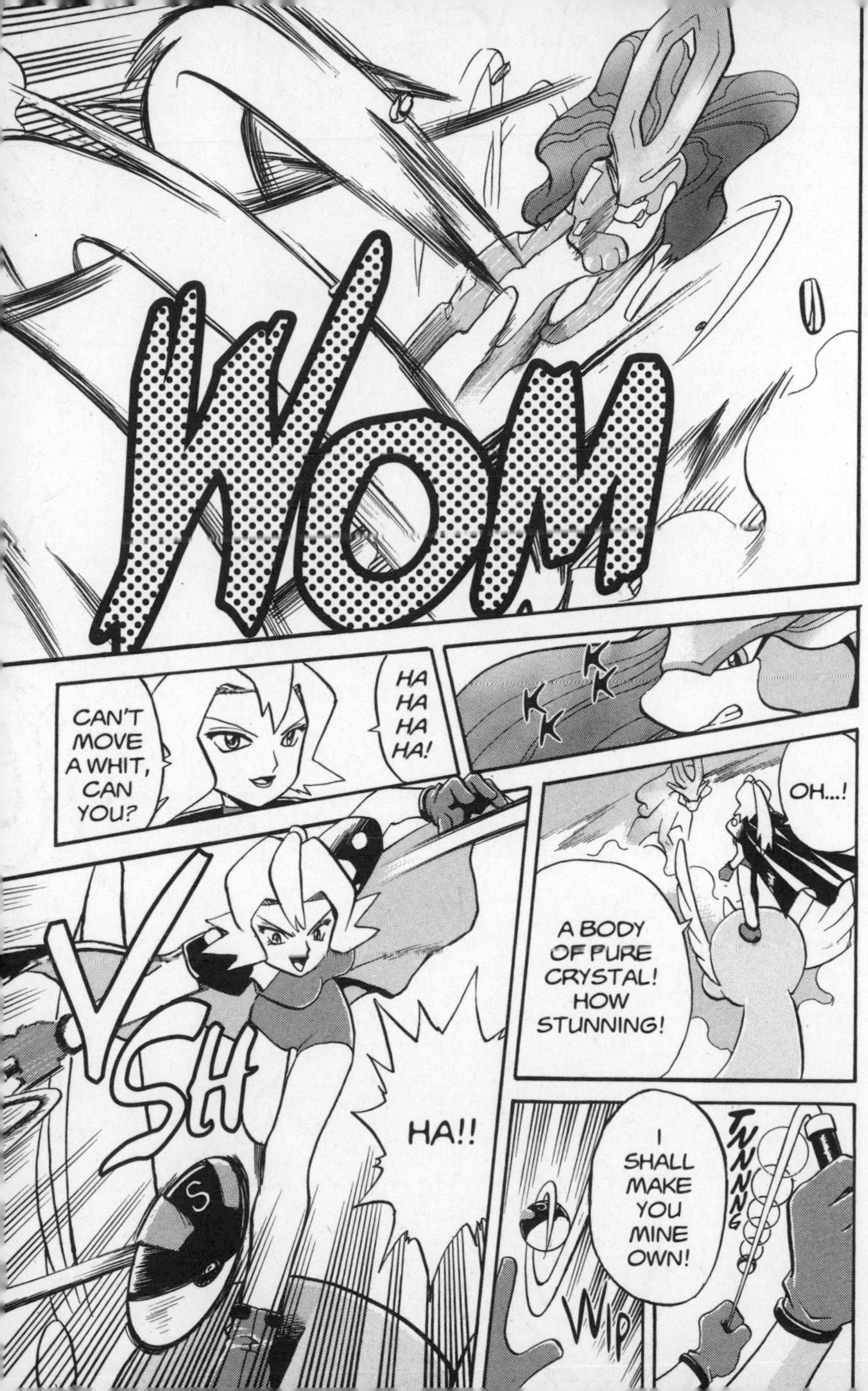
WOM
K K K K K
HA HA HA HA!
CAN'T MOVE A WHIT, CAN YOU?
OH...!
A BODY OF PURE CRYSTAL! HOW STUNNING!
I SHALL MAKE YOU MINE OWN!
TNNNNG
WIP
VSH
HA!!

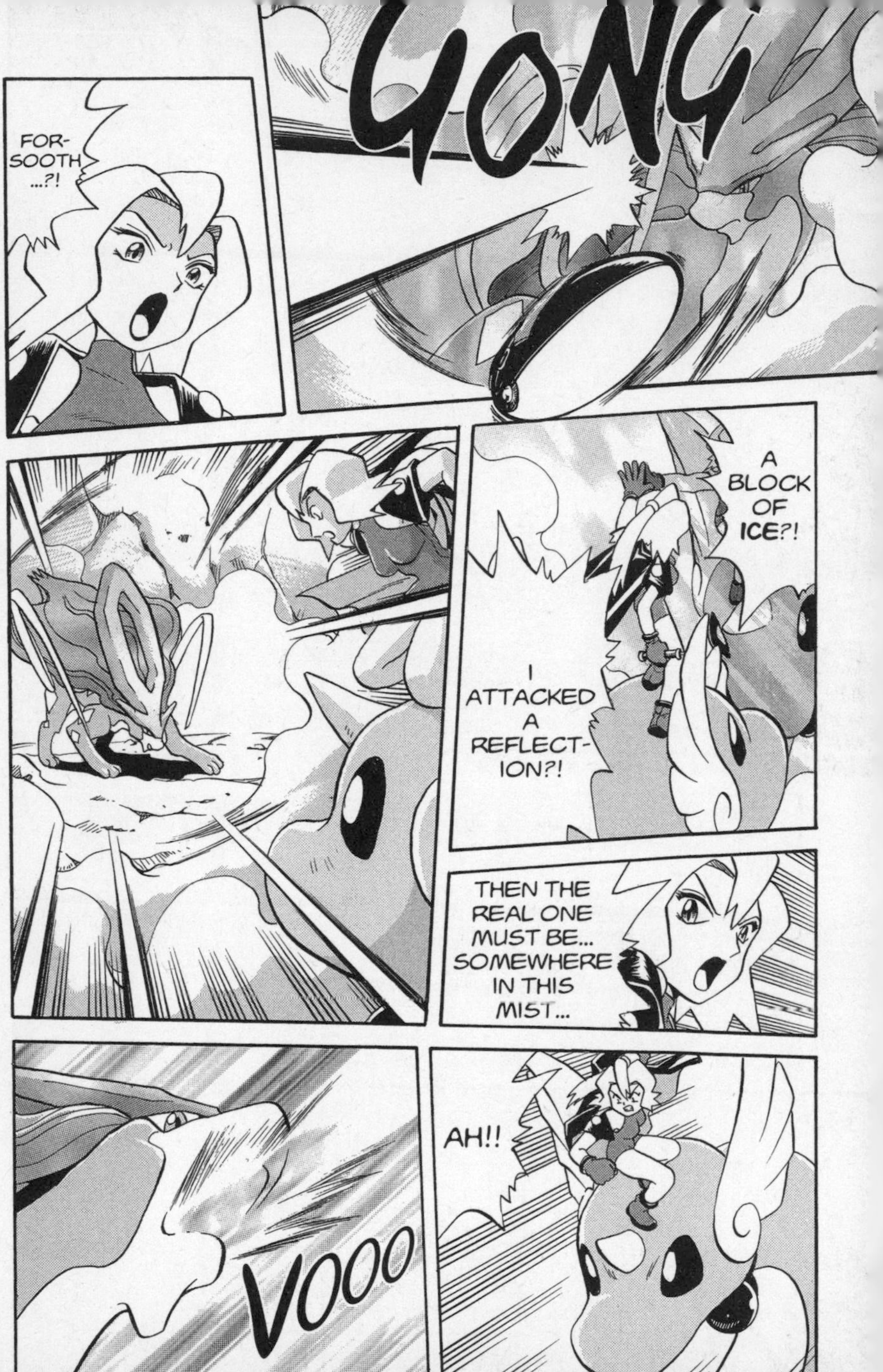
GONG
FOR-SOOTH ...?!
A BLOCK OF ICE?!
I ATTACKED A REFLECT-ION?!
THEN THE REAL ONE MUST BE... SOMEWHERE IN THIS MIST...
AH!!
VOOO

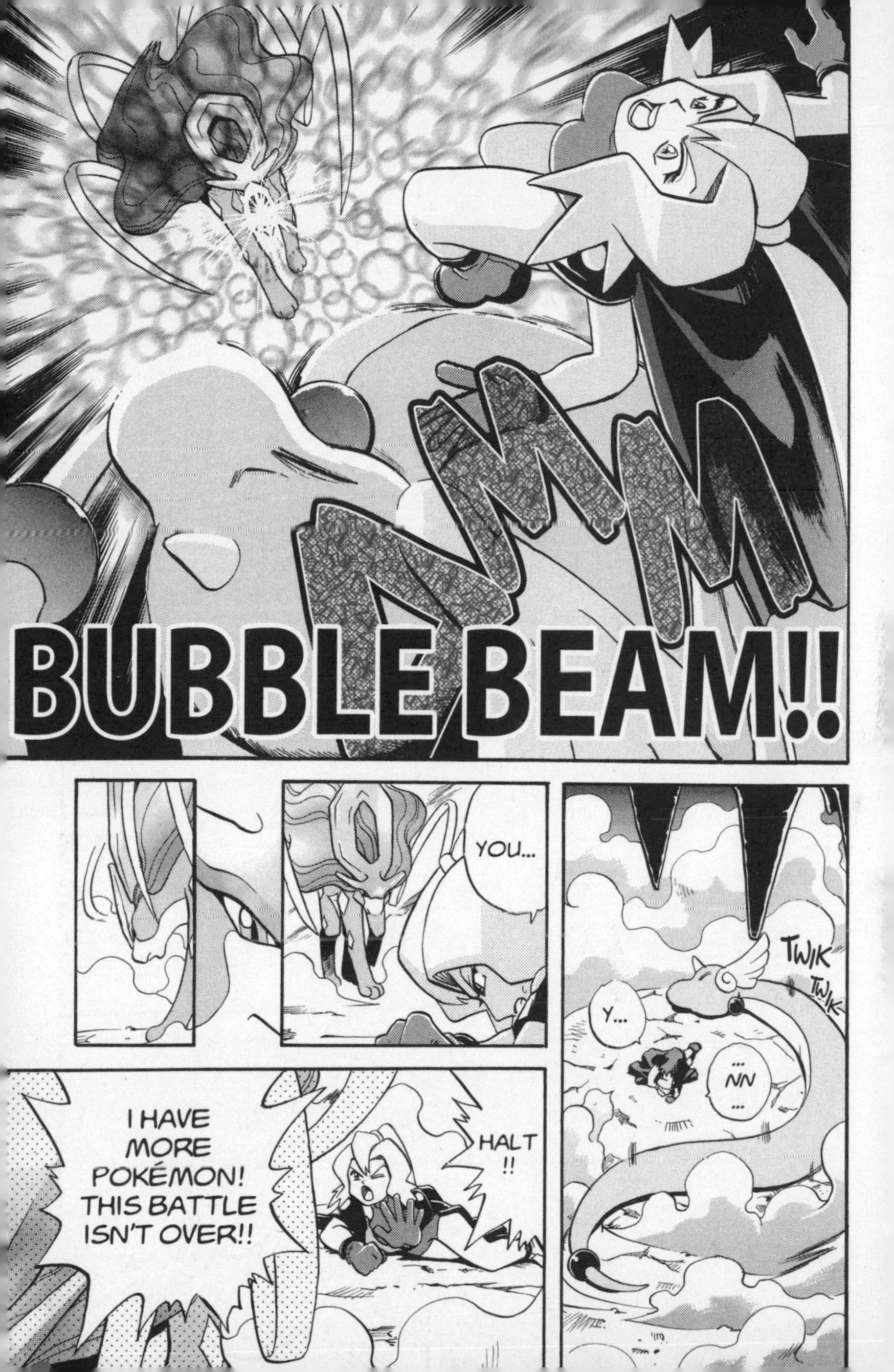
BUBBLE BEAM!!
TWIK TWIK
Y...
...NN...
YOU...
HALT!!
I HAVE MORE POKÉMON! THIS BATTLE ISN'T OVER!!

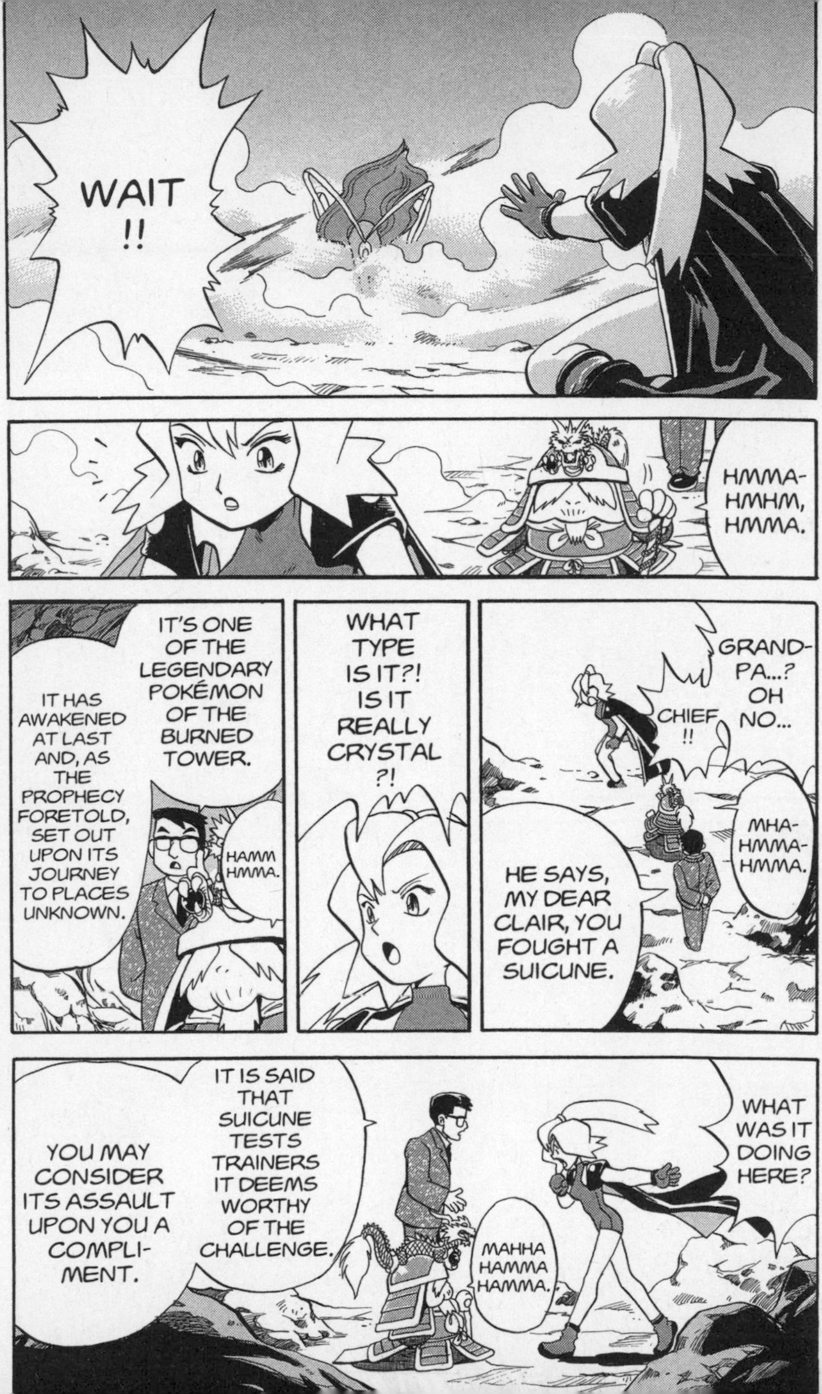
WAIT !!
HMMA-HMHM, HMMA.
GRAND-PA...? OH NO...
CHIEF !!
MHA-HMMA-HMMA.
HE SAYS, MY DEAR CLAIR, YOU FOUGHT A SUICUNE.
WHAT TYPE IS IT?! IS IT REALLY CRYSTAL ?!
HAMM HMMA.
IT'S ONE OF THE LEGENDARY POKÉMON OF THE BURNED TOWER.
IT HAS AWAKENED AT LAST AND, AS THE PROPHECY FORETOLD, SET OUT UPON ITS JOURNEY TO PLACES UNKNOWN.
WHAT WAS IT DOING HERE?
MAHHA HAMMA HAMMA.
IT IS SAID THAT SUICUNE TESTS TRAINERS IT DEEMS WORTHY OF THE CHALLENGE.
YOU MAY CONSIDER ITS ASSAULT UPON YOU A COMPLI-MENT.

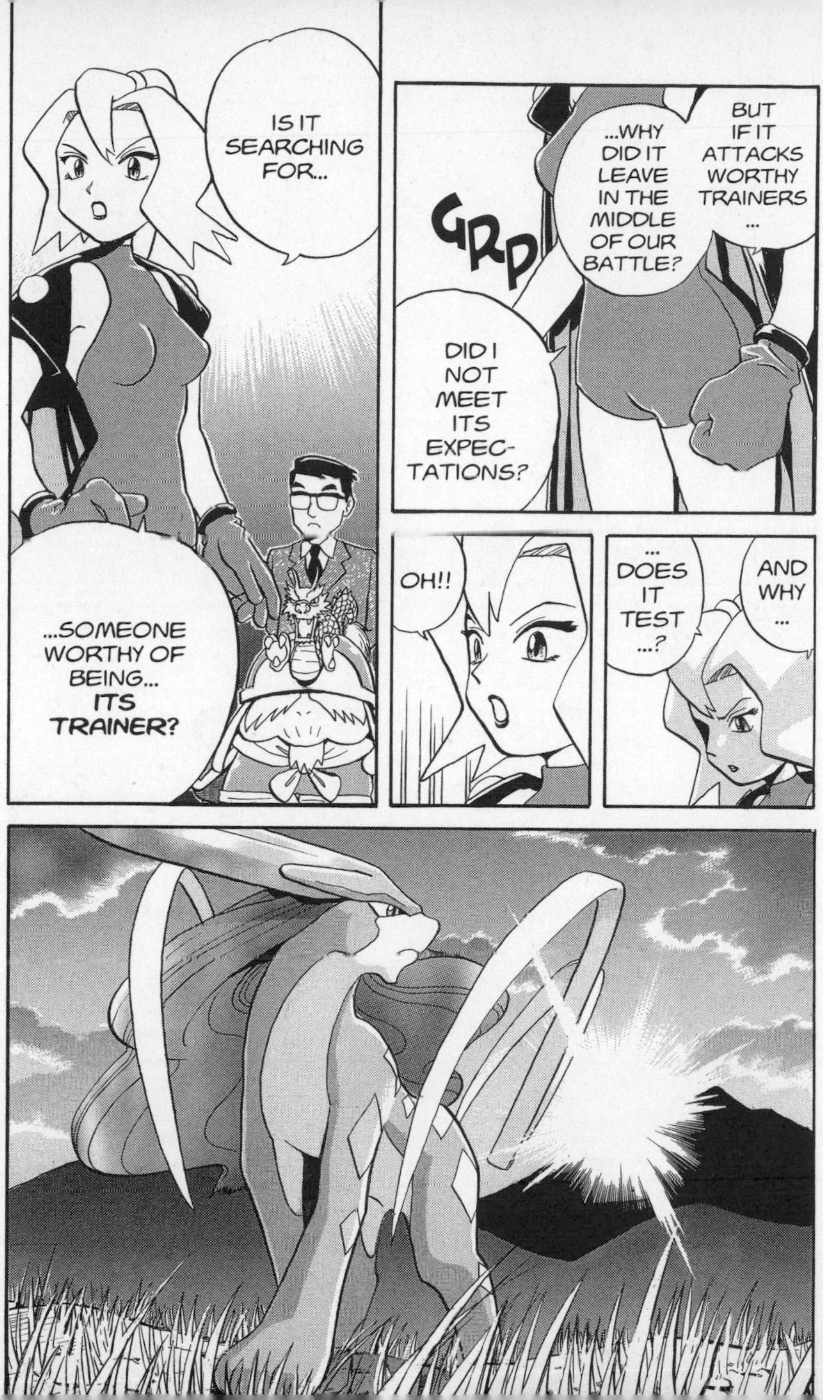
BUT IF IT ATTACKS WORTHY TRAINERS...
...WHY DID IT LEAVE IN THE MIDDLE OF OUR BATTLE?
GRP
DID I NOT MEET ITS EXPEC-TATIONS?
AND WHY...
...DOES IT TEST...?
OH!!
IS IT SEARCHING FOR...
...SOMEONE WORTHY OF BEING... ITS TRAINER?

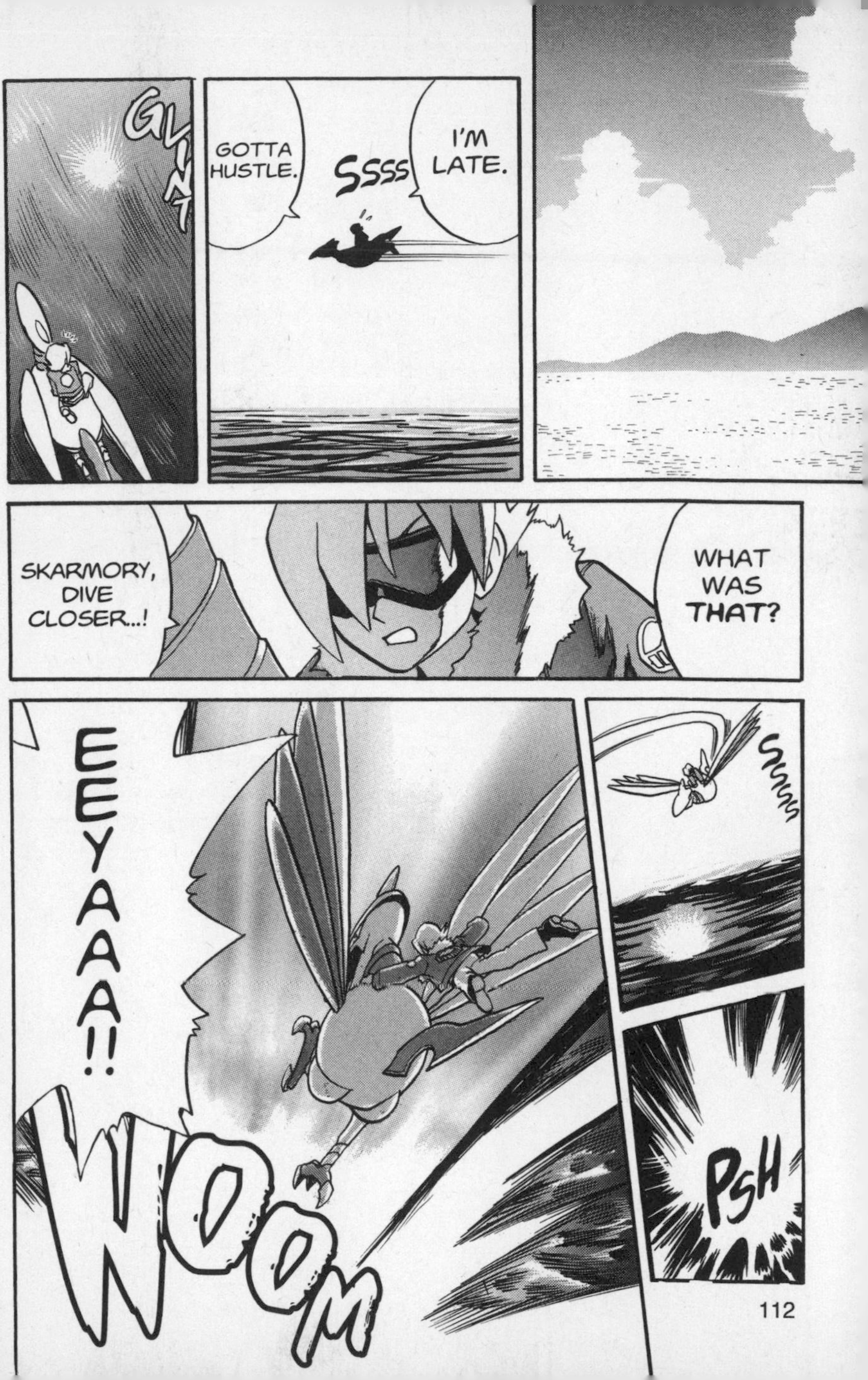
I'M LATE.
SSSS
GOTTA HUSTLE.
GLINT
WHAT WAS THAT?
SKARMORY, DIVE CLOSER...!
PSH
EEYAAAA!!
WOOM

124 Scrappy Skarmory

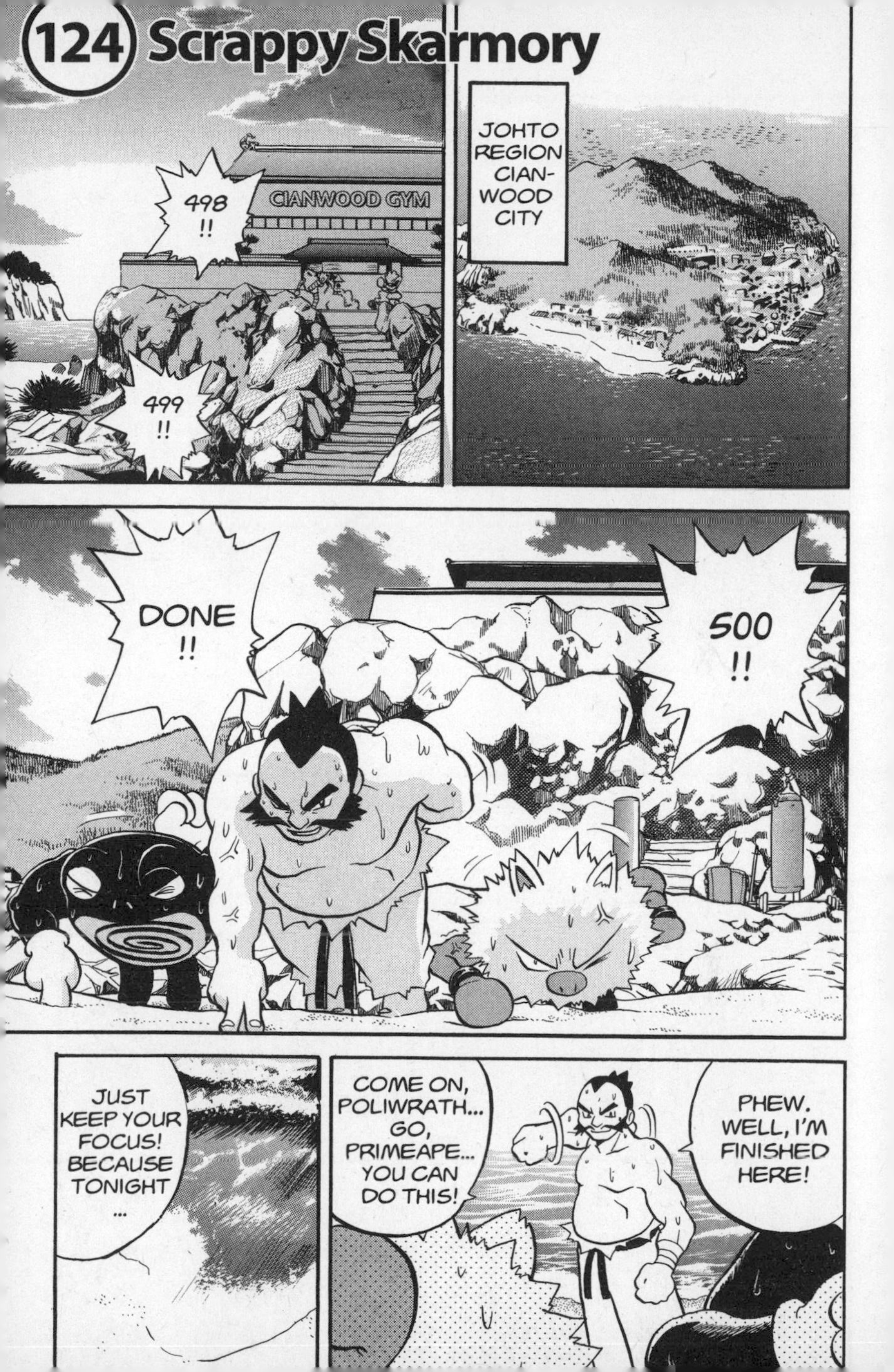
JOHTO REGION CIANWOOD CITY
CIANWOOD GYM
498 !!
499 !!
500 !!
DONE !!
PHEW. WELL, I'M FINISHED HERE!
COME ON, POLIWRATH... GO, PRIMEAPE... YOU CAN DO THIS!
JUST KEEP YOUR FOCUS! BECAUSE TONIGHT ...

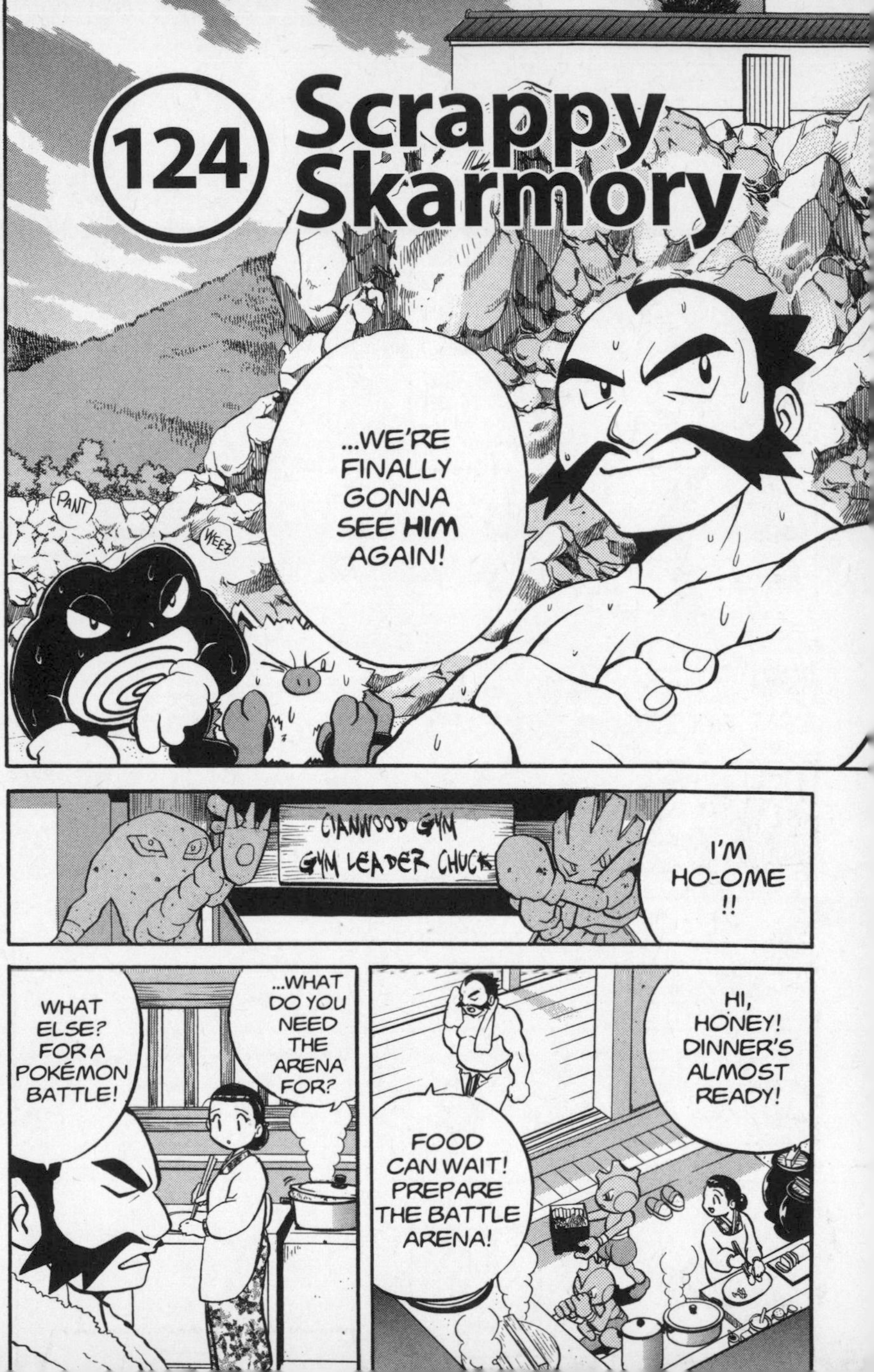
124 Scrappy Skarmory
...WE'RE FINALLY GONNA SEE HIM AGAIN!
PANT
WEEZ
CIANWOOD GYM
GYM LEADER CHUCK
I'M HO-OME !!
HI, HONEY! DINNER'S ALMOST READY!
FOOD CAN WAIT! PREPARE THE BATTLE ARENA!
...WHAT DO YOU NEED THE ARENA FOR?
WHAT ELSE? FOR A POKÉMON BATTLE!

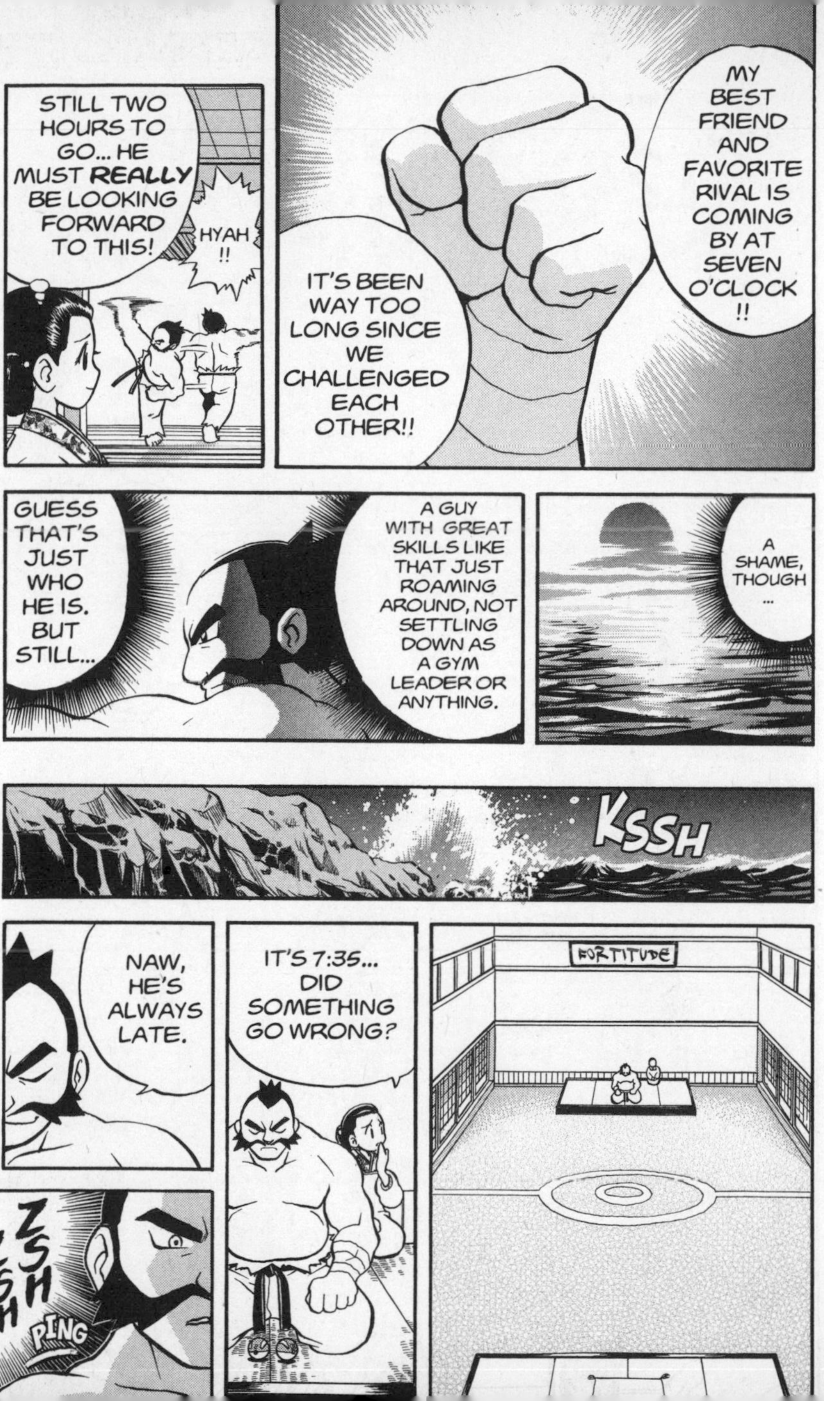

MY BEST FRIEND AND FAVORITE RIVAL IS COMING BY AT SEVEN O'CLOCK !!
IT'S BEEN WAY TOO LONG SINCE WE CHALLENGED EACH OTHER!!
HYAH !!
STILL TWO HOURS TO GO... HE MUST **REALLY** BE LOOKING FORWARD TO THIS!
A SHAME, THOUGH ...
A GUY WITH GREAT SKILLS LIKE THAT JUST ROAMING AROUND, NOT SETTLING DOWN AS A GYM LEADER OR ANYTHING.
GUESS THAT'S JUST WHO HE IS. BUT STILL...
KSSH
FORTITUDE
IT'S 7:35... DID SOMETHING GO WRONG?
NAW, HE'S ALWAYS LATE.
ZSH ZSH
PING

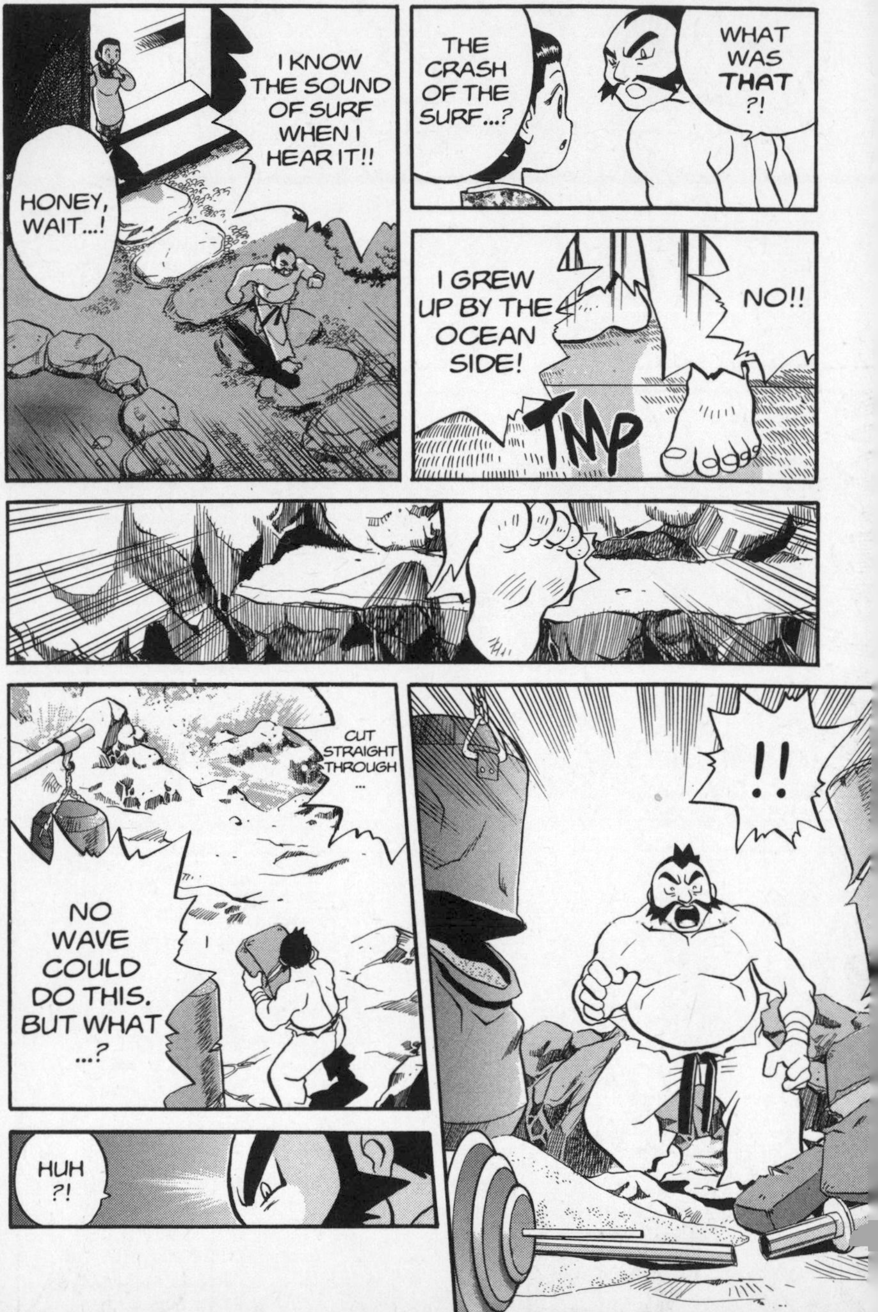
WHAT WAS THAT?!
THE CRASH OF THE SURF...?
NO!!
I GREW UP BY THE OCEAN SIDE!
TMP
I KNOW THE SOUND OF SURF WHEN I HEAR IT!!
HONEY, WAIT...!
!!
CUT STRAIGHT THROUGH...
NO WAVE COULD DO THIS. BUT WHAT...?
HUH?!

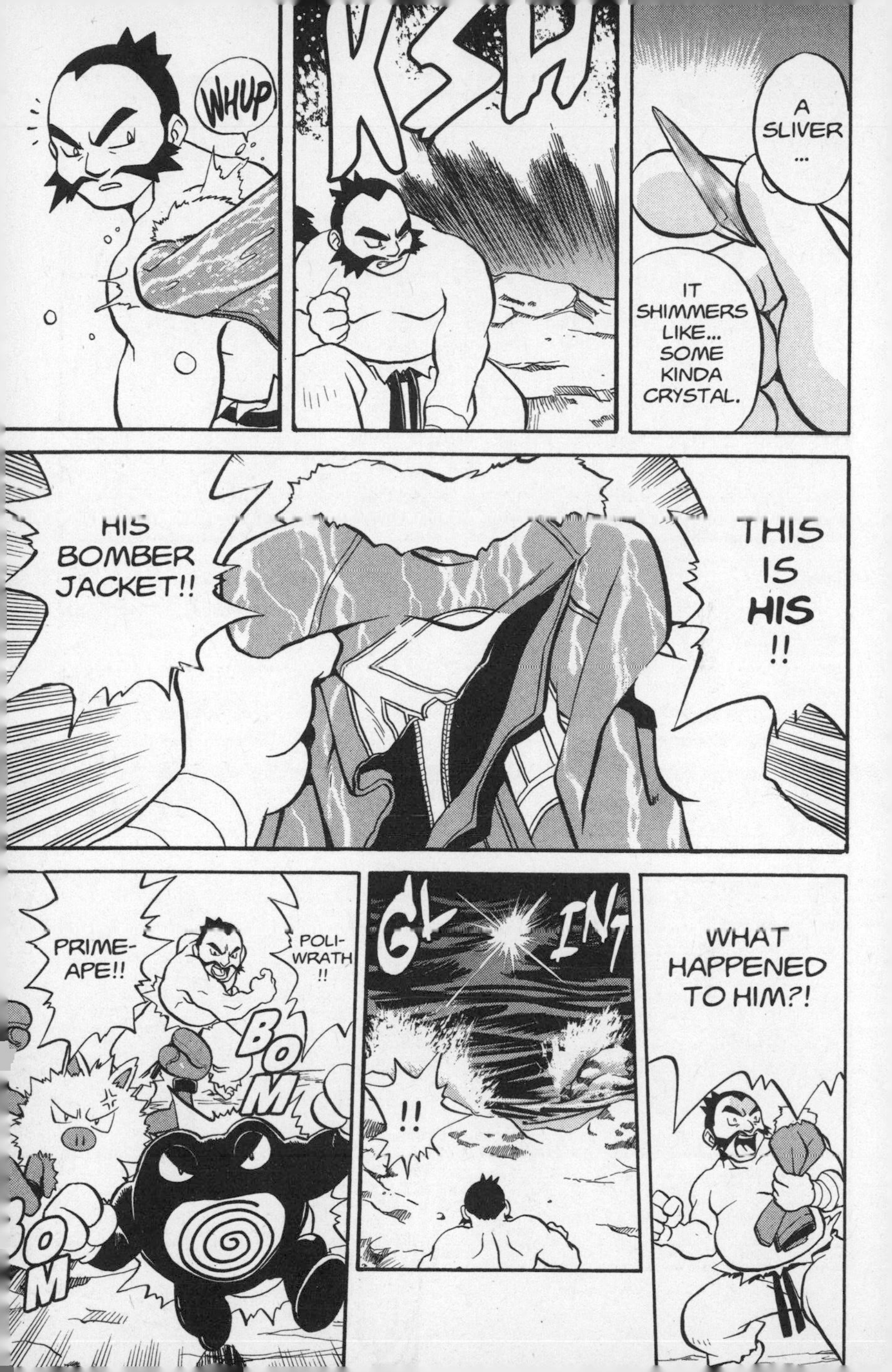
KSH
WHUP
A SLIVER ...
IT SHIMMERS LIKE... SOME KINDA CRYSTAL.
THIS IS HIS !!
HIS BOMBER JACKET!!
WHAT HAPPENED TO HIM?!
GL INT
!!
POLI-WRATH !!
PRIME-APE!!
BOM
BOM

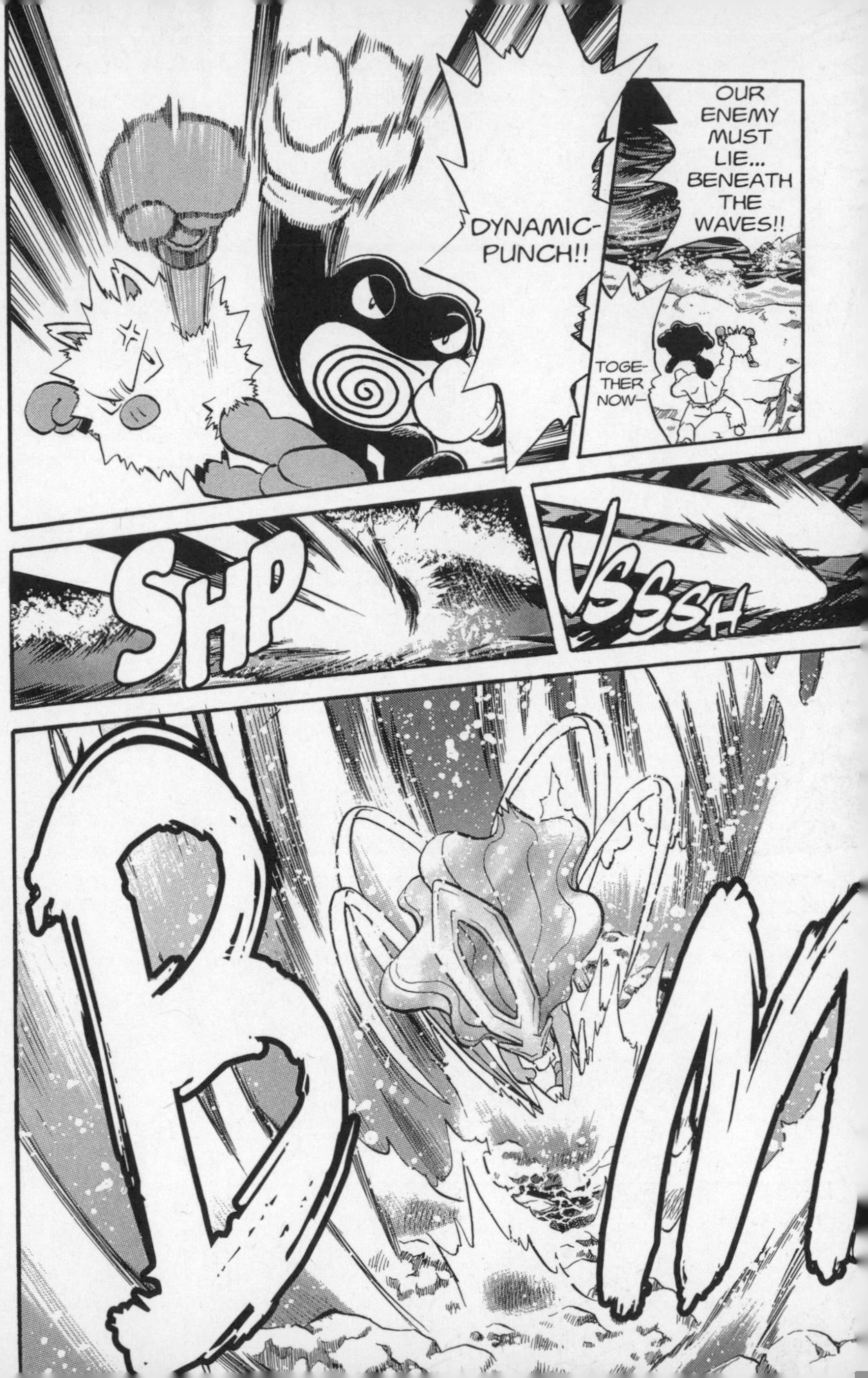
OUR ENEMY MUST LIE... BENEATH THE WAVES!!
TOGE-THER NOW-
DYNAMIC-PUNCH!!
VSSSH
SHP
BAM

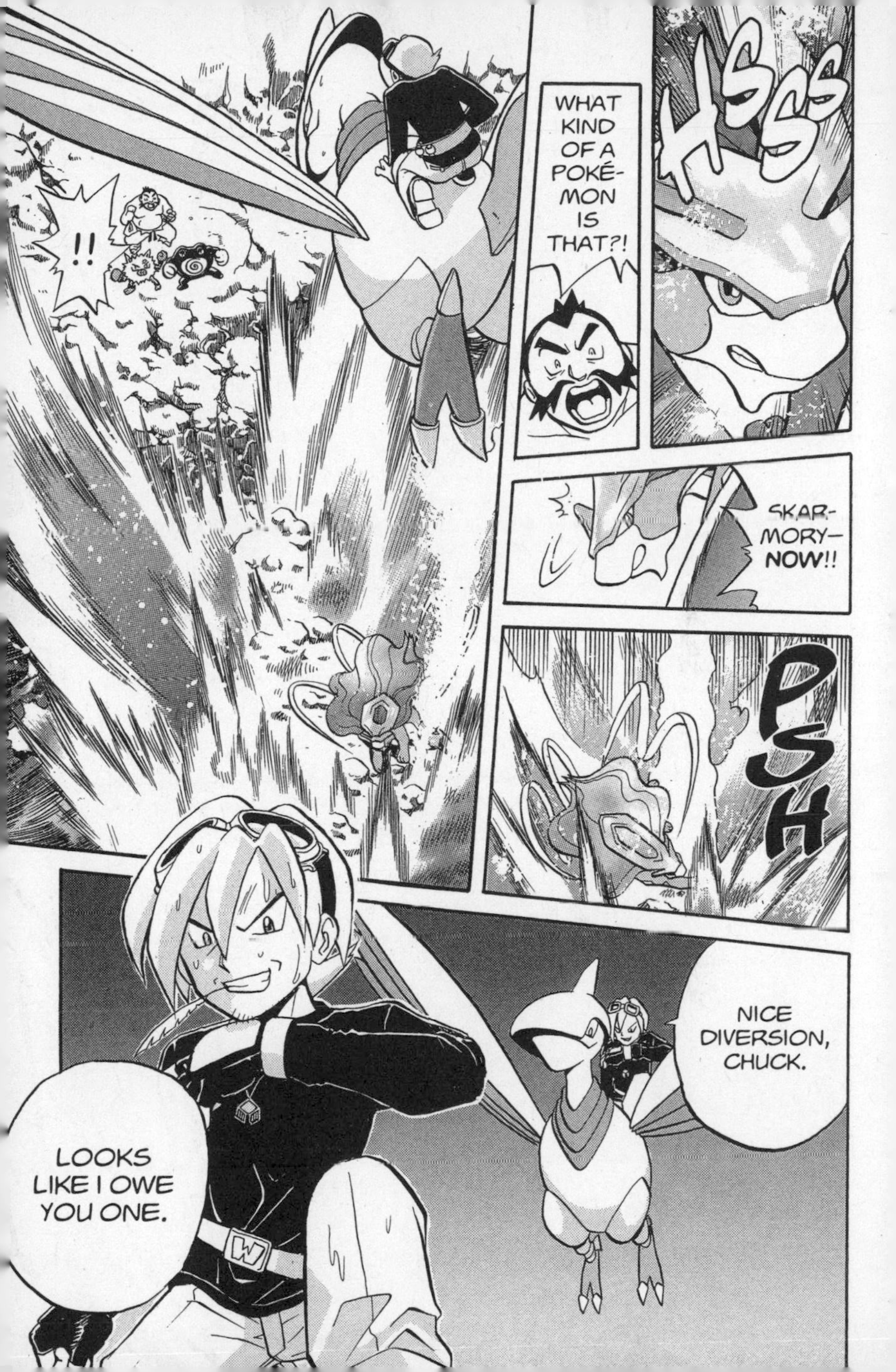
HSSS
WHAT KIND OF A POKÉMON IS THAT?!
!!
SKARMORY— NOW!!
PSH
NICE DIVERSION, CHUCK.
LOOKS LIKE I OWE YOU ONE.

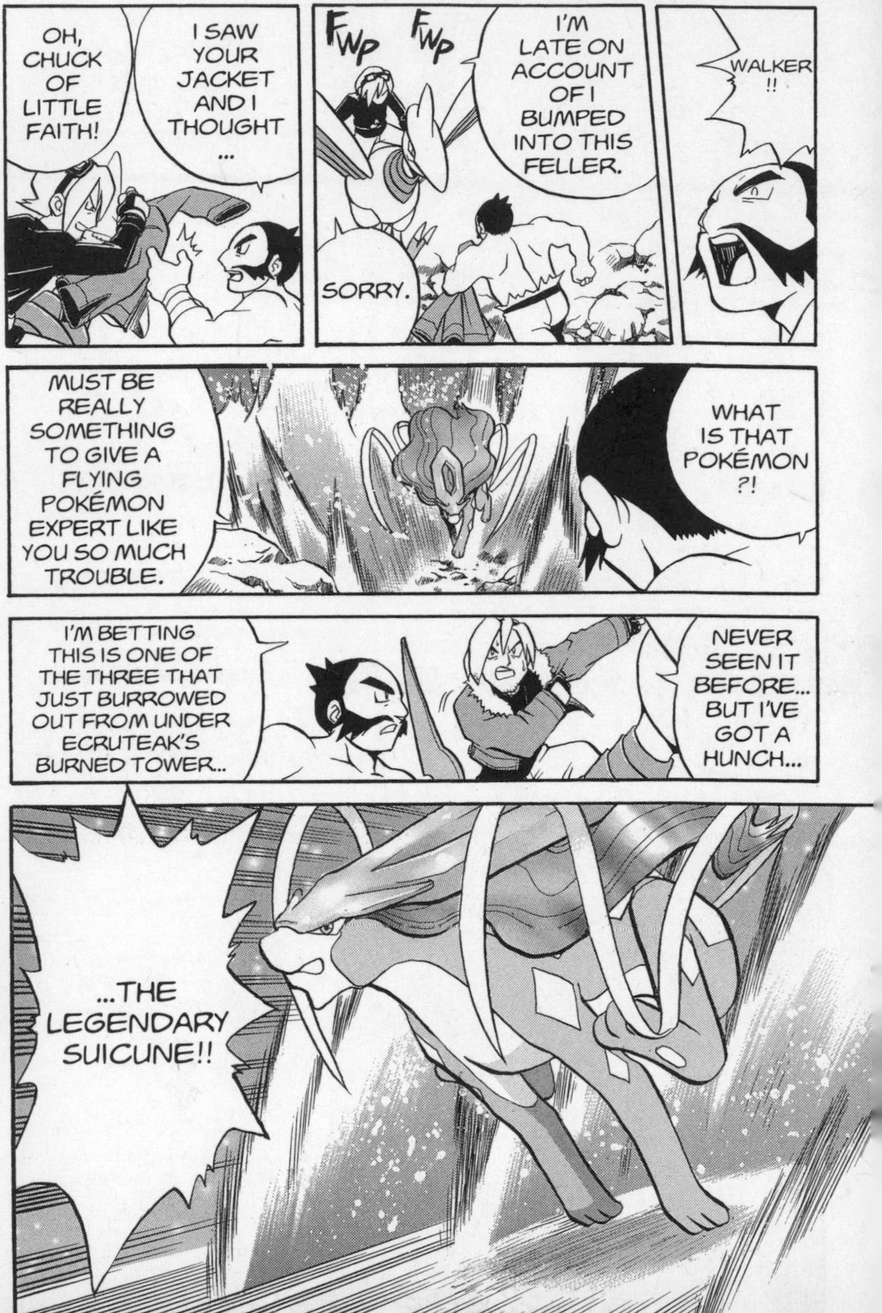
WALKER !!
I'M LATE ON ACCOUNT OF I BUMPED INTO THIS FELLER.
FWP
FWP
SORRY.
I SAW YOUR JACKET AND I THOUGHT ...
OH, CHUCK OF LITTLE FAITH!
WHAT IS THAT POKÉMON ?!
MUST BE REALLY SOMETHING TO GIVE A FLYING POKÉMON EXPERT LIKE YOU SO MUCH TROUBLE.
NEVER SEEN IT BEFORE... BUT I'VE GOT A HUNCH...
I'M BETTING THIS IS ONE OF THE THREE THAT JUST BURROWED OUT FROM UNDER ECRUTEAK'S BURNED TOWER...
...THE LEGENDARY SUICUNE!!

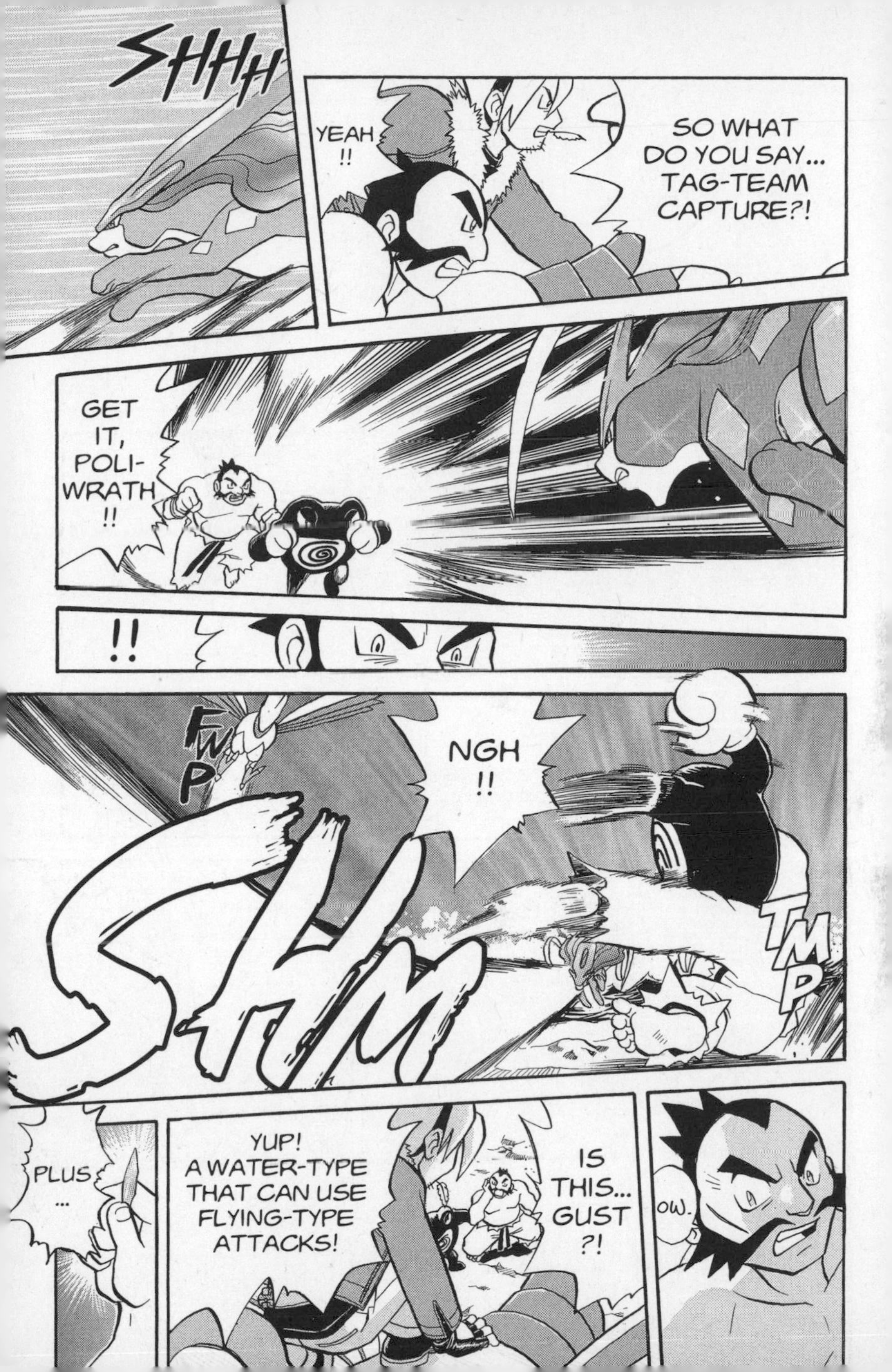
SO WHAT DO YOU SAY... TAG-TEAM CAPTURE?!
YEAH !!
SHHH
GET IT, POLI-WRATH !!
!!
NGH !!
FWP
TMP
SHM
OW.
IS THIS... GUST ?!
YUP! A WATER-TYPE THAT CAN USE FLYING-TYPE ATTACKS!
PLUS ...

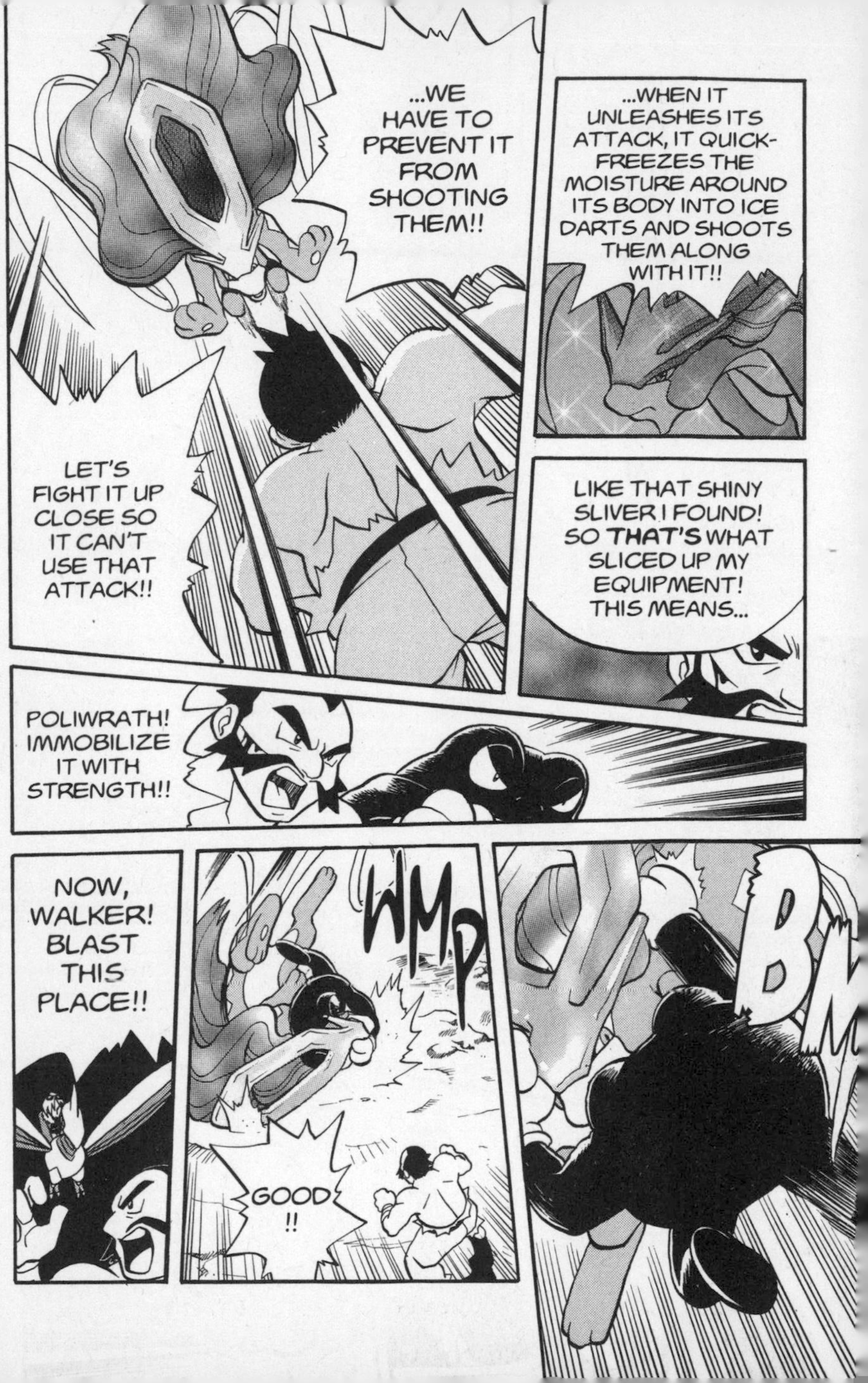
...WHEN IT UNLEASHES ITS ATTACK, IT QUICK-FREEZES THE MOISTURE AROUND ITS BODY INTO ICE DARTS AND SHOOTS THEM ALONG WITH IT!!
LIKE THAT SHINY SLIVER I FOUND! SO **THAT'S** WHAT SLICED UP MY EQUIPMENT! THIS MEANS...
...WE HAVE TO PREVENT IT FROM SHOOTING THEM!!
LET'S FIGHT IT UP CLOSE SO IT CAN'T USE THAT ATTACK!!
POLIWRATH! IMMOBILIZE IT WITH STRENGTH!!
BM
WMP
GOOD !!
NOW, WALKER! BLAST THIS PLACE!!

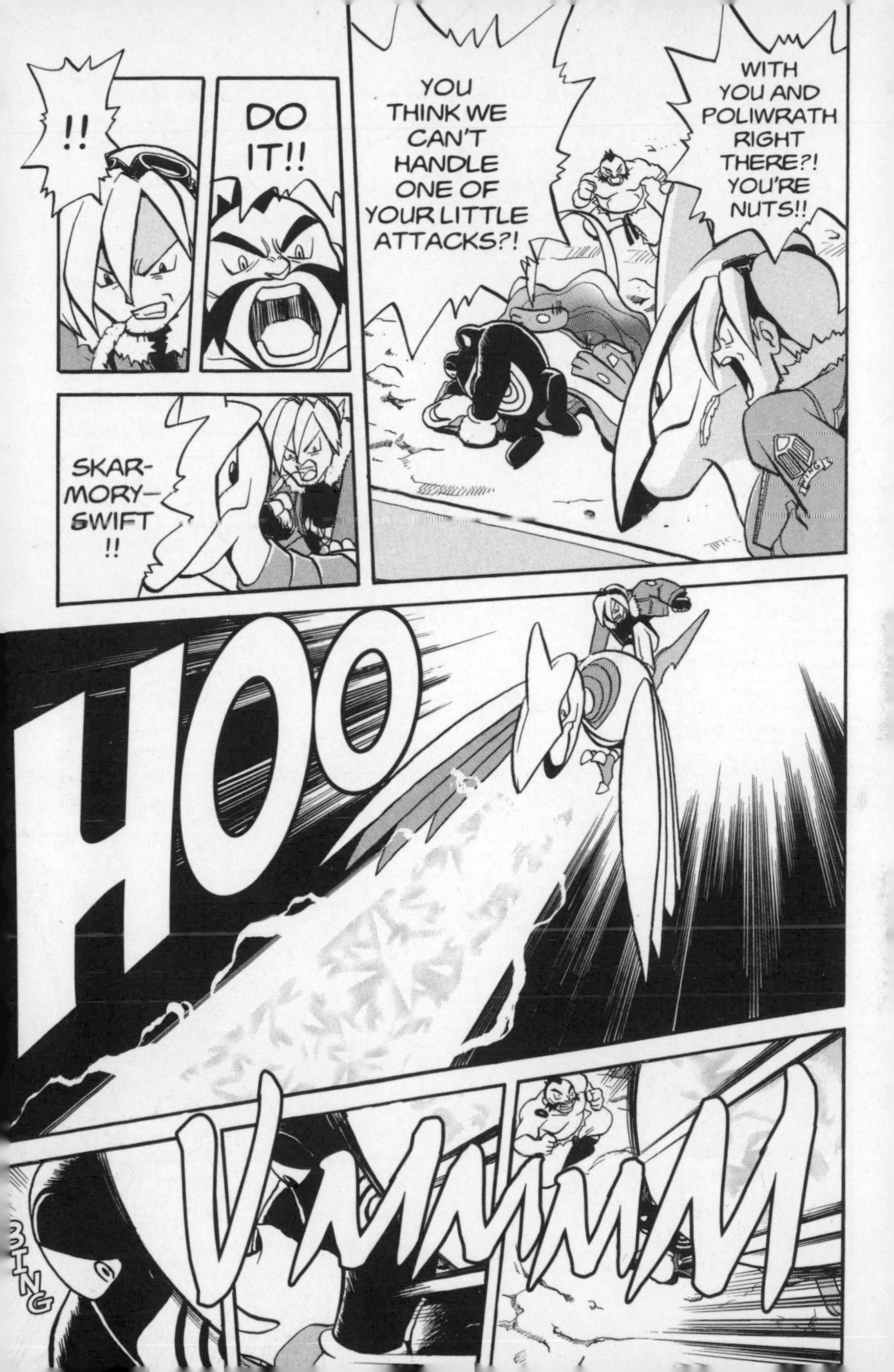
WITH YOU AND POLIWRATH RIGHT THERE?! YOU'RE NUTS!!
YOU THINK WE CAN'T HANDLE ONE OF YOUR LITTLE ATTACKS?!
DO IT!!
!!
SKAR-MORY-SWIFT!!
HOO
VMMMM
BING

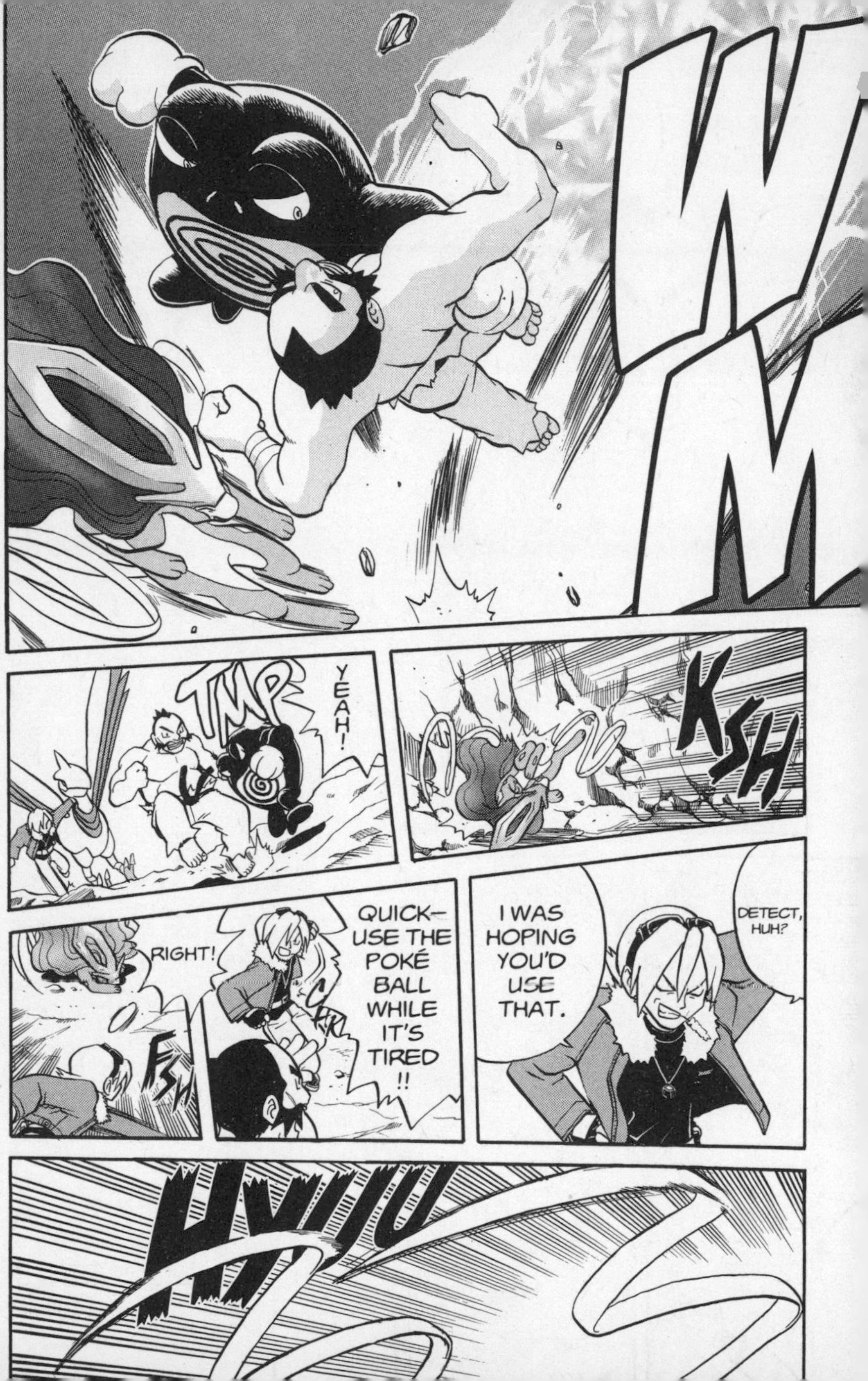
KSH
YEAH!
TMP
DETECT, HUH?
I WAS HOPING YOU'D USE THAT.
QUICK— USE THE POKÉ BALL WHILE IT'S TIRED!!
RIGHT!
HYUU

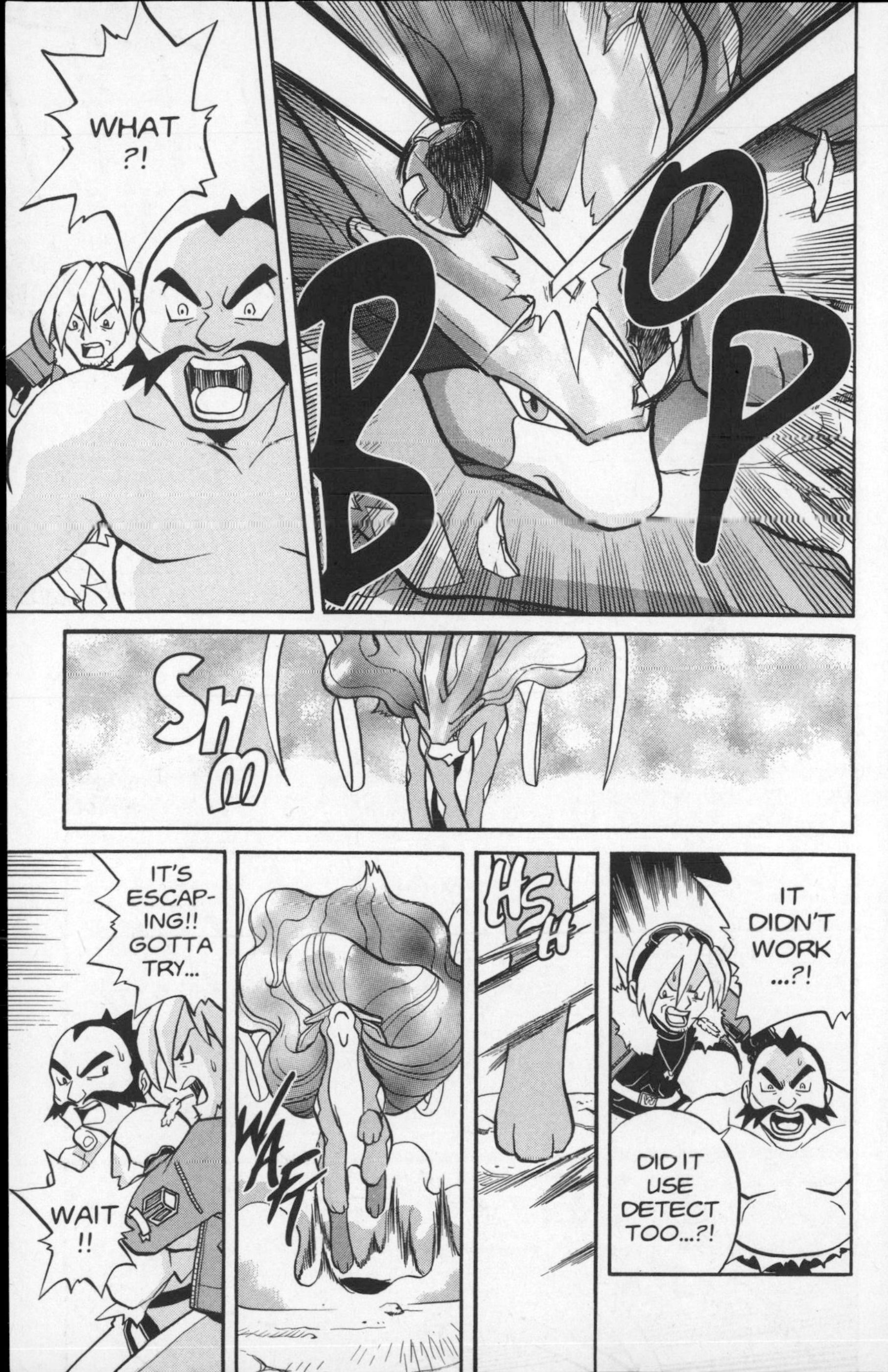
BOOP
WHAT?!
SHM
IT DIDN'T WORK...?!
DID IT USE DETECT TOO...?!
HSH
WAFT
IT'S ESCAPING!! GOTTA TRY...
WAIT!!

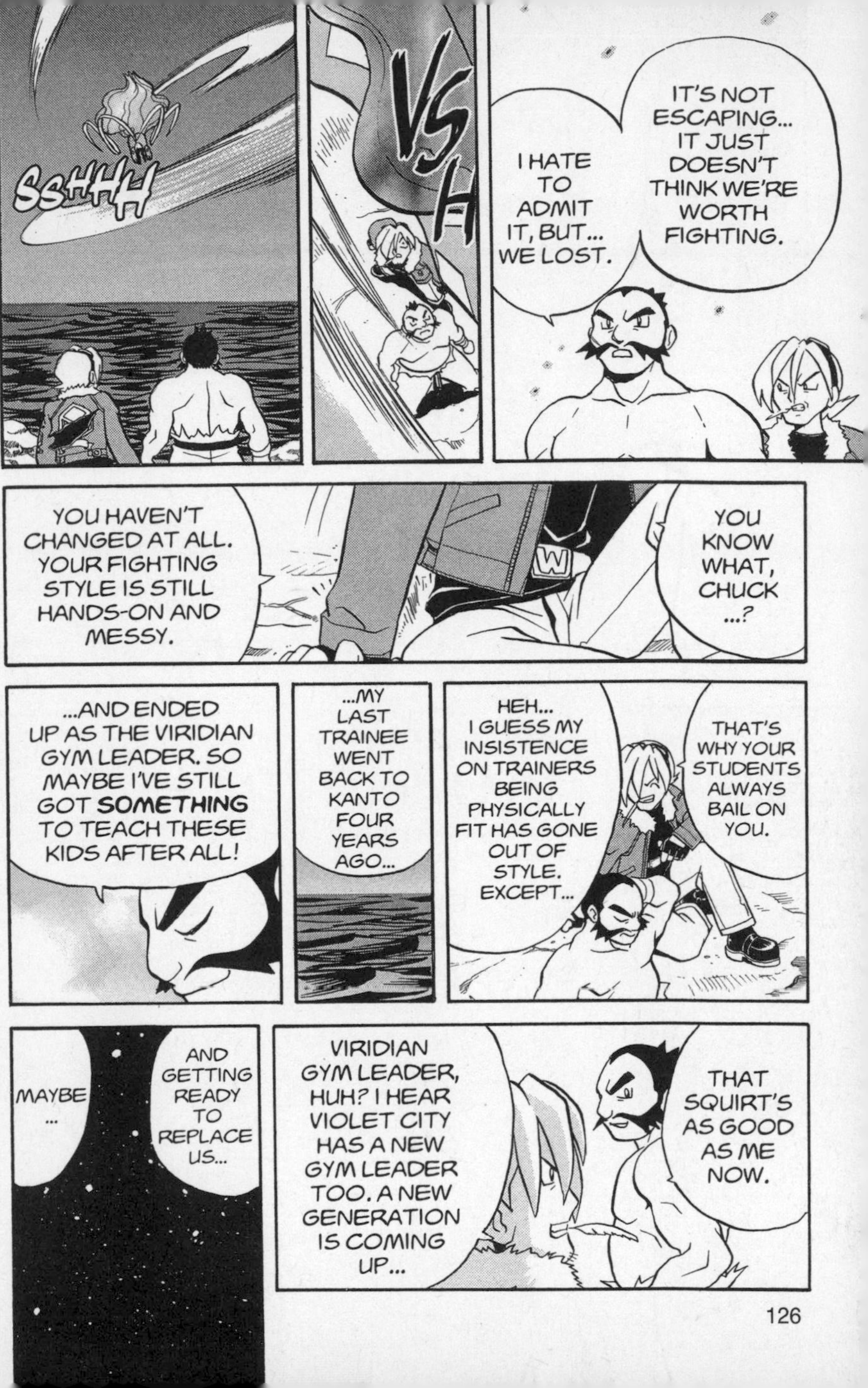
IT'S NOT ESCAPING... IT JUST DOESN'T THINK WE'RE WORTH FIGHTING.
I HATE TO ADMIT IT, BUT... WE LOST.
VSHH
SSHHH
YOU KNOW WHAT, CHUCK ...?
YOU HAVEN'T CHANGED AT ALL. YOUR FIGHTING STYLE IS STILL HANDS-ON AND MESSY.
THAT'S WHY YOUR STUDENTS ALWAYS BAIL ON YOU.
HEH... I GUESS MY INSISTENCE ON TRAINERS BEING PHYSICALLY FIT HAS GONE OUT OF STYLE. EXCEPT...
...MY LAST TRAINEE WENT BACK TO KANTO FOUR YEARS AGO...
...AND ENDED UP AS THE VIRIDIAN GYM LEADER. SO MAYBE I'VE STILL GOT **SOMETHING** TO TEACH THESE KIDS AFTER ALL!
THAT SQUIRT'S AS GOOD AS ME NOW.
VIRIDIAN GYM LEADER, HUH? I HEAR VIOLET CITY HAS A NEW GYM LEADER TOO. A NEW GENERATION IS COMING UP...
AND GETTING READY TO REPLACE US...
MAYBE ...

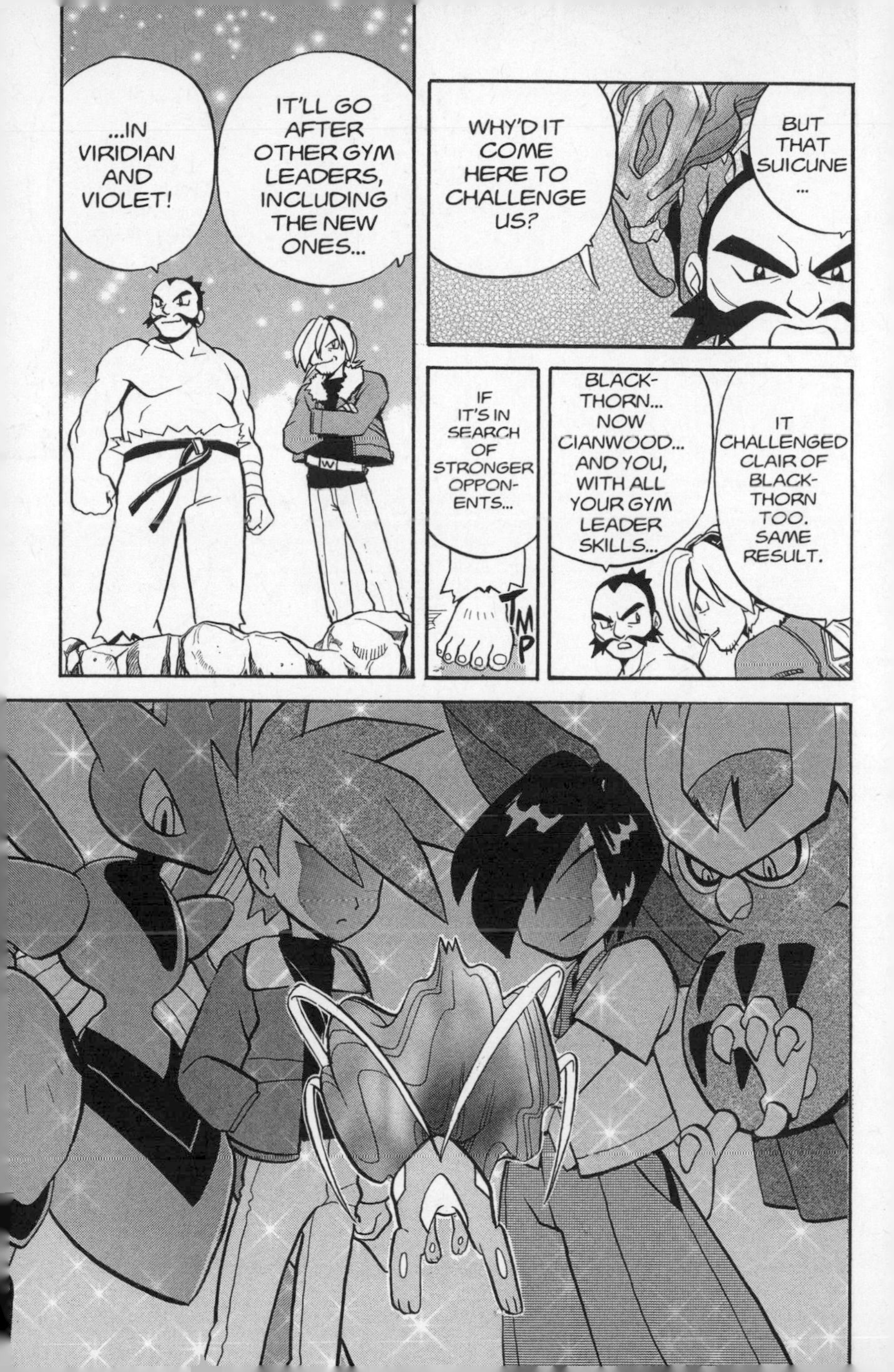
BUT THAT SUICUNE ...
WHY'D IT COME HERE TO CHALLENGE US?
IT CHALLENGED CLAIR OF BLACK-THORN TOO. SAME RESULT.
BLACK-THORN... NOW CIANWOOD... AND YOU, WITH ALL YOUR GYM LEADER SKILLS...
IF IT'S IN SEARCH OF STRONGER OPPON-ENTS...
TMP
IT'LL GO AFTER OTHER GYM LEADERS, INCLUDING THE NEW ONES...
...IN VIRIDIAN AND VIOLET!

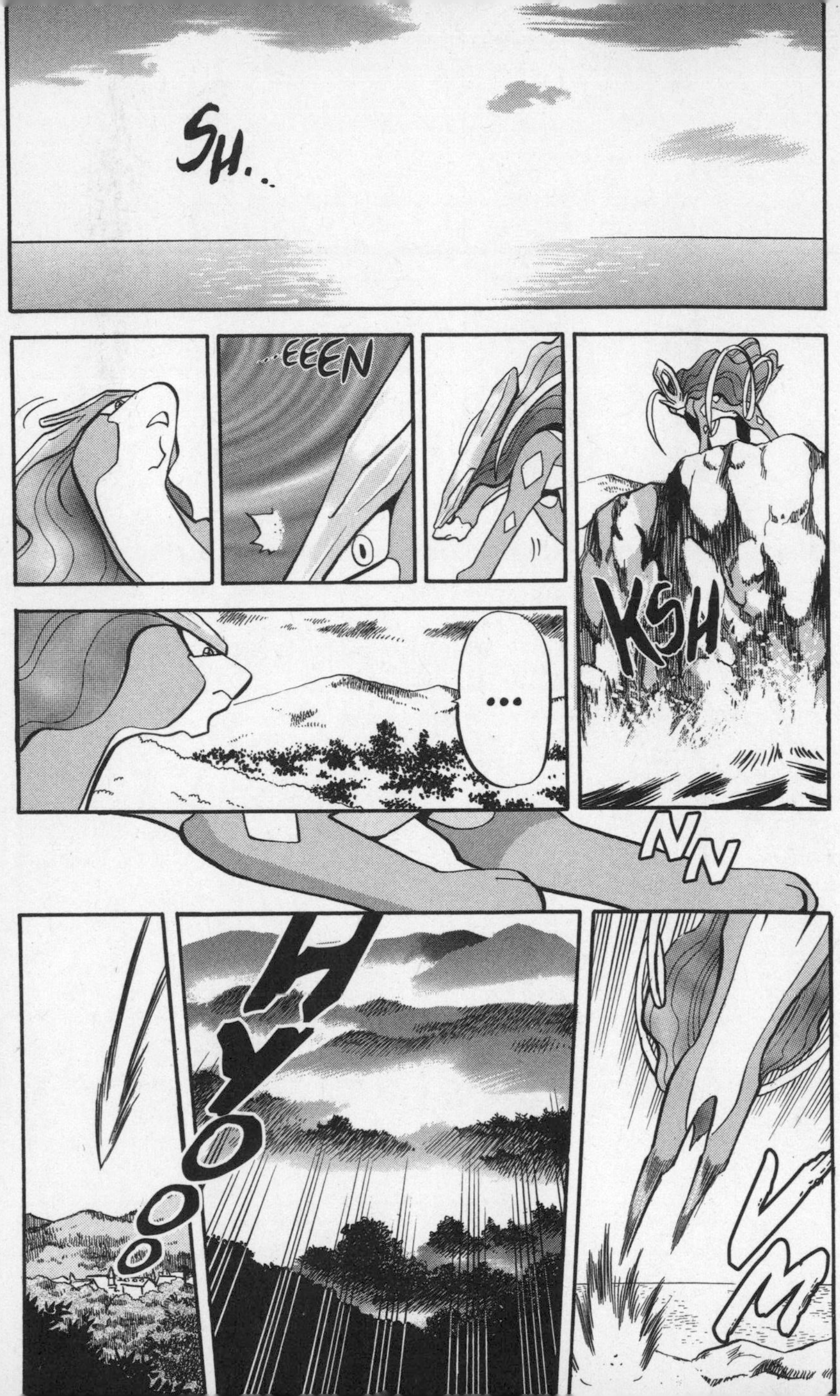
SH...
KSH
...EEEN
...
NN
VM
HYOOO

125 Misdreavus Misgivings

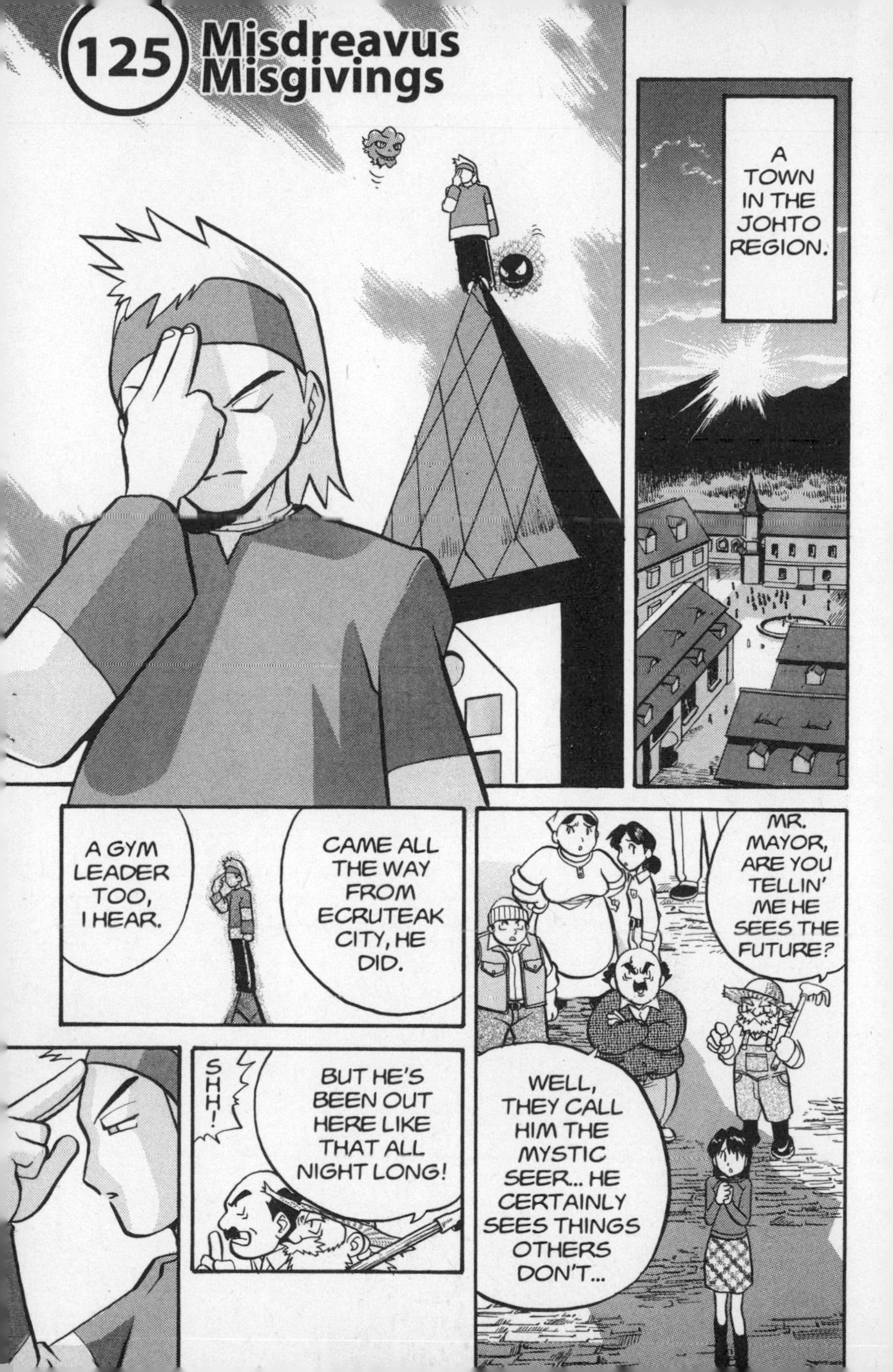
A TOWN IN THE JOHTO REGION.
MR. MAYOR, ARE YOU TELLIN' ME HE SEES THE FUTURE?
WELL, THEY CALL HIM THE MYSTIC SEER... HE CERTAINLY SEES THINGS OTHERS DON'T...
CAME ALL THE WAY FROM ECRUTEAK CITY, HE DID.
A GYM LEADER TOO, I HEAR.
BUT HE'S BEEN OUT HERE LIKE THAT ALL NIGHT LONG!
SHH!

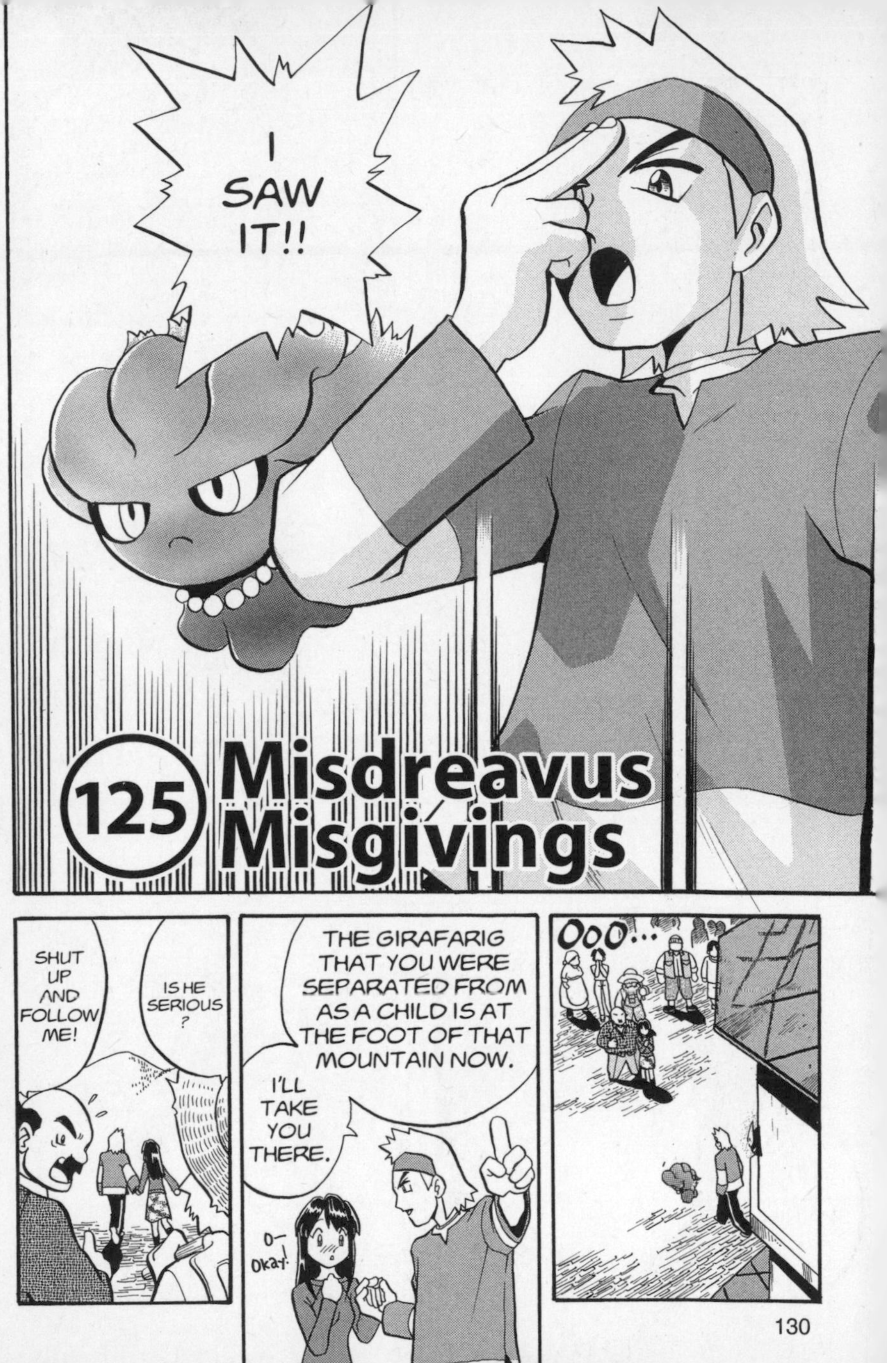
I SAW IT!!
125 Misdreavus Misgivings
OOO...
THE GIRAFARIG THAT YOU WERE SEPARATED FROM AS A CHILD IS AT THE FOOT OF THAT MOUNTAIN NOW.
I'LL TAKE YOU THERE.
O-OKAY!
IS HE SERIOUS?
SHUT UP AND FOLLOW ME!

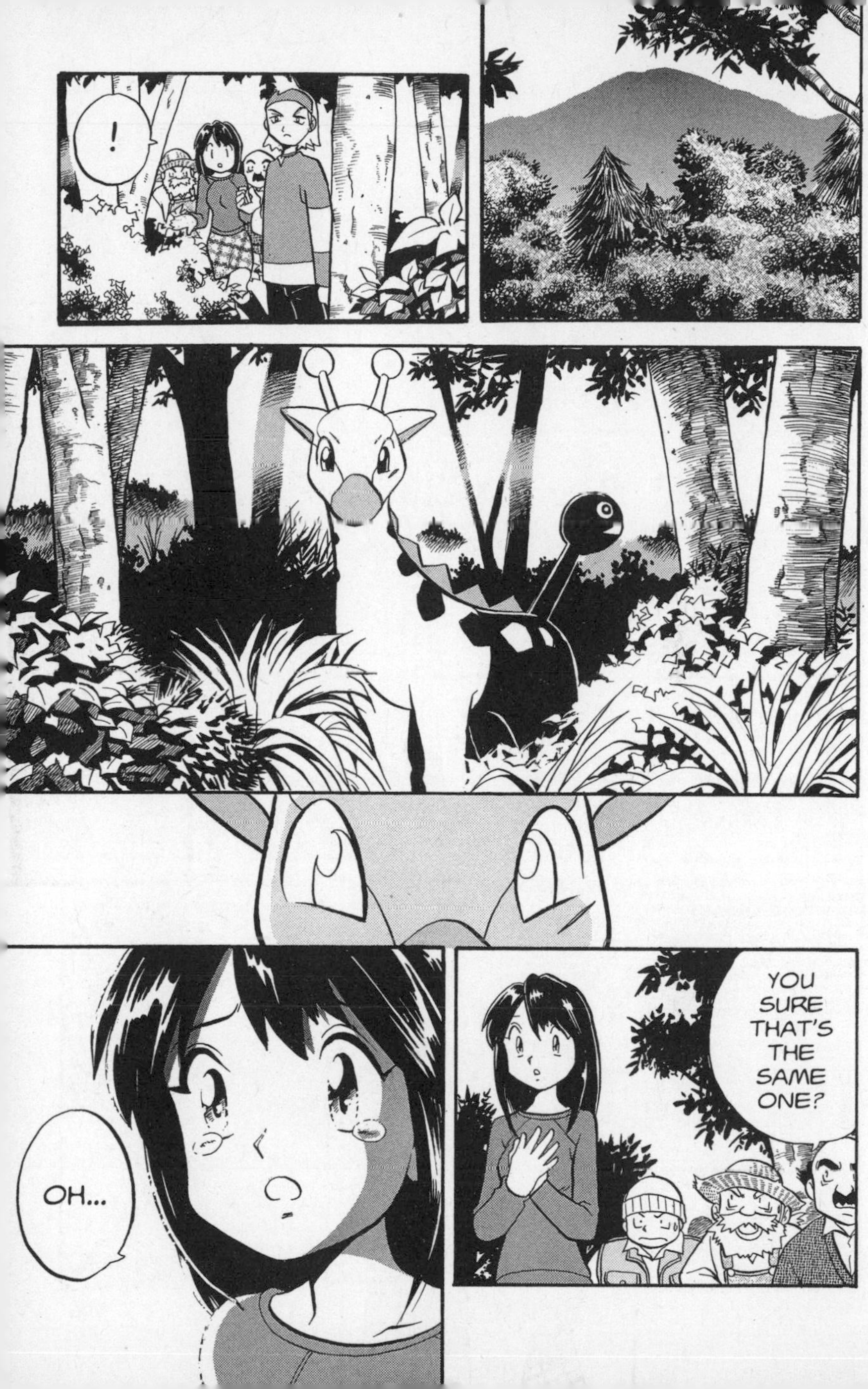
!
YOU SURE THAT'S THE SAME ONE?
OH...

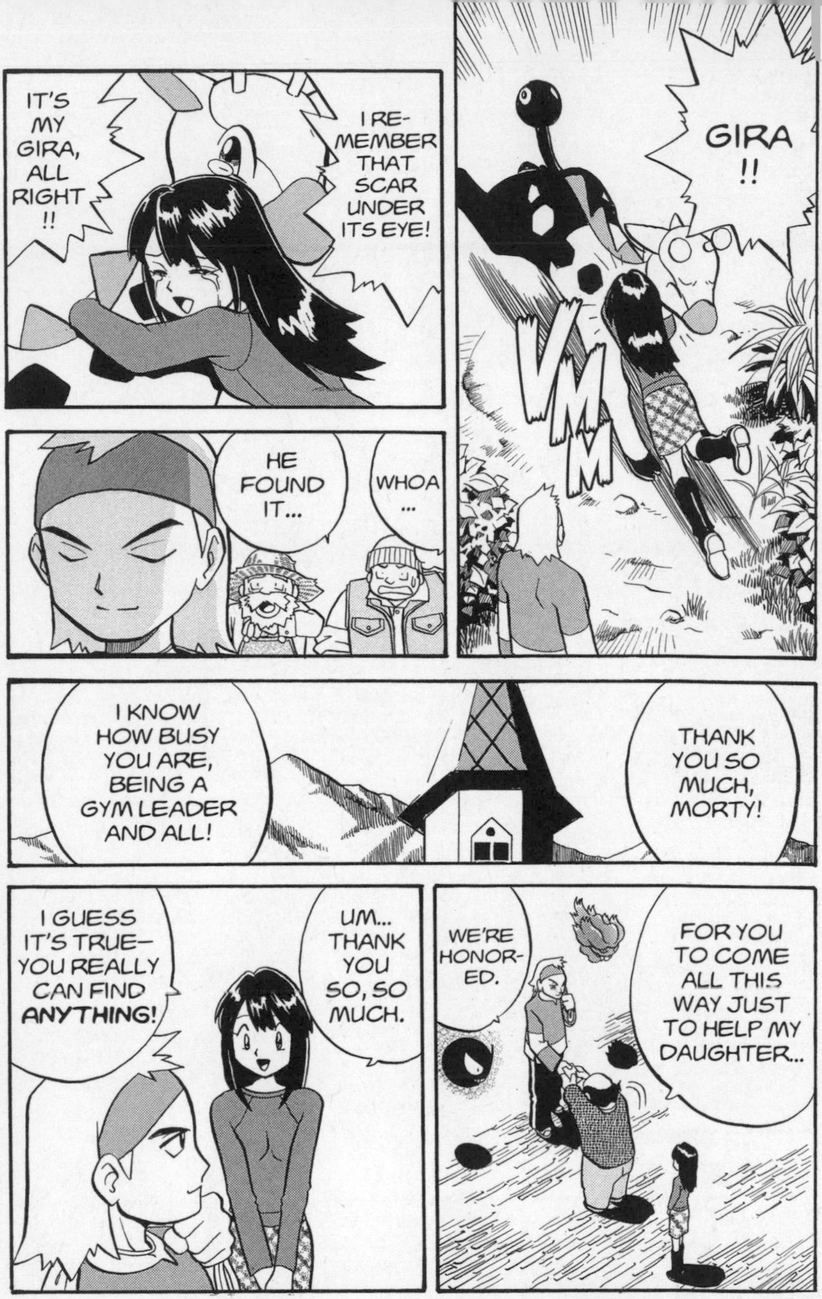
GIRA !!
VMM
I REMEMBER THAT SCAR UNDER ITS EYE!
IT'S MY GIRA, ALL RIGHT !!
WHOA ...
HE FOUND IT...
THANK YOU SO MUCH, MORTY!
I KNOW HOW BUSY YOU ARE, BEING A GYM LEADER AND ALL!
FOR YOU TO COME ALL THIS WAY JUST TO HELP MY DAUGHTER...
WE'RE HONORED.
UM... THANK YOU SO, SO MUCH.
I GUESS IT'S TRUE— YOU REALLY CAN FIND **ANYTHING**!

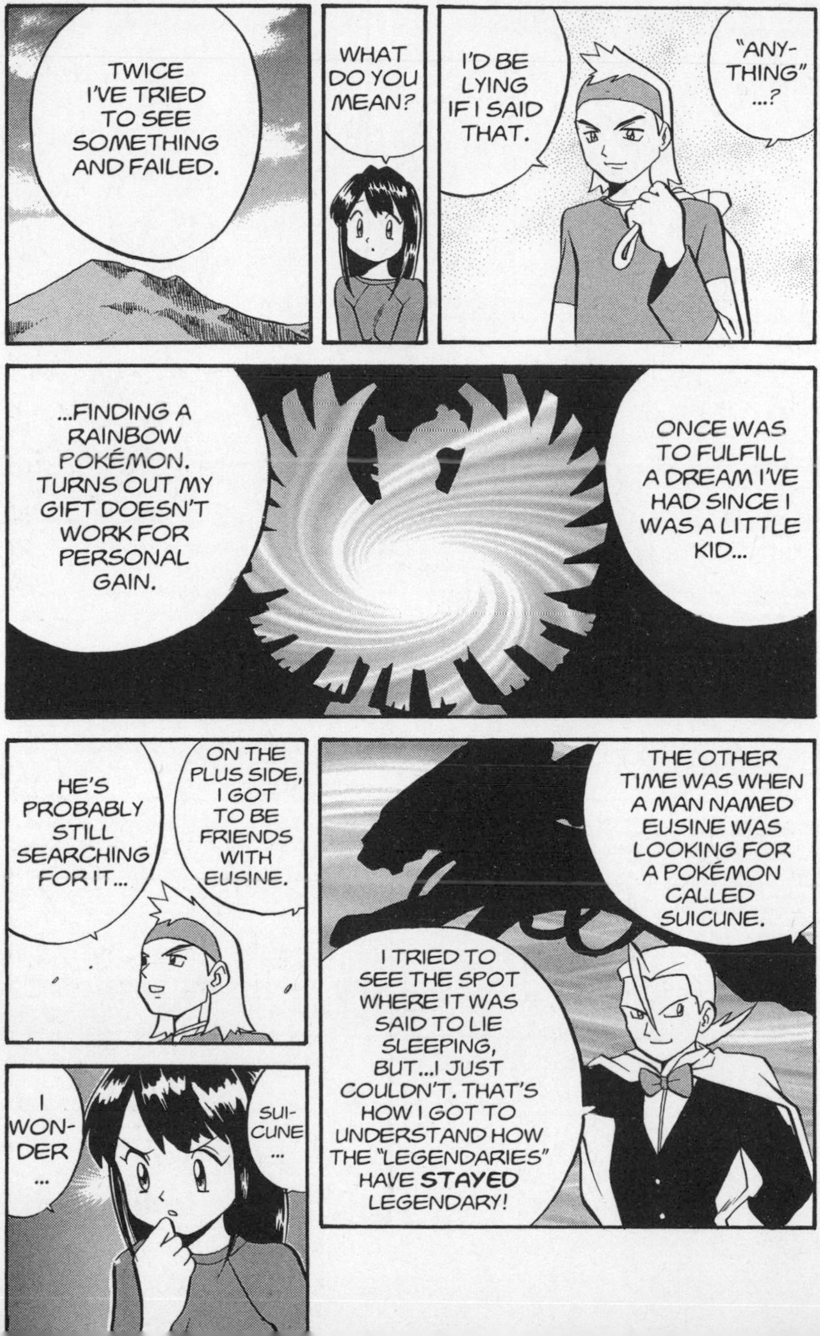
"ANY-THING" ...?
I'D BE LYING IF I SAID THAT.
WHAT DO YOU MEAN?
TWICE I'VE TRIED TO SEE SOMETHING AND FAILED.
ONCE WAS TO FULFILL A DREAM I'VE HAD SINCE I WAS A LITTLE KID...
...FINDING A RAINBOW POKÉMON. TURNS OUT MY GIFT DOESN'T WORK FOR PERSONAL GAIN.
THE OTHER TIME WAS WHEN A MAN NAMED EUSINE WAS LOOKING FOR A POKÉMON CALLED SUICUNE.
I TRIED TO SEE THE SPOT WHERE IT WAS SAID TO LIE SLEEPING, BUT...I JUST COULDN'T. THAT'S HOW I GOT TO UNDERSTAND HOW THE "LEGENDARIES" HAVE **STAYED** LEGENDARY!
ON THE PLUS SIDE, I GOT TO BE FRIENDS WITH EUSINE.
HE'S PROBABLY STILL SEARCHING FOR IT...
SUI-CUNE ...
I WON-DER ...

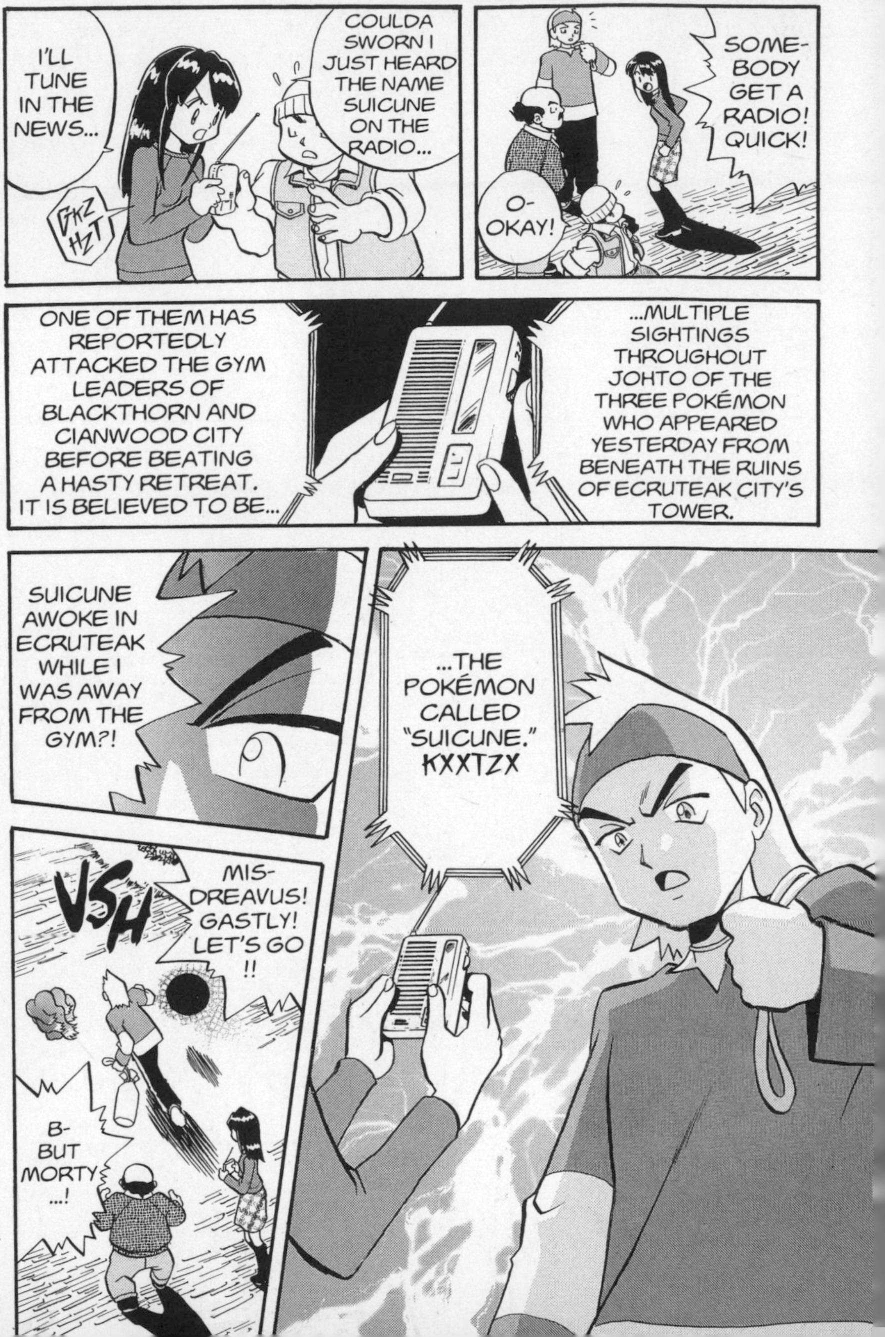
SOME-BODY GET A RADIO! QUICK!
O-OKAY!
COULDA SWORN I JUST HEARD THE NAME SUICUNE ON THE RADIO...
I'LL TUNE IN THE NEWS...
GKZ HZT
...MULTIPLE SIGHTINGS THROUGHOUT JOHTO OF THE THREE POKÉMON WHO APPEARED YESTERDAY FROM BENEATH THE RUINS OF ECRUTEAK CITY'S TOWER.
ONE OF THEM HAS REPORTEDLY ATTACKED THE GYM LEADERS OF BLACKTHORN AND CIANWOOD CITY BEFORE BEATING A HASTY RETREAT. IT IS BELIEVED TO BE...
...THE POKÉMON CALLED "SUICUNE." KXXTZX
SUICUNE AWOKE IN ECRUTEAK WHILE I WAS AWAY FROM THE GYM?!
MIS-DREAVUS! GASTLY! LET'S GO !!
VSH
B-BUT MORTY ...!

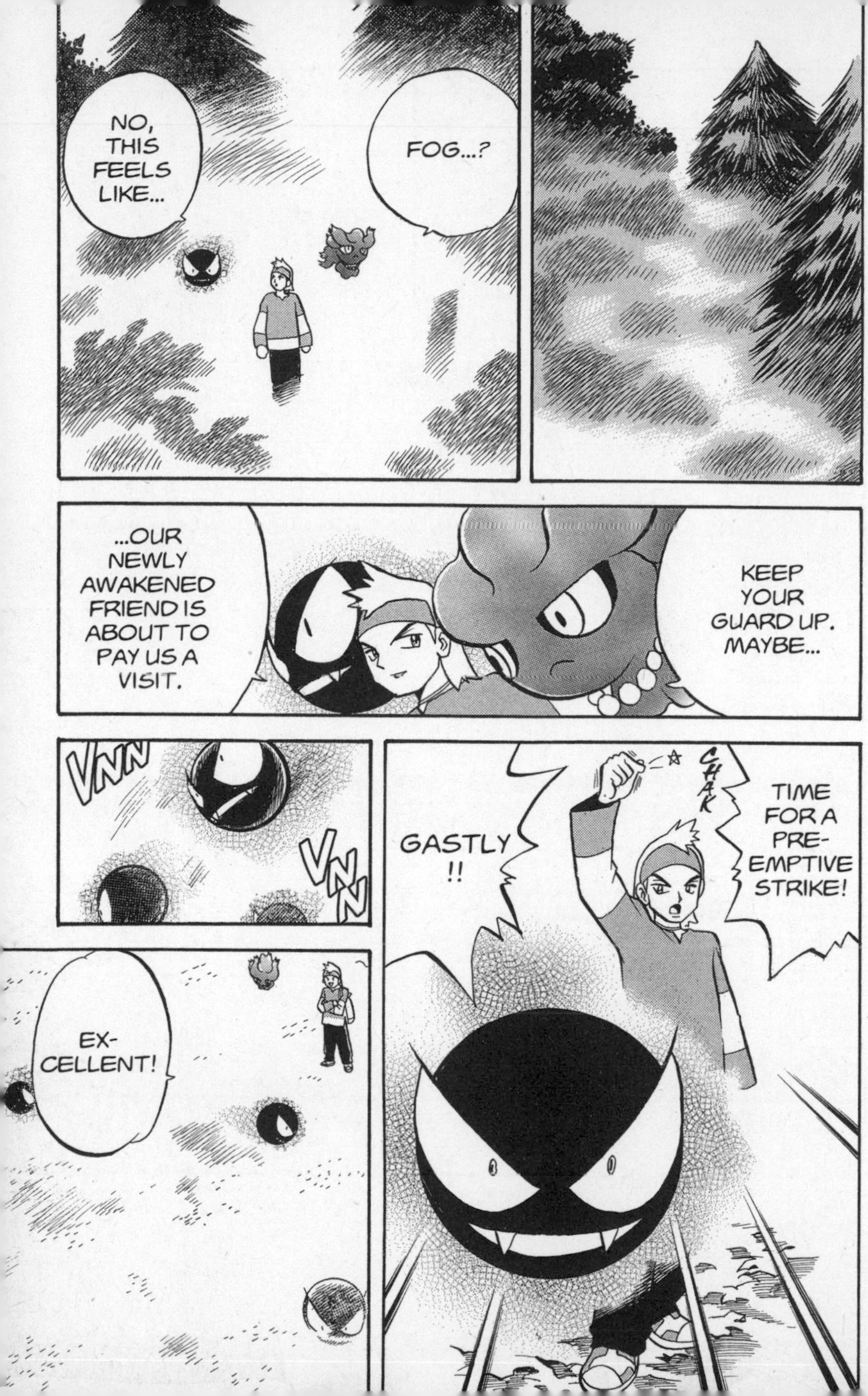
FOG...?
NO, THIS FEELS LIKE...
KEEP YOUR GUARD UP. MAYBE...
...OUR NEWLY AWAKENED FRIEND IS ABOUT TO PAY US A VISIT.
CHAK
TIME FOR A PRE-EMPTIVE STRIKE!
GASTLY!!
VNN
VNN
EX-CELLENT!

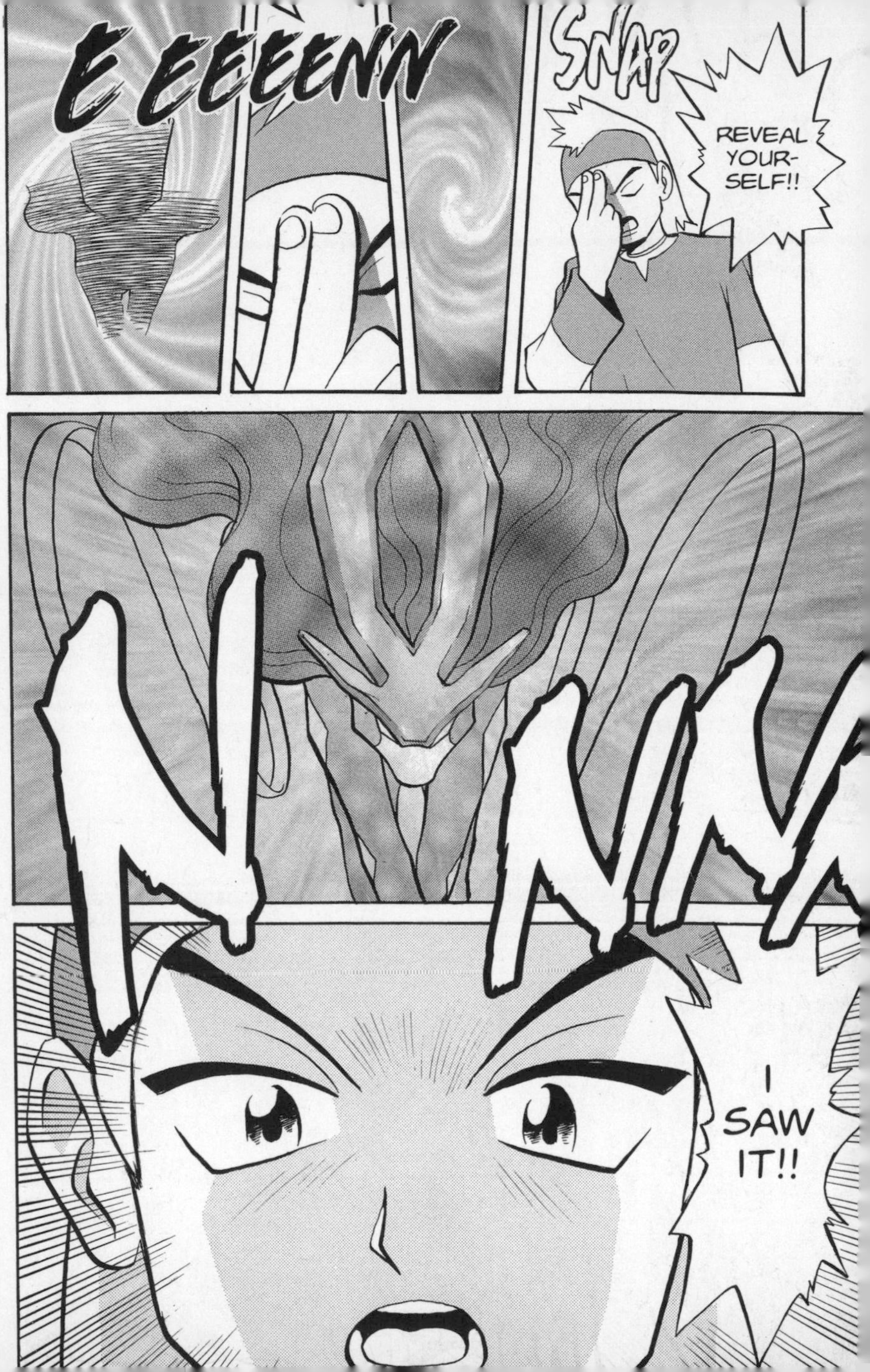
SNAP
REVEAL YOURSELF!!
E EEEENN
NNN
I SAW IT!!

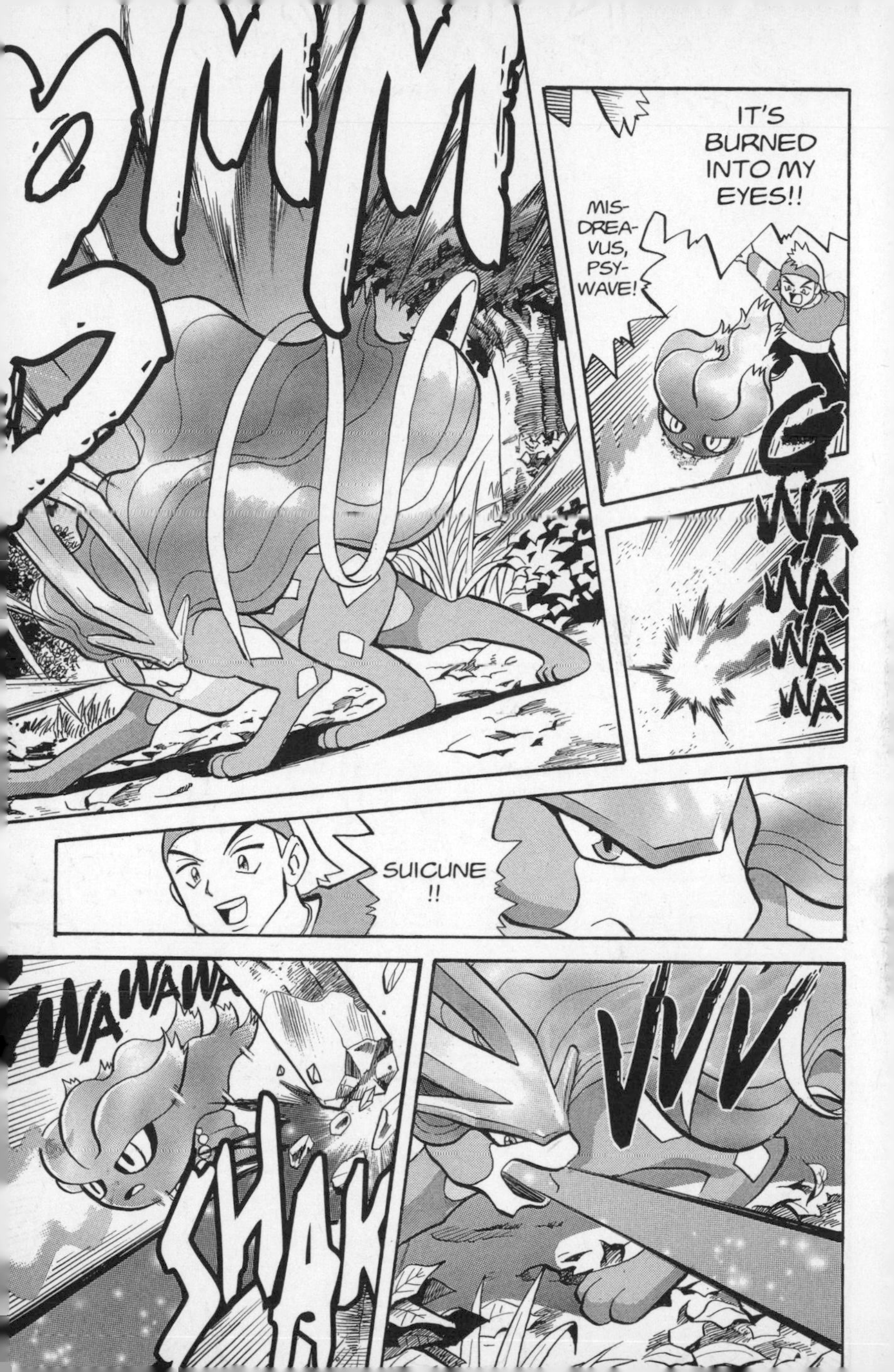
IT'S BURNED INTO MY EYES!!
MIS-DREA-VUS, PSY-WAVE!
GWA WA WA WA
SUICUNE !!
VVV
WAWAWA
SHAK

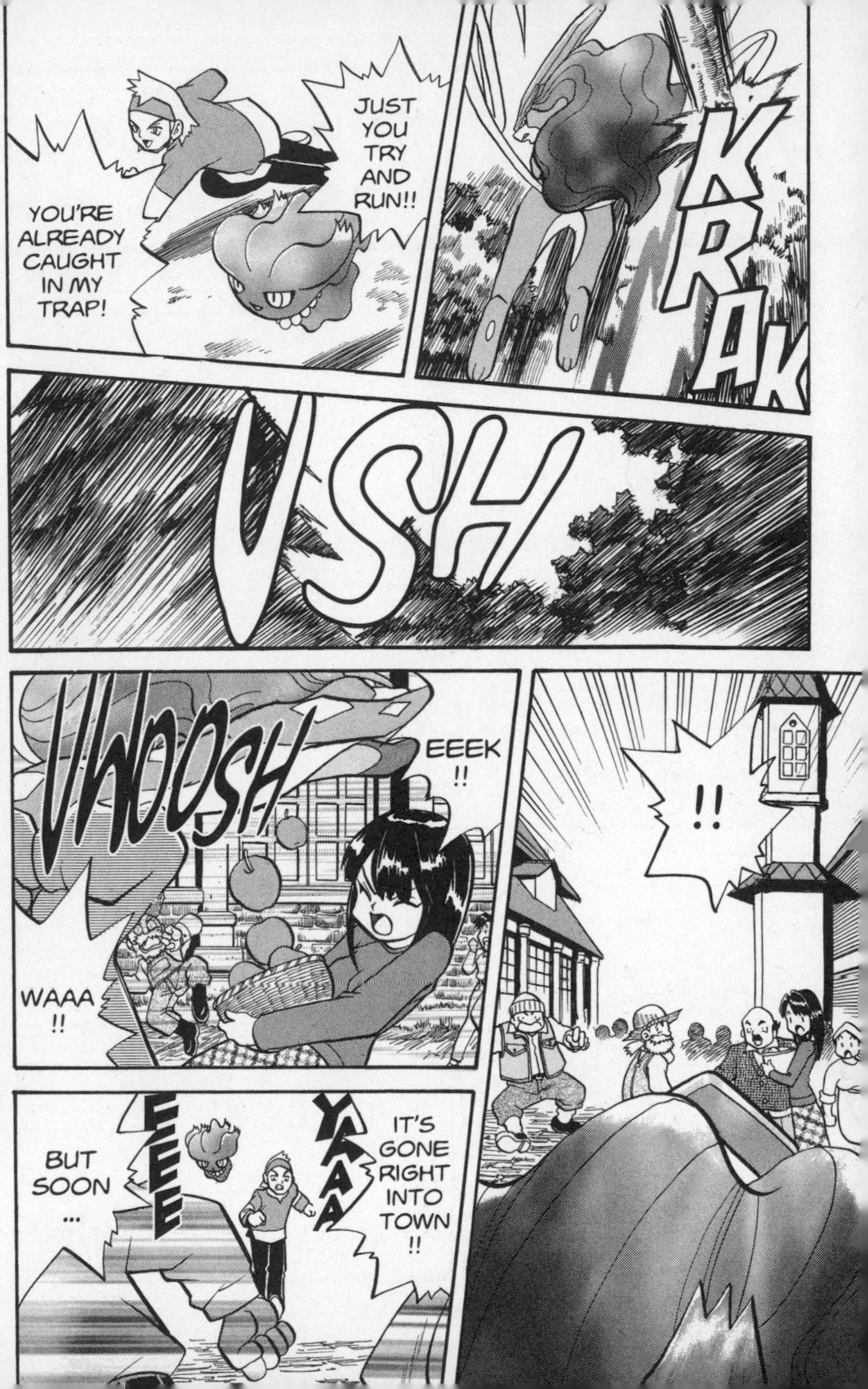
KRAK
JUST YOU TRY AND RUN!!
YOU'RE ALREADY CAUGHT IN MY TRAP!
VSH
!!
EEEK !!
WHOOSH
WAAA !!
IT'S GONE RIGHT INTO TOWN !!
YAAAA
EEEE
BUT SOON ...

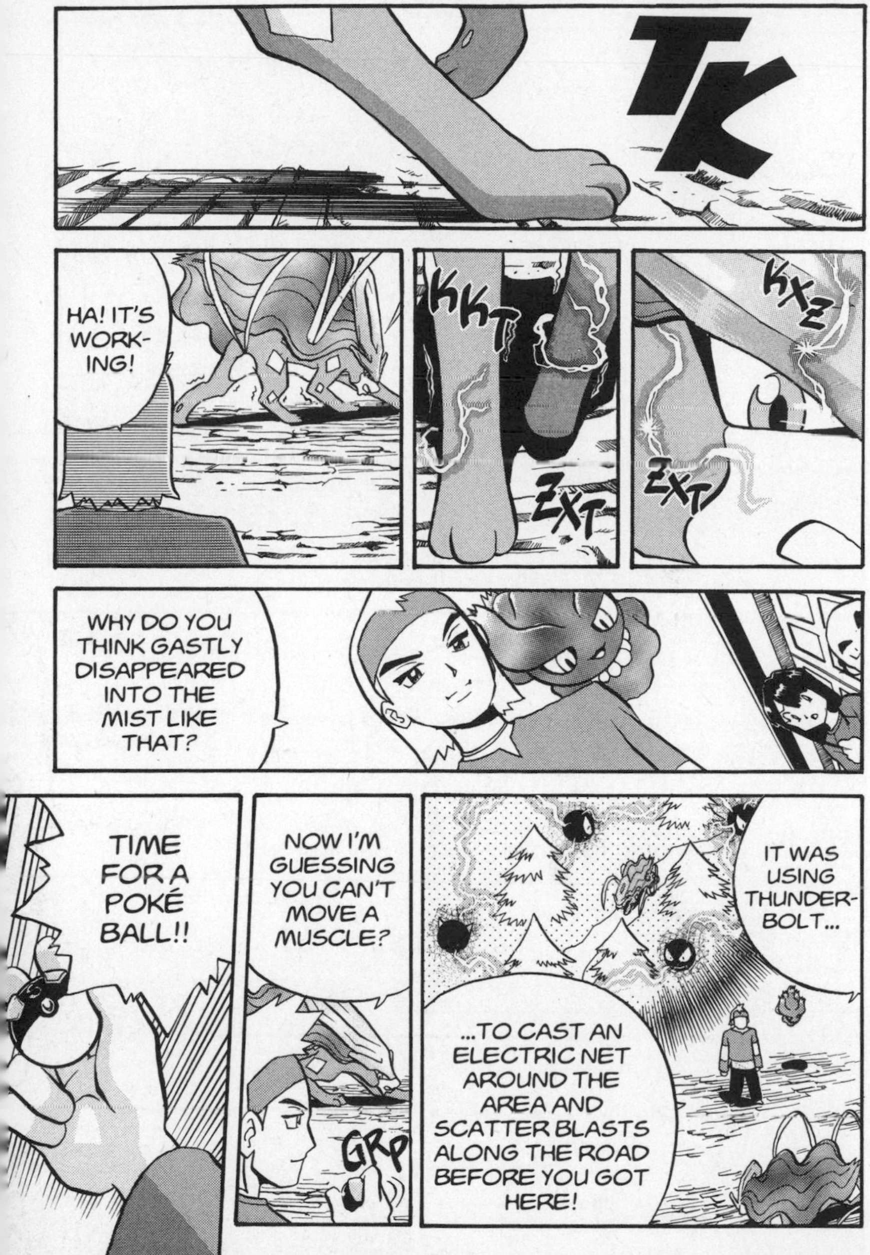
TK
KXZ
ZXT
KKT
ZXT
HA! IT'S WORKING!
WHY DO YOU THINK GASTLY DISAPPEARED INTO THE MIST LIKE THAT?
IT WAS USING THUNDERBOLT...
...TO CAST AN ELECTRIC NET AROUND THE AREA AND SCATTER BLASTS ALONG THE ROAD BEFORE YOU GOT HERE!
NOW I'M GUESSING YOU CAN'T MOVE A MUSCLE?
GRP
TIME FOR A POKÉ BALL!!

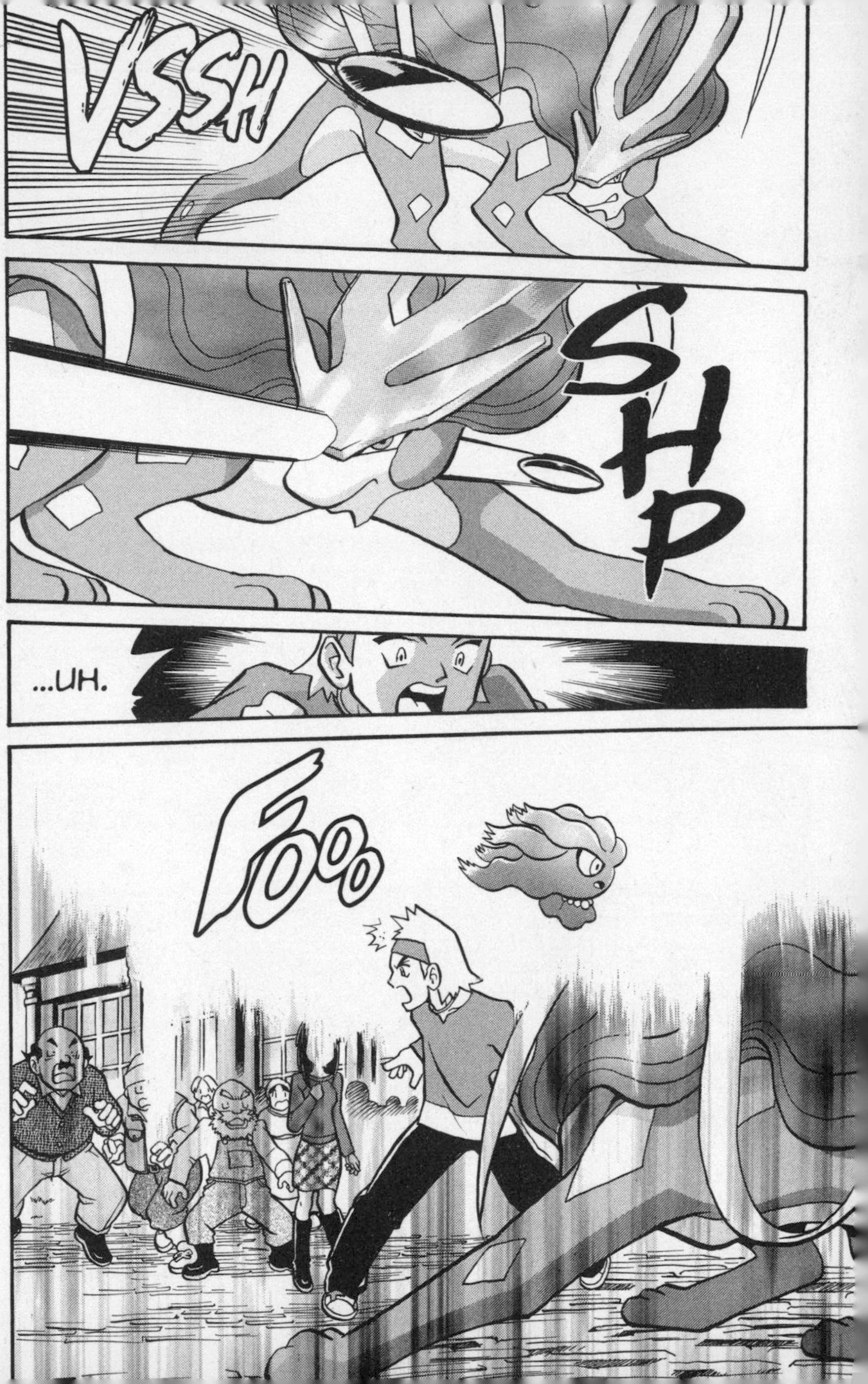
VSSH
SHP
...UH.
FOO

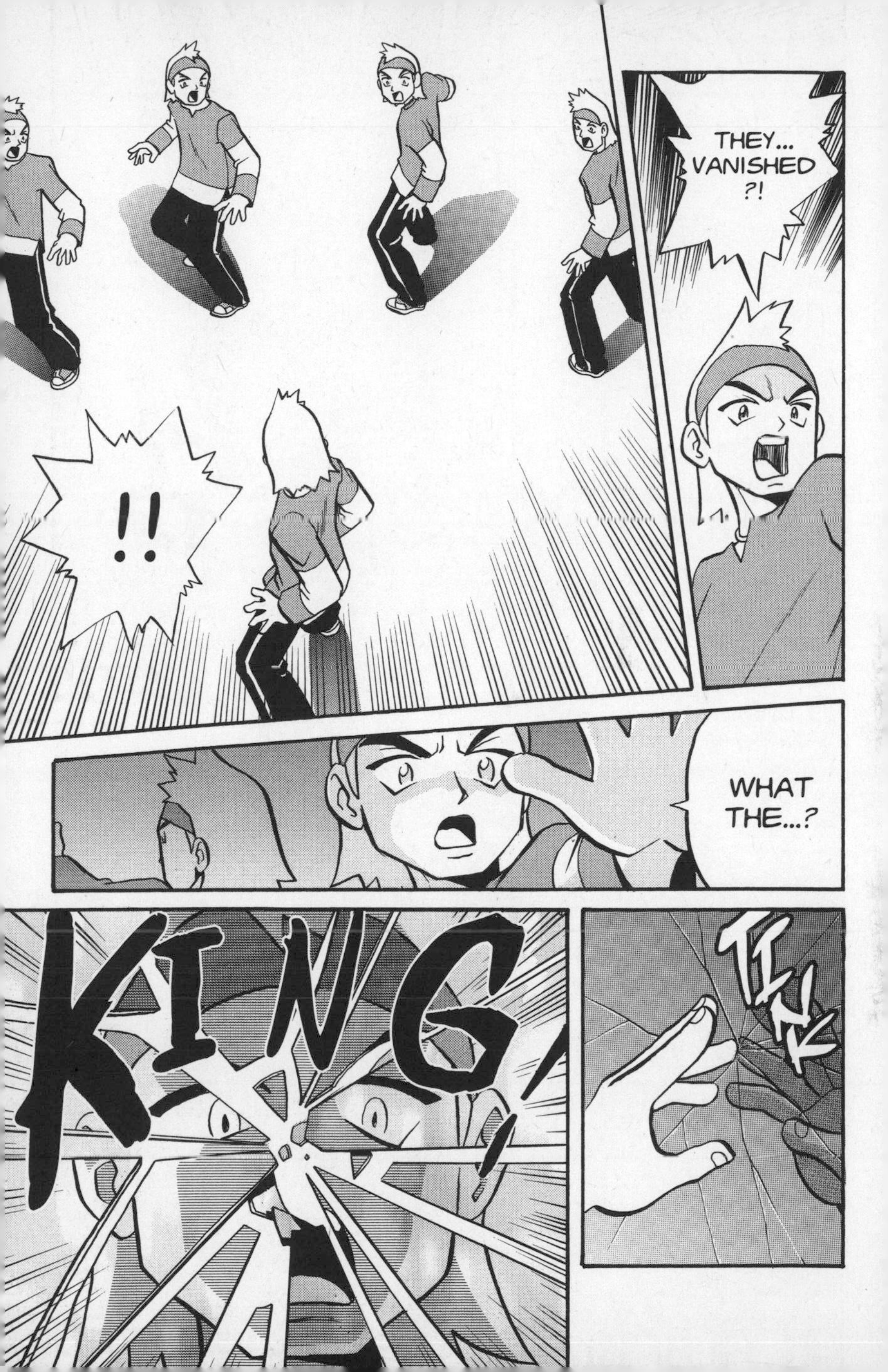
THEY... VANISHED ?!
!!
WHAT THE...?
TINK
KING

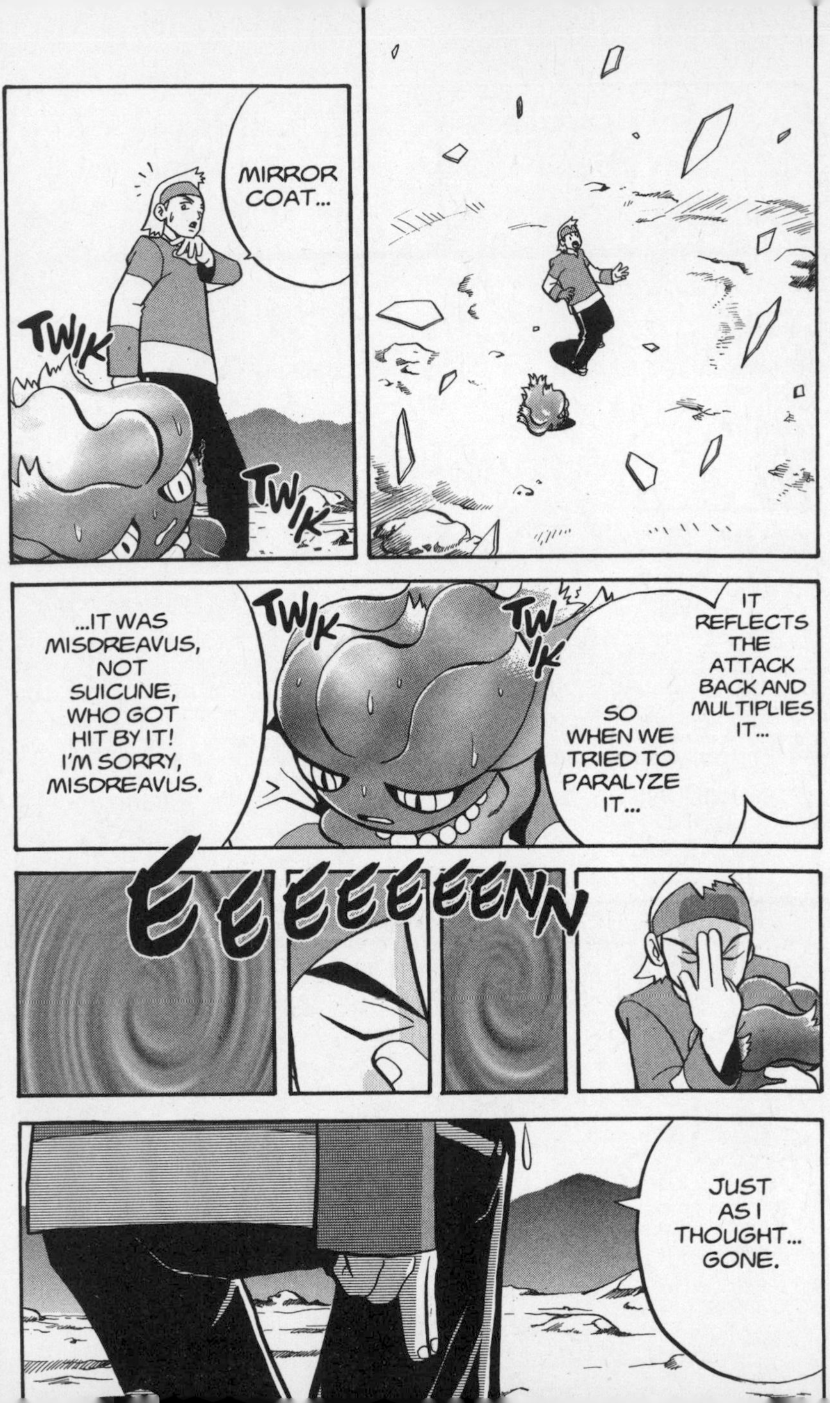
MIRROR COAT...
TWIK
TWIK
IT REFLECTS THE ATTACK BACK AND MULTIPLIES IT...
SO WHEN WE TRIED TO PARALYZE IT...
TWIK
TWIK
...IT WAS MISDREAVUS, NOT SUICUNE, WHO GOT HIT BY IT! I'M SORRY, MISDREAVUS.
EEEEEEEENN
JUST AS I THOUGHT... GONE.

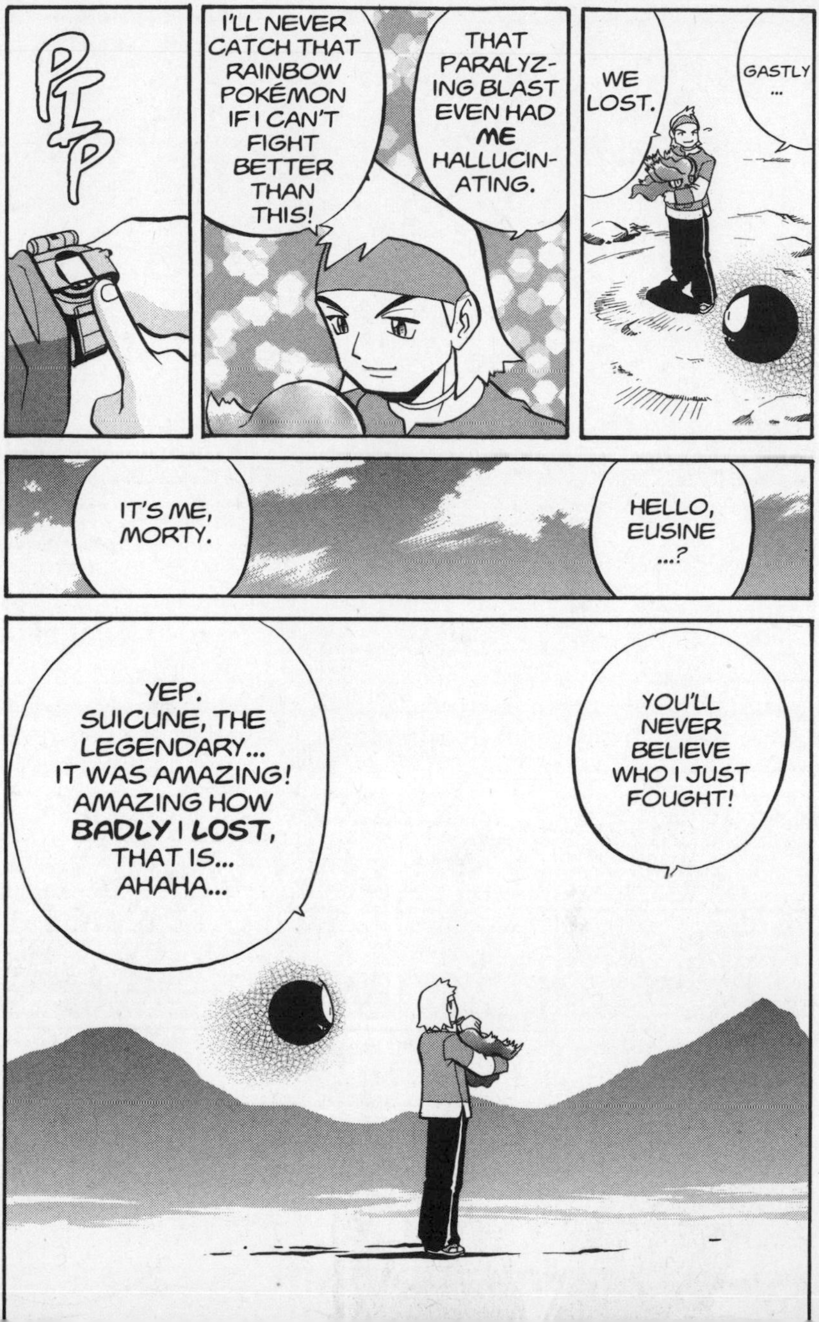
GASTLY ...
WE LOST.
THAT PARALYZING BLAST EVEN HAD **ME** HALLUCINATING.
I'LL NEVER CATCH THAT RAINBOW POKÉMON IF I CAN'T FIGHT BETTER THAN THIS!
PIP
HELLO, EUSINE ...?
IT'S ME, MORTY.
YOU'LL NEVER BELIEVE WHO I JUST FOUGHT!
YEP. SUICUNE, THE LEGENDARY... IT WAS AMAZING! AMAZING HOW **BADLY** I **LOST**, THAT IS... AHAHA...

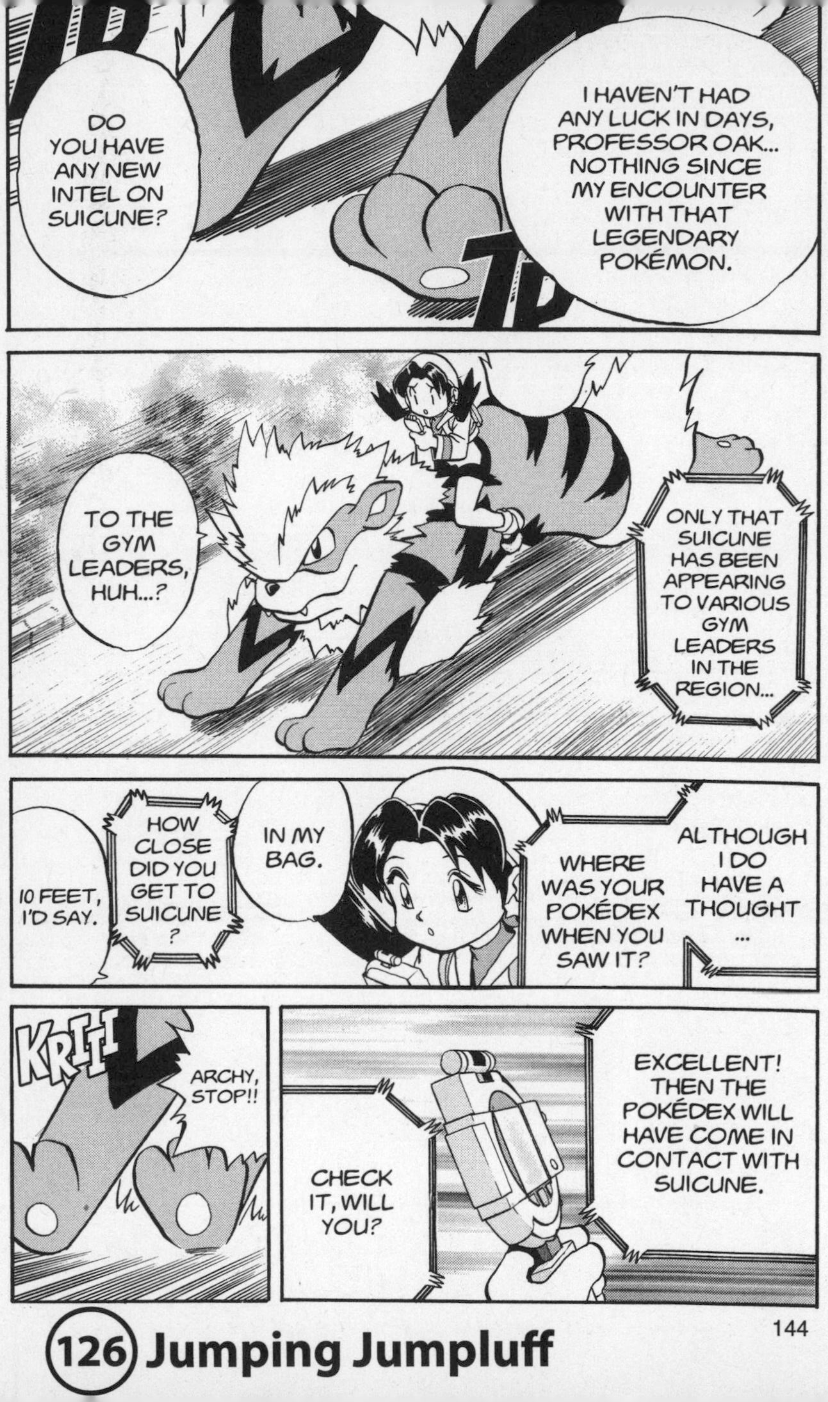
I HAVEN'T HAD ANY LUCK IN DAYS, PROFESSOR OAK... NOTHING SINCE MY ENCOUNTER WITH THAT LEGENDARY POKÉMON.
DO YOU HAVE ANY NEW INTEL ON SUICUNE?
ONLY THAT SUICUNE HAS BEEN APPEARING TO VARIOUS GYM LEADERS IN THE REGION...
TO THE GYM LEADERS, HUH...?
ALTHOUGH I DO HAVE A THOUGHT ...
WHERE WAS YOUR POKÉDEX WHEN YOU SAW IT?
IN MY BAG.
HOW CLOSE DID YOU GET TO SUICUNE ?
10 FEET, I'D SAY.
EXCELLENT! THEN THE POKÉDEX WILL HAVE COME IN CONTACT WITH SUICUNE.
CHECK IT, WILL YOU?
KRIII
ARCHY, STOP!!

126 Jumping Jumpluff

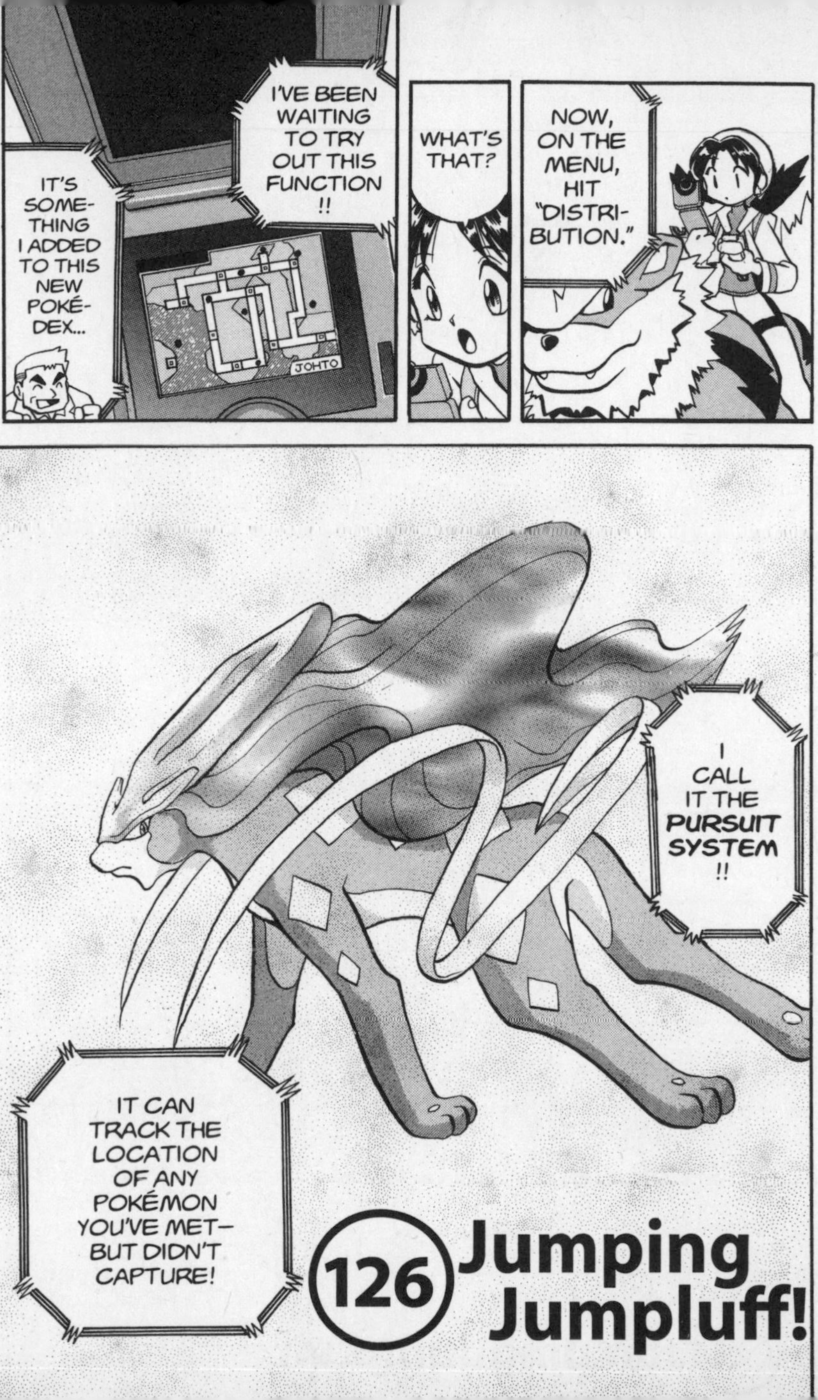
NOW, ON THE MENU, HIT "DISTRIBUTION."
WHAT'S THAT?
I'VE BEEN WAITING TO TRY OUT THIS FUNCTION !!
IT'S SOME-THING I ADDED TO THIS NEW POKÉ-DEX...
JOHTO
I CALL IT THE PURSUIT SYSTEM !!
IT CAN TRACK THE LOCATION OF ANY POKÉMON YOU'VE MET—BUT DIDN'T CAPTURE!
126 Jumping Jumpluff!

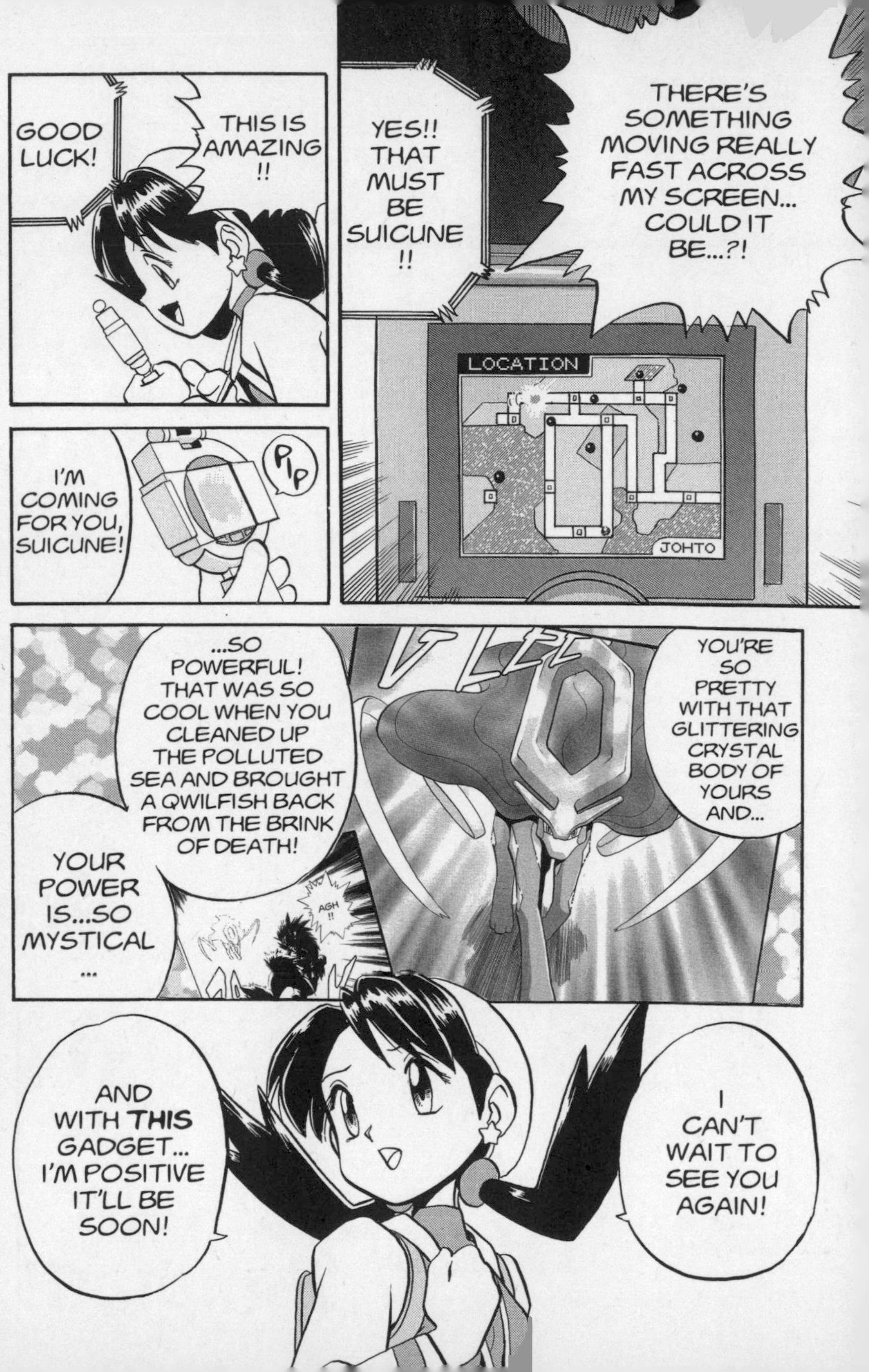

THERE'S SOMETHING MOVING REALLY FAST ACROSS MY SCREEN... COULD IT BE...?!
YES!! THAT MUST BE SUICUNE!!
LOCATION
JOHTO
THIS IS AMAZING!!
GOOD LUCK!
PIP
I'M COMING FOR YOU, SUICUNE!
YOU'RE SO PRETTY WITH THAT GLITTERING CRYSTAL BODY OF YOURS AND...
...SO POWERFUL! THAT WAS SO COOL WHEN YOU CLEANED UP THE POLLUTED SEA AND BROUGHT A QWILFISH BACK FROM THE BRINK OF DEATH!
AGH!!
YOUR POWER IS...SO MYSTICAL...
I CAN'T WAIT TO SEE YOU AGAIN!
AND WITH **THIS** GADGET... I'M POSITIVE IT'LL BE SOON!

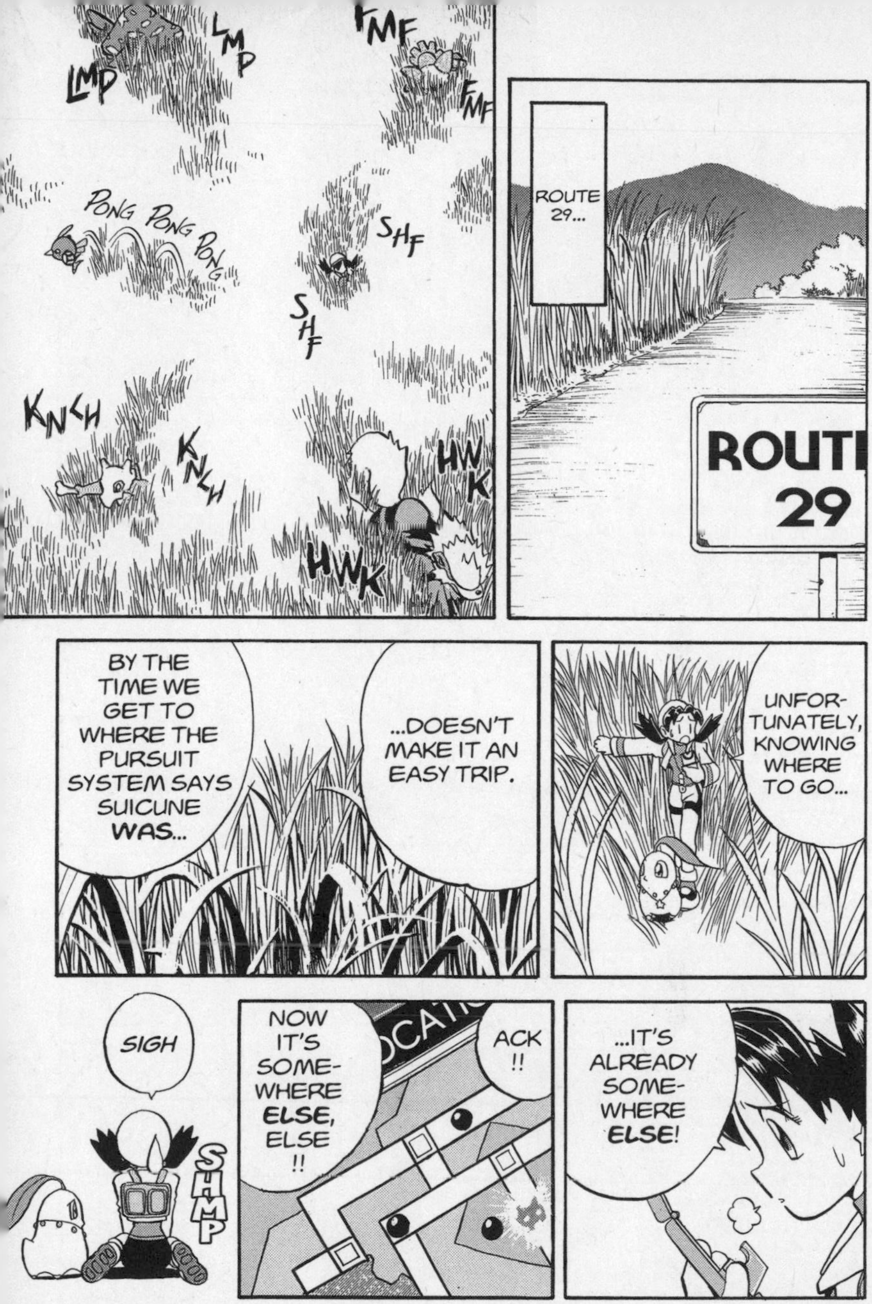

ROUTE 29...
ROUTE 29
FMF
FMF
LMP
LMP
SHF
SHF
PONG PONG PONG
HWK
HWK
KNCH
KNCH
UNFOR-TUNATELY, KNOWING WHERE TO GO...
...DOESN'T MAKE IT AN EASY TRIP.
BY THE TIME WE GET TO WHERE THE PURSUIT SYSTEM SAYS SUICUNE **WAS**...
...IT'S ALREADY SOME-WHERE **ELSE**!
ACK !!
NOW IT'S SOME-WHERE **ELSE**, ELSE !!
SIGH
SHMP

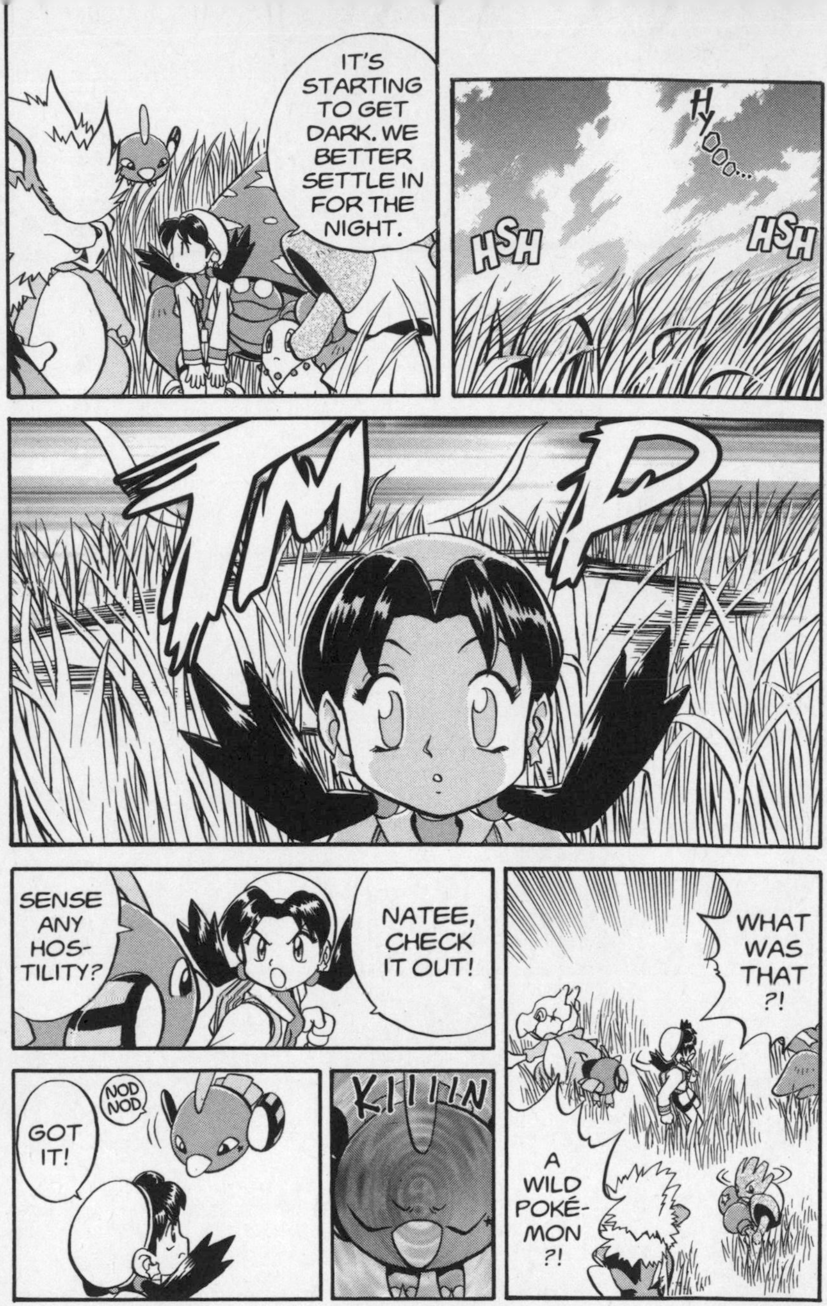
HYOOO...
HSH
HSH
IT'S STARTING TO GET DARK. WE BETTER SETTLE IN FOR THE NIGHT.
TMP
WHAT WAS THAT?!
A WILD POKÉMON?!
NATEE, CHECK IT OUT!
SENSE ANY HOS-TILITY?
KIIIN
NOD NOD
GOT IT!

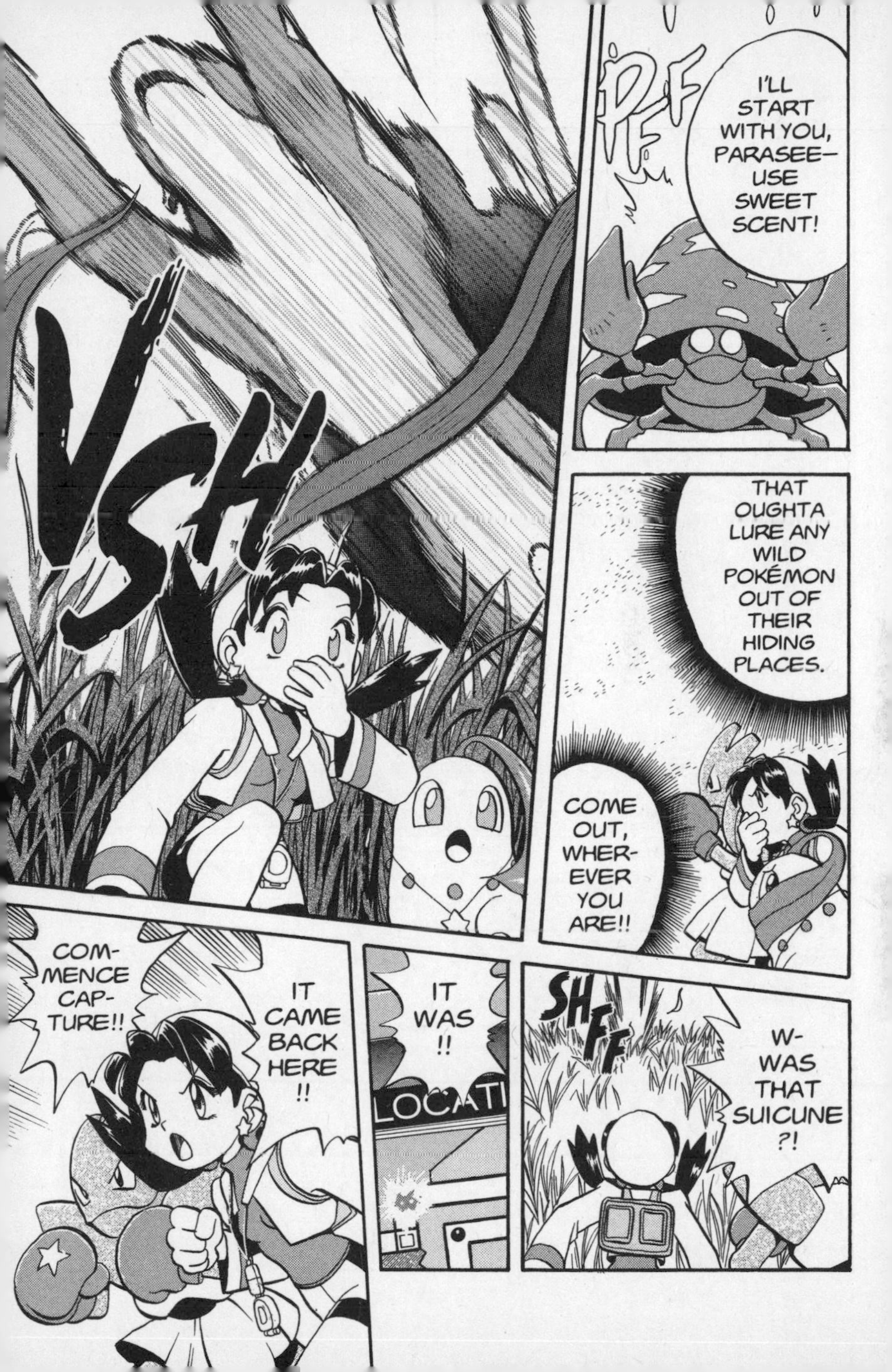
PFF
I'LL START WITH YOU, PARASEE—USE SWEET SCENT!
THAT OUGHTA LURE ANY WILD POKÉMON OUT OF THEIR HIDING PLACES.
COME OUT, WHEREVER YOU ARE!!
VSH
SHFF
W-WAS THAT SUICUNE?!
IT WAS!!
LOCATI
IT CAME BACK HERE!!
COMMENCE CAPTURE!!

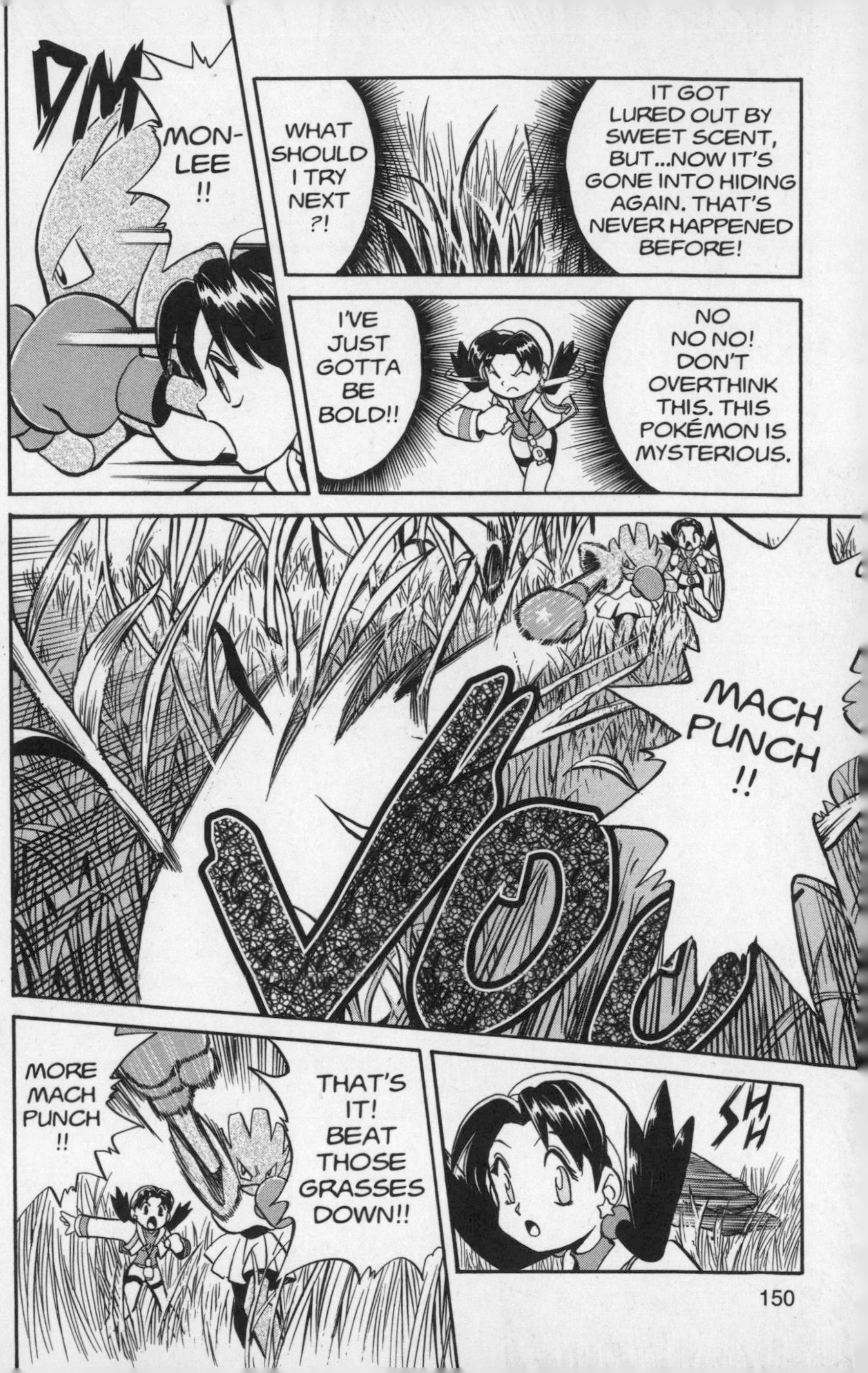
IT GOT LURED OUT BY SWEET SCENT, BUT...NOW IT'S GONE INTO HIDING AGAIN. THAT'S NEVER HAPPENED BEFORE!
WHAT SHOULD I TRY NEXT ?!
NO NO NO! DON'T OVERTHINK THIS. THIS POKÉMON IS MYSTERIOUS.
I'VE JUST GOTTA BE BOLD!!
DM
MON-LEE !!
MACH PUNCH !!
SHH
THAT'S IT! BEAT THOSE GRASSES DOWN!!
MORE MACH PUNCH !!

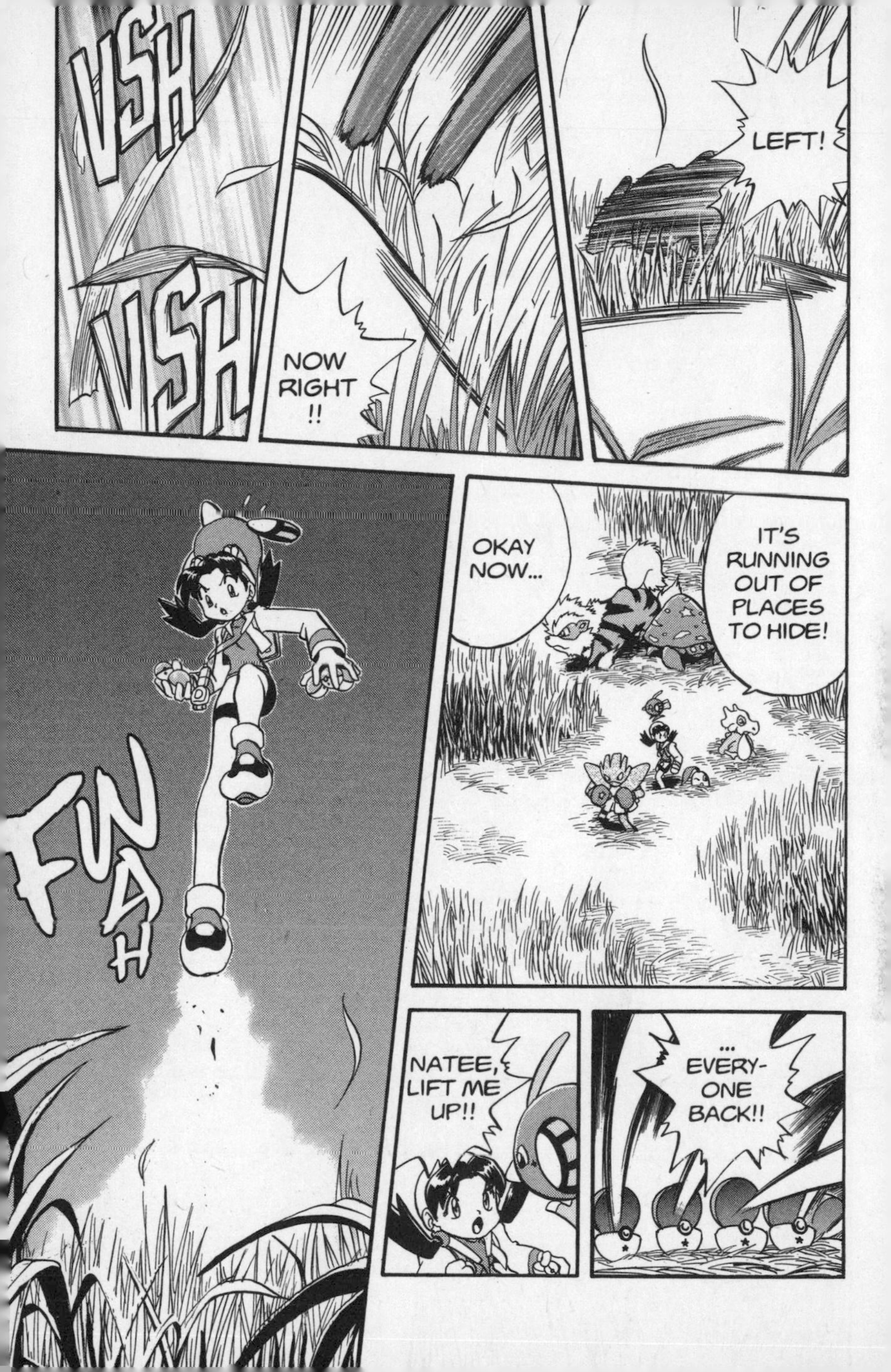
LEFT!
NOW RIGHT !!
VSH
VSH
IT'S RUNNING OUT OF PLACES TO HIDE!
OKAY NOW...
... EVERY-ONE BACK!!
NATEE, LIFT ME UP!!
FWAH

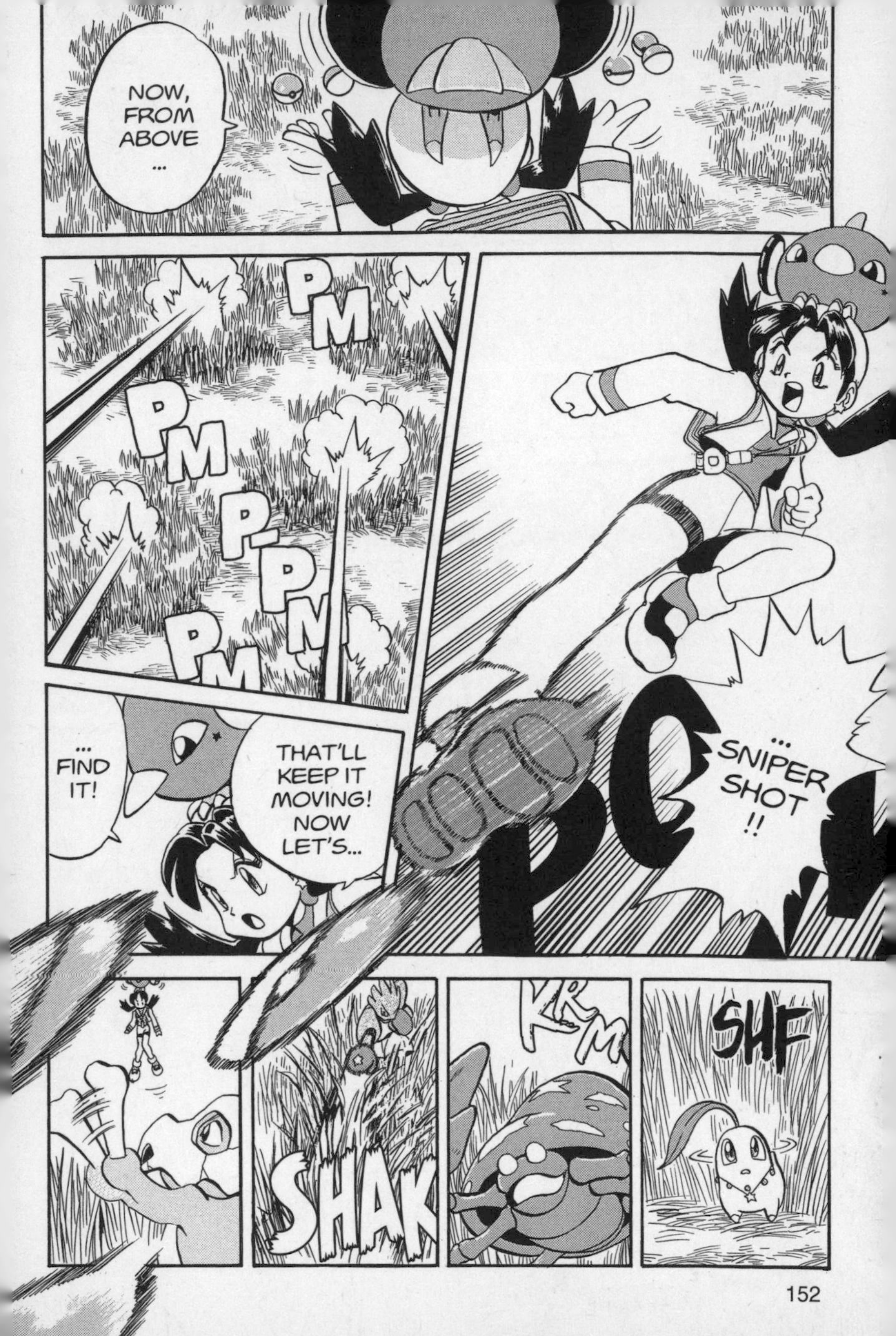
NOW, FROM ABOVE ...
... SNIPER SHOT !!
PM
PM
P-PM
PM
THAT'LL KEEP IT MOVING! NOW LET'S...
... FIND IT!
SHF
KRM
SHAK

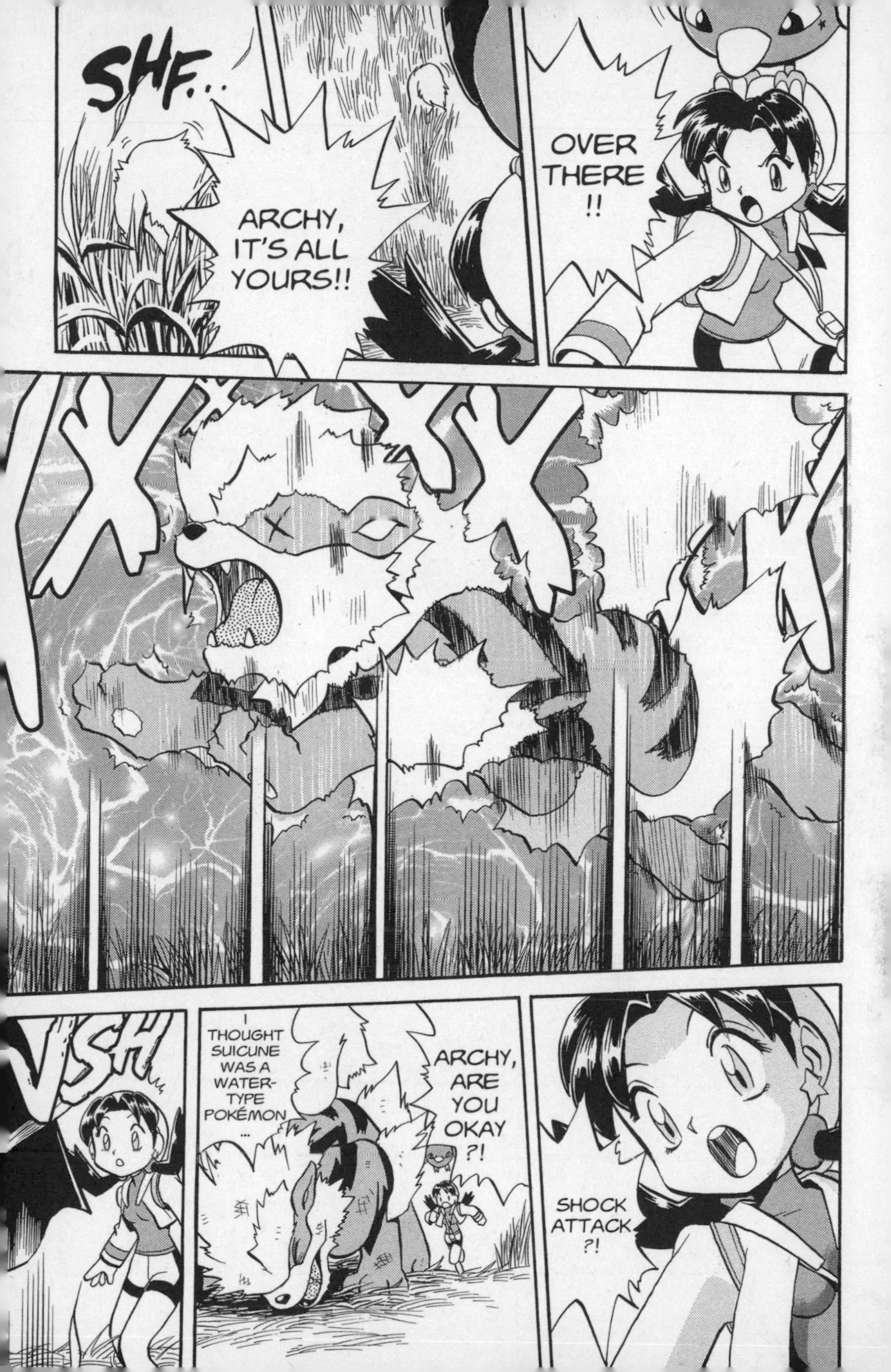
OVER THERE !!
SHF...
ARCHY, IT'S ALL YOURS!!
SHOCK ATTACK ?!
ARCHY, ARE YOU OKAY ?!
I THOUGHT SUICUNE WAS A WATER-TYPE POKÉMON ...

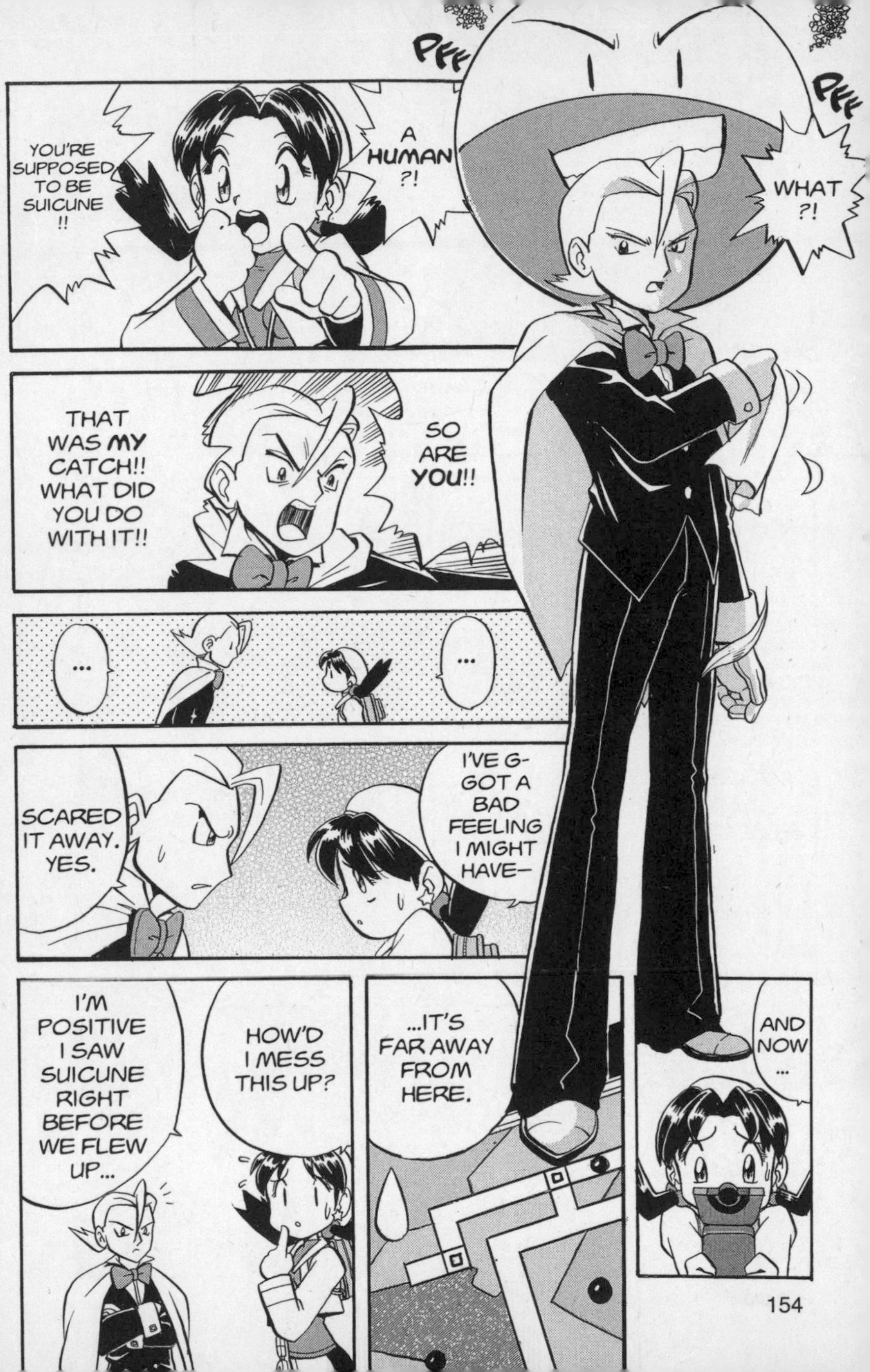
PFF
PFF
WHAT ?!
A HUMAN ?!
YOU'RE SUPPOSED TO BE SUICUNE !!
SO ARE YOU!!
THAT WAS MY CATCH!! WHAT DID YOU DO WITH IT!!
...
...
I'VE G-GOT A BAD FEELING I MIGHT HAVE—
SCARED IT AWAY. YES.
AND NOW ...
...IT'S FAR AWAY FROM HERE.
HOW'D I MESS THIS UP?
I'M POSITIVE I SAW SUICUNE RIGHT BEFORE WE FLEW UP...

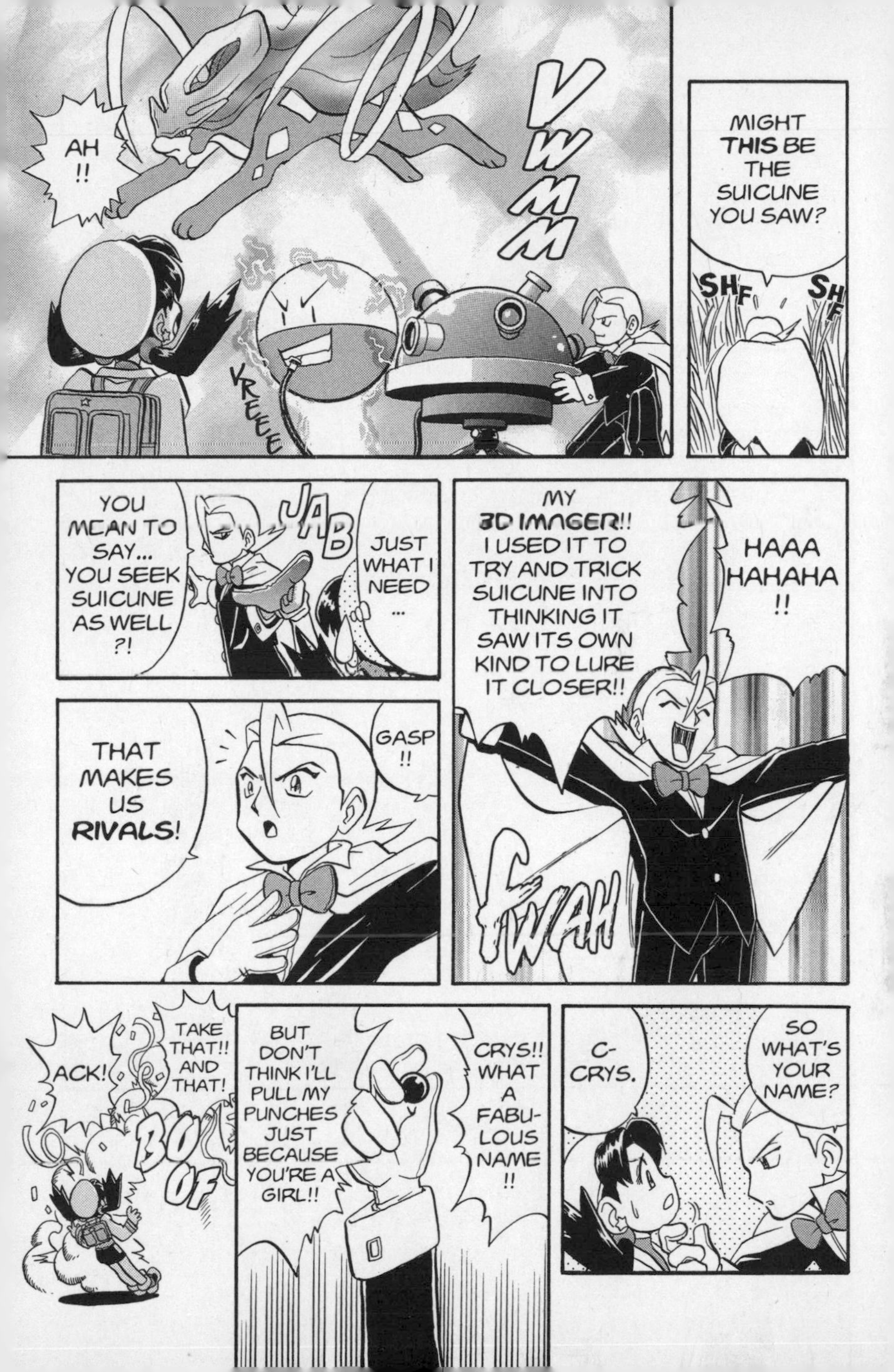
MIGHT THIS BE THE SUICUNE YOU SAW?
SHF SHF
VWMMM
AH !!
VREEEE
MY 3D IMAGER!! I USED IT TO TRY AND TRICK SUICUNE INTO THINKING IT SAW ITS OWN KIND TO LURE IT CLOSER!!
HAAA HAHAHA !!
FWAH
JUST WHAT I NEED ...
YOU MEAN TO SAY... YOU SEEK SUICUNE AS WELL ?!
JAB
GASP !!
THAT MAKES US RIVALS!
SO WHAT'S YOUR NAME?
C-CRYS.
CRYS!! WHAT A FABULOUS NAME !!
BUT DON'T THINK I'LL PULL MY PUNCHES JUST BECAUSE YOU'RE A GIRL!!
TAKE THAT!! AND THAT!
ACK!
BOOF

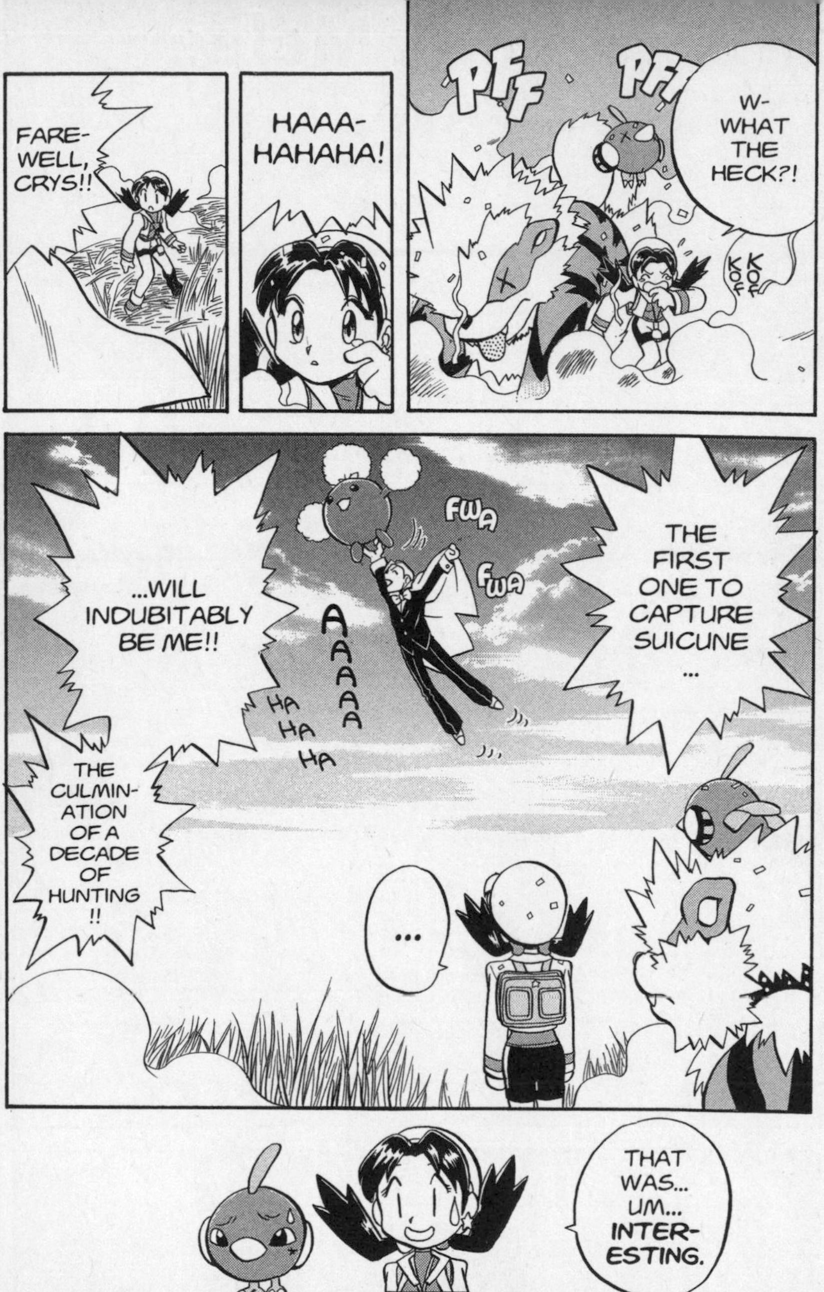
PFF
PFF
W-WHAT THE HECK?!
KOFF KOFF
HAAA-HAHAHA!
FARE-WELL, CRYS!!
THE FIRST ONE TO CAPTURE SUICUNE ...
FWA
FWA
...WILL INDUBITABLY BE ME!!
AAAAAA
HA HA HA
THE CULMIN-ATION OF A DECADE OF HUNTING !!
...
THAT WAS... UM... INTER-ESTING.

127 Miltank Melee

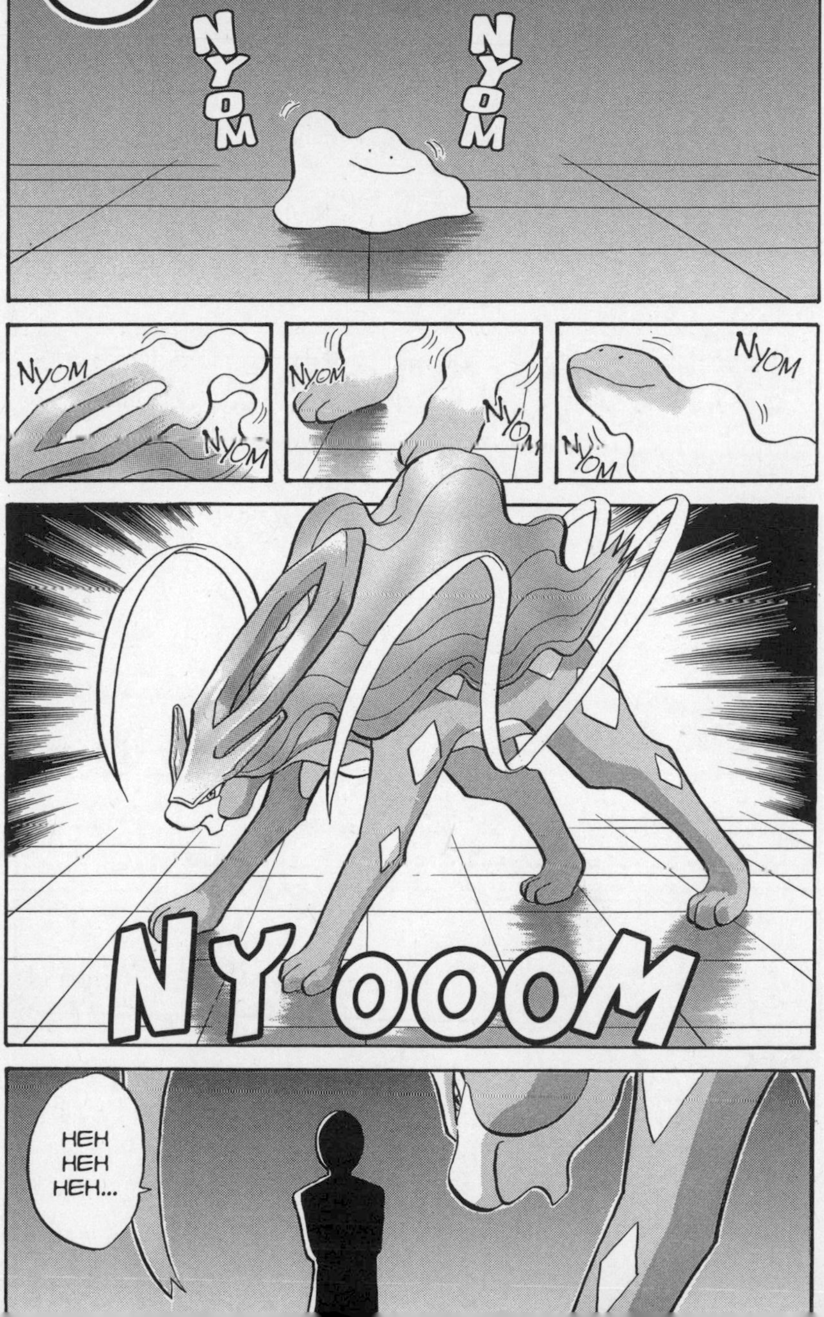

NYOM
NYOM
NYOM
NYOM
NYOM
NYOM
NYOM
NYOM
NYOOOM
HEH HEH HEH...

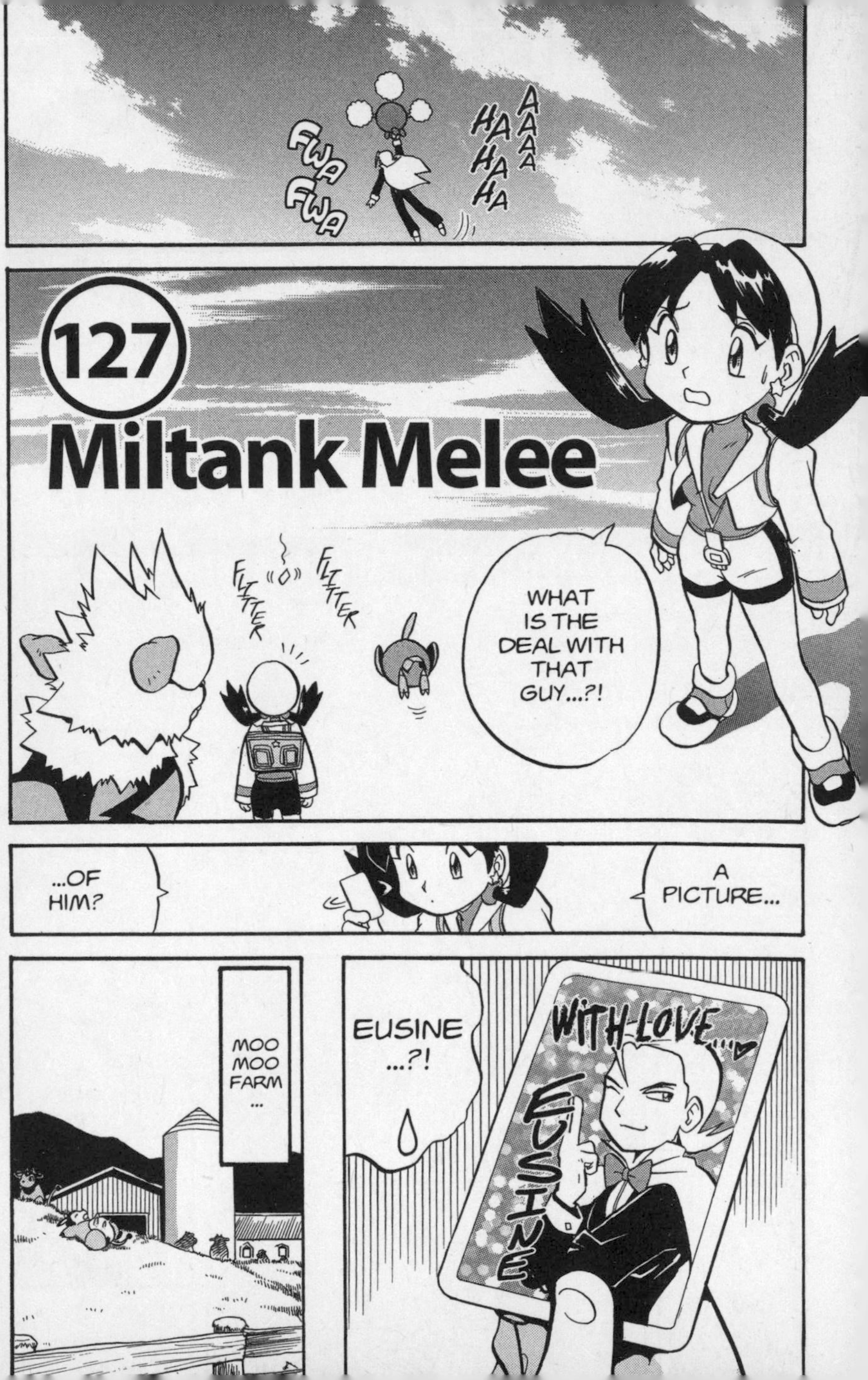

HA HA HA HA AAAA
FWA FWA
127
Miltank Melee
WHAT IS THE DEAL WITH THAT GUY...?!
FLITTER
FLITTER
A PICTURE...
...OF HIM?
WITH LOVE...
EUSINE
EUSINE ...?!
MOO MOO FARM ...

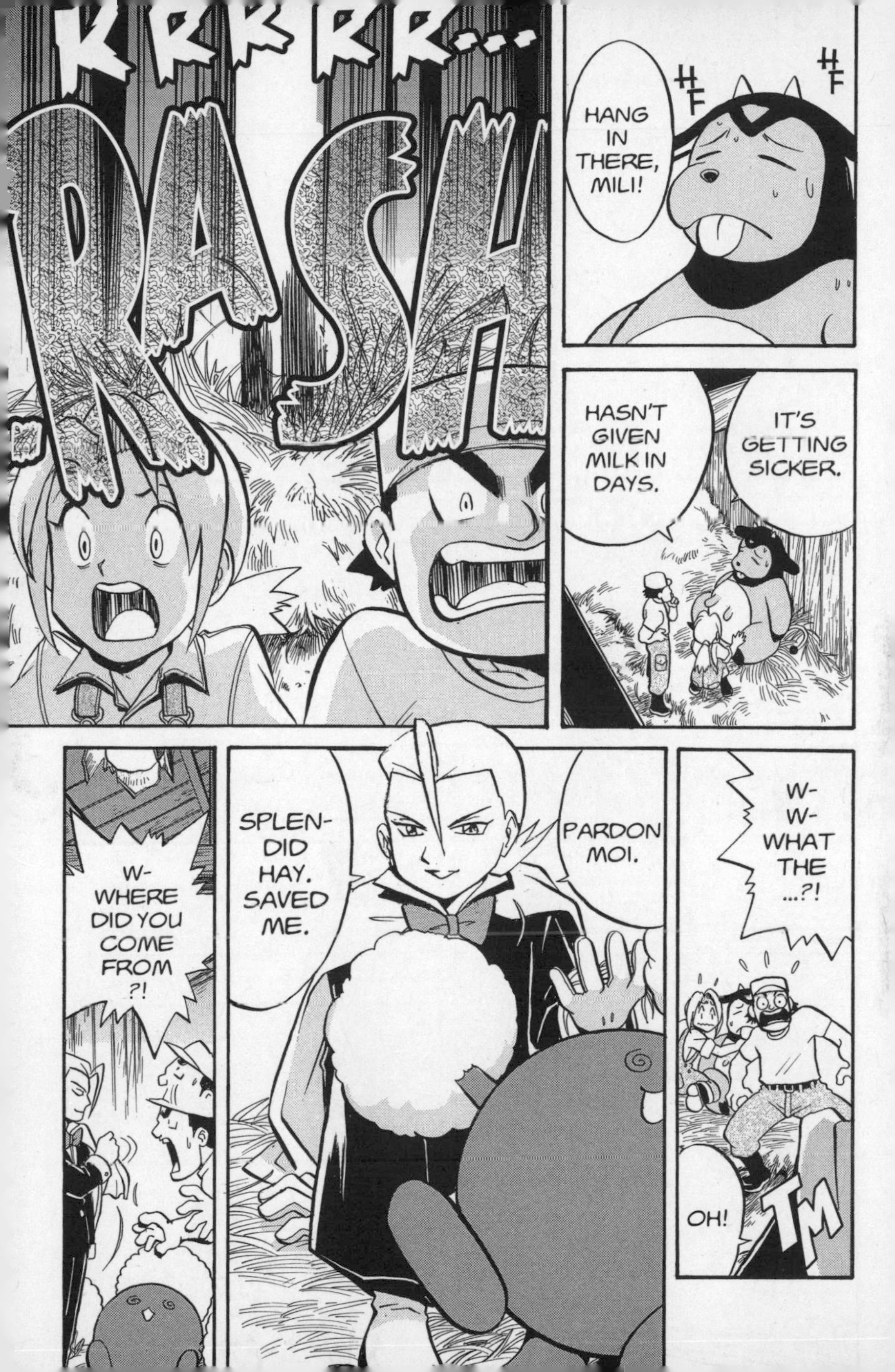
HF HF
HANG IN THERE, MILI!
IT'S GETTING SICKER.
HASN'T GIVEN MILK IN DAYS.
KRK RR...
RASH
W-W-WHAT THE ...?!
OH!
TM
PARDON MOI.
SPLEN-DID HAY. SAVED ME.
W-WHERE DID YOU COME FROM ?!

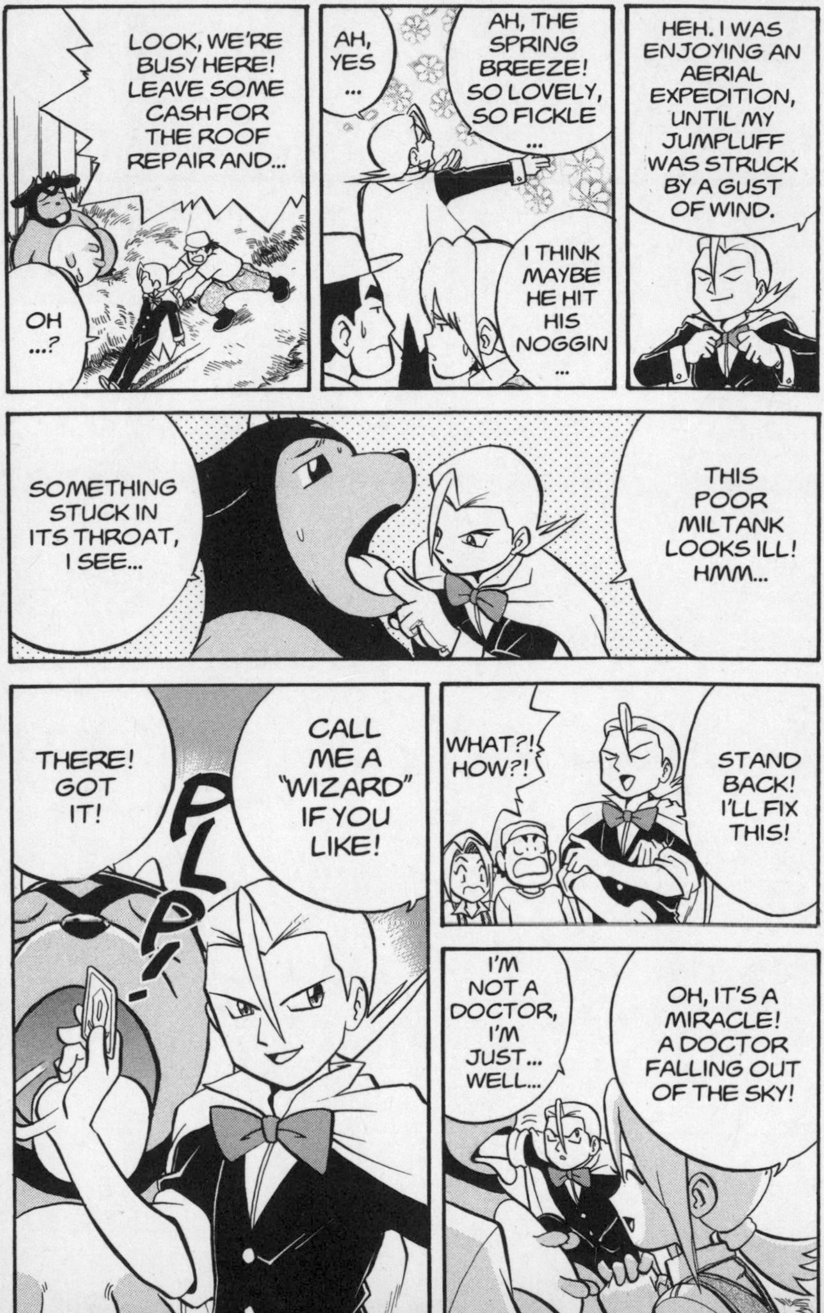
HEH. I WAS ENJOYING AN AERIAL EXPEDITION, UNTIL MY JUMPLUFF WAS STRUCK BY A GUST OF WIND.
AH, THE SPRING BREEZE! SO LOVELY, SO FICKLE...
AH, YES...
I THINK MAYBE HE HIT HIS NOGGIN...
LOOK, WE'RE BUSY HERE! LEAVE SOME CASH FOR THE ROOF REPAIR AND...
OH...?
THIS POOR MILTANK LOOKS ILL! HMM...
SOMETHING STUCK IN ITS THROAT, I SEE...
STAND BACK! I'LL FIX THIS!
WHAT?! HOW?!
OH, IT'S A MIRACLE! A DOCTOR FALLING OUT OF THE SKY!
I'M NOT A DOCTOR, I'M JUST... WELL...
CALL ME A "WIZARD" IF YOU LIKE!
THERE! GOT IT!
PLP!

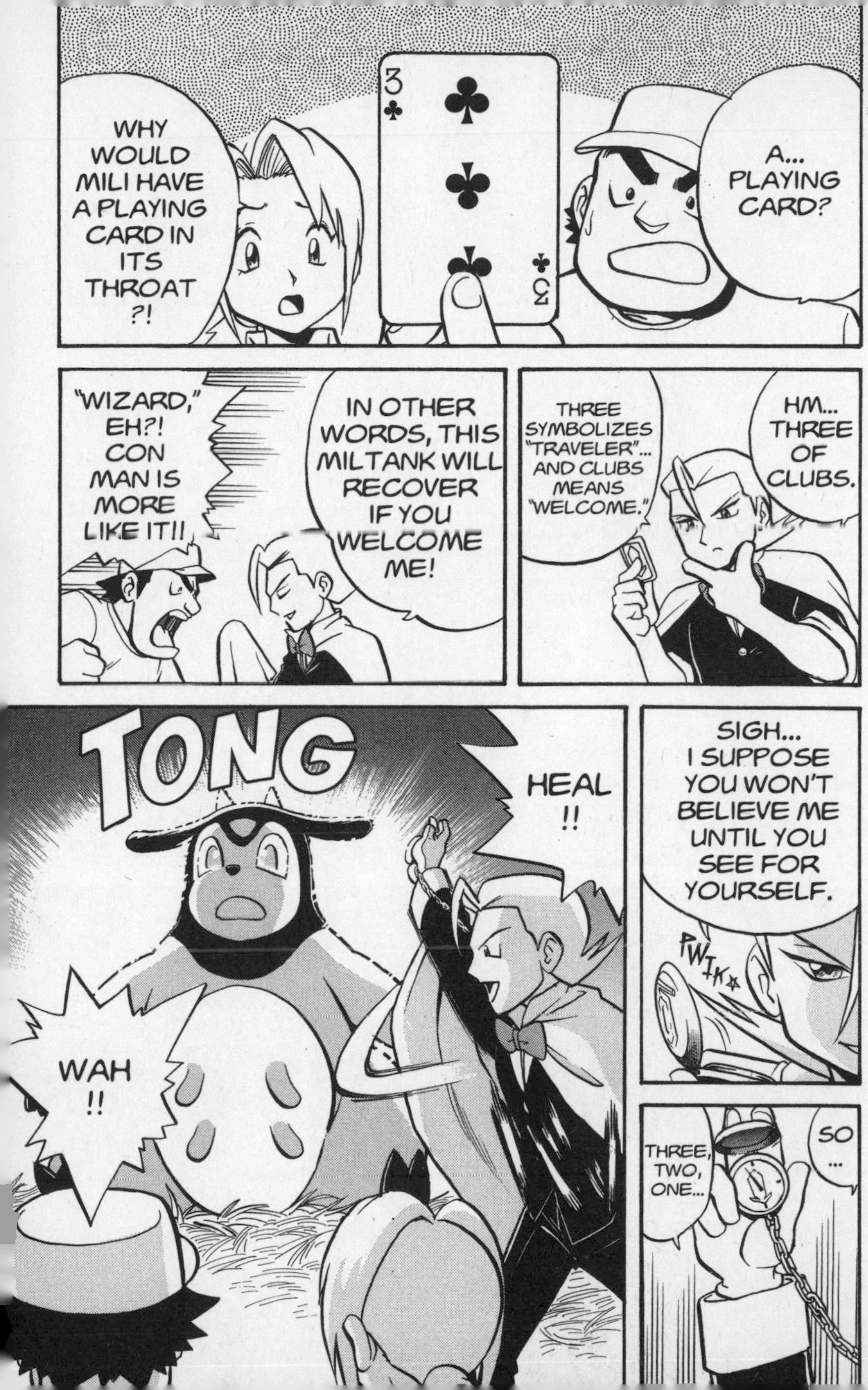
A... PLAYING CARD?
WHY WOULD MILI HAVE A PLAYING CARD IN ITS THROAT ?!
HM... THREE OF CLUBS.
THREE SYMBOLIZES "TRAVELER"... AND CLUBS MEANS "WELCOME."
IN OTHER WORDS, THIS MILTANK WILL RECOVER IF YOU WELCOME ME!
"WIZARD," EH?! CON MAN IS MORE LIKE IT!!
SIGH... I SUPPOSE YOU WON'T BELIEVE ME UNTIL YOU SEE FOR YOURSELF.
PWIK
SO...
THREE, TWO, ONE...
HEAL!!
TONG
WAH!!

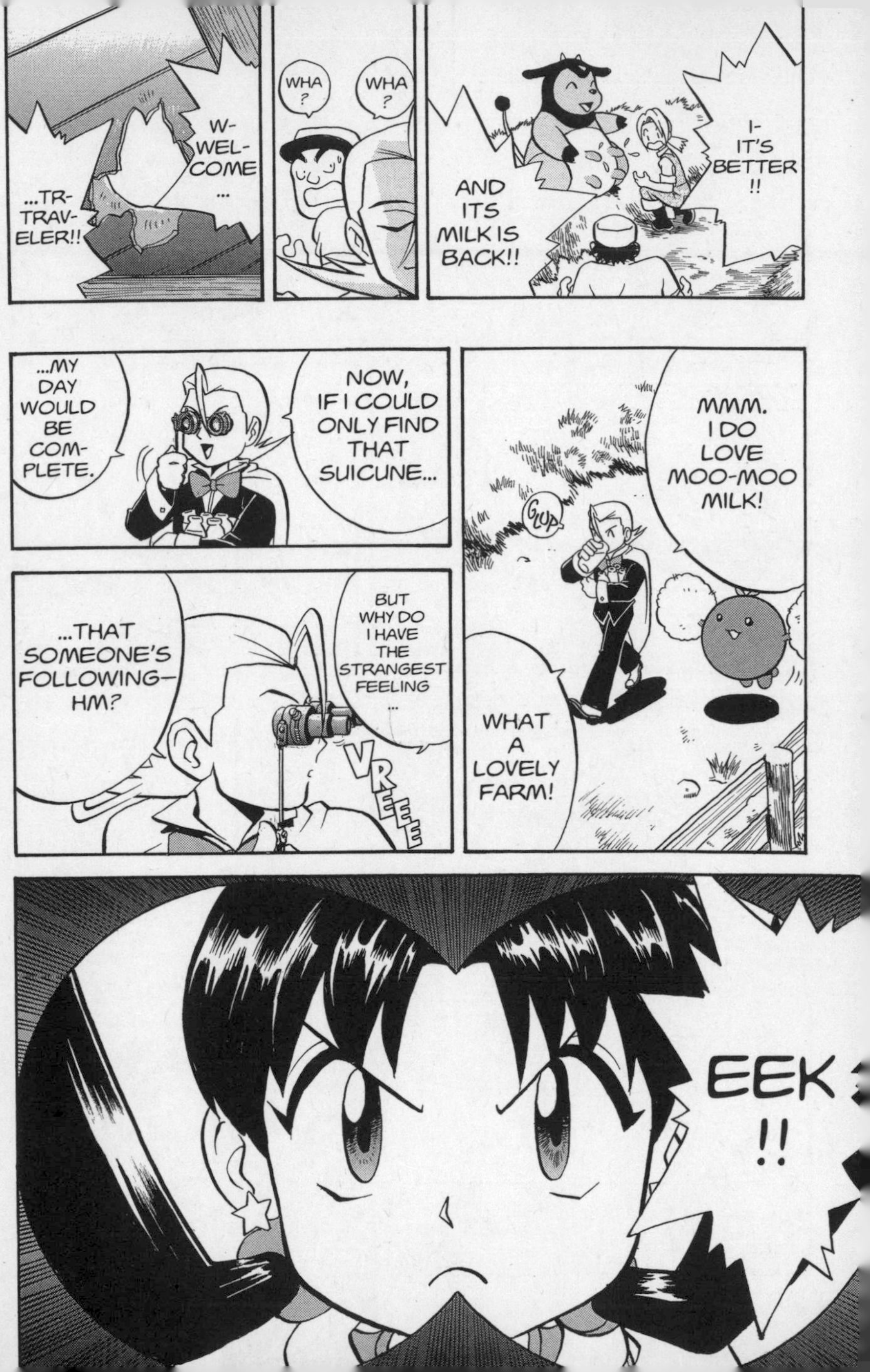
I- IT'S BETTER !!
AND ITS MILK IS BACK!!
WHA ?
WHA ?
W- WEL- COME ...
...TR- TRAV- ELER!!
MMM. I DO LOVE MOO-MOO MILK!
GLUP
WHAT A LOVELY FARM!
NOW, IF I COULD ONLY FIND THAT SUICUNE...
...MY DAY WOULD BE COM- PLETE.
BUT WHY DO I HAVE THE STRANGEST FEELING ...
...THAT SOMEONE'S FOLLOWING— HM?
VREEE
EEK !!

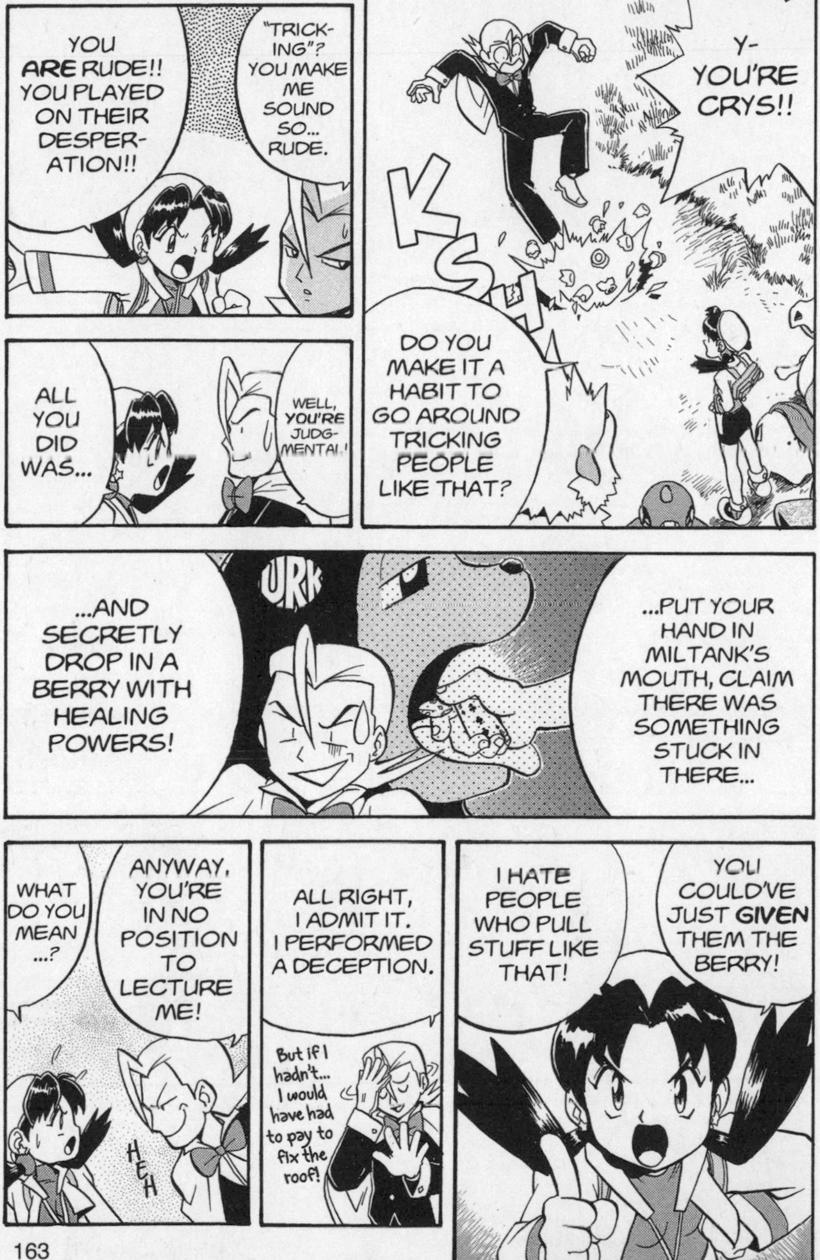
Y- YOU'RE CRYS!!
KSSH
DO YOU MAKE IT A HABIT TO GO AROUND TRICKING PEOPLE LIKE THAT?
"TRICK-ING"? YOU MAKE ME SOUND SO... RUDE.
YOU ARE RUDE!! YOU PLAYED ON THEIR DESPER-ATION!!
WELL, YOU'RE JUDG-MENTAL!
ALL YOU DID WAS...
...PUT YOUR HAND IN MILTANK'S MOUTH, CLAIM THERE WAS SOMETHING STUCK IN THERE...
URK
...AND SECRETLY DROP IN A BERRY WITH HEALING POWERS!
YOU COULD'VE JUST GIVEN THEM THE BERRY!
I HATE PEOPLE WHO PULL STUFF LIKE THAT!
ALL RIGHT, I ADMIT IT. I PERFORMED A DECEPTION.
But if I hadn't... I would have had to pay to fix the roof!
ANYWAY, YOU'RE IN NO POSITION TO LECTURE ME!
WHAT DO YOU MEAN ...?
HEH

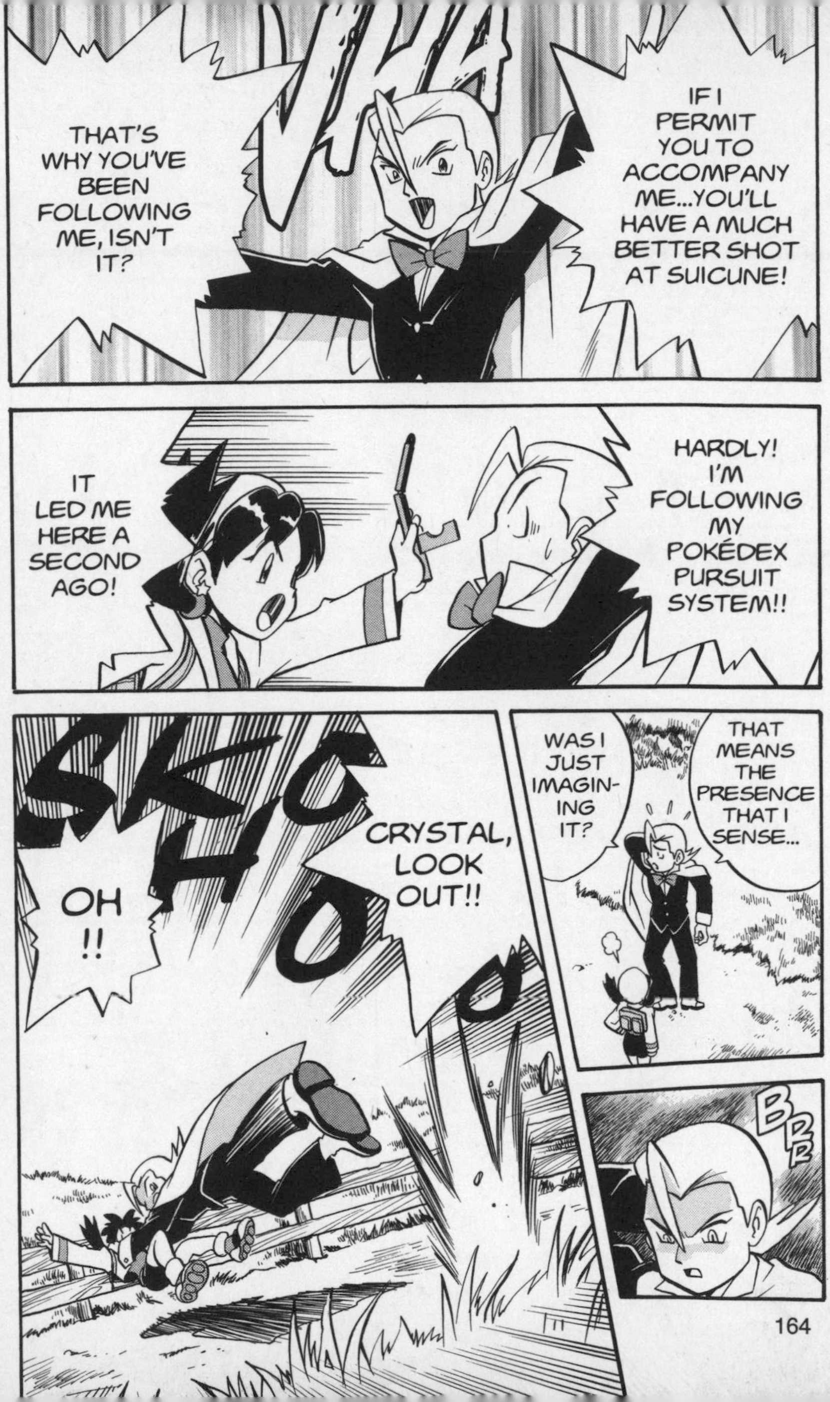
IF I PERMIT YOU TO ACCOMPANY ME...YOU'LL HAVE A MUCH BETTER SHOT AT SUICUNE!
THAT'S WHY YOU'VE BEEN FOLLOWING ME, ISN'T IT?
HARDLY! I'M FOLLOWING MY POKÉDEX PURSUIT SYSTEM!!
IT LED ME HERE A SECOND AGO!
THAT MEANS THE PRESENCE THAT I SENSE...
WAS I JUST IMAGINING IT?
BRR
CRYSTAL, LOOK OUT!!
OH !!

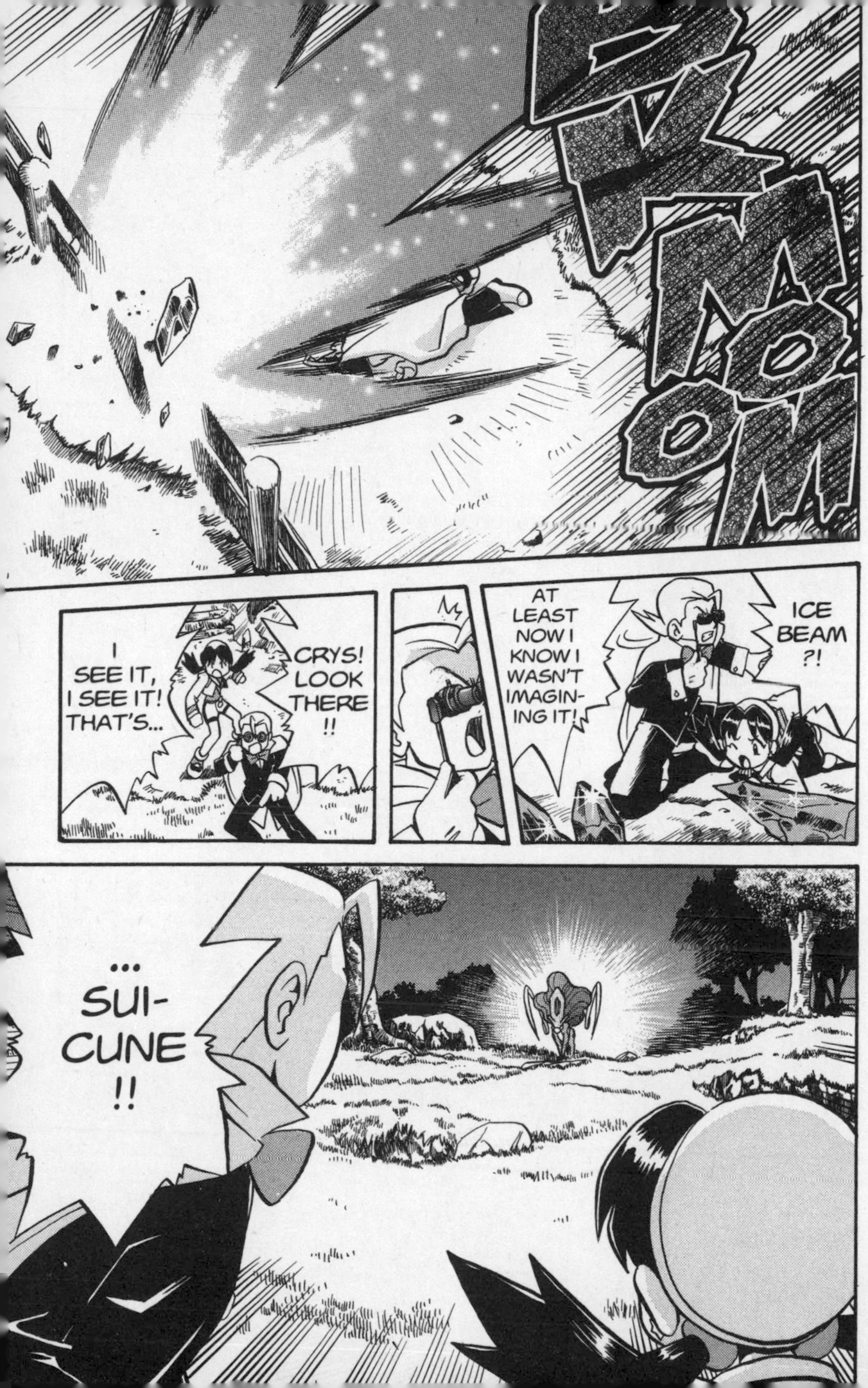
ICE BEAM ?!
AT LEAST NOW I KNOW I WASN'T IMAGIN-ING IT!
CRYS! LOOK THERE !!
I SEE IT, I SEE IT! THAT'S...
... SUI-CUNE !!

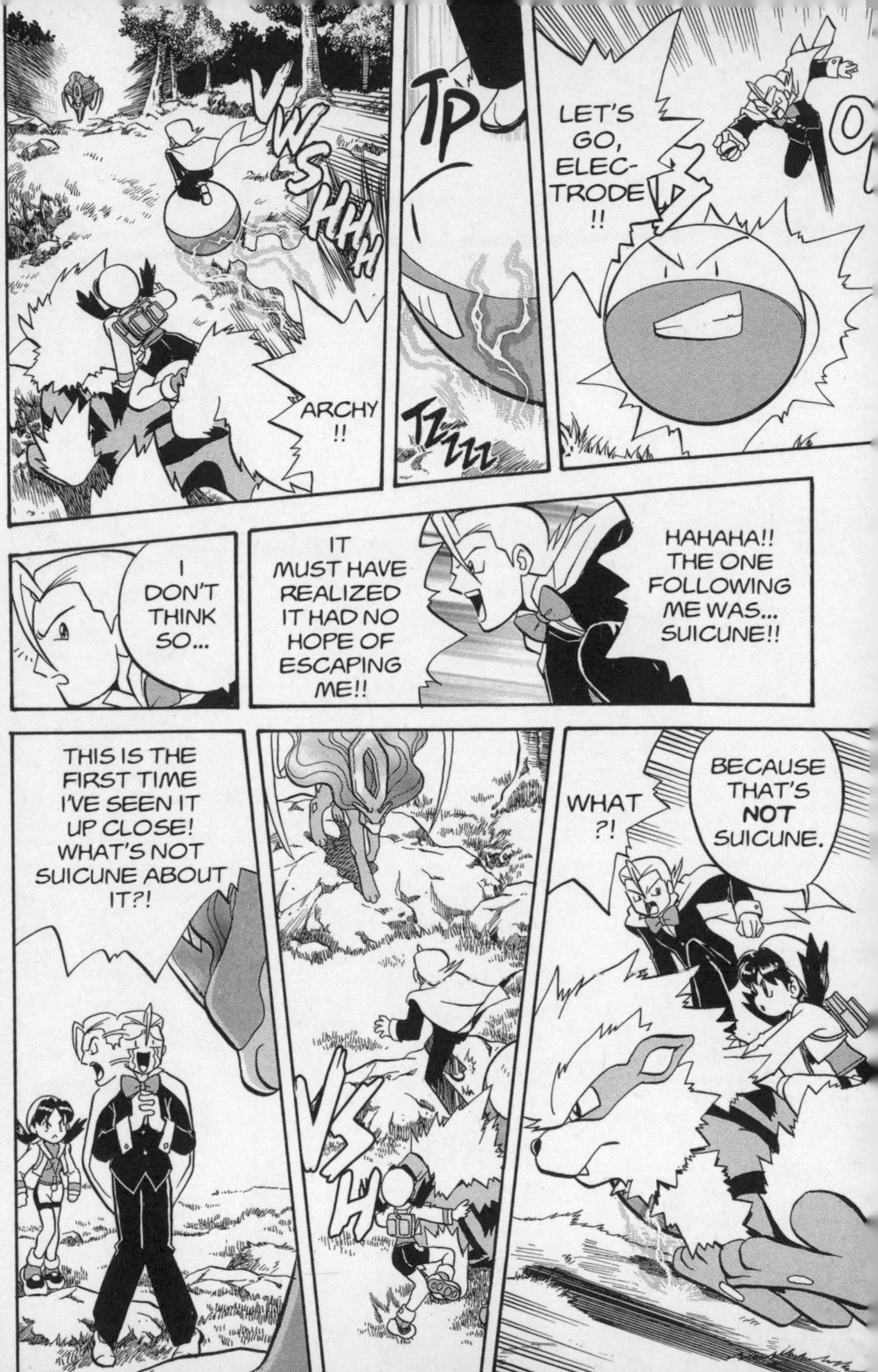
LET'S GO, ELECTRODE!!
TP
TZZZZ
VWSHHHH
ARCHY!!
HAHAHA!! THE ONE FOLLOWING ME WAS... SUICUNE!!
IT MUST HAVE REALIZED IT HAD NO HOPE OF ESCAPING ME!!
I DON'T THINK SO...
BECAUSE THAT'S **NOT** SUICUNE.
WHAT?!
VSH
THIS IS THE FIRST TIME I'VE SEEN IT UP CLOSE! WHAT'S NOT SUICUNE ABOUT IT?!

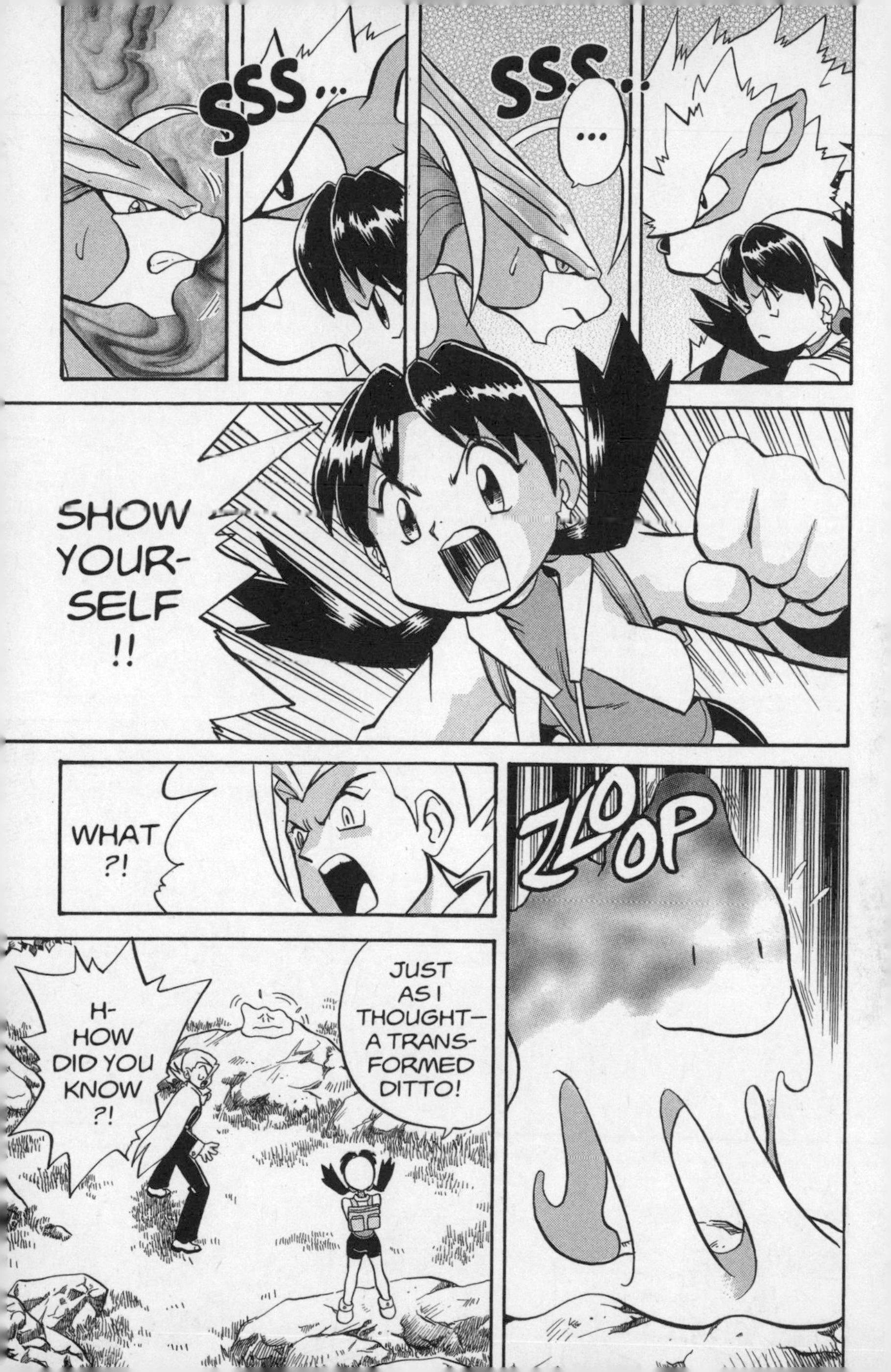
SSS...
...
SSS...
SHOW YOURSELF!!
ZLOOP
WHAT?!
JUST AS I THOUGHT—A TRANSFORMED DITTO!
H-HOW DID YOU KNOW?!

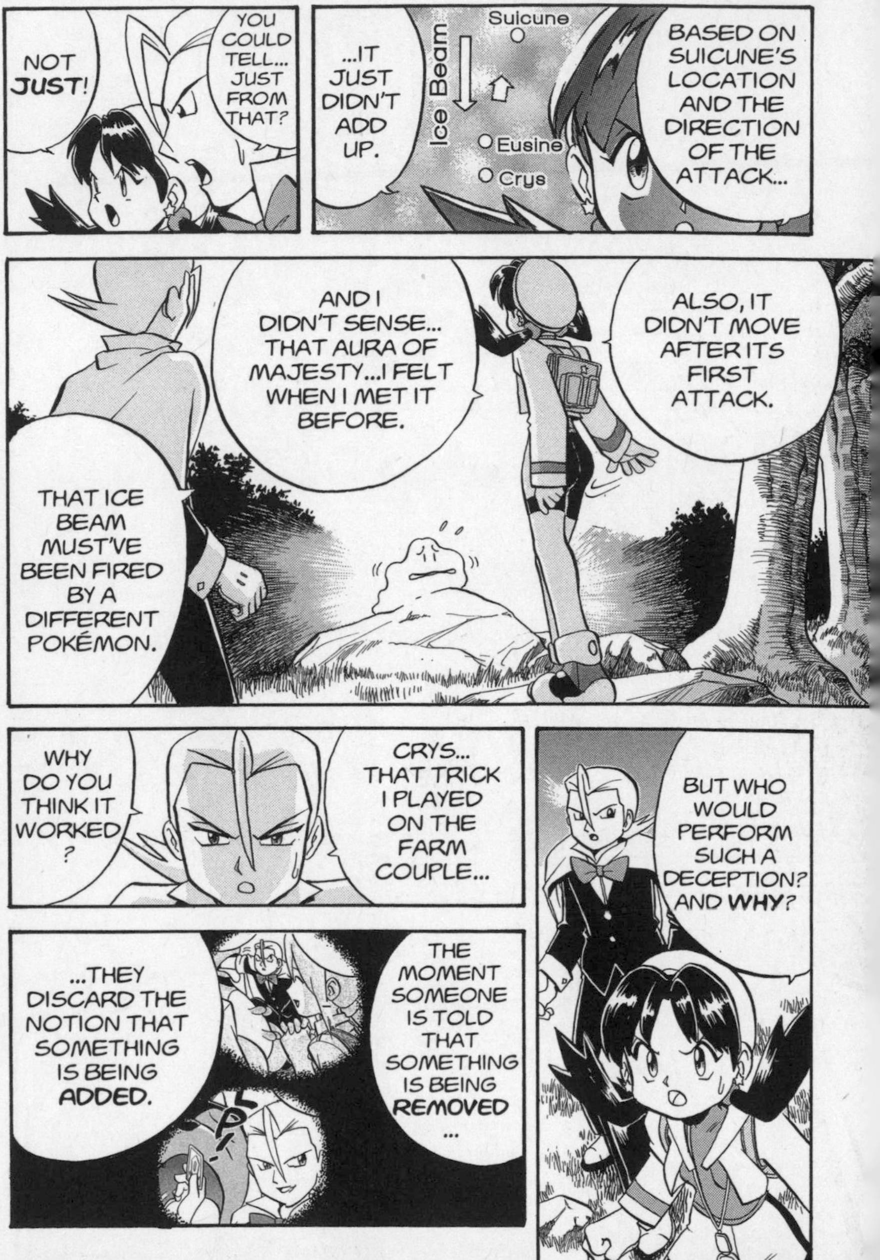
BASED ON SUICUNE'S LOCATION AND THE DIRECTION OF THE ATTACK...
Suicune
Ice Beam
Eusine
Crys
...IT JUST DIDN'T ADD UP.
YOU COULD TELL... JUST FROM THAT?
NOT **JUST**!
ALSO, IT DIDN'T MOVE AFTER ITS FIRST ATTACK.
AND I DIDN'T SENSE... THAT AURA OF MAJESTY...I FELT WHEN I MET IT BEFORE.
THAT ICE BEAM MUST'VE BEEN FIRED BY A DIFFERENT POKÉMON.
BUT WHO WOULD PERFORM SUCH A DECEPTION? AND **WHY**?
CRYS... THAT TRICK I PLAYED ON THE FARM COUPLE...
WHY DO YOU THINK IT WORKED?
THE MOMENT SOMEONE IS TOLD THAT SOMETHING IS BEING **REMOVED**...
...THEY DISCARD THE NOTION THAT SOMETHING IS BEING **ADDED**.

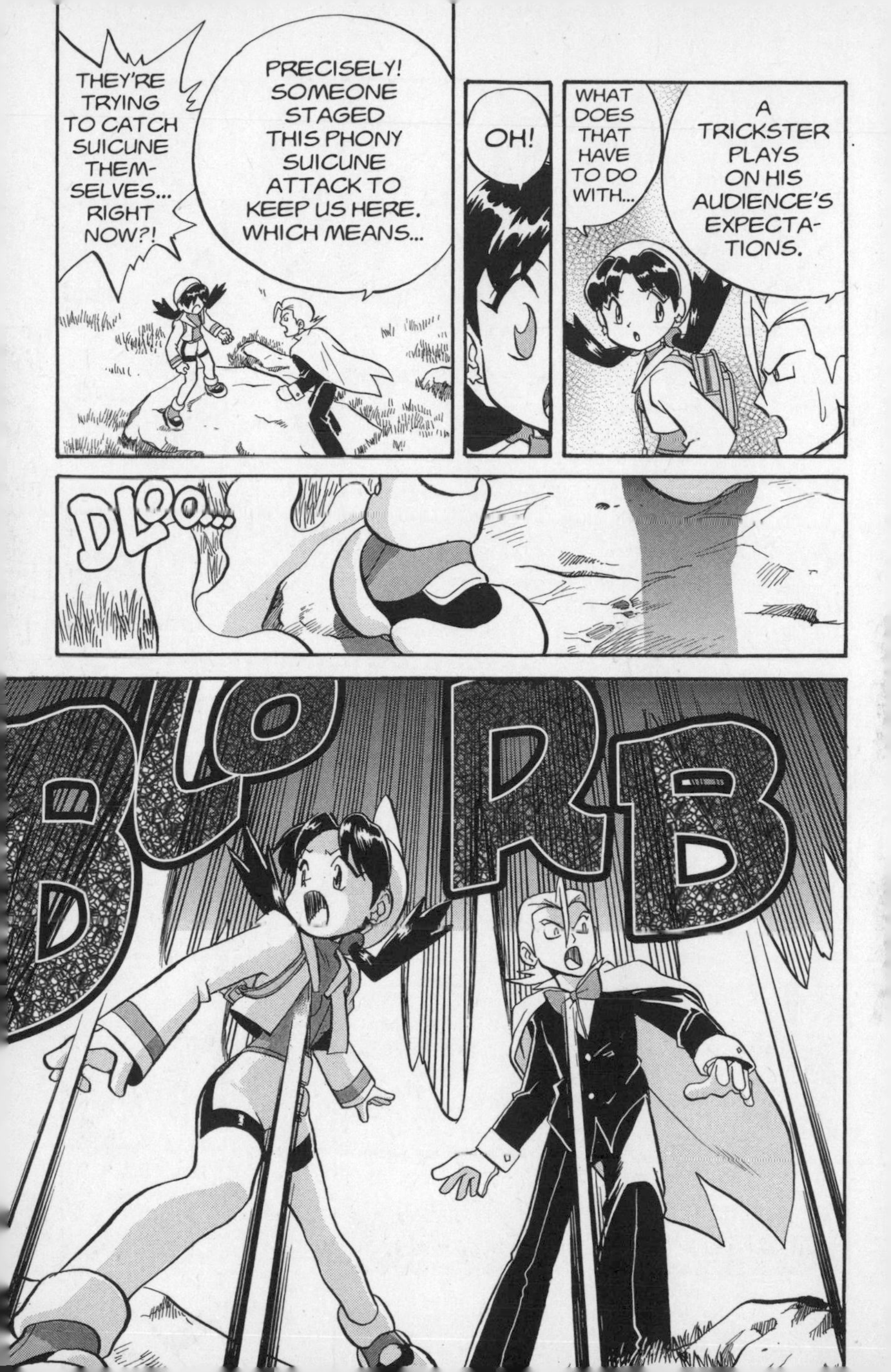
A TRICKSTER PLAYS ON HIS AUDIENCE'S EXPECTATIONS.
WHAT DOES THAT HAVE TO DO WITH...
OH!
PRECISELY! SOMEONE STAGED THIS PHONY SUICUNE ATTACK TO KEEP US HERE. WHICH MEANS...
THEY'RE TRYING TO CATCH SUICUNE THEMSELVES... RIGHT NOW?!
DLOO...
BLORB

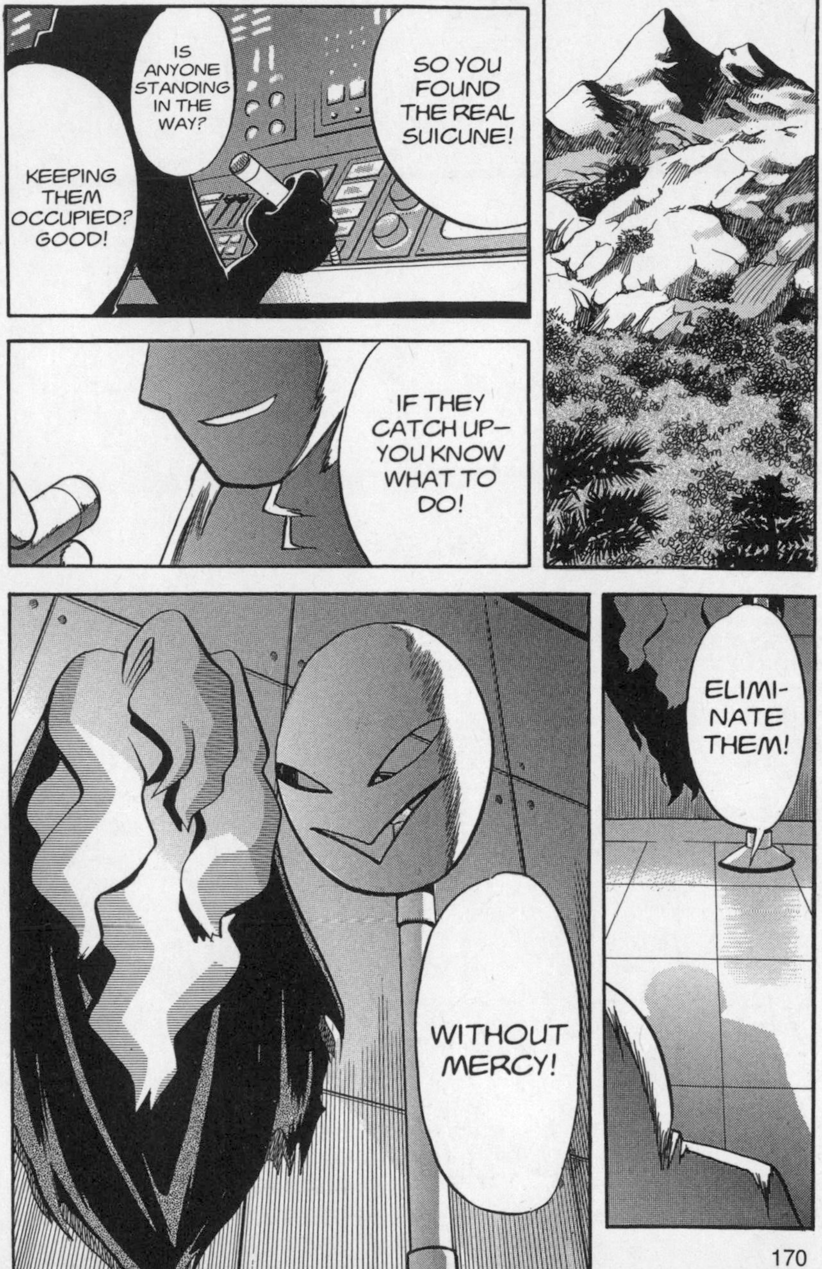
SO YOU FOUND THE REAL SUICUNE!
IS ANYONE STANDING IN THE WAY?
KEEPING THEM OCCUPIED? GOOD!
IF THEY CATCH UP—YOU KNOW WHAT TO DO!
ELIMI-NATE THEM!
WITHOUT MERCY!

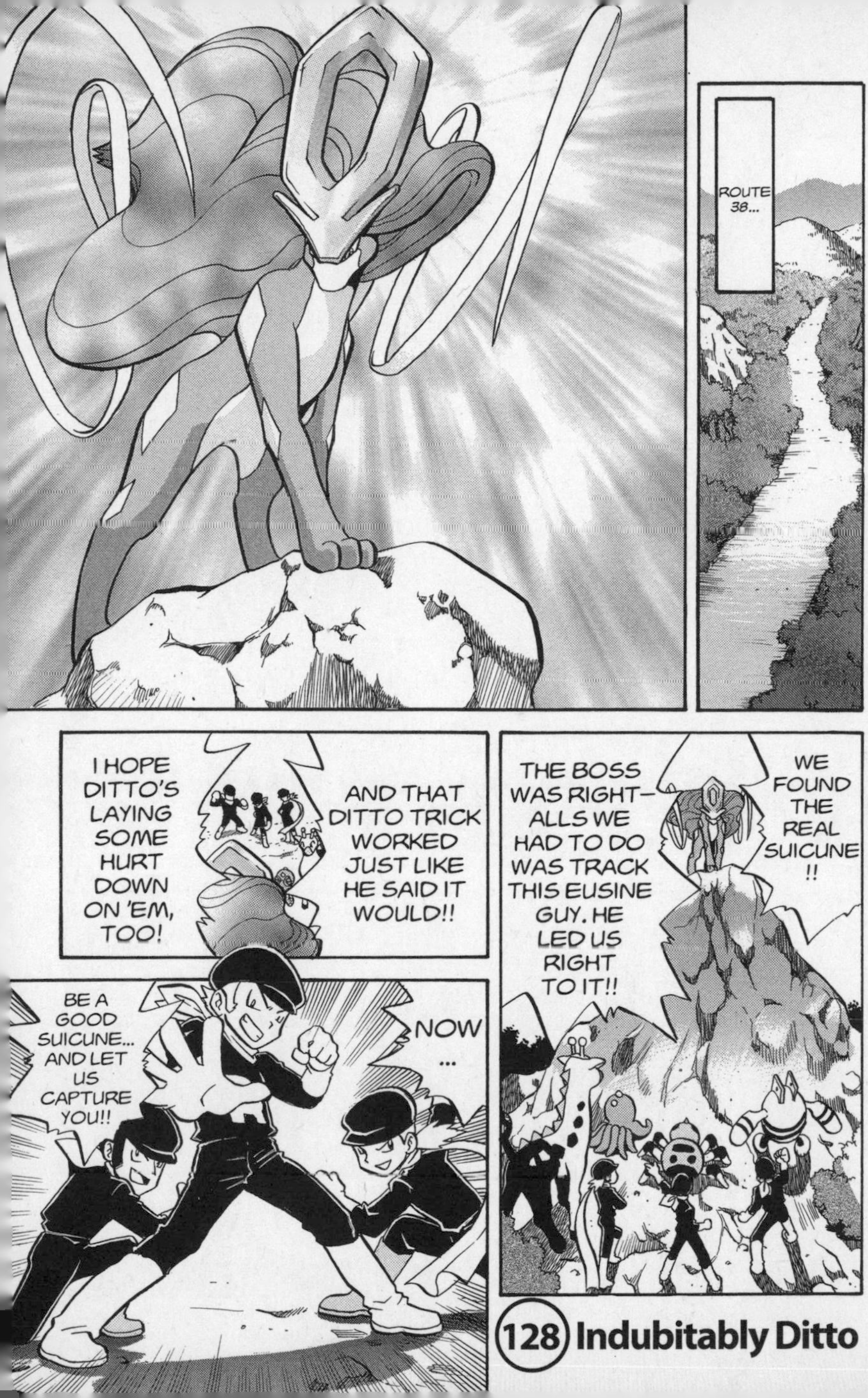
ROUTE 38...
WE FOUND THE REAL SUICUNE!!
THE BOSS WAS RIGHT—ALLS WE HAD TO DO WAS TRACK THIS EUSINE GUY. HE LED US RIGHT TO IT!!
AND THAT DITTO TRICK WORKED JUST LIKE HE SAID IT WOULD!!
I HOPE DITTO'S LAYING SOME HURT DOWN ON 'EM, TOO!
NOW...
BE A GOOD SUICUNE... AND LET US CAPTURE YOU!!

128 Indubitably Ditto

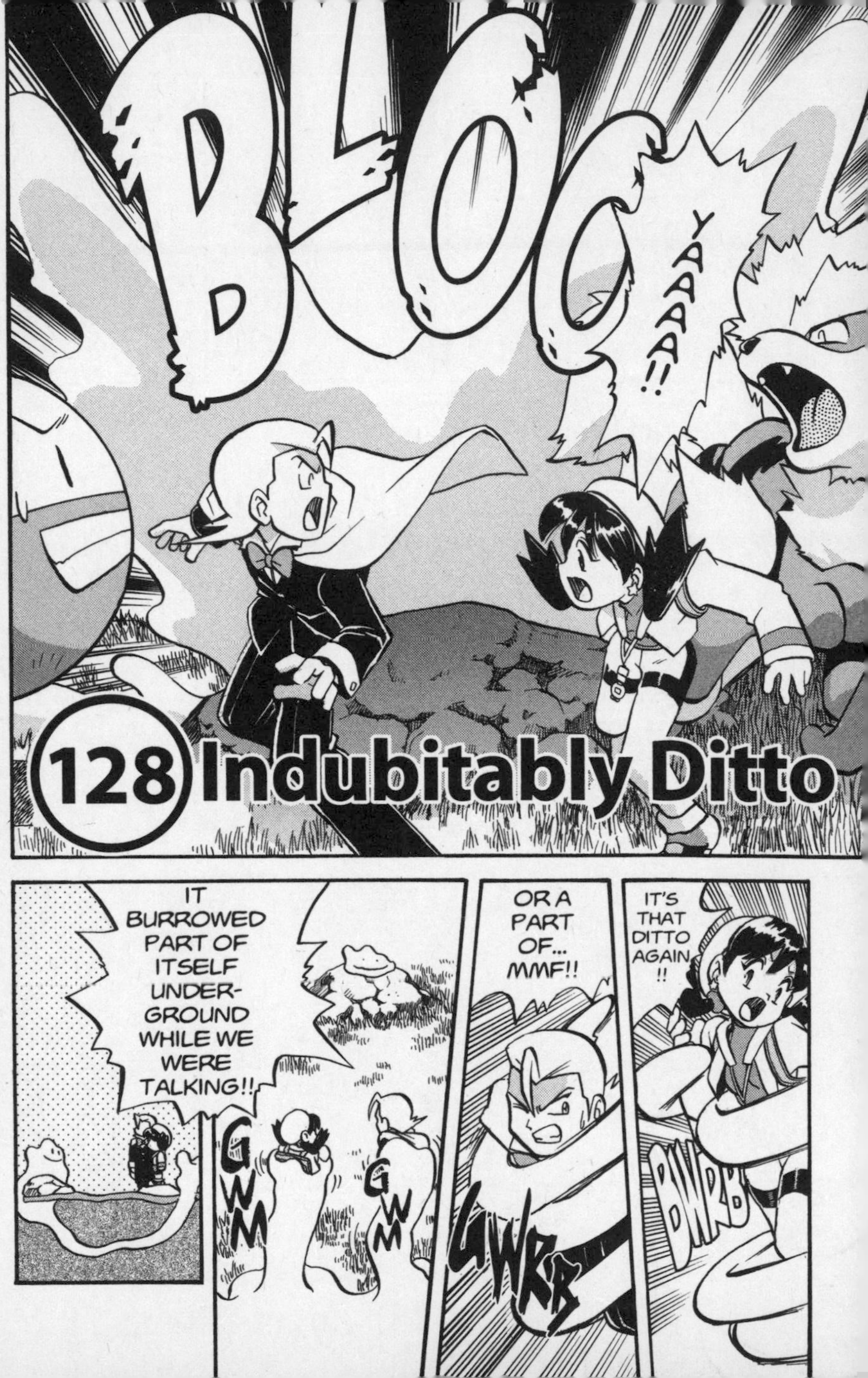
BLOO
YAAAAA!!
128 Indubitably Ditto
IT'S THAT DITTO AGAIN!!
OR A PART OF... MMF!!
IT BURROWED PART OF ITSELF UNDER-GROUND WHILE WE WERE TALKING!!
GWM
GWM

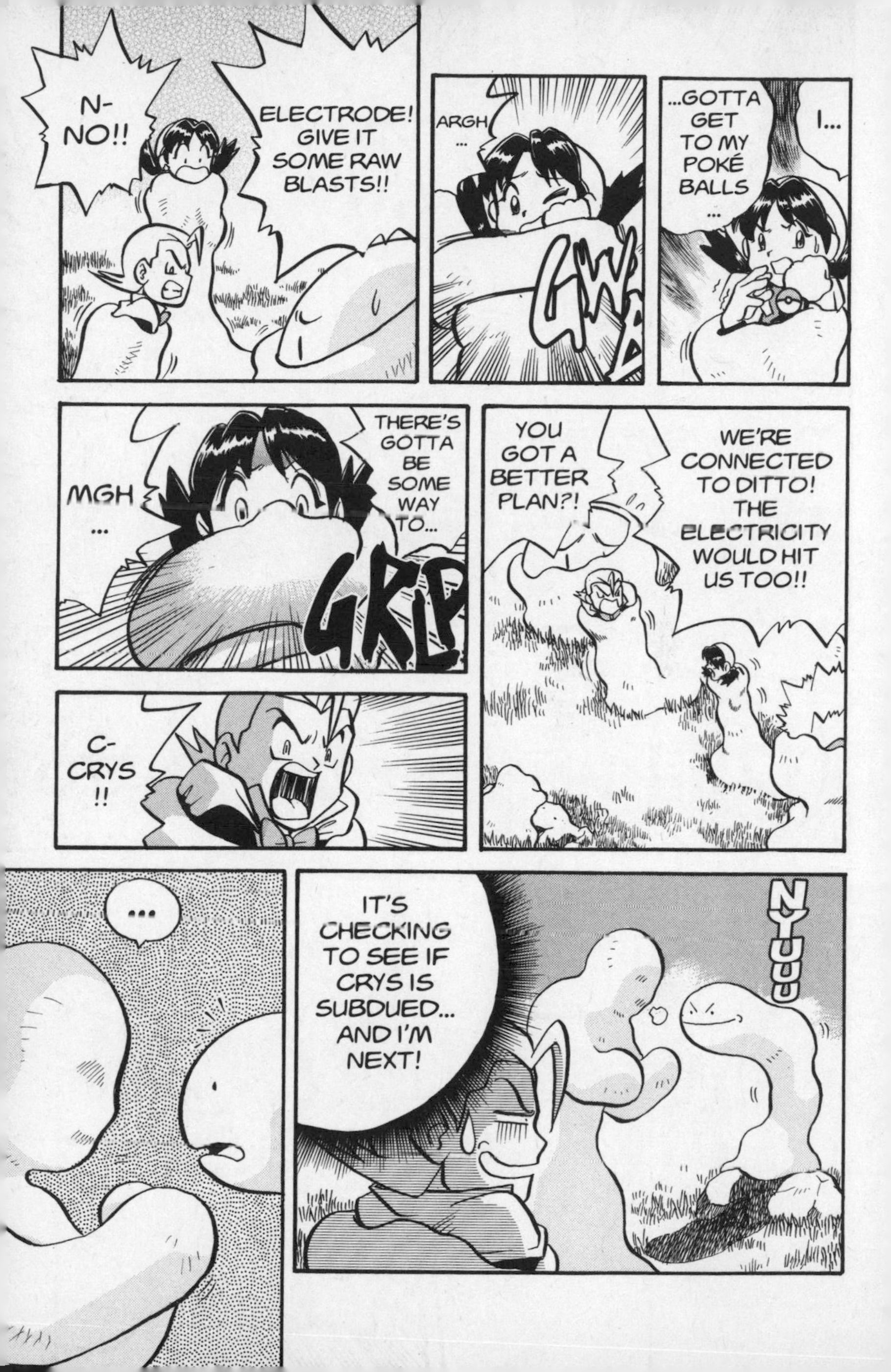
I...
...GOTTA GET TO MY POKÉ BALLS ...
ARGH ...
ELECTRODE! GIVE IT SOME RAW BLASTS!!
N- NO!!
WE'RE CONNECTED TO DITTO! THE ELECTRICITY WOULD HIT US TOO!!
YOU GOT A BETTER PLAN?!
THERE'S GOTTA BE SOME WAY TO...
MGH ...
GRIP
C- CRYS !!
NYUUU
IT'S CHECKING TO SEE IF CRYS IS SUBDUED... AND I'M NEXT!
...

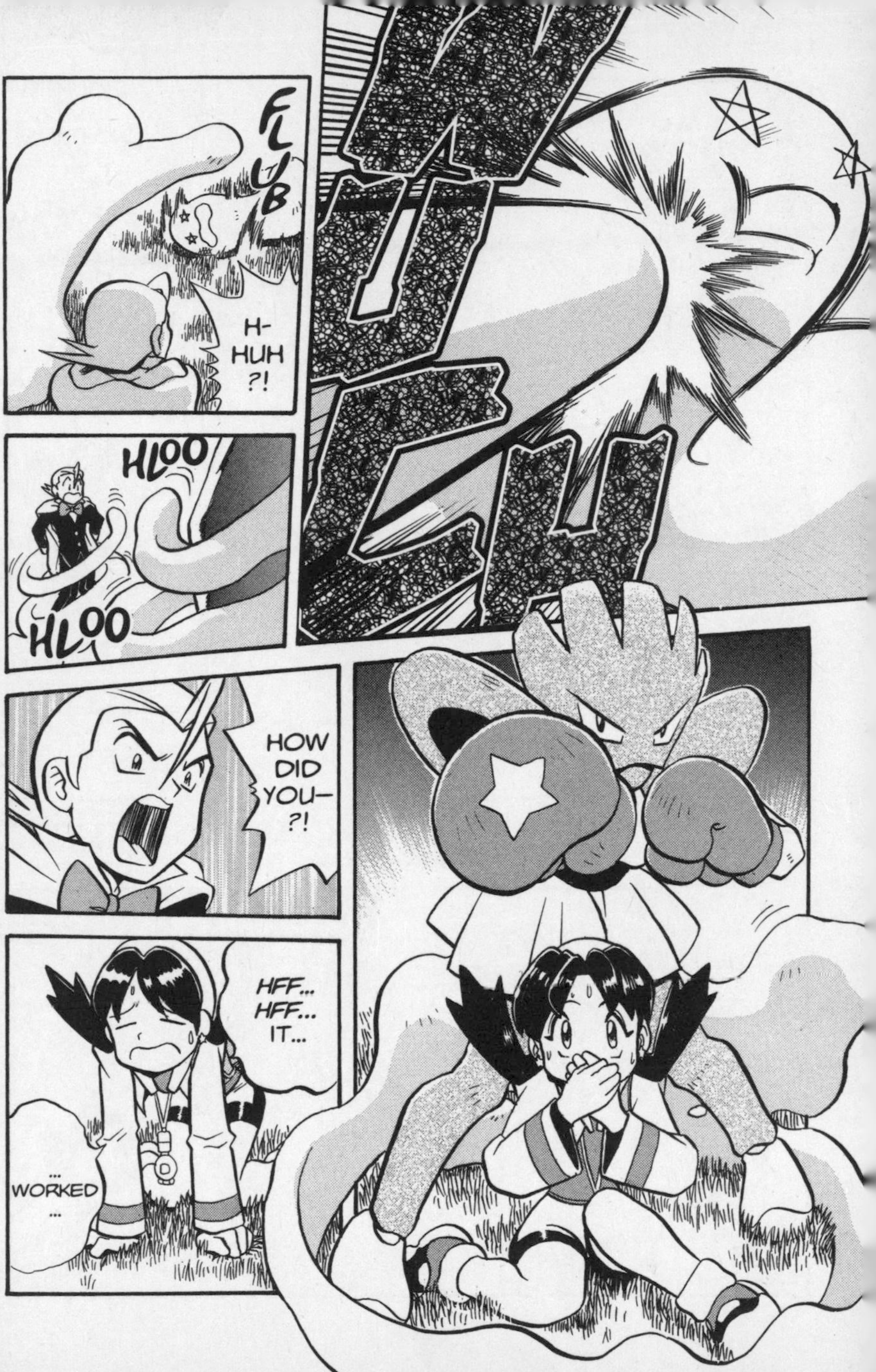
FLUB
H-HUH ?!
HLOO
HLOO
HOW DID YOU— ?!
HFF... HFF... IT...
...WORKED...

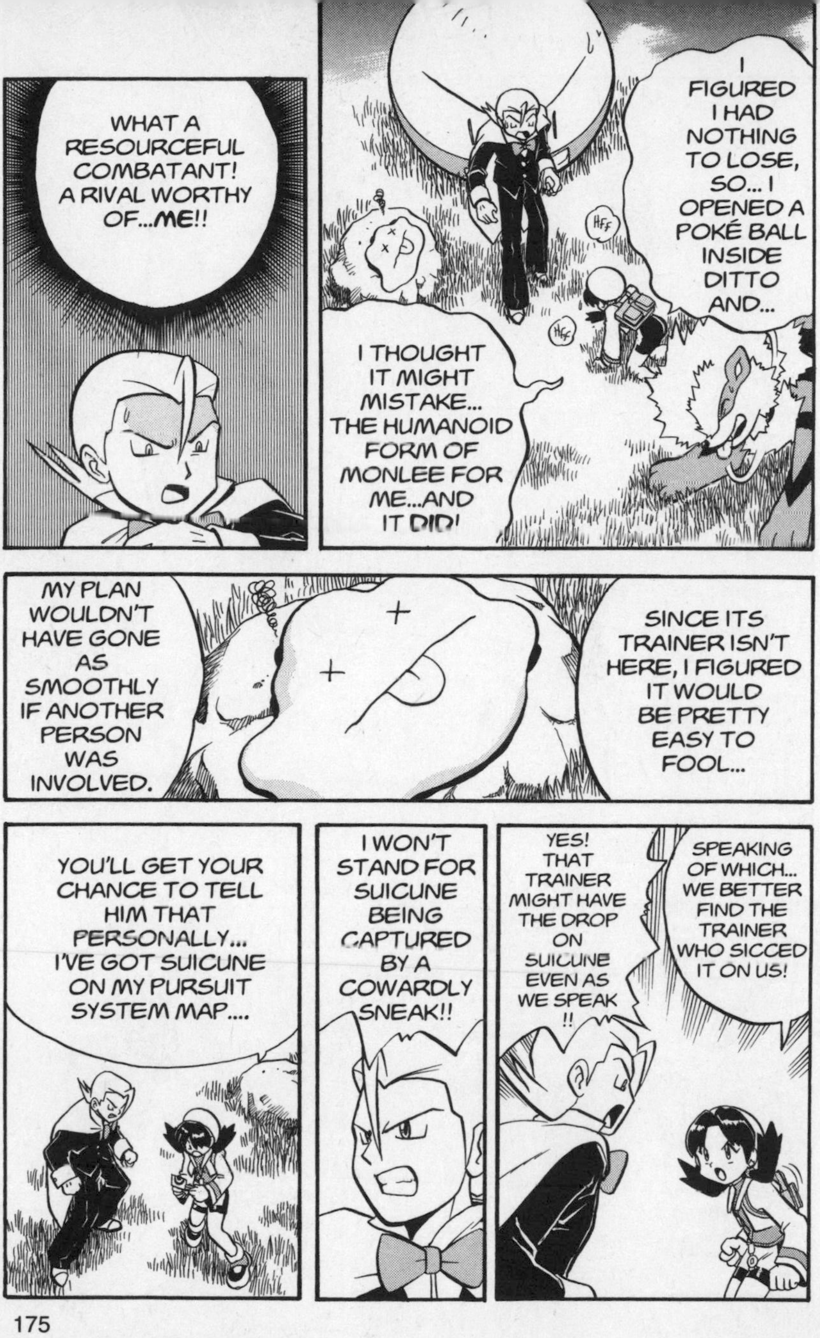

I FIGURED I HAD NOTHING TO LOSE, SO... I OPENED A POKÉ BALL INSIDE DITTO AND...
HFF
HFF
I THOUGHT IT MIGHT MISTAKE... THE HUMANOID FORM OF MONLEE FOR ME...AND IT DID!
WHAT A RESOURCEFUL COMBATANT! A RIVAL WORTHY OF...ME!!
SINCE ITS TRAINER ISN'T HERE, I FIGURED IT WOULD BE PRETTY EASY TO FOOL...
MY PLAN WOULDN'T HAVE GONE AS SMOOTHLY IF ANOTHER PERSON WAS INVOLVED.
SPEAKING OF WHICH... WE BETTER FIND THE TRAINER WHO SICCED IT ON US!
YES! THAT TRAINER MIGHT HAVE THE DROP ON SUICUNE EVEN AS WE SPEAK !!
I WON'T STAND FOR SUICUNE BEING CAPTURED BY A COWARDLY SNEAK!!
YOU'LL GET YOUR CHANCE TO TELL HIM THAT PERSONALLY... I'VE GOT SUICUNE ON MY PURSUIT SYSTEM MAP....

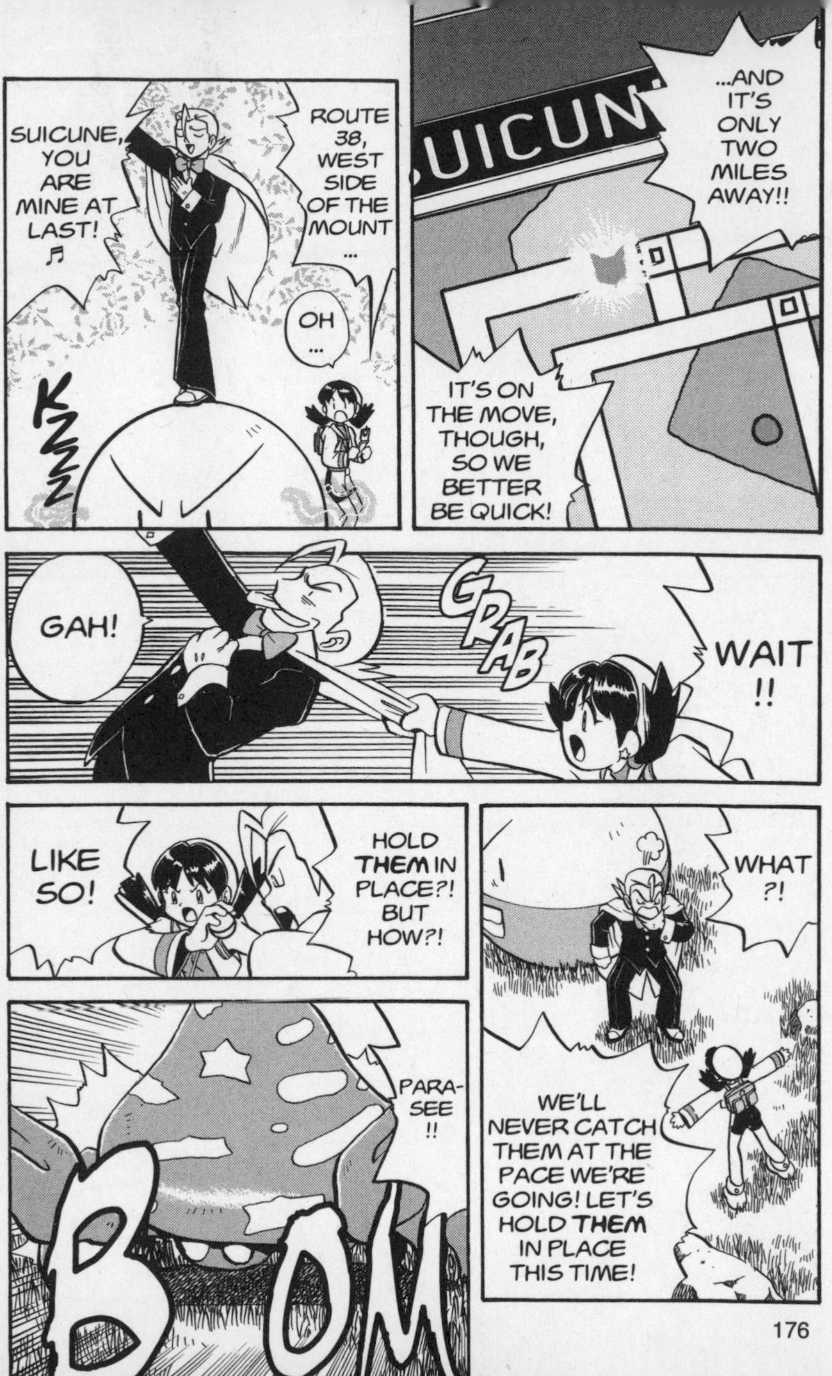
SUICUN
...AND IT'S ONLY TWO MILES AWAY!!
IT'S ON THE MOVE, THOUGH, SO WE BETTER BE QUICK!
ROUTE 38, WEST SIDE OF THE MOUNT ...
SUICUNE, YOU ARE MINE AT LAST! ♫
OH ...
KZZZ
WAIT !!
GRAB
GAH!
WHAT ?!
WE'LL NEVER CATCH THEM AT THE PACE WE'RE GOING! LET'S HOLD THEM IN PLACE THIS TIME!
HOLD THEM IN PLACE?! BUT HOW?!
LIKE SO!
PARA-SEE !!
BOOM

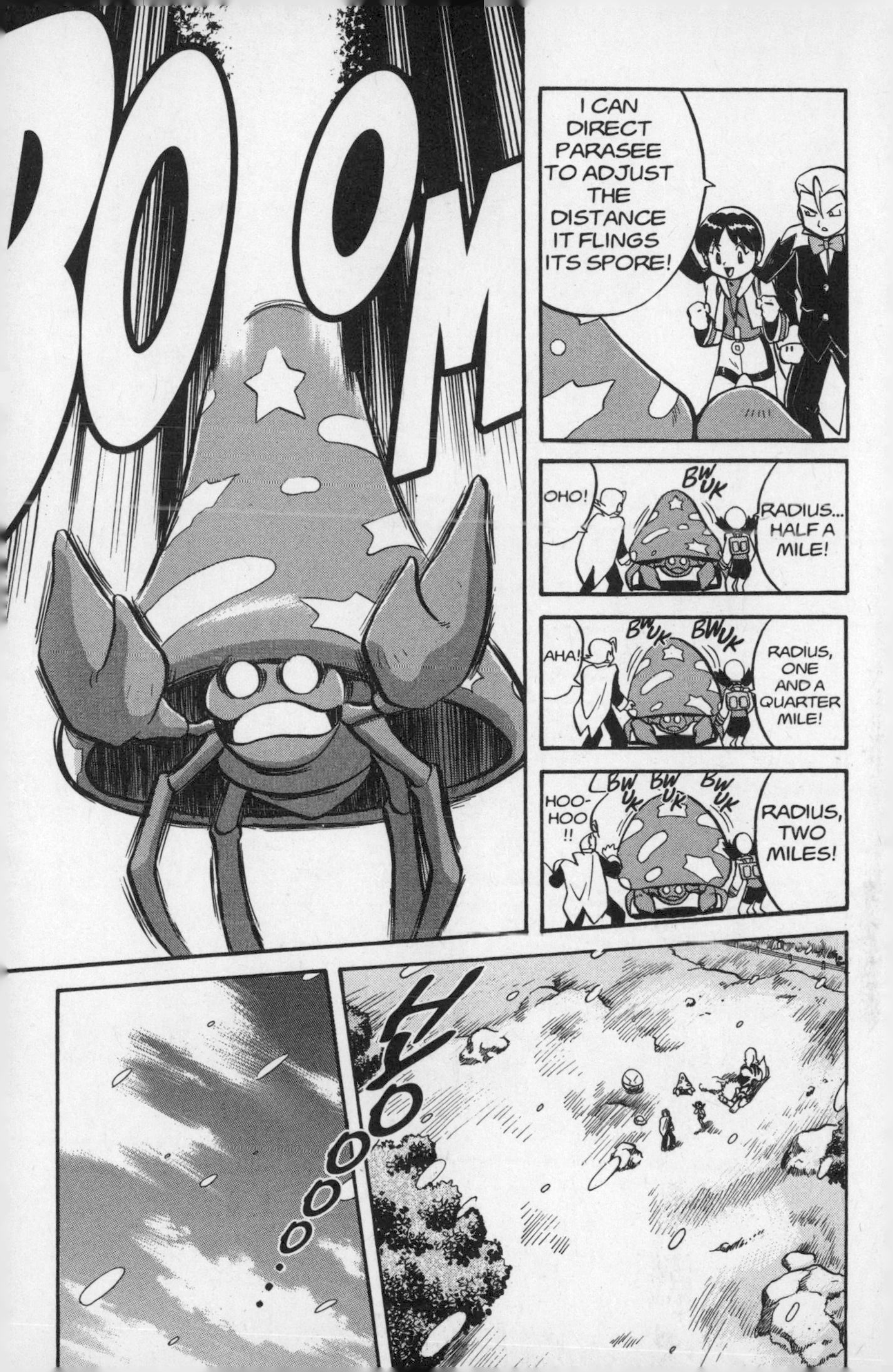
I CAN DIRECT PARASEE TO ADJUST THE DISTANCE IT FLINGS ITS SPORE!
RADIUS... HALF A MILE!
BWUK
OHO!
RADIUS, ONE AND A QUARTER MILE!
BWUK
BWUK
AHA!
RADIUS, TWO MILES!
BWUK
BWUK
BWUK
HOO-HOO !!
BOOM

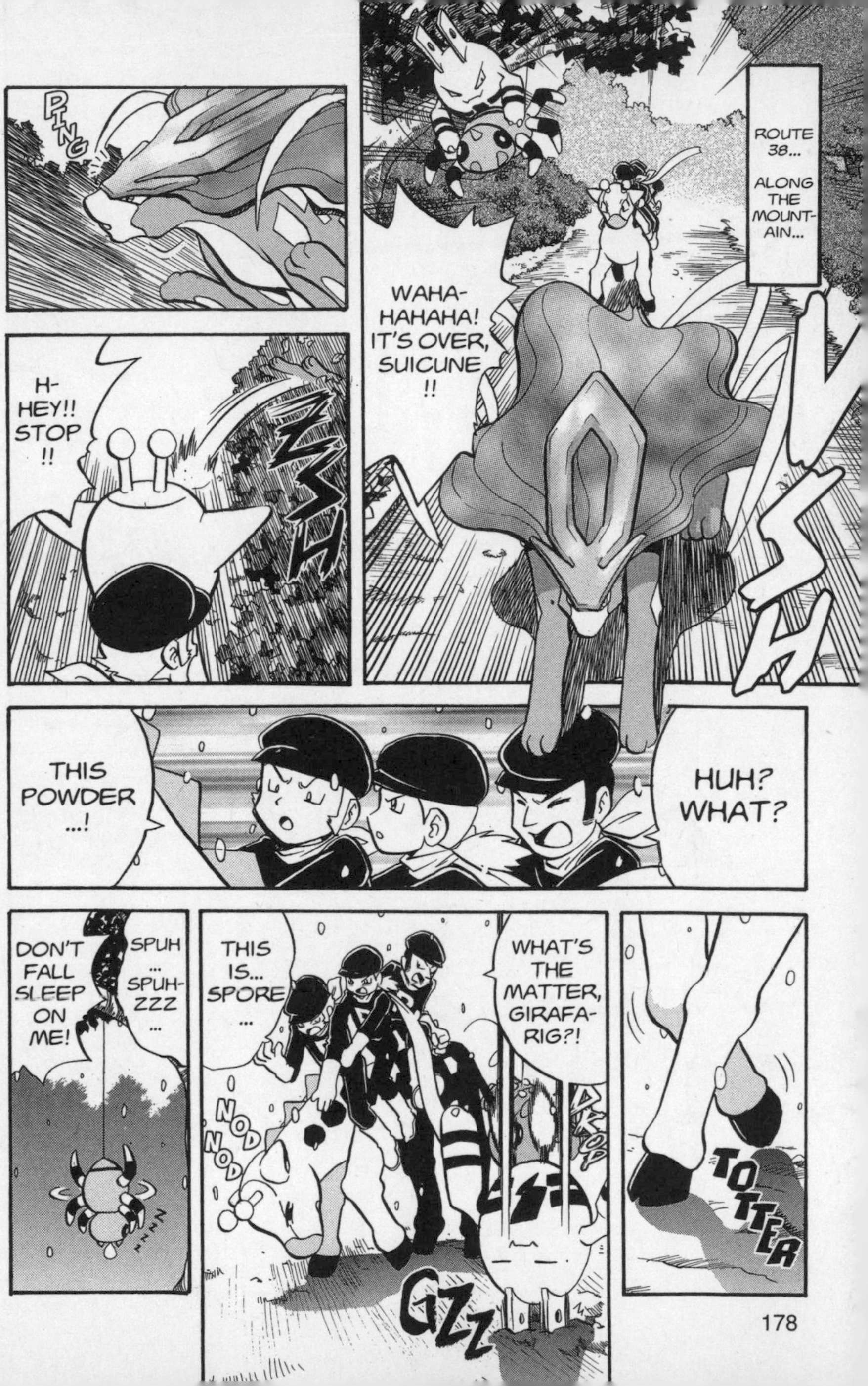

ROUTE 38... ALONG THE MOUNT-AIN...
WAHA-HAHAHA! IT'S OVER, SUICUNE!!
PING
H-HEY!! STOP!!
HUH? WHAT?
THIS POWDER...!
TOTTER
WHAT'S THE MATTER, GIRAFA-RIG?!
THIS IS... SPORE...
NOD NOD
GZZ
SPUH... SPUH-ZZZ...
DON'T FALL SLEEP ON ME!

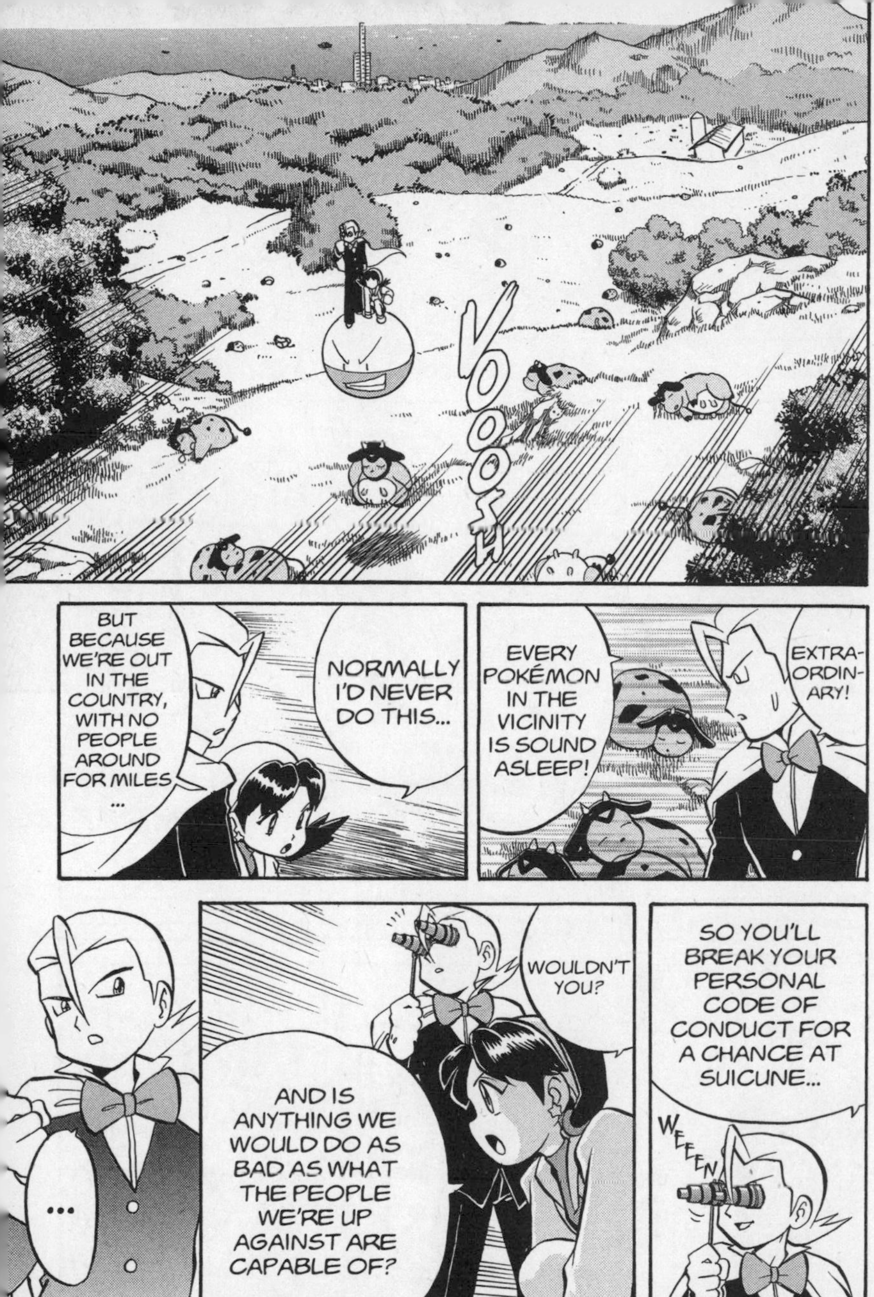
VOOOSH
EXTRA-ORDINARY!
EVERY POKÉMON IN THE VICINITY IS SOUND ASLEEP!
NORMALLY I'D NEVER DO THIS...
BUT BECAUSE WE'RE OUT IN THE COUNTRY, WITH NO PEOPLE AROUND FOR MILES...
SO YOU'LL BREAK YOUR PERSONAL CODE OF CONDUCT FOR A CHANCE AT SUICUNE...
WEEEN
WOULDN'T YOU?
AND IS ANYTHING WE WOULD DO AS BAD AS WHAT THE PEOPLE WE'RE UP AGAINST ARE CAPABLE OF?
...

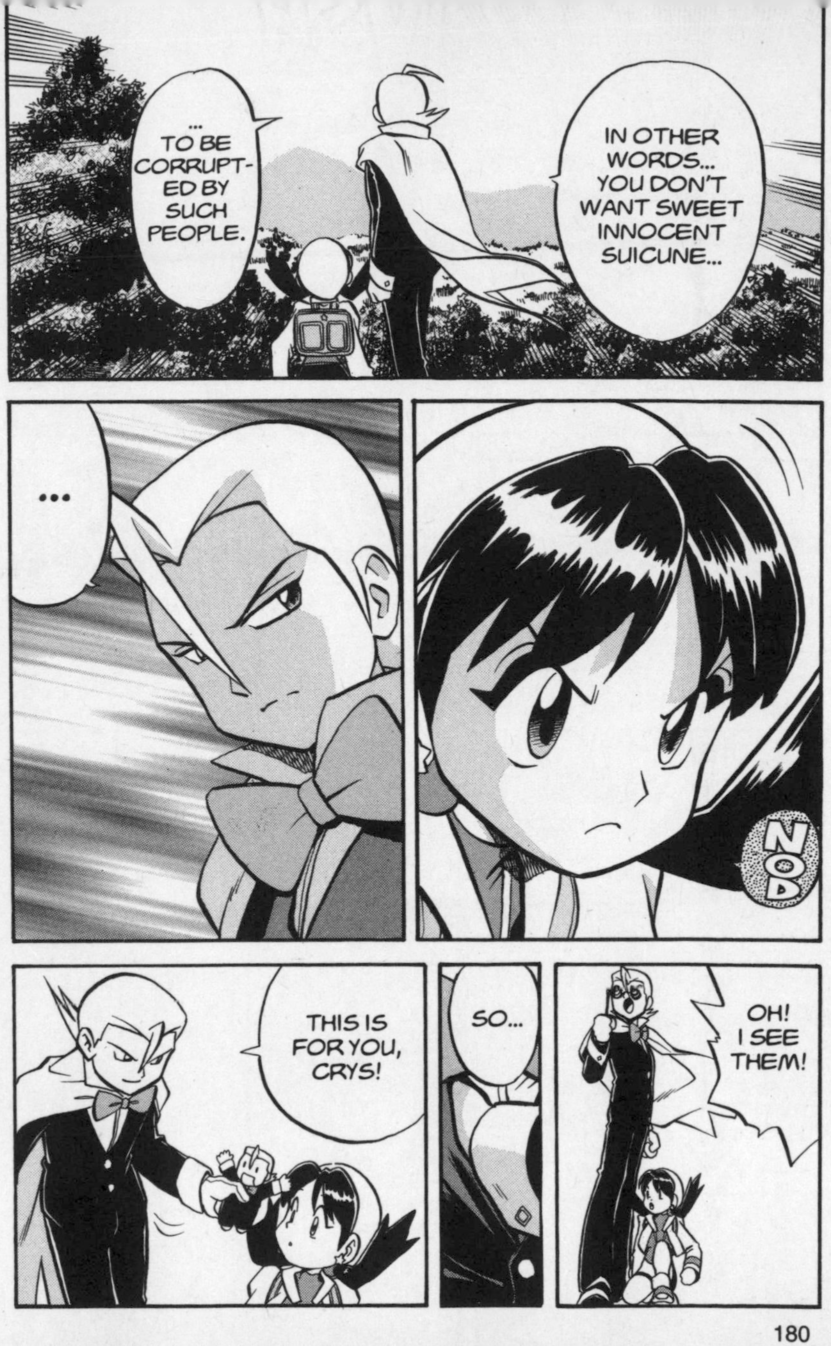
IN OTHER WORDS... YOU DON'T WANT SWEET INNOCENT SUICUNE...
... TO BE CORRUPTED BY SUCH PEOPLE.
NOD
...
OH! I SEE THEM!
SO...
THIS IS FOR YOU, CRYS!

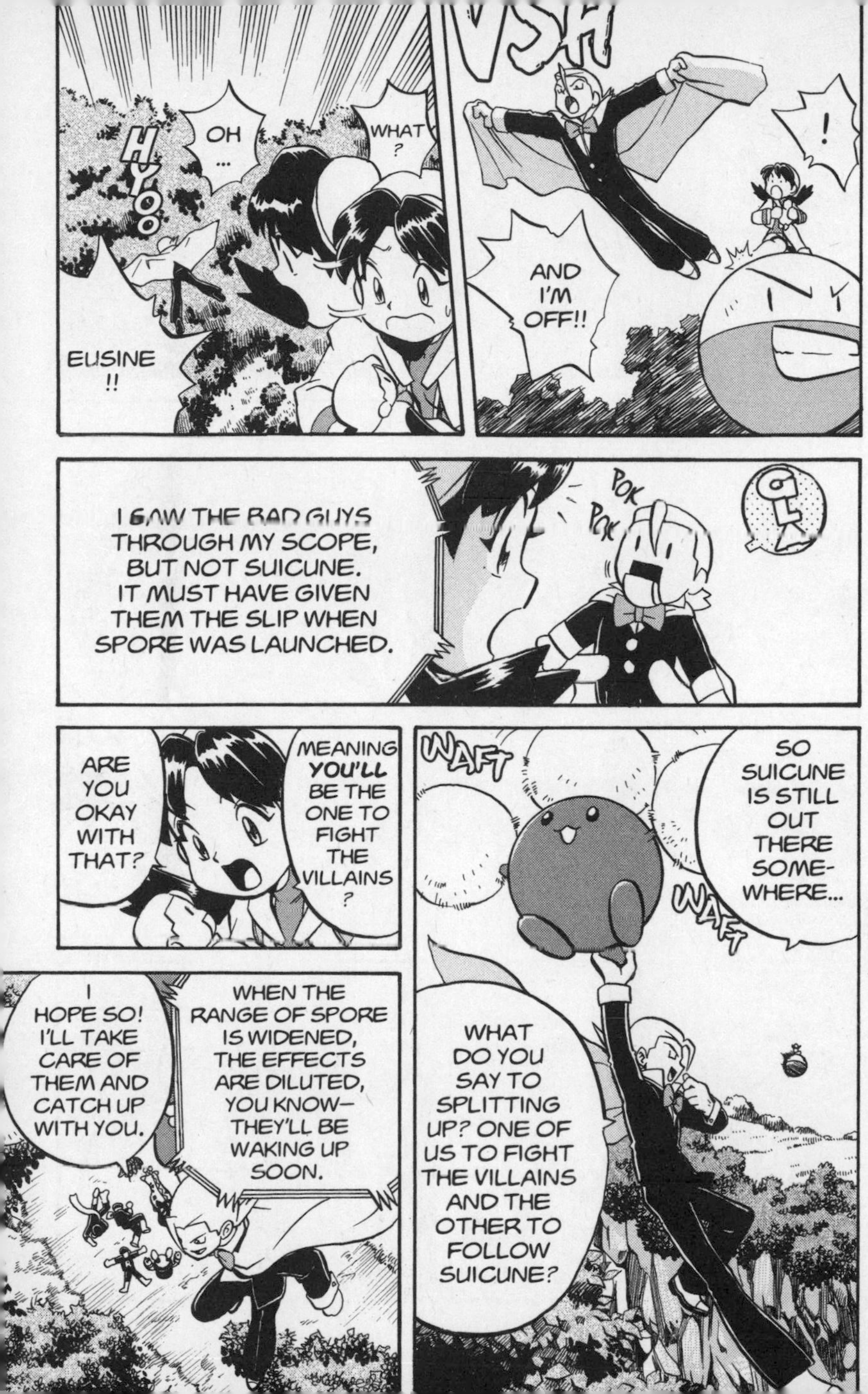
VSH
!
AND I'M OFF!!
WHAT?
OH...
HYOO
EUSINE!!
GL
POK POK
I SAW THE BAD GUYS THROUGH MY SCOPE, BUT NOT SUICUNE. IT MUST HAVE GIVEN THEM THE SLIP WHEN SPORE WAS LAUNCHED.
SO SUICUNE IS STILL OUT THERE SOME-WHERE...
WAFT
WAFT
WHAT DO YOU SAY TO SPLITTING UP? ONE OF US TO FIGHT THE VILLAINS AND THE OTHER TO FOLLOW SUICUNE?
MEANING YOU'LL BE THE ONE TO FIGHT THE VILLAINS?
ARE YOU OKAY WITH THAT?
WHEN THE RANGE OF SPORE IS WIDENED, THE EFFECTS ARE DILUTED, YOU KNOW—THEY'LL BE WAKING UP SOON.
I HOPE SO! I'LL TAKE CARE OF THEM AND CATCH UP WITH YOU.

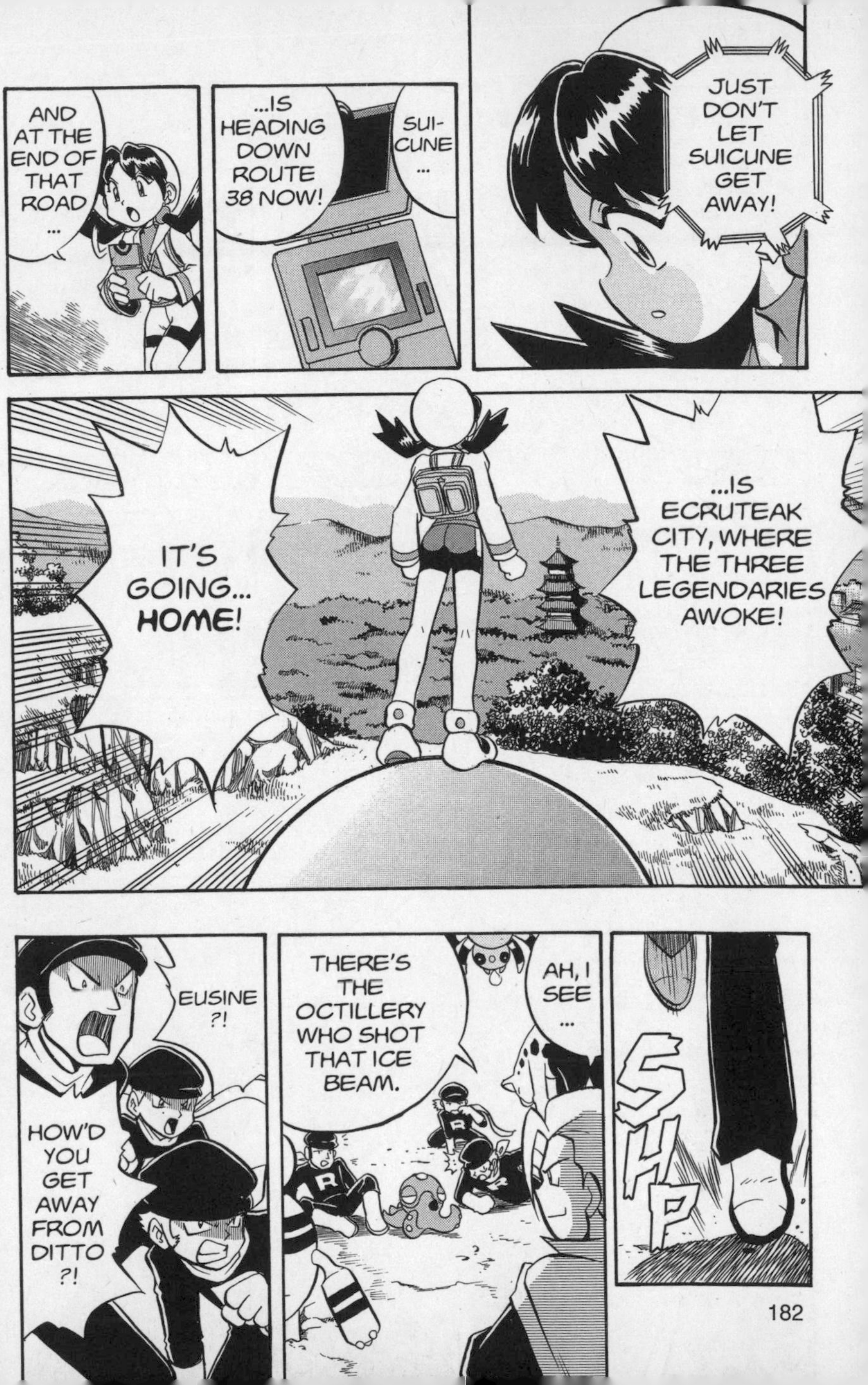

JUST DON'T LET SUICUNE GET AWAY!
SUI-CUNE...
...IS HEADING DOWN ROUTE 38 NOW!
AND AT THE END OF THAT ROAD...
...IS ECRUTEAK CITY, WHERE THE THREE LEGENDARIES AWOKE!
IT'S GOING... **HOME!**
SHP
AH, I SEE...
THERE'S THE OCTILLERY WHO SHOT THAT ICE BEAM.
EUSINE?!
HOW'D YOU GET AWAY FROM DITTO?!

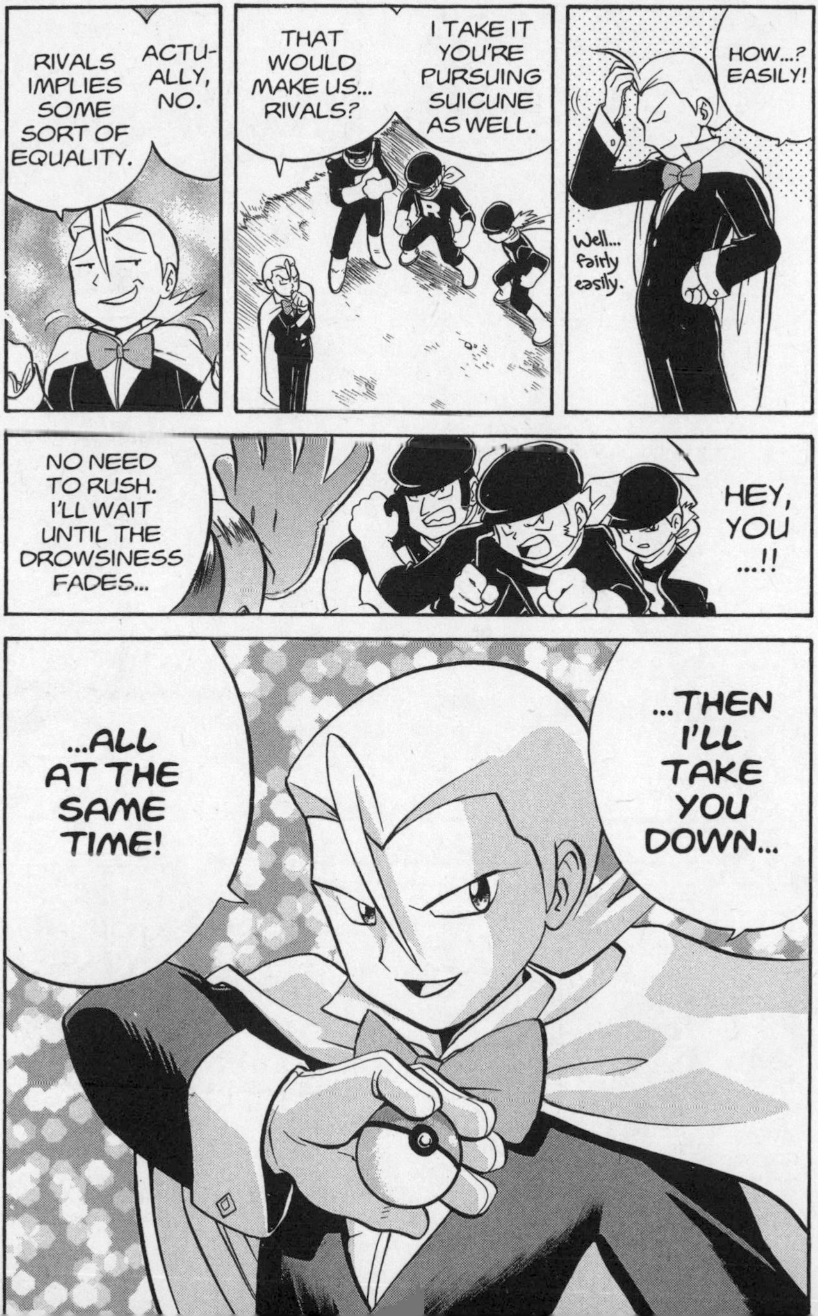
HOW...? EASILY!
Well... fairly easily.
I TAKE IT YOU'RE PURSUING SUICUNE AS WELL.
THAT WOULD MAKE US... RIVALS?
ACTU-ALLY, NO.
RIVALS IMPLIES SOME SORT OF EQUALITY.
HEY, YOU ...!!
NO NEED TO RUSH. I'LL WAIT UNTIL THE DROWSINESS FADES...
...THEN I'LL TAKE YOU DOWN...
...ALL AT THE SAME TIME!

129 Great Girafarig

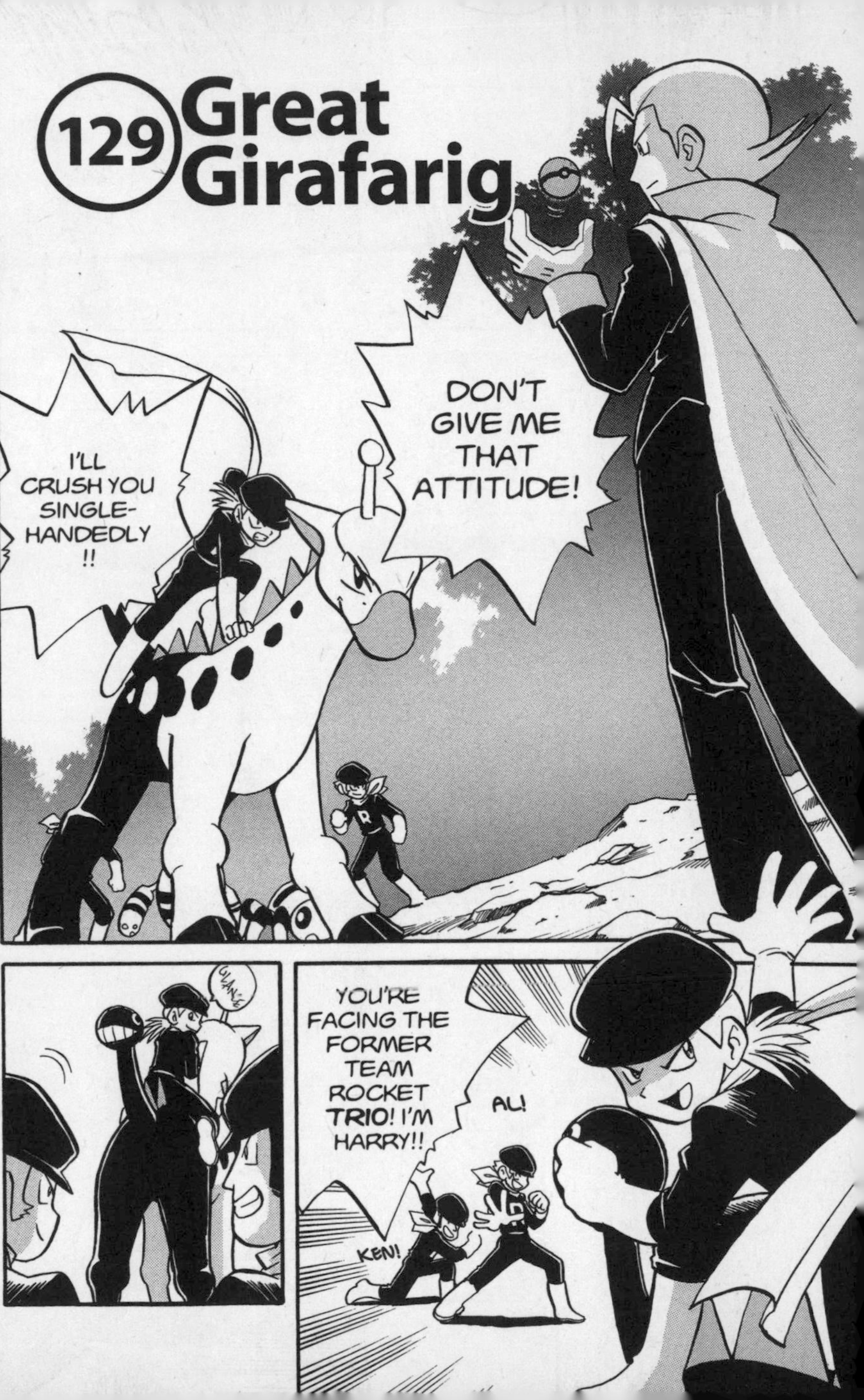
DON'T GIVE ME THAT ATTITUDE!
I'LL CRUSH YOU SINGLE-HANDEDLY!!
YOU'RE FACING THE FORMER TEAM ROCKET TRIO! I'M HARRY!!
AL!
KEN!
GLANCE

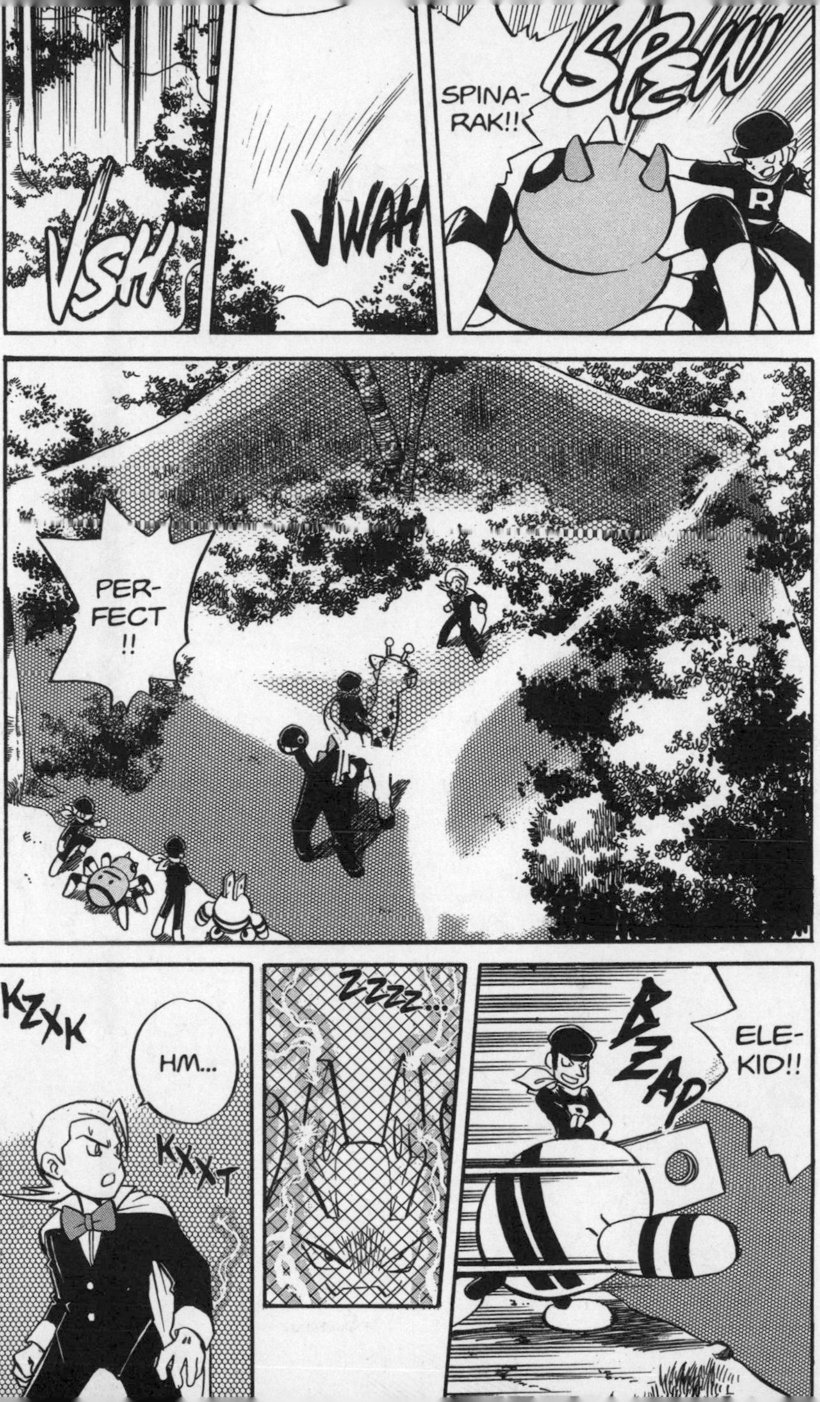
SPEW
SPINA-RAK!!
VWAH
VSH
PER-FECT!!
ELE-KID!!
BZZAP
ZZZZ...
KZXK
HM...
KXXT

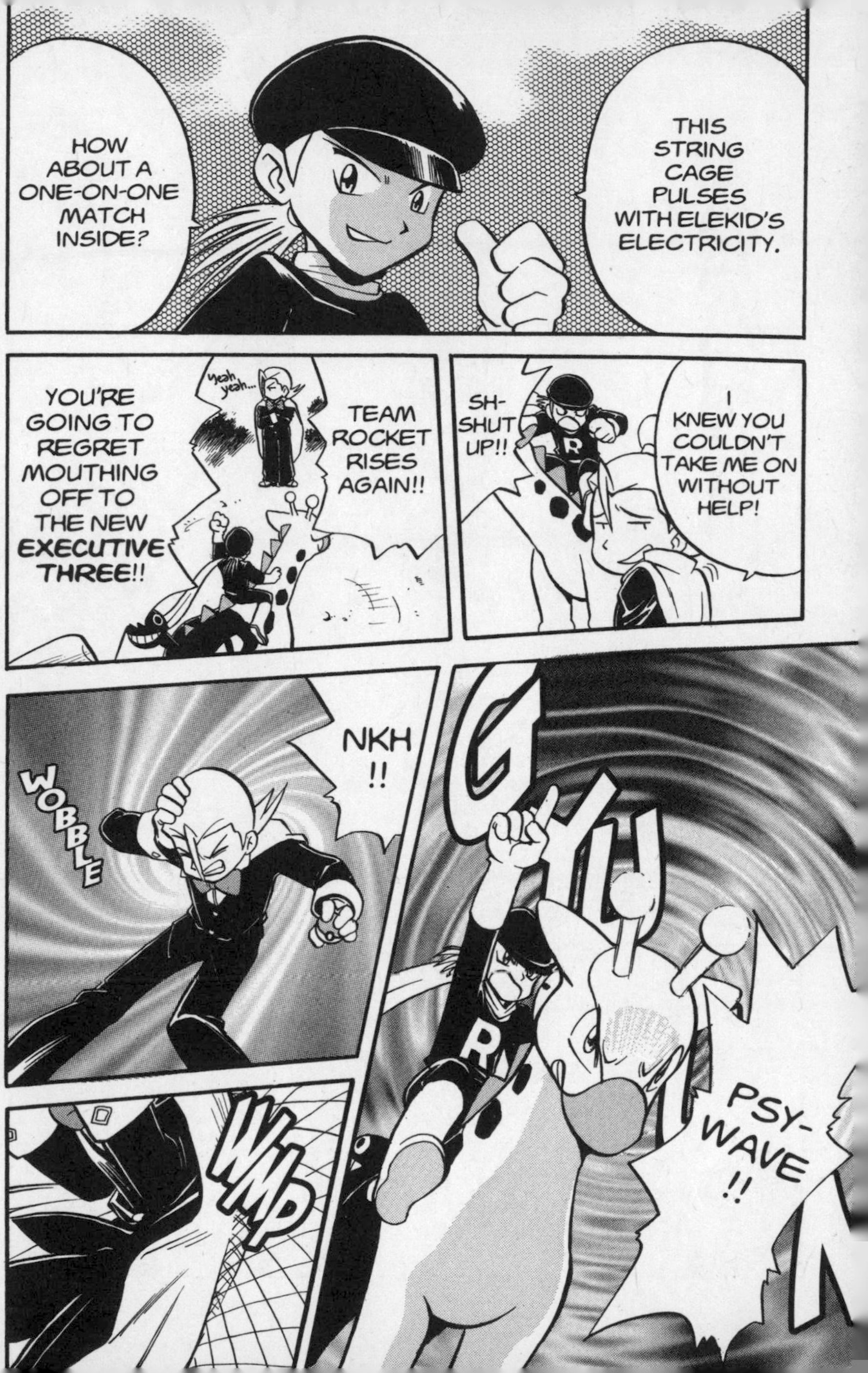

THIS STRING CAGE PULSES WITH ELEKID'S ELECTRICITY.
HOW ABOUT A ONE-ON-ONE MATCH INSIDE?
I KNEW YOU COULDN'T TAKE ME ON WITHOUT HELP!
SH- SHUT UP!!
TEAM ROCKET RISES AGAIN!!
yeah yeah...
YOU'RE GOING TO REGRET MOUTHING OFF TO THE NEW EXECUTIVE THREE!!
GYU
PSY-WAVE!!
NKH!!
WOBBLE
WMP

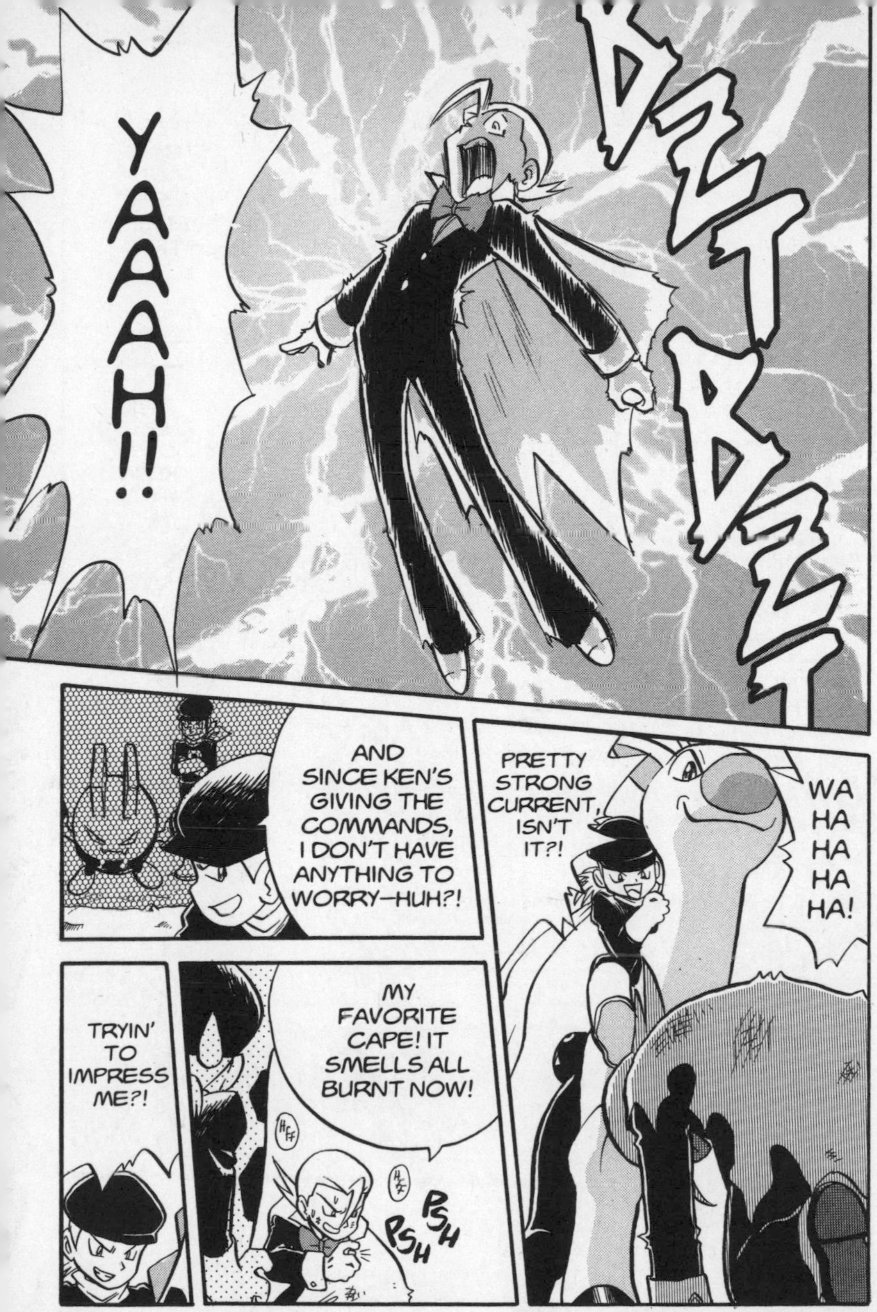
YAAAH!!
WA HA HA HA HA HA!
PRETTY STRONG CURRENT, ISN'T IT?!
AND SINCE KEN'S GIVING THE COMMANDS, I DON'T HAVE ANYTHING TO WORRY—HUH?!
MY FAVORITE CAPE! IT SMELLS ALL BURNT NOW!
PSH PSH
TRYIN' TO IMPRESS ME?!

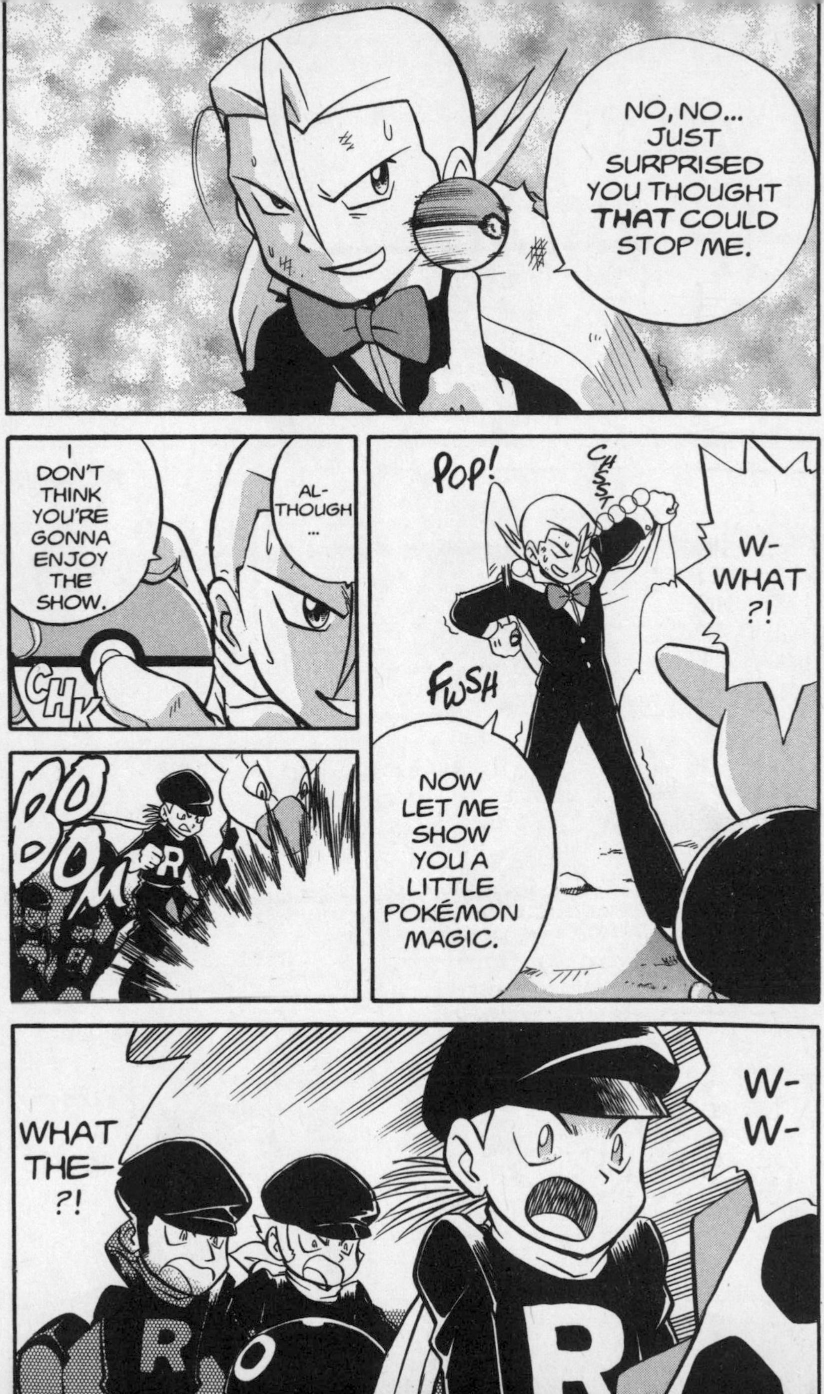
NO, NO... JUST SURPRISED YOU THOUGHT THAT COULD STOP ME.
W-WHAT?!
CHSST
POP!
FWSH
NOW LET ME SHOW YOU A LITTLE POKÉMON MAGIC.
AL-THOUGH...
I DON'T THINK YOU'RE GONNA ENJOY THE SHOW.
CHK
BOOM
W-W-
WHAT THE—?!

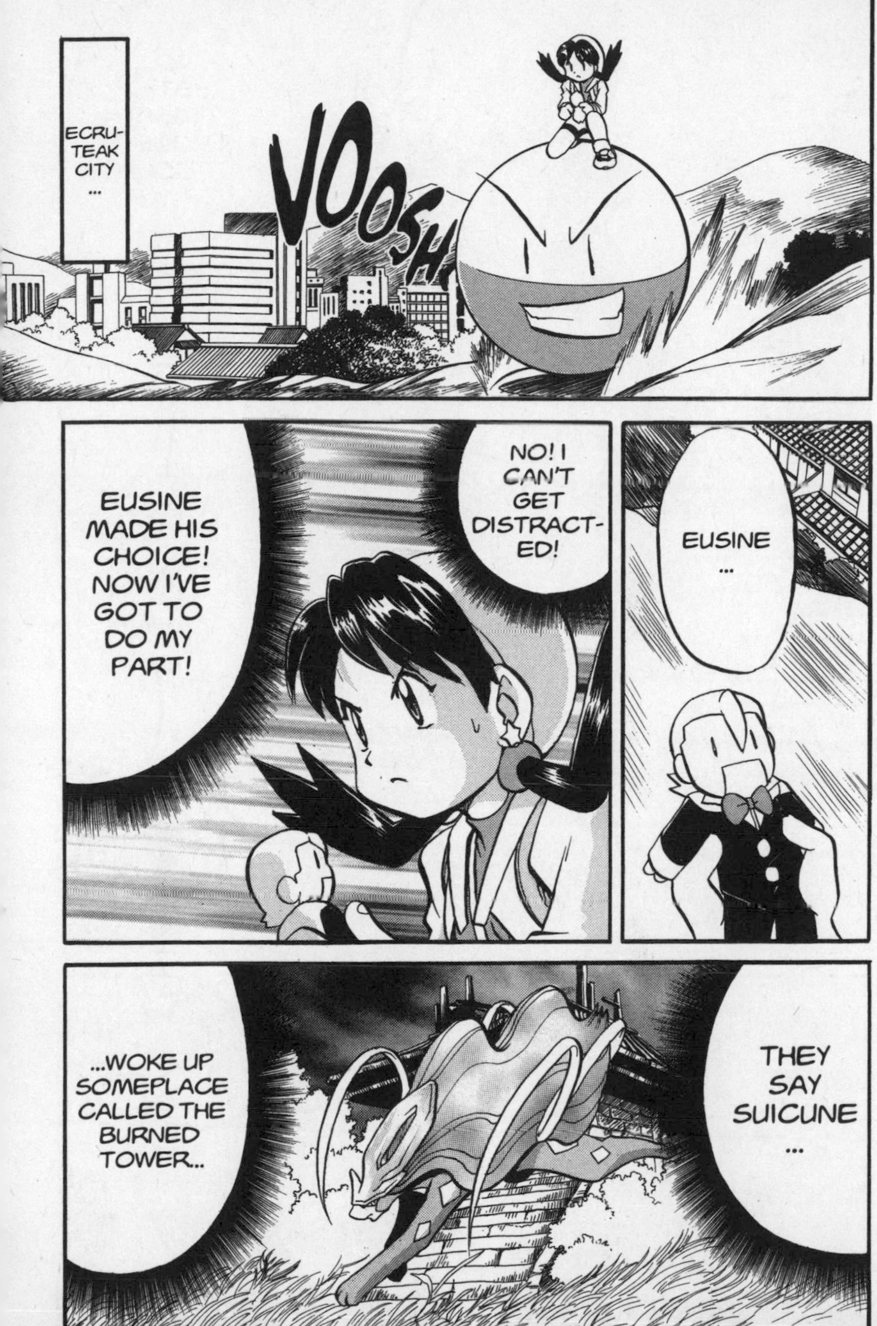
ECRU-TEAK CITY ...
VOOSH
EUSINE ...
NO! I CAN'T GET DISTRACT-ED!
EUSINE MADE HIS CHOICE! NOW I'VE GOT TO DO MY PART!
THEY SAY SUICUNE ...
...WOKE UP SOMEPLACE CALLED THE BURNED TOWER...

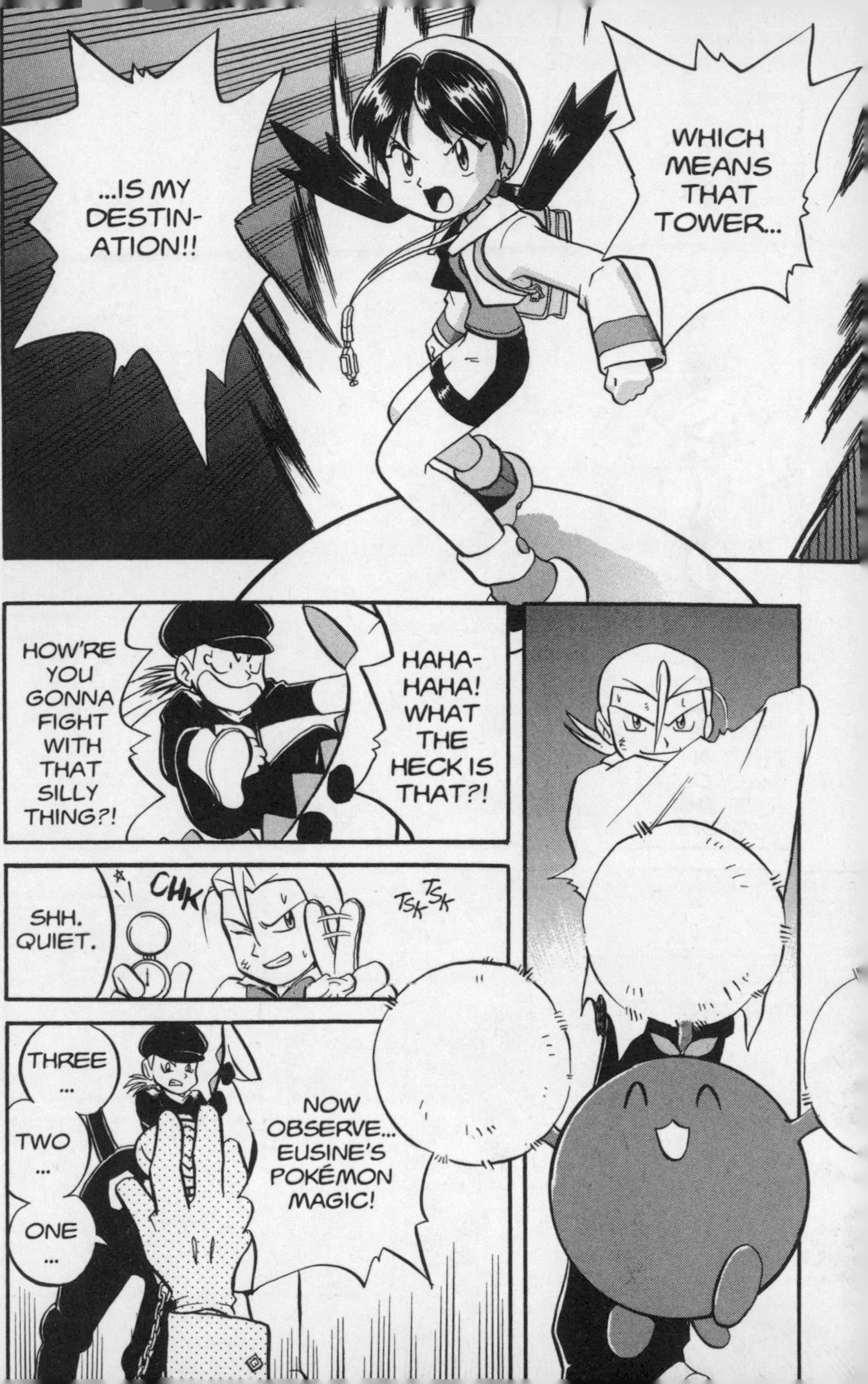

WHICH MEANS THAT TOWER...
...IS MY DESTINATION!!
HAHA-HAHA! WHAT THE HECK IS THAT?!
HOW'RE YOU GONNA FIGHT WITH THAT SILLY THING?!
TSK TSK
CHK
SHH. QUIET.
NOW OBSERVE... EUSINE'S POKéMON MAGIC!
THREE ...
TWO ...
ONE ...

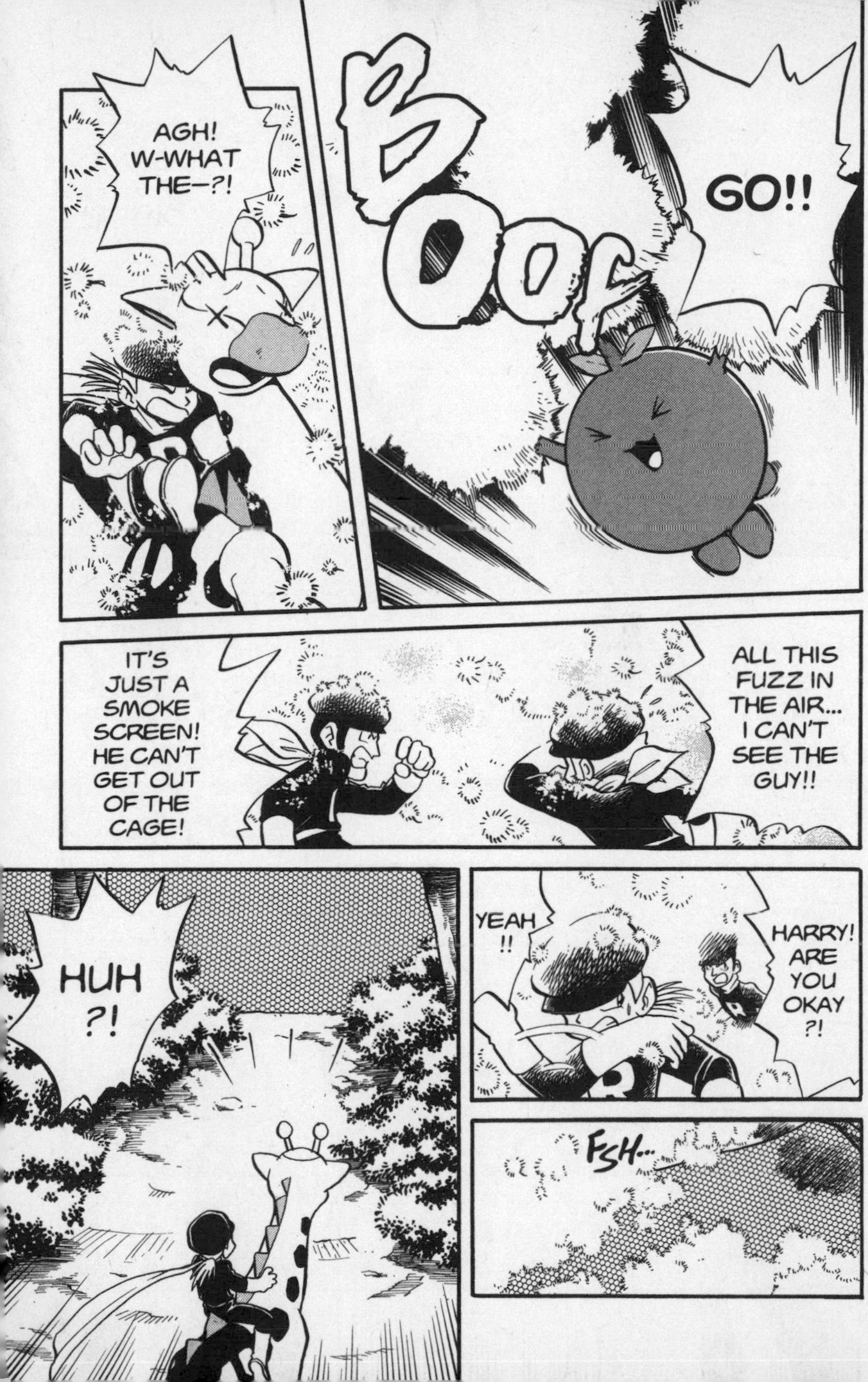
GO!!
BOOF
AGH! W-WHAT THE—?!
ALL THIS FUZZ IN THE AIR... I CAN'T SEE THE GUY!!
IT'S JUST A SMOKE SCREEN! HE CAN'T GET OUT OF THE CAGE!
HARRY! ARE YOU OKAY ?!
YEAH !!
FSH...
HUH ?!

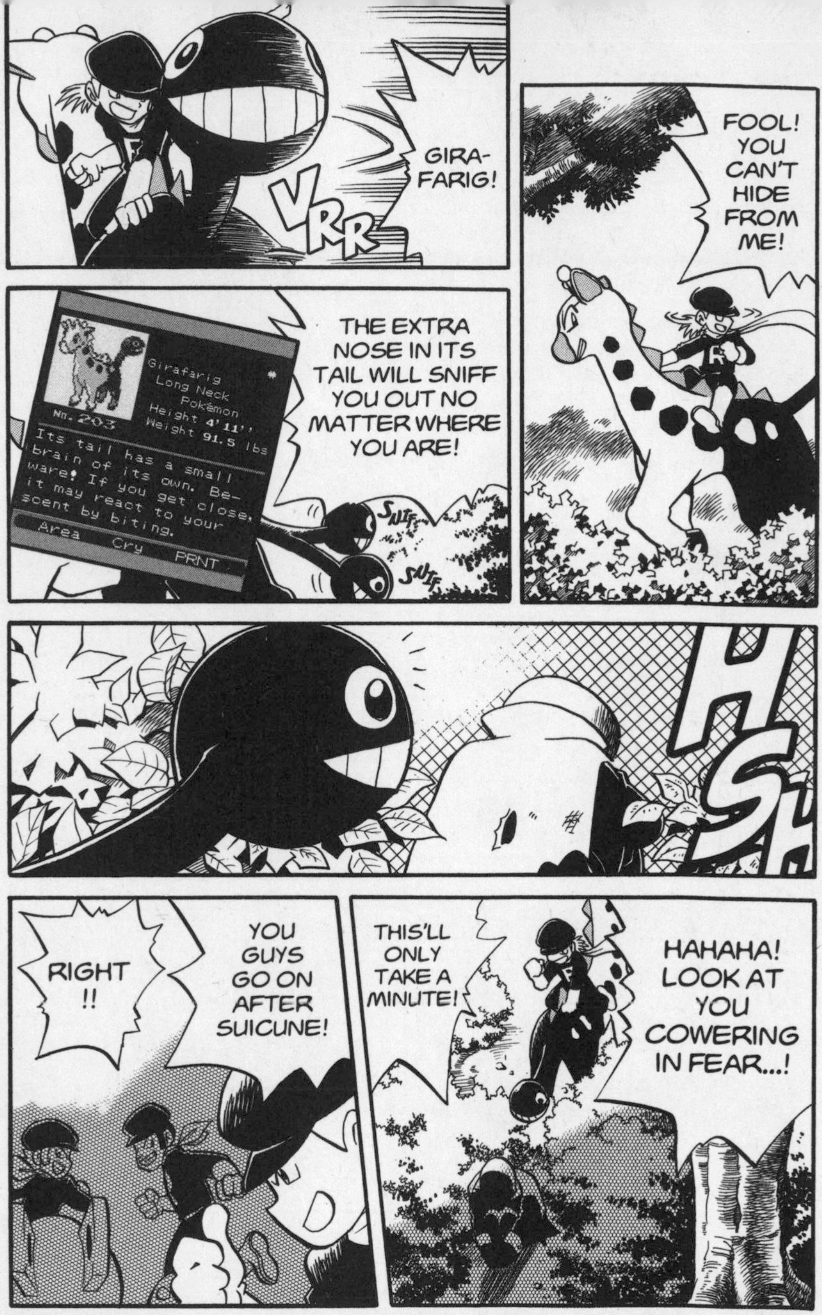
FOOL! YOU CAN'T HIDE FROM ME!
GIRA-FARIG!
VRR
Girafarig
Long Neck Pokémon
Height 4'11''
Weight 91.5 lbs
No. 203
Its tail has a small brain of its own. Beware! If you get close, it may react to your scent by biting.
Area Cry PRNT
THE EXTRA NOSE IN ITS TAIL WILL SNIFF YOU OUT NO MATTER WHERE YOU ARE!
SNIFF
SNIFF
HAHAHA! LOOK AT YOU COWERING IN FEAR...!
THIS'LL ONLY TAKE A MINUTE!
YOU GUYS GO ON AFTER SUICUNE!
RIGHT!!

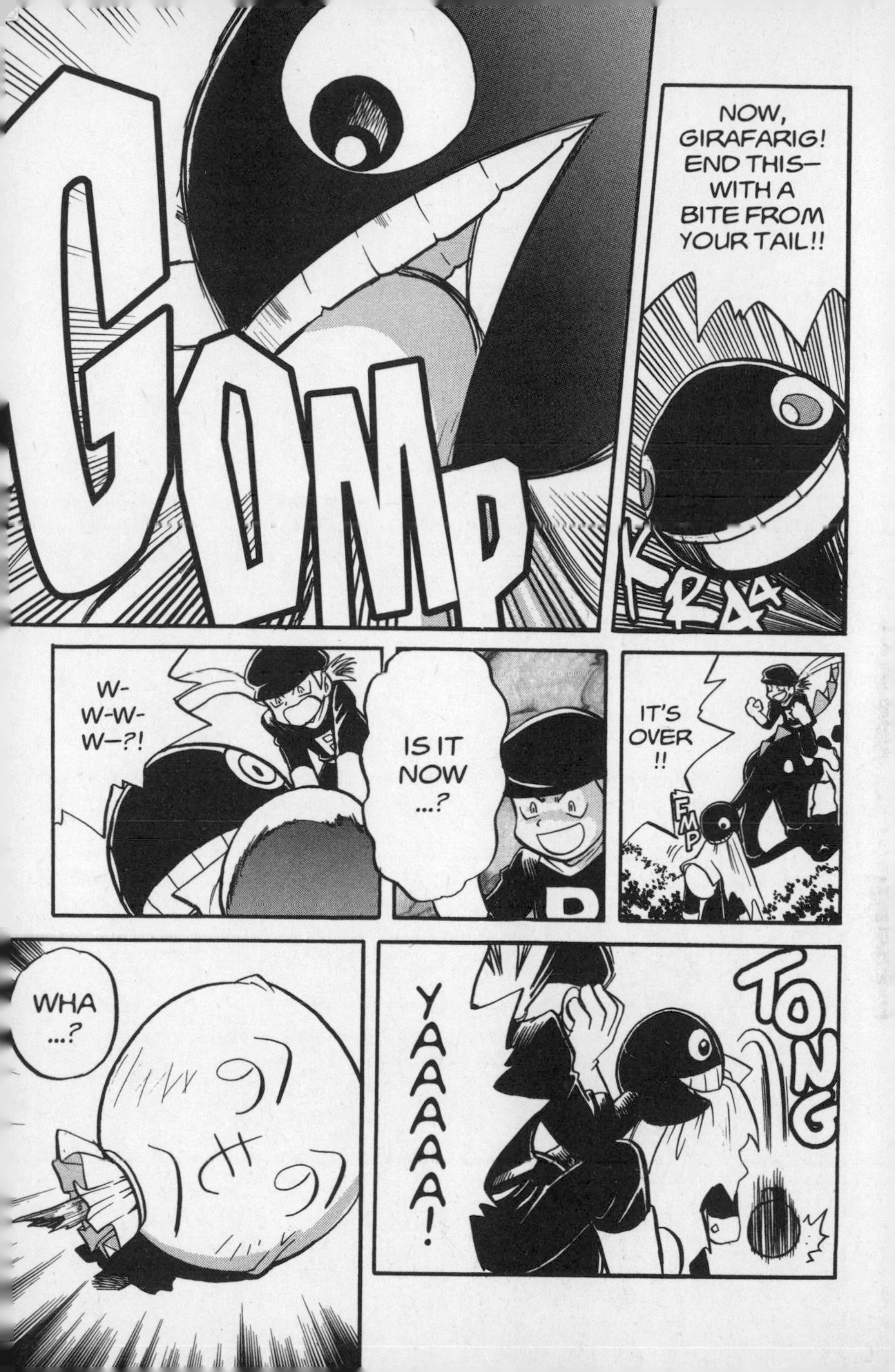
NOW, GIRAFARIG! END THIS— WITH A BITE FROM YOUR TAIL!!
GOMP
IT'S OVER !!
FMP
IS IT NOW ...?
W- W-W- W—?!
TONG
YAAAAA!
WHA ...?

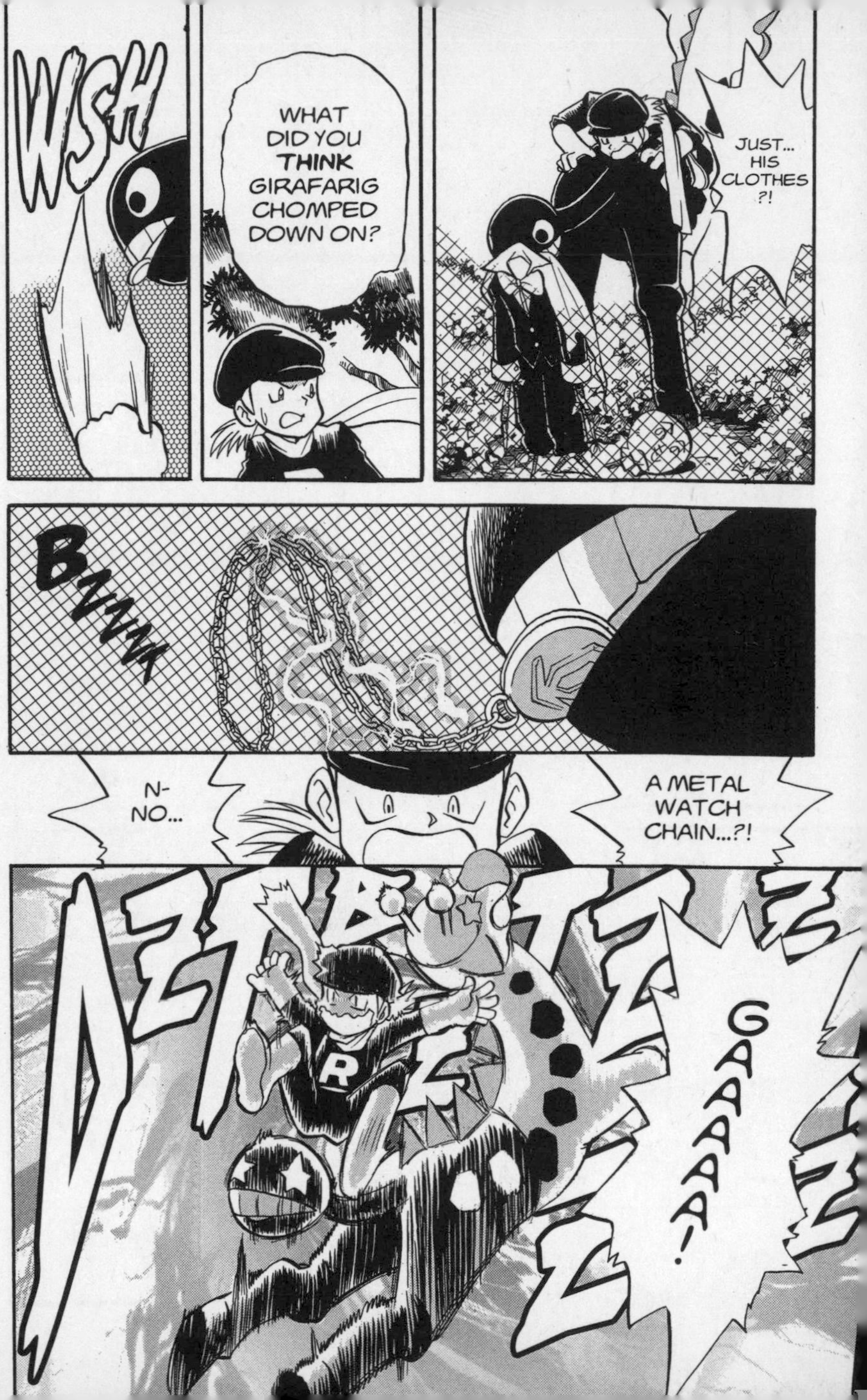
JUST... HIS CLOTHES?!
WHAT DID YOU **THINK** GIRAFARIG CHOMPED DOWN ON?
WSH
BZZZK
A METAL WATCH CHAIN...?!
N- NO...
GAAAAAA!

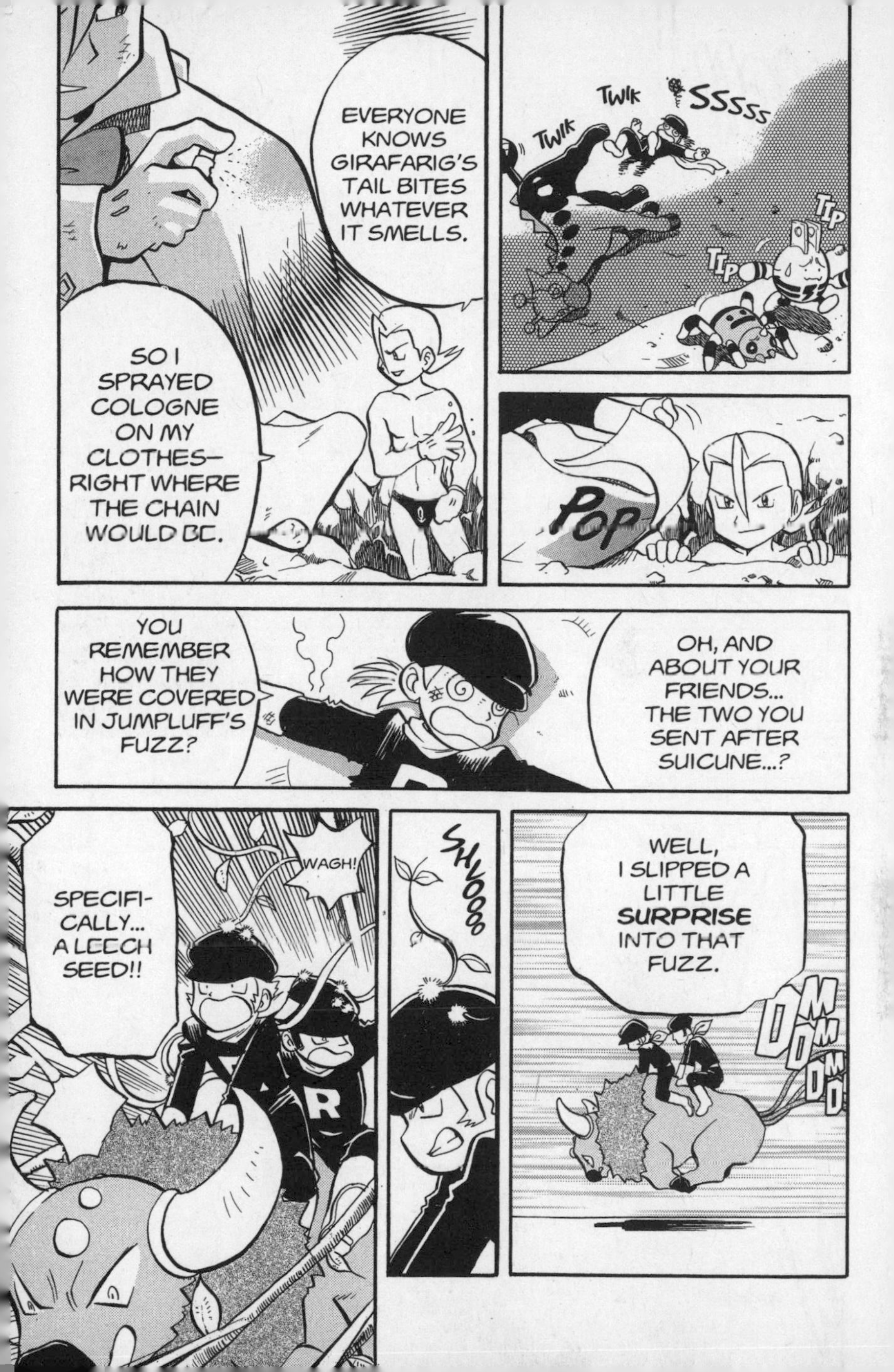
TWIK
TWIK
SSSSS
TIP
TIP
POP
EVERYONE KNOWS GIRAFARIG'S TAIL BITES WHATEVER IT SMELLS.
SO I SPRAYED COLOGNE ON MY CLOTHES—RIGHT WHERE THE CHAIN WOULD BE.
OH, AND ABOUT YOUR FRIENDS... THE TWO YOU SENT AFTER SUICUNE...?
YOU REMEMBER HOW THEY WERE COVERED IN JUMPLUFF'S FUZZ?
WELL, I SLIPPED A LITTLE **SURPRISE** INTO THAT FUZZ.
DM DM DM D!
SHVOOOO
WAGH!
SPECIFI-CALLY... A LEECH SEED!!

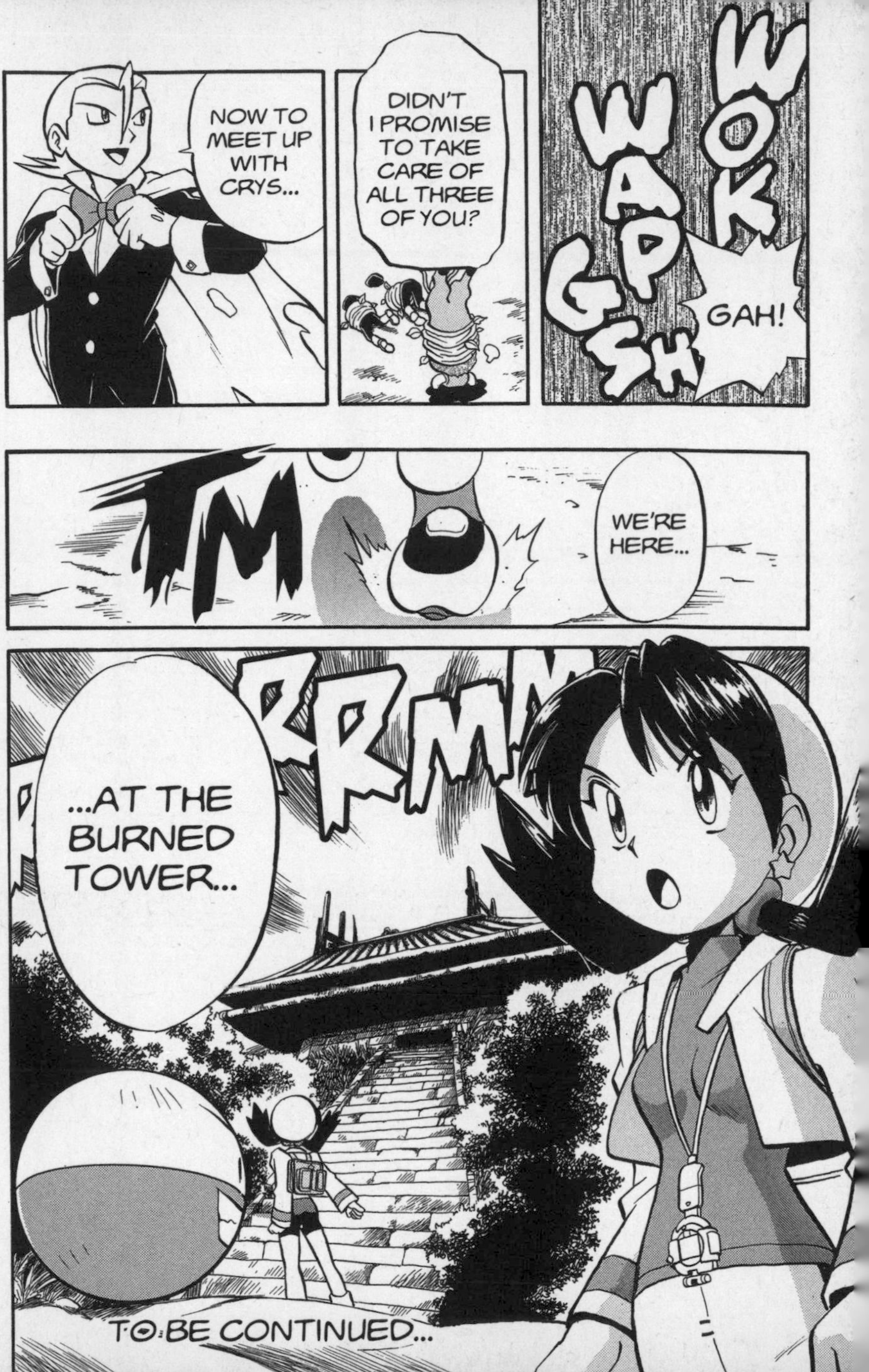
WOK
WAP
GUSH
GAH!
DIDN'T I PROMISE TO TAKE CARE OF ALL THREE OF YOU?
NOW TO MEET UP WITH CRYS...
WE'RE HERE...
TM
...AT THE BURNED TOWER...
TO BE CONTINUED...

TO BE CONTINUED

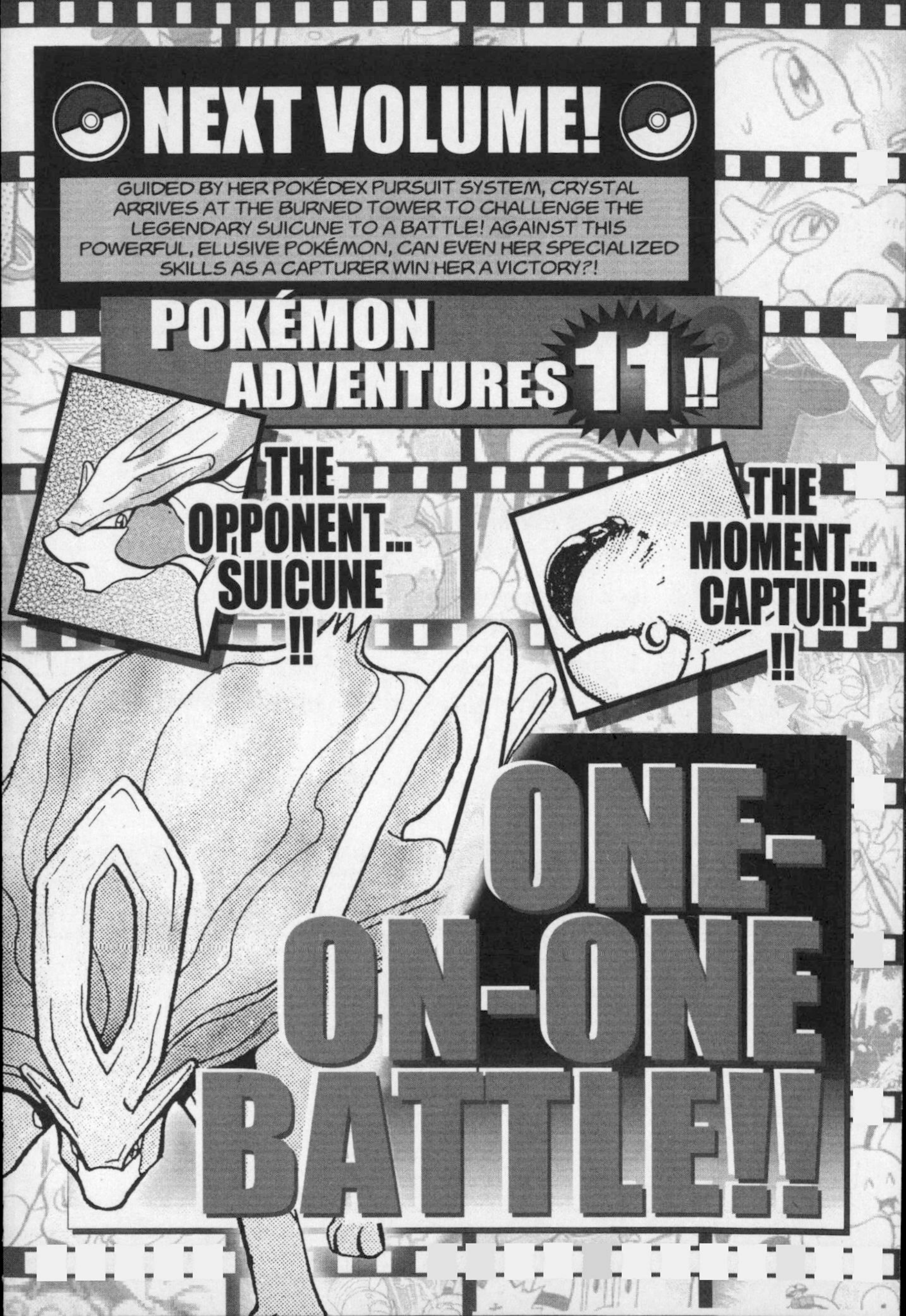
NEXT VOLUME!
GUIDED BY HER POKÉDEX PURSUIT SYSTEM, CRYSTAL ARRIVES AT THE BURNED TOWER TO CHALLENGE THE LEGENDARY SUICUNE TO A BATTLE! AGAINST THIS POWERFUL, ELUSIVE POKÉMON, CAN EVEN HER SPECIALIZED SKILLS AS A CAPTURER WIN HER A VICTORY?!
POKÉMON ADVENTURES 11!!
THE OPPONENT... SUICUNE!!
THE MOMENT... CAPTURE!!
ONE-ON-ONE BATTLE!!

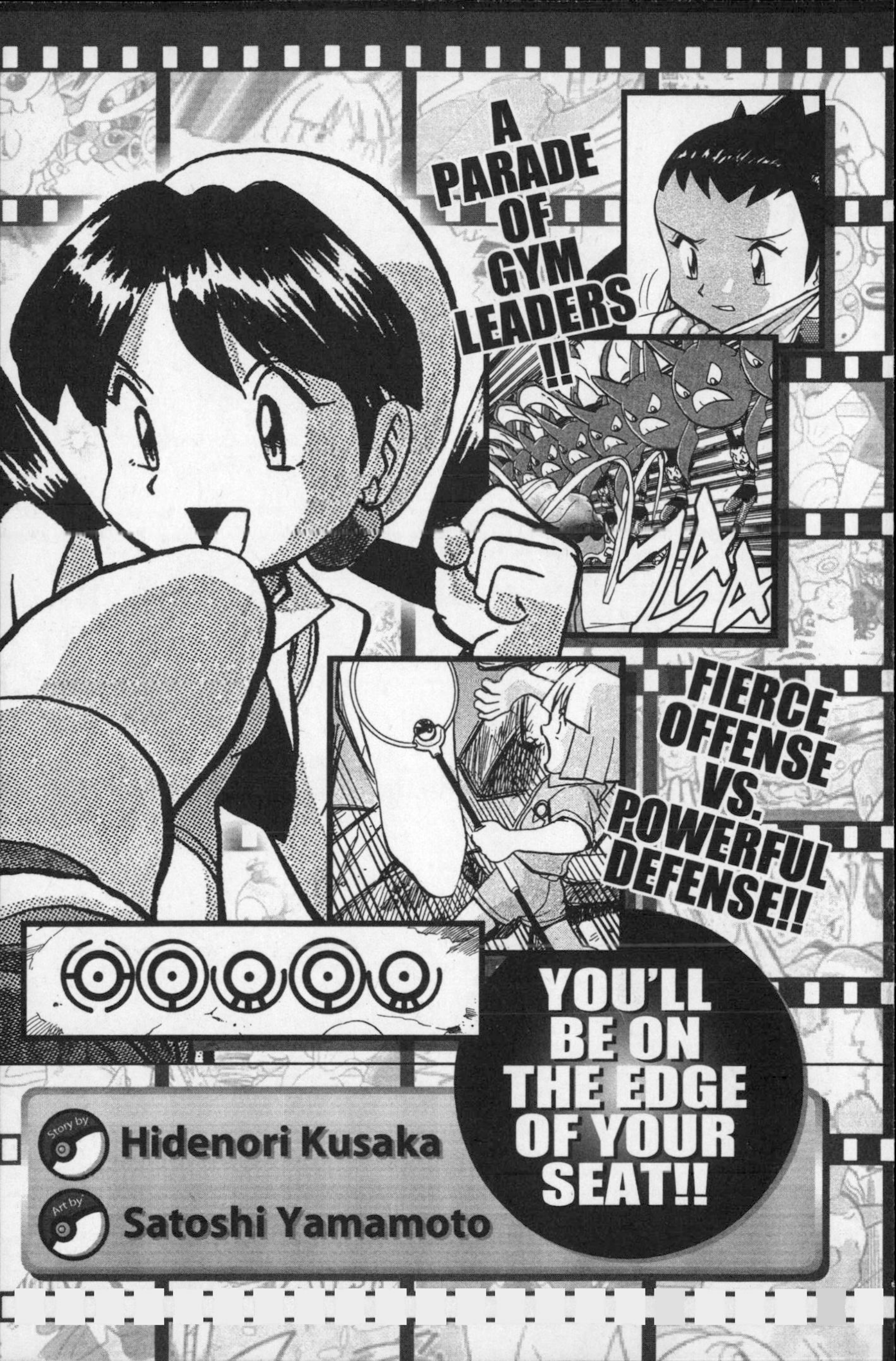
A PARADE OF GYM LEADERS!!
FIERCE OFFENSE VS. POWERFUL DEFENSE!!
YOU'LL BE ON THE EDGE OF YOUR SEAT!!
Story by Hidenori Kusaka
Art by Satoshi Yamamoto

POKÉMON ADVENTURES!

CRYS'S TRAVELS, INCLUDING HER CAPTURES AND PURSUIT OF SUICUNE.

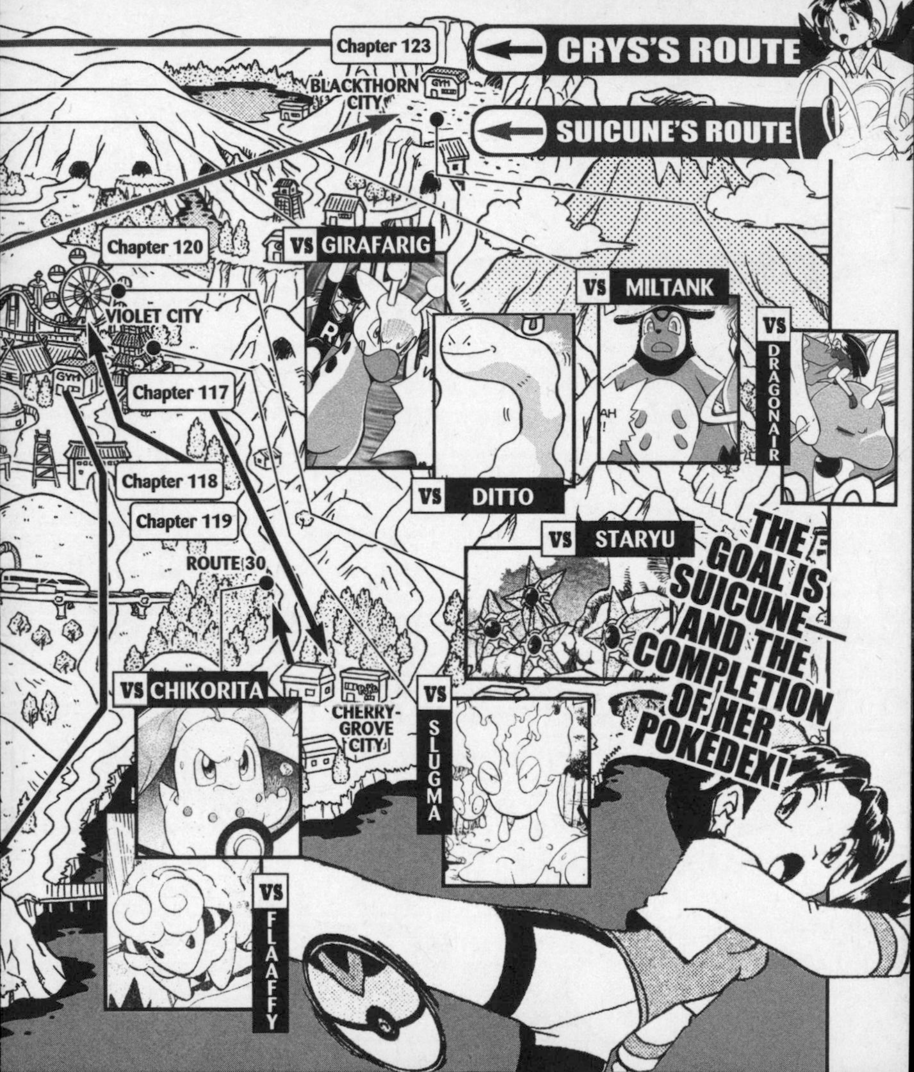

CRYS'S ROUTE
SUICUNE'S ROUTE
Chapter 123
BLACKTHORN CITY
GYM
Chapter 120
VS GIRAFARIG
VIOLET CITY
VS MILTANK
VS DRAGONAIR
Chapter 117
VS DITTO
Chapter 118
Chapter 119
VS STARYU
THE GOAL IS SUICUNE—AND THE COMPLETION OF HER POKÉDEX!
ROUTE 30
VS CHIKORITA
CHERRY-GROVE CITY
VS SLUGMA
VS FLAAFFY

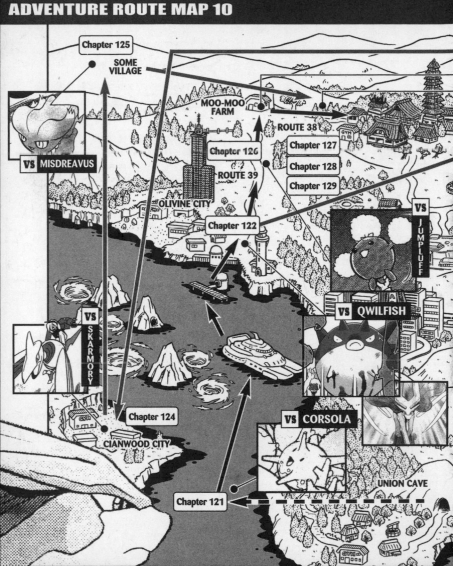

"GOTTA CATCH 'EM ALL!!"
ADVENTURE ROUTE MAP 10

Chapter 125

SOME VILLAGE

MOO-MOO FARM

ROUTE 38

Chapter 127

Chapter 128

Chapter 129

Chapter 126

ROUTE 39

VS MISDREAVUS

OLIVINE CITY

Chapter 122

VS JUMPLUFF

VS QWILFISH

VS SKARMORY

Chapter 124

Chapter 121

CIANWOOD CITY

VS CORSOLA

UNION CAVE

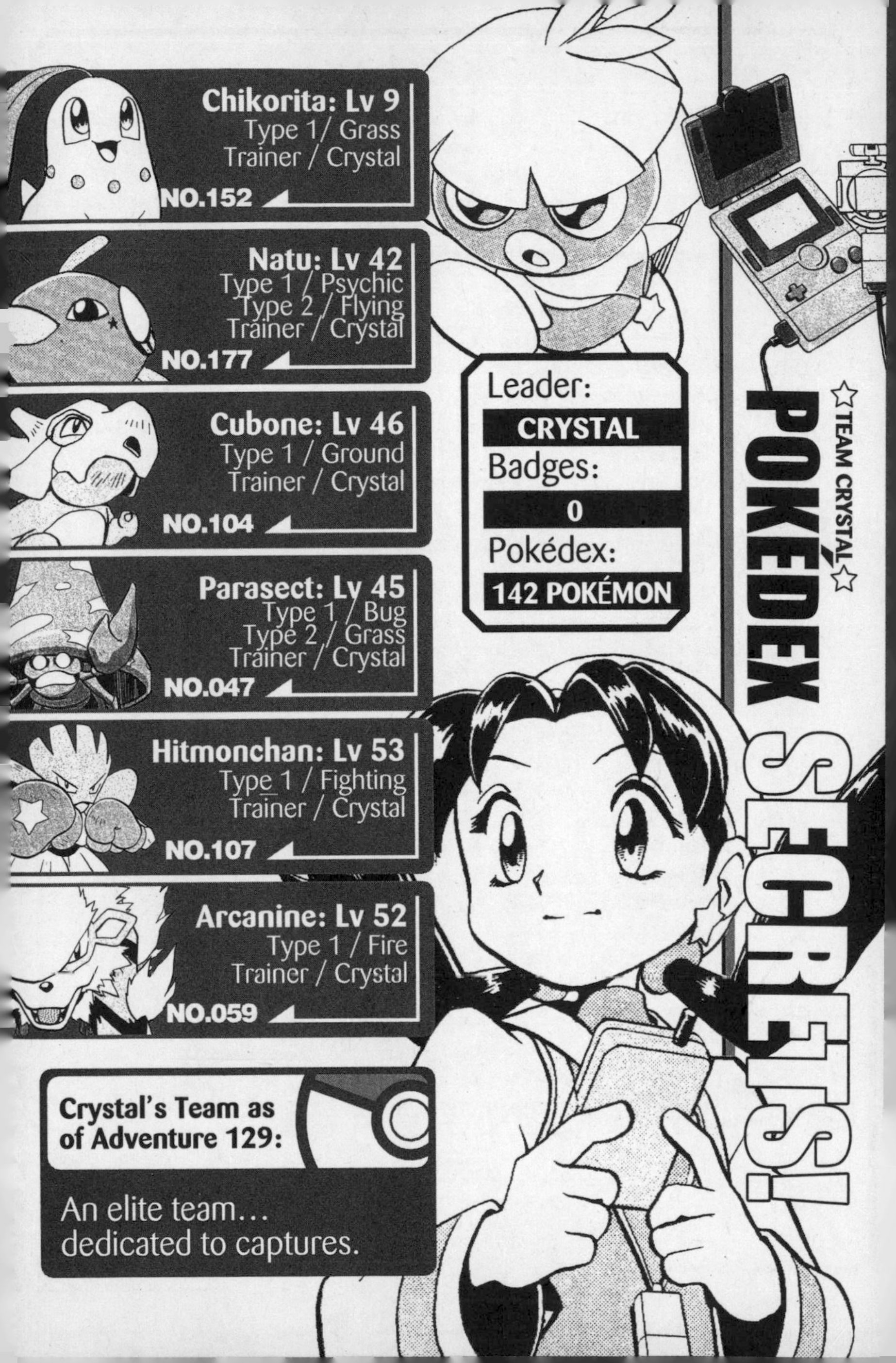
☆TEAM CRYSTAL☆
POKÉDEX SECRETS!
Leader:
CRYSTAL
Badges:
0
Pokédex:
142 POKÉMON
Chikorita: Lv 9
Type 1/ Grass
Trainer / Crystal
NO.152
Natu: Lv 42
Type 1 / Psychic
Type 2 / Flying
Trainer / Crystal
NO.177
Cubone: Lv 46
Type 1 / Ground
Trainer / Crystal
NO.104
Parasect: Lv 45
Type 1 / Bug
Type 2 / Grass
Trainer / Crystal
NO.047
Hitmonchan: Lv 53
Type 1 / Fighting
Trainer / Crystal
NO.107
Arcanine: Lv 52
Type 1 / Fire
Trainer / Crystal
NO.059
Crystal's Team as of Adventure 129:
An elite team…
dedicated to captures.

Pokédex

▶ 152	🔵 Chikorita	166	🔵 Ledian	071	🔵 Victreebel
153	– – – – –	167	🔵 Spinarak	187	🔵 Hoppip
154	– – – – –	168	🔵 Ariados	188	🔵 Skiploom
155	– – – – –	074	🔵 Geodude	189	🔵 Jumpluff
156	– – – – –	075	🔵 Graveler	046	🔵 Paras
157	– – – – –	076	🔵 Golem	047	🔵 Parasect
158	– – – – –	041	🔵 Zubat	060	🔵 Poliwag
159	– – – – –	042	🔵 Golbat	061	🔵 Poliwhirl
160	– – – – –	169	🔵 Crobat	062	🔵 Poliwrath
016	🔵 Pidgey	173	🔵 Cleffa	186	🔵 Politoed
017	🔵 Pidgeotto	035	🔵 Clefairy	129	🔵 Magikarp
018	🔵 Pidgeot	036	🔵 Clefable	130	🔵 Gyarados
021	🔵 Spearow	174	🔵 Igglybuff	118	🔵 Goldeen
022	🔵 Fearow	039	🔵 Jigglypuff	119	🔵 Seaking
163	🔵 Hoothoot	040	🔵 Wigglytuff	079	🔵 Slowpoke
164	🔵 Noctowl	175	– – – – –	080	🔵 Slowbro
019	🔵 Rattata	176	– – – – –	199	🔵 Slowking
020	🔵 Raticate	027	🔵 Sandshrew	043	🔵 Oddish
161	🔵 Sentret	028	🔵 Sandslash	044	🔵 Gloom
162	🔵 Furret	023	🔵 Ekans	045	🔵 Vileplume
172	– – – – –	024	🔵 Arbok	182	🔵 Bellossom
025	– – – – –	206	🔵 Dunsparce	096	🔵 Drowzee
026	🔵 Raichu	179	🔵 Mareep	097	🔵 Hypno
010	🔵 Caterpie	180	🔵 Flaaffy	063	🔵 Abra
011	🔵 Metapod	181	🔵 Ampharos	064	🔵 Kadabra
012	🔵 Butterfree	194	🔵 Wooper	065	🔵 Alakazam
013	🔵 Weedle	195	🔵 Quagsire	132	🔵 Ditto
014	🔵 Kakuna	092	🔵 Gastly	204	🔵 Pineco
015	🔵 Beedrill	093	🔵 Haunter	205	🔵 Forretress
165	🔵 Ledyba	094	🔵 Gengar	029	🔵 Nidoran ♀
		201	🔵 Unown	030	🔵 Nidorina
		095	🔵 Onix	031	🔵 Nidoqueen
		208	🔵 Steelix	032	🔵 Nidoran ♂
		069	🔵 Bellsprout		⋮
		070	🔵 Weepinbell		

Number Found:

143

Number Captured:

142

It's been a week since she started—and her Pokédex is filling up fast!!

Message from
Hidenori Kusaka

The new character who appears in this volume is a special one for me. Since I first started working on Pokémon manga, I've wanted to create some kind of capturing expert. As someone who agonizes over never catching the "legendaries," I thought it would be nice if I could at least capture them in the book! (LOL) That's how the idea for "The Capturer" came to be.

Message from
Satoshi Yamamoto

Nice to meet you! Satoshi Yamamoto here. I'll be drawing this manga starting with volume 10. Not knowing a single thing about Pokémon, I got really into trying to draw the main girl well…so into it that before I knew what was happening, it was time for the book to go to print. Here's to a long relationship with everyone!

More Adventures Coming Soon...

Crystal is well into her journey to fill Professor Oak's latest Pokédex when she meets the Legendary Pokémon Suicune. Will she be the Trainer who finally captures it?

And whatever happened to the missing Gold and Silver? Will they ever be found?

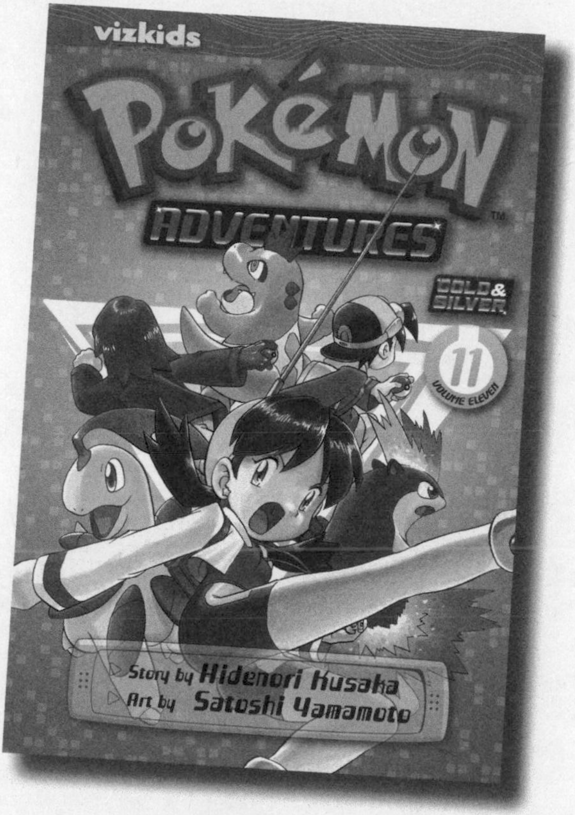

vizkids
POKéMON
ADVENTURES
GOLD & SILVER
11
VOLUME ELEVEN
Story by Hidenori Kusaka
Art by Satoshi Yamamoto

AVAILABLE NOW!

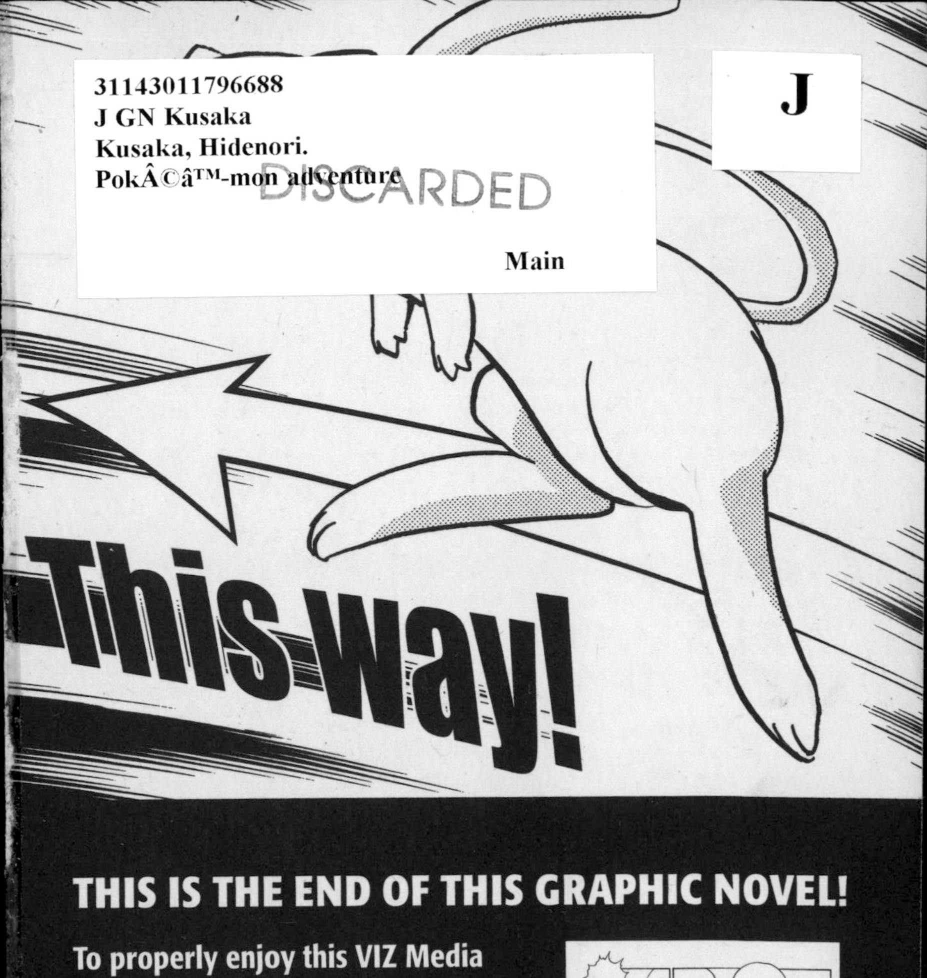
This way!

THIS IS THE END OF THIS GRAPHIC NOVEL!

To properly enjoy this VIZ Media graphic novel, please turn it around and begin reading from right to left.

This book has been printed in the original Japanese format in order to preserve the orientation of the original artwork. Have fun with it!

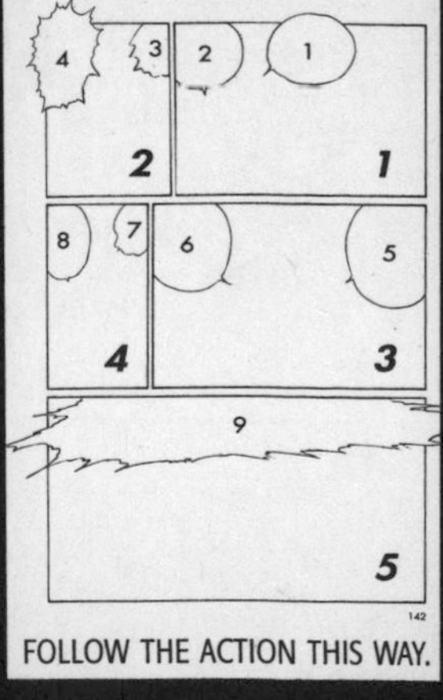
FOLLOW THE ACTION THIS WAY.